PLAIN ENGLISH

RACHEL SPANGLER

Bywater
BOOKS

2022

Bywater Books First Edition: February 2022

Print ISBN: 978-1-61294-243-8

Cover Design by TreeHouse Studio

Printed in the United States of America on acid-free paper.

Bywater Books
PO Box 3671
Ann Arbor MI 48106-3671
www.bywaterbooks.com

This novel is a work of fiction. Names, characters, places, and
incidents are the product of the author's imagination.

For Susie who continues to move and shift and grow alongside me.
This, and so many other things, are all your fault.

CHAPTER ONE

Pip rolled over, her head sinking into a cooler spot on the pillow and something softer. The smell of jasmine seeped into her sleep-shrouded senses. She inhaled more deeply, and a little tickle fluttered against the end of her nose. She didn't want to be awake yet, but her mind struggled to process the discordant details, and doing so caused the haze of slumber to burn away, leaving her more vulnerable to awareness.

Light shone a yellowish orange through closed eyelids, suggesting morning had made its assault. Her lips parted on a sigh, and something shifted across her outstretched arm, suggesting that wherever she found herself when she opened her eyes, she wouldn't find herself alone. The thought didn't disturb her so much as the realization that she would indeed need to wake up fully to process the where and the who, or perhaps how she'd gotten into this position.

Opening one eyelid a sliver, she waited for the light of the room and the fog of sleep to counterbalance, but as her surroundings came into focus, a few more details slipped into place: stone walls, a lush duvet, high arcing windows of leaded glass, the morning rays across a Persian rug.

Castle.

That narrowed her location down significantly. The bed wasn't her own, as the canopy overhead was maroon instead of emerald, which meant probably not her castle. While the realization assured her she wasn't someplace terribly unusual, it didn't offer enough details to whittle anything to a fine point. She opened her other eye, searching for clues. A chaise lounge stretched along one window, next to a washstand with an ornate gilded mirror. Decorative swirls rose to a crest containing the outline of a lion, mouth open, mane flowing.

The Penchant Lion.

Her memory returned in a rush. Vic's party—no, her premiere. They'd shown her cousin's movie on a giant screen hung from the great stone walls of the outer bailey. People had come from all over. There'd been speeches and dancing in the gardens, but Pip had attended a more intimate gathering for the family, cast, and crew where everyone toasted her cousin's success and that of her beautiful bride. Champagne had flowed right into gin o'clock by the time she found herself in conversation with an American actress.

She inhaled another deep pull of jasmine as her mind shifted from how and where to whose head lay heavy on her arm. There'd been many Americans last night, all brash and beautiful, such an enthralling breed with their intriguing mix of awe at their surroundings and their confidence in themselves. Images flickered through Pip's mind the way the movie had played across the screen. So many witty conversations, so many flawless faces. She smiled at the mental replay of getting close enough to the film's star, to have her singer wife shoot daggers from her eyes and lips. That one had diva written all over her, and because there should only be one diva in any given bed, Pip had turned toward something softer.

The same softness brushing against her now.

The young up-and-coming starlet with green eyes and strawberry blond hair curling over exposed shoulders. The details returned in full now as Pip distinctly remembered this woman declaring there'd been so many lesbians on the set of the film she'd started to wonder what all the fuss was about; so Pip offered to clear that question up for her.

She suffered a fleeting pang of temptation to linger long enough to see whether she'd settled the woman's query, but given the way the starlet had clung to her into the morning hours, she suspected she knew the answer. With the final mystery solved, the story no longer held her interest.

Pip had never been one for a long denouement, but even if she were prone to lassitude, the longer she lazed about, the more likely her chance of meeting her aunt at breakfast. The thought was enough to turn even the warmest body cool against her bare skin. Every minute that ticked by only worsened her odds of escaping without some exchange requiring pleasantries or protocol. She shivered lightly. Even though she remained under the comfort of the duvet physically, mentally she'd already gone.

She slipped from under the covers with little more than a backward glance, then lifted her rucksack off the settee before padding naked into the spacious bathroom. She splashed some water on her face, then went about her morning routine as quickly and quietly as possible. Within minutes she stood before the mirror in her trusty travel outfit of olive-green cargo pants and a brown Henley. By the time she slipped on her helmet, she'd be absolutely unrecognizable to anyone who'd seen her the night before.

Then reaching into the rucksack one more time she pulled out two cards. One she inked for the starlet still asleep in her bed, telling her, tongue in cheek, that if she ever wanted to go south from there she should give her a call. Then she added the number to her formal residence, but not her personal mobile phone. The other note she addressed to her "Most Favourite Cousin Ever," asking Vic to please stow the rest of her things until she passed back through, whenever that may be.

With that, Pip exited the other side of the washroom, without any further thought to the things she left behind.

With a cursory glance down toward the staterooms, she slunk along the wall, her footsteps light and quick until she found the door handle inlaid in the wood panelling. She gave a twist and pushed with her shoulder until she eased backward into a narrow servants' corridor running parallel to the one used by anyone even remotely related to her. Closing the door softly, she took one more step backward and tripped over something or, rather, someone.

Stumbling back, she caught hold of the person, gripping them tightly in an attempt to keep her backside from hitting the hardwood.

Only when certain she could remain upright did she register the stunning beauty in her arms. She flashed her most disarming smile on pure reflex before recognition filtered in that the waist she currently clutched belonged to Sophia LeBlanc, famous actress, director, and wife to one of the few relatives she actually cared for.

Sophia eyed her suspiciously. "Good morning, Lady Mulgrave."

She grimaced and stepped back. "Please don't call me that before 7 a.m."

"It's 8:45."

"Then please don't call me that ever," she said. "In fact, I'm aware you don't know me well, but would you mind not calling me anything right now, or even maybe not telling anyone you saw me this morning?"

"That depends." Sophia drew out the phrase in her distinctly American accent. "Who are you running from?"

"Is there an answer that gets me out of here more quickly than the others?"

Sophia snorted. "Seeing as how I'm currently avoiding my mother-in-law, I certainly have sympathies to share."

"Ah yes, my aunt is very much the reason I learned to use this particular passageway many years ago."

Sophia nodded agreeably. "Seeing as I'm prone to support family avoidance, can I safely assume that's your valid excuse and you're not sneaking out on the up-and-coming actress I saw you leave the party with last night?"

Pip rubbed the back of her neck. "Does it have to be an either/or proposition? I'm more of a both/and kind of queer."

The corners of Sophia's mouth quirked up. "I did sort of get that sense even in my limited knowledge of your escapades."

Pip didn't question or defend herself against whatever hung behind that comment. "So, you never saw me?"

Sophia glanced over her shoulder, then shrugged. "So long as if you get caught, you never saw me."

She nodded solemnly. "On my honour."

Sophia rolled her eyes. "I'm not sure what that's worth, but go ahead and make your escape."

Pip dropped her chin to her chest, clicked her heels, then took off again, thinking she already liked her cousin's new wife a great deal more than she liked most of her other extended family members.

Hopping lightly down a flight of wooden stairs, she exited the residence and slipped on her aviator sunglasses, now relatively secure in her ability to blend in with the staff cleaning up from the festivities the night before. She weaved between gardeners already patching the grounds and beefy boys loading tables into a lorry until she reached the garage and roused a young redheaded man staring dreamily at the array of luxury vehicles filling the former stables.

He snapped to attention, but she held up a hand and shook her head, not wanting to draw attention to herself this close to freedom. "No worries. I'm here for the bike, the Triumph if there's more than one."

He grinned. "No ma'am, and honestly I've been sitting here wondering where that one came from."

"It probably comes from some deep-seated desire to unnerve my parents."

"Wow."

"It's more fun than therapy, mate." She slapped him on the shoulder. "And better for picking up women, too, which is why I must be off."

"Right." He nodded. Then his eyes lit up. "It's in the last stall on the right. Would you like me to fetch it?"

"I'd be more likely to let you take a spin with my date than my ride."

"Well, anytime you want to arrange that, let me know." He seemed to remember himself and added an awkward, "Ma'am."

"Stranger things have happened." She laughed lightly as she ambled through the old stone barn and wondered how the Penchants managed to find such amiable people when her own parents kept trotting out the same stodgy staff.

As she reached the back stall, all other thoughts fell away when her gaze landed on her baby. The motorcycle stood gleaming, a polished military olive-green with a smooth brown saddle-leather seat. Its large tires had tread for rough road, and the low handlebars shone silver into a newly regripped throttle.

"Good morning, gorgeous." Pip mumbled the greeting she hadn't managed to afford last night's lover.

She grabbed her black half-shell helmet off a side hook and swung her leg over the seat, settling against the subtle grooves her thighs had worn in the leather. Then with a light leap she kicked down and relished the engine rumble purring underneath her.

Rolling her head from side to side, the tension slipped from her shoulders. In all her trips to various spas, she'd never had a massage that shook the knots from her muscles the way 650 cc's could.

She revved the engine, listening for any notes out of tune, then eased the bike forward and down the main line of the stable. She offered a little salute to the attendant when he stared lustily at the ride and not at her before turning toward the main gate. It swung wide to accommodate her, and she felt the whole of Great Britain open to her as well.

⥷ ⥷ ⥷

Pip rode down the long military road, enjoying the rattle of her wheels across the cobblestones until she reached a fork. She chose at random, turning right toward the old city walls and between long row houses, until she reached the Bondgate and rolled right out into the small market town and then into the countryside.

At some point she had it in the back of her mind to head north. The last week in August the Fringe Festival would be in its final throes throughout Edinburgh, but no one she cared to see would be out this early on a Sunday morning. While she loved the city more than any other, she ceded its middays to the families as they flooded the streets with balloons and prams queuing up to see magicians, jugglers, and bagpipers. She'd wait until night to search out the storytellers, radical queers, and belly dancers, with the occasional fire-eater thrown in for effect. In general, Pip preferred Edinburgh after dark, when the crooked streets and cobblestones cast in low light lent an equalizing mystique to everyone. No one down those back alleys ever called her "ma'am" or "Lady" anything, but dark came late and disappeared early this far up the coast, so she surrendered instead to the pull of the sea.

Leaning her body into a lazy curve, she zipped down a rural road along a babbling brook. Pip didn't know the area well, but all rivers in this part of the country wandered their way to the great North Sea, and if she kept on in the same general direction as the stream, they'd both hit salt water soon.

The road rose and fell like the fields on either side of her, but her eyes remained fixed on the baby blue of the horizon until it blended with the deeper azure of water shimmering in the distance. A picturesque estuary appeared amid rushes and reeds. Sailboats dotted the scene, and around the bend a village sprang up like a painting in a storybook. Such subtle, simple, sublime beauty. Pip arced almost all the way through a roundabout before easing upright and straight on toward the quaint scene.

A stone bridge loomed before her, too narrow for two cars, and currently completely filled with a lorry. She eased off the throttle, creating both the time and space for clearance, but when she upshifted again, nothing caught.

The absence of acceleration registered even before the sound came. Only a little whine, but she recognized it with the tuned ear of a parent who could pick out her own child's whimper in a crowded nursery.

She downshifted again, her toe searching for purchase, but her foot just clicked lower into an empty sort of place, and her stomach dropped right along with it.

"Damn it."

To her right, the bank of the estuary dropped off at a precarious angle, and dead ahead the road inclined on a gentle rise the bike no longer had enough thrust to crest. The large open sheep field to the left offered her only viable option.

Using the last of her momentum, Pip swerved sharply and hopped the kerb. Landing in the grass, she skidded across rough ground, rattling her teeth and her headlight. A low fence loomed dead ahead, and she had a mere sliver of a second to make the decision as to whether she wanted to test the old unstoppable force, immovable object theorem before deciding to lay the bike, and by extension herself, down in the mud and muck.

Closing her eyes, she tightened her jaw and eased into the slide with about as much grace as Bambi on ice, but when the scraping and the friction and the grind of her body between steel and soil all slowed to a stop, she hopped up, relatively unscathed.

Searching her extremities, she found the lower right leg of her trousers shredded and her jacket well scuffed at the elbow, but none of her limbs hurt nearly as badly as the sight of her bike, battered if not completely broken, in a trail of dirt, oil, and adrenaline.

She stood over the tangled mess, breath heavy, pulse racing, and brain spinning like the back tire. There went her baby. There went her plans. There went her great escape. Throwing back her head, she growled, allowing the sound to rumble into the echo of her engine, growing in both its volume and guttural qualities until she shouted the entirety of her thoughts on the subject.

"Fuck, bugger, wanker, hell, and piss."

CHAPTER TWO

Claire Bailey stared at the surreal sight mere meters from her garden fence. Everything had happened so quickly she might not even have believed what she'd just seen, if not for the person standing in an open and otherwise utterly unremarkable field hurling profanities at a piece of wreckage.

She rubbed the sleep out of her eyes and replayed the last sixty seconds. She'd merely stepped outside the back door of her gallery to check the morning light, but she'd no sooner set her bare feet on the cool stone when a motorcycle had rocketed off the road, launching both itself and its rider into her grandfather's field before tipping over and skidding to a steaming stop.

She'd held her breath, worried she'd just witnessed a vehicular death statistic in real time, but the rider had popped up with startling speed, stared heavenward for a hot second, then unloaded the most over-the-top, nonsensical string of curse words she'd ever heard.

The rapid succession of surreal events sent a bubble of laughter through her core, and before she could catch herself, it came right out of her lips.

It wasn't funny, not entirely, but as her heart raced with adrenaline-laced relief Claire couldn't help herself, and she didn't manage to keep quiet about her inappropriate amusement either. Her sharp cackle reverberated across the still landscape, and the rider wasn't nearly far enough away to not notice.

Turning their head at the sound, they stared at Claire with a startled kind of insolence that caused her breath to catch every bit as much as the initial wreck.

"Do you find this humorous?"

She shook her head. She had a second ago, but not anymore. Not in the face of the most dangerously good-looking human she'd ever been this close to. And honestly, they weren't even that close, but even at a distance of twenty yards, she felt trapped in the tractor beam of the most electric blue eyes she'd ever seen.

The rider took a few steps closer, and Claire fought the urge to back up as more stunning details came into focus. The subtle curve of hips and breasts, the sharp cut of an angular jaw, cheekbones that seemed almost clichéd in their nobility.

"I lost control and crashed." The voice was richer, smoother than one might expect from someone who'd recently suffered a near-death experience.

"I saw."

"You saw?" The rider looked around as though silently asking whether this was really happening, and Claire at least identified with that impulse. "Seriously? That's all you've got? I could've broken my neck."

"Seeing as how you hopped up like a little meerkat popping out of a hole, it hadn't occurred to me that you'd severed your spinal cord."

"Meerkat?" The rider snorted and strode forward until she reached a small hedge marking the edge of the pasture and the boundary to Claire's garden. "Some people might have considered it polite to check if I'd been injured before laughing at a stranger who'd come through a harrowing event."

Claire shrugged. "I probably would have if I'd had another second or two, but your grasp on a rather wide array of obscenities gave the impression you'd survive the trauma."

"Obscenities?" An arched eyebrow, a little hint of a smile, the complete absence of genuine embarrassment, all played quickly across the most flawless of faces. "You heard that?"

"The entire village probably heard."

"Well then." The rider unsnapped the chin strap of a black helmet and lifted it gingerly before shaking out a head of dark brown hair, the length of which feathered impeccably along the shorter side and revealed a hint of auburn in the places where sunlight shone through the lighter layers.

Claire's mouth went dry at the effortless perfection of that move, and the seeming impossibility of anyone's hair looking so unsullied after being smashed under a helmet during a motorcycle wreck. The situation became only more absurd as the almost mythical creature before her dipped low in a stately bow, then said smoothly, "Humblest apologies if my coarse vocabulary caused offence. It appears I forgot myself."

"Forgot yourself?" Claire scoffed. "This can't be real. You can't be real."

"Believe me. I'd rather a great many things about my morning up until this point weren't real, but this moment isn't one of them."

"Oh, lord. Do you have a concussion?"

"I don't recall hitting my head when I laid the bike down, but I suppose one can't be too careful with these things. Perhaps I should take a seat and you could ask me a few questions to be certain."

Claire rolled her eyes. That was entirely too smooth to be genuine, and a thousand alarms sounded in the back of her brain, but then again, could anyone that good-looking ever manage to be sincere about anything? This woman, and she did seem to be a woman, exuded an effortless blend of femininity and masculinity in ways that sparked both envy and attraction across the spectrum. Still, she supposed none of those qualities changed the dictates of socially acceptable manners. She'd never actually been in a similar situation, but she suspected that asking to sit down for a few minutes after crashing violently into someone's field wasn't an unreasonable request.

She sighed and stepped over to unlatch her garden gate. "Thank you, Ms. . . . ?"

"Claire."

"I'm in your debt, Ms. Claire."

"No Ms., just Claire."

"Ah, you haven't a surname?"

"Of course I do, but I'm not sure I want to give it to strange people who've proved themselves reckless and of poor judgment."

"Very well. I shall call you just Claire and you may call me . . . erm . . . Flip until I've repaired my image in your eyes."

"Flip?" She noted the pause mid-introduction and immediately pegged the moniker as an alias, or an all-out lark, but she gestured to a wooden table and a couple of rickety deck chairs. "What kind of name is Flip?"

"The kind that suits me." Flip gave a brash smile before adding, "And I always do what suits me."

"That's the most unsurprising fact of this morning."

"Why?"

She took the seat opposite and inched it back, a bit eager for any distance she could get from the magnetic pull across the table. "You seem like someone who's used to getting their way."

"I'd love to hear what makes you think so."

"Nope." She shook her head. "We're in concussion protocol here. I'll ask the questions."

Flip leaned back and crossed one leg over the other. "Fire away."

"What day is it?"

"Sunday."

"No, what's the date?"

"Hmm, August . . . something."

"That's an inspiring start."

"Ask me something I'd know on, like, an average sort of day."

"I thought I had. How about 'where are you?'"

"Ah, well, that's . . . I assume still in Northland?"

"Can you narrow it to something smaller than an entire region?"

Flip pondered for entirely too long. "South of Edinburgh?"

"That's not actually more specific, as all of England falls south of Edinburgh." Claire sat forward as a hint of concern crept in. "Where do you live?"

"Could we do a different one?"

"You don't know where you live?"

"No, I do." Flip defended herself quickly. "I simply don't know if saying will help my case."

"Because you live in what . . . a prison? A mental ward?"

Flip laughed. "While at times I've thought so, it's not actually horrible . . . most days. But it's complex."

"Fine. What questions can you answer?"

"Do you want to know what's currently showing at the National Theatre? Or something about the duke's crest? Or how about the fifth person in line for succession to the throne?"

"Why would anyone know those things in the first place, much less hold onto them after a head trauma?" Something didn't add up, and Claire simply didn't know enough about concussions to be sure what kind of memories a person lost, but that list of completely irrelevant trivia didn't seem nearly as important as dates and addresses. She needed meaningful details, and then she needed to get this beautiful distraction back on the road to far away. She glanced toward the field, and her eyes fell on something a little closer to both of them. "Tell me about the motorcycle."

Flip's smile turned slow and happy in the first genuine expression Claire had seen on her yet.

"She's a 1961 Triumph TR6 Trophy with an original four-stroke twin parallel engine and a four-speed transmission." Flip's eyes crinkled at the corners, her voice taking on what might've been considered a youthful enthusiasm if not for the low, sexy timbre it dropped into as performance blended into real passion. "She's outfitted with an updated suspension and refurbished seat to comfortably accommodate two people, so long as they're willing to move as one and lean into whatever curves the road has in store for us."

Flip eyed her more steadily under long, dark lashes. A hint of challenge, and maybe an underlying hope sparked between them. Claire didn't quite manage to back away fast enough, and she felt the singe of something hot sinking under her skin.

"Nope, no, nuh-uh." She pushed back from the table. She didn't need to hear this walking thirst-trap talk in low, intimate tones, not about anything, but especially not about curves, and leaning, or two moving as one.

"Excuse me?"

"No concussion." She shook her head. "I mean I think you're *fine*."

Flip's eyebrows rose, and her cocky grin returned. "How fine?"

"Ugh, I didn't mean to emphasize *fine*, like, I meant . . . like, not your looks, but 'fine' as in 'not injured.' I think you are, medically speaking, very much . . ." She flicked her eyes over Flip's lanky frame, resting too long on the subtle curve of her hips, and couldn't stop herself from realizing that's where she'd hold on if she did ever ride double on that road they'd been talking about.

"A *fine* specimen?" Flip offered to finish the sentence for her, and then with her tongue firmly in her cheek, added, "medically speaking, of course."

"Sure, yeah. You're well enough to walk back over to your wreck of a super old motorcycle."

Flip grimaced, and her complexion paled to the point where Claire's basic human decency flared again.

"Are you in pain?"

"Only the emotional kind." Flip groaned as she pushed back from the table. "But you're right. I must attend to my baby."

"Your baby? Please tell me you mean your ancient bike?"

"It's not ancient. It's a classic, and yes, I prefer it to most infants I've met. It doesn't come with wet nappies."

"No, it merely tries to break your neck when you hit a bump."

"I didn't hit a bump. I'm a much better driver than that."

Claire pursed her lips to keep from smiling. Flip didn't seem

14

quite as threatening to her better judgment when flustered and pouty.

"I actually stayed in remarkable control for the situation. However, the mechanical issue that forced my hand in the first place wasn't helped by anything that came after."

"And by 'after' you mean crashing? The crashing didn't help the problems your antique toy was having in the first place?"

Flip gritted her teeth. "If you must phrase things in such a blunt way, I suppose your baseline facts aren't incorrect."

"I don't know if 'must' is the right term, so much as 'genuinely enjoy.'"

Flip's eyes narrowed. "Are you some sort of masochist?"

Claire laughed again, this time not from shock, but from actual amusement. "You're not the first person to ask me that question."

"And?"

"Sadly, you won't be around long enough to find out."

Flip sighed. "Perhaps you're right, but may I bother you to use your phone?"

"What's wrong with yours?"

"Mine's dead."

"Because you're a Time Lord?"

"What?"

"You don't have a workable mobile, you don't know the date or where you are, your vocabulary is a bit too formal, your home address is 'complex,' and you're driving a rickety motorcycle from the 1950s. Time Lord seems as valid an option as any."

Flip raised a hand as if she planned to start a rebuttal, then merely smiled—a genuine, broad, timeless expression that made Claire's knees go a little soft—before nodding. "Actually, yes. Can I trust you to keep my secret?"

Claire's heart gave a disturbing little thump, and she bit her lip to keep herself from making promises to another woman like this while she reached into the pocket of her sweatpants and pulled out her phone. "I don't know if I'm prepared to cover for you yet, but I'm at least intrigued enough to let you make a couple of calls."

❧ ❧ ❧

"Hello, Louisa."

"Pippa? Oh, for the love of God, where are you calling from?"

"Actually, I'm not sure exactly." She glanced around the small garden and the larger field beside it. "But I could tell you how to get here."

"And pray tell, why would I be inclined to go there?"

"Because your favourite sibling needs your help?"

"Oh, is Margie with you?"

"Ouch. How could you say something so hurtful to the tiny little baby who followed you around and always held your hand, and who always lied and said you were visiting me at school even when you were with Geoffrey, especially after I've gone through the trauma of wrecking the Triumph?"

"Oh shit, are you kidding?"

"I'd never joke about something so heinous."

The sadness must've come through her voice because Louisa sobered. "Lord, are you okay? Are you bleeding? Please tell me you're not hurt."

"The masochistic local woman letting me use her phone assures me I don't have a concussion."

Claire snorted on the other side of the garden, proving she was listening even if she'd taken several polite steps away and pretended to watch some sheep amble along a small stream.

"Is this woman a doctor?"

Pip turned to her reluctant host, taking a moment to enjoy the view from behind that understated hourglass frame and the still tousled blond hair that fell halfway down her back and curled only at the tips. "I don't know. Claire, are you a doctor?"

"Do you think I'd be living in a loft above a rural art gallery if I had a medical degree?"

She spoke into the phone again. "That's a no, but apparently I'm currently roadside behind a rural art gallery. That should narrow it down. Google 'rural art gallery' and 'sheep pastures' within fifteen miles of Victoria's."

"You're in Amberwick," Claire said drolly, and Pip noticed a hint of an accent that didn't quite sound local before she added, "Are you always this helpless?"

"Right. Apparently, I wrecked outside a village called Amberwick, and Claire wants to know if I'm always this helpless."

"Yes," Louisa said emphatically.

"No," Pip relayed to Claire. "My sister says I'm actually known for my brilliance, level head, and charisma."

"Are you flirting with this woman?" Louisa asked with new sharpness. "Seriously? An hour after sneaking out on the poor woman from Sophia's movie and leaving your entire family without a word, you seriously want other people to drop what they're doing and . . . what? Come pick you up while you try to pick up someone else?"

"That would be lovely, yes. Also, could you arrange to have the bike brought back to Vic's valet? I'm certain he'll be able to assist me from there."

"You're incorrigible."

"And you love that about me?"

"I'm nearly thirty miles south of Newpeth already."

She hadn't counted on the others leaving around the same time she had. "What about Mum?"

"She was getting ready to head out when I left. She and father fly from Newcastle this afternoon."

"They're going to Margie's today?"

"Yes, and you're on the naughty list for not saying good-bye. You embarrassed everyone to bits, the whole family waiting for you to make an appearance at the table when your most recent conquest came in wearing your tuxedo shirt and asking if we'd seen you."

She grimaced. "I left her a note."

"A note?" Louisa exploded. "Can you even imagine Mother's face, and in front of her sister?"

"Steely rage?"

"Understatement, Pippa. Your penance will last the rest of your life."

"So, what you're saying is I probably shouldn't call the duchess next?"

Louisa actually laughed. "You'd be either braver or dumber than I thought, and that's saying loads."

"Thanks. Isn't there anyone who doesn't hate me left in the area?"

"The only people not totally horrified were Victoria and Sophia, but they're busy."

"Yes, that's perfect." She warmed to the idea. "They're sensible, and they know the region. I'm sure they'd pop over."

"It's kind of a big weekend for them. I'm not sure they want to pop anywhere."

"But Victoria's a good sort. She'll do it if you ask her nicely."

"If *I* ask her? I think you mean when *you* ask her."

"Can't you intercede for me? You know, play the protective big sister card? She'll respect it more coming from you. She's got a younger sibling. You can bond over your sense of responsibility."

"I'm tired of always bailing you out. You need to learn to handle your own affairs instead of leaving everyone else to clean up your messes." A new weariness crept into Louisa's voice. "And the way you treat these women isn't funny. It's embarrassing, and I hate it. You need to take some responsibility."

"You're probably right," Pip said with put-on sincerity, and for some reason shot another glance to Claire, standing with her arms folded and her brow furrowed. "I do want to do better, but I'm imposing on the locals right now, and we both know I'm a terrible bother in these situations. I don't know the area or reputable people to work with. I'm not sure where I'd even begin. Surely someone could at least get the ball rolling to show me how it's done."

"Ugh. You're helpless, but it's not my fault our parents had given up on actual parenting by the time you arrived."

Pip grinned, hearing the last hints of resistance in her sister's voice. "It's not my fault either. No one asked my opinion on our birth order, or any of the other inconvenient facts of my birth, for that matter."

Louisa sighed. "You're the worst."

"And you're the best."

"Which is why I'm going to call Victoria and tell her you're stranded on the side of the road outside Amberwick, but then I wouldn't blame her if she abandons you there."

"Thanks. I love you, too." She disconnected the phone but didn't immediately hand it back. Instead, she dialed a different number and let it ring a couple of times before clicking it off and turning to Claire once more.

"Thank you." She stepped closer to the woman, who still angled away from her. "My sister will call my cousin, and she'll come pick me up, probably."

"Probably?" Claire asked, her cool tone not quite managing to hide the hint of interest underneath the chill.

"It's kind of complicated."

"Like where you live?"

"They're related, yes."

"Why do I get the sense that's just the tip of the old iceberg?"

"The complexity iceberg? Oh, very much indeed."

Claire finally turned to her, fixing her with green eyes, light and flecked with hints of gold. Talk about complex. Pip suspected she could sink a few ships of her own with all the hazards lurking beneath that smooth surface. "It didn't sound like your sister was happy with you."

"No. She may've mentioned that my name has been scrawled atop several shit lists this morning."

"Because you sneaked out of the mental ward again?"

"Something like that," Pip agreed, then added, "I actually did skip out on a family thing this morning, but in my defence all the good parts were over last night. If you knew my aunt you wouldn't want to have breakfast with her either."

"What's so terrible about her?"

"Have you ever seen the evil queen in Snow White?"

19

Claire finally cracked a grudging smile.

"She looks just like that, and she doesn't need to put the poison in any apples. She can deliver it via witty repartee or a withering stare. When I was five years old, I sneaked into her residence to look for her terrifying magic mirror."

"Seriously?"

Pip drew a cross over her heart.

"And that's the family coming to fetch you? Are you sure you wouldn't rather hitchhike wherever you were originally headed?"

"Tempting, but I'm a good soldier. I'd never leave a man behind, and since the bike ranks higher in my estimation than any man I've ever known, I could never abandon her in her hour of need."

Claire glanced over her shoulder toward where the motorcycle lay dug into the ground. "You genuinely love that thing, don't you?"

"She's the love of my life."

"Why?"

Pip's chest filled with a mix of emotions, memories, and mental recall too overwhelming to put into words. "I'm not nearly poetic enough to do her justice, but would you come with me so I could show you?"

Claire gave a noncommittal shrug. "You may've piqued my interest."

Pip's heart gave a little jump as she tried not to let the comment mean too many things. Still, she extended a hand to Claire as she opened the garden gate. Claire, for her part, stared first at Pip's palm, then her eyes, then back again for a whole three seconds before laughing.

"What?"

"I said I'd look at your old heap of metal, Time Lord. I don't need to hold your hand like a damsel exiting a carriage."

"Sorry, I was merely being chivalrous as we passed through the gate."

"I'm not wearing a hoop skirt."

"No." Pip's lips quirked up as she scanned Claire's jogging

trousers and the oversized sweatshirt that hung slightly askew at the neck, casually revealing a tantalizing hint of collarbone. "But I do find this ensemble rather fetching."

Claire rolled her eyes. "If you don't start doing a little more walking and a little less talking, I'll make you sit by the roadside alone."

Pip found the ultimatum amusing, and with someone else, she might have enjoyed testing the boundary, but she wasn't ready to risk her remaining moments with someone who didn't hesitate to answer suave with sass, so she pressed her lips together and led the short way back to where the Triumph lay wounded.

The sight of her baby sprawled undignified in the dirt managed to sober Pip a little, even as Claire stood much closer than she had in the garden.

"This is your prized possession, huh?"

"Without a doubt."

"She's . . . she is a girl, right?"

"A girl?" Pip blustered. "Would you call Meryl Steep a girl? Would you call Helen Mirren a girl? What about Audrey Hepburn? She's a classic. She's timeless. She's a grand dame, a heartbreaker. She's stacked and raw and boundless. This is the same motorcycle Steve McQueen used in *The Great Escape*."

"How great an escape could it have been?"

Pip threw her hands up in the air. "You've got to be kidding me."

Claire cracked a smile. "Yeah, I totally am, but you're a lot easier to rev than this motorcycle at the moment."

Pip shook her head even while fighting a smile. "I'd argue, but what's the use at this point?"

"None whatsoever. And what do you even care?" Claire asked a little more pointedly. "What does my opinion of your vehicular girlfriend even matter?"

Pip started to make a smart remark but bit it off and, cocking her head to the side, stopped to think. She wasn't wrong. In the grand scheme of the morning, Claire's opinion of the Triumph shouldn't even register. Plenty of people in her life didn't share her affinity for, well, anything. What was one more person to find her odd or inappropriate—especially a stranger? She studied Claire more closely, from the eyes that caught her attention to the frame that held it. But she'd had no shortage of pretty women in her life. If mere beauty were enough, Pip would've stayed in bed longer this morning and missed this whole mess entirely.

No. There was more to this woman than even her most appealing physical features. Maybe the way she managed to come across as superior even in lounge clothes? The almost comical condescension in her voice? The set of her arms folded challengingly under the soft swell of her breasts beneath the thin sweatshirt? Or maybe the press of her lips as if trying to suppress a knowing smile? Pip's eyes lingered a second too long on those lips, and when she glanced up again, Claire's eyes had gone a little darker.

She recognized that expression, the attraction, the curiosity, even the wariness, but the people with that look in their eyes usually stepped forward. Claire took a step back, and Pip would be damned if she didn't find herself following her instead of the other way around.

She didn't want to think about how much farther she would've chased this woman across the absurdly quaint setting if not for the sound of tires slowing to a stop behind them.

"Oh lord, you really did muck that up, didn't you?"

Pip sighed without turning around. "Hello, Vic. Thanks for coming."

"Family loyalty and queer sensibilities aside, you'll owe me big time for this one."

She nodded before gesturing over her shoulder. "That's my cousin."

"Thank you for supervising the family delinquent, Ms. . . . ?"

"We're not doing surnames. Apparently, she doesn't find me trustworthy," Pip explained.

"Smart woman." Vic's voice softened. "I'm sorry for any inconvenience, but could we possibly leave this death trap in your field while we arrange for pickup?"

Pip finally turned around. "You can't leave it here unattended."

"Of course you can," Claire cut in. "No one's going to steal a broken hunk of metal, and it's not like anyone could ride off on it."

"Are we really going back to the broken metal bit?"

Claire shrugged, not quite able to keep her smile hidden this time. "The truth hurts."

"It's settled then," Vic said resolutely. "We'll try to make arrangements in a timely manner."

"Timely, as in we'll wait here until a mechanic arrives?"

"Bye, Flip," Claire said.

"Can't we talk this through?"

"Get in the car, Pip," Vic called.

"Pip?" Claire asked, a giggle bubbling up in her voice as she looked her up and down once more.

Pip groaned as a spark of amusement once again supplanted the attraction propelling them together seconds ago, but Claire's smile kept growing, past a smirk, past mirth, all the way to a genuine openness. "Now *that* suits you."

CHAPTER THREE

Claire stood in the same spot for entirely too long, the cold, loamy earth between her toes grounding her in ways she hadn't been able to summon in Pip's presence.

Pip.

She smiled. The name didn't convey the woman's suave or stunning looks, but it certainly fit her personality. Claire doubted the woman ever had a twinge of insecurity in her life. Honestly, even referring to her as a woman seemed reductive. Pip transcended such comfortable classification. Handsome, charming, suave, and boy did she know it. Every move, every deliberate glance, every quick comment carried the confidence of someone used to getting their way.

She shook her head. This wasn't what she'd moved to Amberwick to deal with. She'd had plenty of reservations about leaving her life in London, but fewer distractions of Pip's ilk had landed firmly in the pro column of her emotional ledger.

Turning back to the place she was still struggling to call home, she smiled slightly at the sight of sun shining on the little converted schoolhouse with its stone walls, high peaked roof, and tidy garden. It might not be the type of place she'd dreamed of back in the city, but it was more than she'd ever been able to afford there.

She walked back, relishing the grass under her feet and breathing fresh salt air, other luxuries London never offered. She checked to make sure her gate latched behind her and then tugged open the sliding glass door that always stuck a bit in the middle. Stepping inside, she surveyed the main gallery. Though it was mostly empty save for a few racks of knickknacks left over from its previous life as a tourist shop, Claire could envision much more eventually. Paintings by local artists on every wall. Sculptures on pedestals. Maybe a little nook for books from local authors and photographers. There was still the kitchen from the building's years as a tearoom that would take more refurbishing than she could afford, but maybe someday she'd have a small café, or at least something functional enough to cater gallery shows.

The little bell over the front door chimed, and she turned, eager to greet whatever customer had appeared to help her on her way to her dreams, but as her eyes fell on the familiar face of her grandmother, the expression didn't fade so much as morph into a different kind of warmth. "Good morning, Nan."

"Good morning, love." She kissed Claire's cheek, surrounding her with the scent of warm flour like a cloud of goodness, causing Claire's stomach to rumble. "Oh dear, haven't you eaten yet?"

"No, I slept late and then had a bit of a run-in with a cheeky motorist."

Nan's thin eyebrows shot up.

She waved her hand. "No worries, everyone's fine, but tell Granddad there's an old motorcycle on the edge of his field awaiting pickup for either its repair or its last rites."

"It sounds like quite a bit of excitement."

She nodded. Excitement. She supposed her encounter with Flip, or rather Pip, qualified as such around here. That half hour had certainly been the most exciting of the past few months. Since moving north in the spring, most of her days were spent largely in quiet solitude broken only by shared meals with her grandparents and the occasional tourist popping in to ask if she sold tea towels. A few of them lingered to look at her art, but rarely had any of their perfunctory questions made her feel more than mild engagement.

Pip, on the other hand, inspired myriad feelings, from amusement to suspicion. She hadn't wanted any of those particular emotions, or even welcomed them when they came, but Pip hadn't left her much choice. Her blue eyes and easy confidence simply wouldn't be deterred, and Claire kicked herself for not being able to resist.

She was supposed to be turning a new leaf, getting a fresh start, settling in and settling down.

"Claire?" her nan prodded, only she'd missed the question.

"I'm sorry, what?"

"I asked if you'd like to have Sunday roast at the pub with your grandfather and me tonight. Ester might join us."

She smiled weakly. "That would be lovely."

And it would be. A nice, quiet, comfortable meal with comfortable conversation, and undoubtedly comforting food. Nothing during the early bird hours at the Raven would challenge her at all. Nothing would tempt her to step closer to a flickering flame. Nothing would draw her back toward reckless habits or even encourage her to start Internet searches for enigmatic women called Pip, because she didn't want to do that.

"Good." Nan patted her shoulder lightly. "I worry about you being cooped up here by yourself all the time."

"I thought that was the point. Time and space."

She tutted. "Time and space to grow, to work, to focus on your own art, not to become a hermit at the age of thirty."

"I did intend to get some painting done between the rush of customers."

Nan looked around pointedly.

"You never know," Claire defended herself against the unspoken. "Today could be the day we have a run of tourists wanting to buy a one-of-a-kind souvenir of their summer holidays."

"I like your optimism. Lord knows it must come from my

side of the family."

She grinned, thinking of her granddad's grumpy demeanour. "A little cheer will come in handy when all the art collectors arrive en masse and overwhelm me."

"That's the spirit, but until they do, maybe you could paint some watercolours of the puffins. People love puffins."

She didn't argue. People did love puffins. The postcards bearing the likeness of the seasonal visitors to nearby islands had sold out in the first weeks of the summer holiday season, and several more times since then. If she wanted to spend the rest of her life painting nothing but miniature puffins, she might make enough money to afford a steady diet of tinned beans.

Her stomach rumbled again, and her voice took on a slightly more desperate edge. "What time should I meet you at the Raven?"

"How about five o'clock? You know your granddad won't want to be out too late on a Sunday, not that there's any difference between a weeknight and the weekend now that we're both retired. The man is stuck in his ways." Nan smiled. "But it'll be nice to have a young person to chat with for a bit before we both retire to our separate televisions for the evening."

Claire smiled more genuinely this time. "I'm already looking forward to it."

"Good, now I'll let you get back to your painting." Nan nodded at the blank canvas against the wall near the glass door. "See you this evening."

Claire watched her go, then turned back to the blank square and tried not to see it as taunting her. A clean slate should be exciting. That's what she'd come here for in both the literal and figurative sense. A chance to create something of her own.

She picked up the canvas in one hand and her lightweight easel in the other. She used her foot to nudge open the sliding glass door until the point where it got stuck on the track, and then she sucked in her stomach and scooted her way through the small opening. Of course, nothing was perfect, but as she set up her easel and stared across the open field with its little river and small flock of sheep, she reminded herself she had a job that made her happy if not rich and that provided time for her to feed her soul. She had family nearby that doted on her. She was surrounded by beauty on all sides.

She exhaled some of the tension she'd been carrying since the moment that motorcycle had rocketed off the road, and inhaled some of the peace and purpose this view often provided. Sure, she worried she might indeed turn into the hermit her nan feared she'd become, but there were worse fates for an artist. She had the chance at a good life here.

Taking one long look at the spot where the river bent toward the bridge over the estuary, she closed her eyes and tried to set the image into her mind, but as she attempted to bring the golden light of morning into focus, all she could see was the imprint of electric blue eyes, sparkling with interest in her.

❧ ❧ ❧

"You managed to muck things up quite thoroughly, and as usual your timing is impeccable with the house staff returning to Scotland and all the summer staff exhausted and spread thin after last night's event." Vic sounded more tired than cross as she dropped into an overstuffed chair next to Pip in the Penchant family's personal library.

"I am sorry," Pip said. "I honestly didn't want to impose on one of the few family members I actually like."

"Maybe you could like me a little less during your future escapades, but you'll at least be happy to know I spoke to Charlie, and he can procure a tow for your motorcycle. We'll have it back here by evening, but he'll need a few more days to make arrangements for repairs."

"You don't have to do that," Pip said.

"Nice of you to say after I've already done it."

"No, I mean I appreciate your arranging to have the Triumph brought back here. You and your people don't need to arrange for repairs."

Vic arched an eyebrow. "I'd planned to lend you one of our Land Rovers, but I suppose we could arrange for a tow back to Mulgrave."

Pip didn't quite hide a grimace at the mention of returning home.

"What?"

"It'll be easier to source the parts from Edinburgh, and I don't want to strain your time or resources any further, plus it's Sunday and a tow halfway down the coast would be . . ."

"What?" Vic's smile turned teasing. "Expensive?"

Pip laughed. "I hadn't meant to imply I couldn't cover the cost. I only . . ." She shrugged, not sure what she'd intended. She didn't have a plan, but she didn't want to return home yet either, though with her parents out of the country for the next week, she wasn't sure why. She closed her eyes, and her mind drifted back to the image of a woman barefoot and distant in a field, arms crossed, mouth tight, eyes full of mischief. "I guess I thought it would be easiest on everyone if I stayed here until the repairs were done."

"Easiest on everyone." Vic repeated the claim, making it sound rather dubious.

"I'd stay out of your way and handle the repairs myself so as not to bother your staff."

"And how long do you expect those repairs to take?"

Pip lifted a shoulder and cocked her head to the side as she scrunched up her face, hoping that the expression made it look as though she were doing some detailed projections and mental math. In reality, the only calculations she could focus on at the moment were the ones that might provide her a valid excuse to see Claire again, for at least long enough to figure out what she found so alluring about the woman's prickly demeanour. "It might take a while."

Vic leaned forward. "'A while' is properly vague, and you intend to stay here during that time? Not run off to God knows where and leave my people to clean up your messes?"

"I would never."

Vic shook her head. "Says the person who ducked out of here this morning, leaving a wake of awkwardness. What's changed all of a sudden that makes you want to stay?"

Pip pushed away an image of Claire with her hip cocked to the side, her smile restrained but persistent. She wouldn't win any sympathies from Vic there, so she tried an ever-popular appeal instead. "Didn't you mention the duchess is headed back to Scotland this afternoon?"

"I did."

"There you have it. That's what changed."

Vic snorted and stood. "Well played. I can't deny I'm eager for a more relaxed mind-set around here myself, but I hadn't intended on company."

"I'm not company. I'm family." Pip flashed her most winning smile. "Besides, do you even know anyone more relaxed than I?"

"Not anyone I share any DNA with."

"Then I'll fit right in. You'll hardly know I'm here. Please, Vic. Can't I stay long enough to make the repairs?"

Vic sighed, but her expression softened. Then she reached out and tousled Pip's hair. "I suppose you can stay a bit longer if you promise to stay out of trouble."

Pip grinned. "I promise I'll do my best."

CHAPTER FOUR

If Claire could have pushed back from the table to forcibly separate herself from the temptation to lick her plate clean, she would have. However, she'd chosen to sit in the corner of a booth, giving the movable chairs to her grandparents and imperilling herself for a whole array of table-manner sins. She couldn't help it. The roast chicken, potatoes, carrots, and parsnips were slathered in the richest, most flavourful gravy she'd ever eaten and came with a ginormous Yorkshire pudding. She was aware enough to realize that any meal of this magnitude might've blown her mind after a week of noodles microwaved in foam cups served alongside Pop-Tarts, but she also suspected this Sunday roast would hold up against even the best restaurants in the city.

To prove the point, she ran a finger along the plate and stuck it in her mouth while her grandparents' attention was focused on the story their friend Ester was telling about some big to-do at the local castle last night.

"You know, we got our own preview of the film months ago, but I thought it a nice touch to let the wider community be part of the British release."

"Indeed," her grandmother agreed. "I hear the reviews

have been stellar."

"Oh, they are. I do wish more of them would mention the filming locations, but I suppose the word is getting out. Emma said they're going to film some scenes for a Disney series up by the Abbey next month."

Claire did her best to follow the conversation. She wasn't living on another planet. All of Northland had filmmaking fever these days, but she'd arrived in town many months after the movie crew had left, and she hadn't been part of the early preview. She didn't know any of the power players most of the town had brushed elbows with, other than Emma Volant.

She glanced over to where her newest friend sat at the bar sipping a hard cider and making eyes at her wife, who bustled between one table and another. Emma looked up in time to see Claire watching, and her expression brightened. She raised her eyebrow in unspoken invitation, then patted the bar stool next to her.

"Do you all mind if I go chat with Emma?" Claire asked her companions.

"Not at all," Ester said quickly.

"Emma could come over here," her granddad suggested, but then he winked at her.

"No, you go along, love," Nan said. "I'm glad the two of you have hit it off."

"I thought they might," Ester said almost conspiratorially. "It seems our plans to create a village of artistic types is off to quite the start."

"That was my idea," Granddad claimed.

"You didn't even know any artists until a couple of years ago."

Claire shook her head and slipped out of the booth. She'd heard this all before. The entire village liked to take credit for Emma's arrival, her marriage, and her career advancement. To hear them tell it, they'd collectively drawn back Cupid's bow and loosed the arrow. The stories got bigger as time went on, along with their many escapades during the lead-up to and filming of Emma's book-turned-movie throughout the region.

"Are they gossiping about the big event at the castle last night?" Emma asked as soon as Claire's butt hit the stool beside her.

"Incessantly." She made a show of being exhausted. "Was it everything they imagined and more?"

Emma's face contorted. "When the duchess does something, she does it all the way, and she does nothing with as much gusto as party planning."

"I love how you make the phrase 'party planning' sound like waterboarding."

"Maybe not quite that bad, but close." Emma shivered. "I love that the movies are getting made, and they mean so much to the area, but the whole thing's exhausting."

"Champagne problems."

Emma bumped her shoulder. "I know, right? No one feels sorry for the little introvert writer. I just wish I weren't so awkward in front of a crowd."

"I'm sure it's not that bad."

"You don't know. You get to stay in your lovely gallery, painting in peace and quiet. Do you know how much I envy you these days?"

"I'd trade you a bit of my solitude for a few of your royalties."

"If you could make that deal, I'd gladly pay—"

"There you are, Volant. You owe me a drink!"

They both turned toward the booming interruption, as did the entire pub, as Charlie McKay burst through the door.

"Good lord, Charles," Brogan snapped. "It's a business, not a barn."

"Sorry." He managed to look properly chastised by his big sister, but that didn't keep him from making a beeline toward the bar.

"Quite an entrance there," Emma said. "Why do I owe you a drink?"

"Because I've put in wicked work hours all week, and then just when I'm ready to fall into my own bed and sleep the sleep of a dead man, more of your distinguished guests get reckless and suddenly it's 'Charlie, be a good chap and dig them out all afternoon and into the bloody evening.'"

"Aw, poor baby." Emma laughed. "I'm sorry you had to do actual work this week instead of zipping all over the county in the duke's Land Rovers, but I can't take responsibility for anything post-party. I don't go near that family's drama."

"I'd like to not go near it either, but this afternoon it came covered in dirt and motor oil."

"Dirt and motor oil?" Claire asked. The phrase hit a little too close to where her mind kept wandering.

"Oh, hi, Claire," Charlie said as if noticing her for the first time.

"Why this afternoon?" Emma pulled him back. "Vic said everyone would leave right after breakfast."

Claire's interest piqued at the name Vic, accompanied by the memory of the stunning woman in the Land Rover that morning. Surely there had to be some mistake, though, because her neighbours seemed to be talking about the castle dwellers up the road, and Pip had called the Vic who came to get her "cousin." She gave a subtle nod to the gene pool that managed to produce the two of them, though completely different in their colouring and carriage, and yet both shockingly attractive.

"Everyone was supposed to leave, but there was some sort of hubbub with a family member, and you know I can't share the details, but it's no great secret that the fallout involved me digging an absurdly expensive motorcycle out of a sheep field for two hours."

"For your boss's family?" Claire asked.

"Aye."

"And for clarity, your boss is . . .?"

Charlie stood a little straighter. "I'm in the employ of the Duke of Northland, though I mostly fall under the purview of Lady Victoria Penchant. If she were into such titles, one might call me her personal valet, but I also oversee transport for her movie business. Sometimes I do maintenance on the family fleet, but the motorcycle today was way beyond my skills."

The hair on the back of her arms stood on end. "Because it was so badly wrecked, or because it was so old?"

"I wouldn't call it old. Classic maybe. Trust me, if I could've fixed it, I would have. Then I would've risked my job for a chance to take the long way back to the castle. God, I bet she corners like a—"

"Okay." Claire rolled her eyes. She'd heard enough about the damn bike for one day. She didn't need Charlie to wax poetic while she tried to solve a much bigger equation. If Vic were Pip's cousin, and this Vic in question was actually Lady Victoria Penchant, then that meant Pip wasn't merely deliriously good-looking and sharp-witted. She was also . . . nobility . . . or . . .? Claire didn't really understand all the titles, but at the very least Pip was related to the local nobility?

She turned from Charlie to Emma, who both stared at her expectantly, but she couldn't manage to form any coherent questions without leading her to answers she wasn't sure she wanted. Thankfully, she didn't have to sit in the awkwardness for too long before her phone buzzed.

She didn't recognize the number on the screen, but she was so eager for a distraction she accepted the call anyway. "Hello?"

"Hello, Claire?"

"Yes."

"This is Pip, erm, Flip, whichever you prefer."

She didn't know how to respond.

"You know, from this morning."

Still nothing.

"I wrecked my prized possession in your field, we did this charming bit around concussion protocol. Honestly, I thought I'd made more of an impression."

"How did you get my mobile number?"

"Ah, I must admit, when you let me borrow your phone, in addition to calling my sister, I also dialled my own number so I could have yours. I understand that might seem presumptuous, but I assure you I wanted only to properly thank you for your hospitality."

Claire managed a little scoffing sound. "My hospitality overwhelmed you and inspired gratitude, did it?"

"You were a regular Florence Nightingale," Pip said, and Claire could hear the smile in her voice. "And since it seems as though I'll be in the area longer than expected, I hoped to take you out for a drink or perhaps dinner to show my appreciation."

Claire's palms began to sweat. She didn't need this. She was honest enough to admit to herself that a part of her might want it, but that was a bad part, a traitorous part, a part with a history of horrible judgment in similar situations. No, wanting to have dinner with someone like Pip only served as the strongest evidence of why she should say no.

"Claire?" Pip asked.

"Yes?"

"Do we have a spotty connection, or have I made some grievous social error?"

"No, I may have made some misjudgments of my own, though."

"How so?"

"Hmm, where to even begin?" She rewound the morning's interactions in her mind until she hit on something solid. "How about last names?"

"What about them?" Pip's voice grew a little higher.

"It might be time to share them now."

Pip groaned.

"Yeah." The reaction confirmed Claire's fears. "You do have a full name, don't you?"

"I do indeed, but if I tell it to you, everything will change, so I want you to promise you'll still go to dinner with me after I say it."

"Still? That implies I agreed to go in the first place, which I didn't."

Pip laughed. "Then I suppose I'm under no obligation to answer your question."

Claire gritted her teeth and glanced at Charlie and Emma, who were both doing a rather poor job of hiding the fact that they were totally eavesdropping. She couldn't blame them. She had no one but herself to blame for this predicament, and as much as she didn't love the quid pro quo aspect of this dinner date she had little faith in her ability to withstand her own curiosity. "Fine."

"Fine? As in you'll tell me your full name and let me take you to dinner at your earliest convenience?"

"Fine. My name is Claire Bailey, and I'm free in the evening . . . pretty much always."

"It's lovely to formally make your acquaintance," Pip said with an interesting mix of triumph and trepidation. "I'm Lady Phillipa Anne Marion Farne-Sacksley of Mulgrave, but please call me Pip when I pick you up at seven tomorrow evening."

Claire put her head down on the bar as the words worked their way into her brain with all the force of an ice pick. She had to say something, but every one of her better angels asked her to end all this right now. Only she'd promised she wouldn't. Keeping promises had to be a good thing, right?

"Claire, you're making me question the connection again."

"I'm here."

"And?"

"Goodnight, Pip."

She disconnected the phone and dropped it next to her head on the bar.

A warm, gentle hand landed on her back with a sympathetic pat. "You want to talk about it?" Emma asked softly.

"I probably need to do," Claire managed weakly, "but first I think you owe me a drink now, too."

Chapter Five

Pip pulled up in front of the building for the first time. It appeared to be an old stone schoolhouse, but the sign designated it as an art gallery and gift shop.

Curious.

In the garden yesterday, with Claire in her casual attire and bare feet, Pip assumed she'd just woken and stepped out her back door. It hadn't occurred to her that this might be Claire's place of work. And if so, would she still be here past business hours?

She'd sensed the hesitance in Claire's voice during their phone call. She would've had to be deaf not to, but she hadn't even considered the possibility of being stood up. Things like that didn't happen to her, but then again, nothing about Claire meshed with Pip's usual experience with women. She found herself both nervous and excited about that fact as she climbed out of the borrowed Land Rover and headed toward the shop's entrance.

She reached the door, not sure if she should knock as if she were at someone's home or walk in like a business. Thankfully, Claire spared her the awkwardness by stepping out to greet her.

"Good evening, Ms. Bailey." Pip hoped the warmth of the

greeting could be explained by politeness, and not by the way her body temperature ratcheted up at the sight of Claire's tight jeans and subtlest hint of cleavage at the V-neck of her teal shirt. The ensemble wasn't as formal as Pip's own trousers and the light blue oxford she'd left open at the collar, but she doubted anyone would balk at such simple beauty.

Claire's eyes skimmed her once over before meeting her own. "Should I assume you weren't planning to eat in the village?"

"Whatever gave you that idea?"

"You're a bit overdressed for a pub or beer garden, and those are our only real options unless you wanted takeaway fish and chips or curry."

"All stellar choices . . ." Pip got the sense that coming off as overly formal might make Claire more skittish. "But I'd intended to head into Newpeth. I've heard the castle gardens have a lovely restaurant, though I've never—"

"Nope."

"Pardon?"

"You're not taking me to dinner at your cousin's castle."

"No, of course not. I meant an actual restaurant in the gardens, which are—"

"Part of the castle," Claire said flatly.

"Castle adjacent," Pip admitted weakly, "though I've never even been in the restaurant, and I hear it's lovely with nice views, and—it's still a no, isn't it?"

Claire shook her head. "Sorry, but I'm not comfortable going to dinner on your home field. There's too much of a power dynamic there. It gives you an emotional advantage."

"Technically, Penchant castle is my cousin's home field."

"Any castle or grounds you have at your personal disposal works to your advantage, and I'm sure there are a great many women in your circles who'd eat that sort of thing up, but I'm not one of them."

"I've started to gather as much." Pip smiled, remembering why she'd felt drawn to Claire in the first place. "What did you have in mind instead?"

"Neutral territory. Someplace small, local, and casual."

She nodded thoughtfully as if giving the matter some consideration, but in reality letting Claire pick the restaurant didn't constitute any major concession. "Very well, why don't you choose a place you feel offers the appropriate amount of neutrality, and I promise I'll be content to simply be in your company."

Claire sighed.

"What?"

"That was graceful."

"Thank you?" Pip laughed. "Would you rather I stumbled or perhaps stamped my foot and demanded you bend to my will?"

Claire finally smiled. "Maybe. I would've found that more amusing, but since you've decided to be mature about it, now I will too."

"Does that mean we won't be eating curry with our fingers as we hover over a park bench?"

"Not tonight. Let's go to the Raven."

With a nod of agreement Pip extended her arm for Claire to take, only to be met with a little chuckle and a shake of the head. She dropped her elbow and hoped her cheeks didn't colour too much as she tried another angle. "Why don't you lead the way?"

Claire seemed more comfortable with that plan and set off at a moderate pace, leaving Pip to fall in beside her as they strolled through the middle of a small roundabout and down a slight incline onto the main street of a picturesque village. Long row houses rose a couple of stories high on either side of them, many with flower boxes or brightly painted doors. Crooked little alleyways and open carriage arches offered alternating glimpses of either the estuary or the sea, and somewhere up ahead a church bell tolled the hour from its pretty spire.

"Your village is quite lovely. Am I correct it's the one where Victoria and Sophia shot their recent movie?"

"Yes, and while the locals do seem fond of your cousin, around here it's referred to as Emma's movie."

"Emma?"

"She wrote the book it's based on, and she lives in the village."

"Well done, her."

"This is her second movie adaption, and while I wasn't living here for either of them, she's a point of pride for most village residents."

"As she should be, and now that you mention it, I do believe my newest and favourite in-law, Sophia, was part of that first movie as well. I seem to remember stories around her and Vic's courtship that left the family quite scandalized."

"I wouldn't know." Claire directed them down a narrow cobblestone offshoot. "I don't hang out with movie stars or the nobility they offend."

"Pity," Pip said airily as Claire pulled on a low wooden door. "Sophia's arrival made for interesting dinner conversations."

They stepped into the pub, and a greeting went up from somewhere to the right of them before Pip's eyes even adjusted to the dimmer light.

She turned to see an older woman sitting at a table with a middle-aged man.

"Hello, Ester," Claire said warmly, "and hi, Will. How was the water today?"

"Smooth as glass," the man said in an almost dreamy tone. "You'll have to come with me next time. Your nan said you wanted to paint more puffins."

"She wants me to paint more puffins."

He laughed, and his cheeks pushed his dark beard almost to the corners of his eyes. "I see."

"Who knows?" Claire said, a lightness in her voice. "I may give in one of these days."

"Oh hi, Claire." A redheaded woman came from somewhere in the back and took up a place behind the bar.

"Claire's here?" someone asked from the direction the woman had come from, and a second later a pretty blonde came in as well.

"Do you know the entire pub?" Pip asked.

Claire shrugged. "It's a small village."

A young man pushed open the door they'd used. He looked so similar to the woman behind the bar that Pip did a double take as he nearly bumped into them.

"What er ya blocking the doorway for?" he said with a grin. "Can't make up your mind, Claire?"

Pip turned to her date with an accusatory scoff. "What was it you were saying about neutral territory?"

Claire managed a sheepish grin, but before she could offer up any defence, the young man stopped in his tracks and straightened up.

"Lady Mulgrave," he said stiffly, "my apologies."

Her chest tightened as she finally recognized him as Vic's valet. "No worries."

"Can I get you a table or a drink, ma'am?" he offered quickly.

Claire raised an eyebrow pointedly. "Yes, Lady Mulgrave, would you like to stay here, or did you want to have another discussion about level playing fields?"

Pip's shoulders fell slightly, but she managed to lift her chin as she nodded toward an empty booth in the corner. "Fair enough."

✺ ✺ ✺

Maybe Claire hadn't thought this through. She hadn't wanted to let Pip get too far into her comfort zone, but in bringing her to the Raven, she may have inadvertently let the woman too far into her own. She hadn't expected to see her relaxed and at ease in a small-town pub, making easy conversation and passing the evening amiably amid Claire's new friends and neighbours. She also hadn't expected her to tuck right into a shockingly large portion of Brogan's bangers and mash with gusto, while Claire took smaller, more deliberate bites of her pork medallions.

Pip didn't seem to mind the extra time, though. She sat across from her, a pint of cider in one hand, and her other arm draped casually across the back of the booth as she kept up more

42

than her half of the conversation. Her hair looked darker in the dim light and had been brushed back so only one strand fell across her perfectly smooth forehead, giving a purposefully rakish appeal that set Claire's teeth on edge.

Maybe she should've let Pip drive them to the castle after all. At least there Claire would've felt out of place. She needed one of them to, and after less than an hour Pip had made herself at home here. Or maybe women like Pip could feel at home anywhere.

"So, you weren't raised here in the village?" Pip asked, keeping with her trend of amiably prying questions.

"No, my childhood was much more convoluted than that."

"How so?"

"My mum was raised here, but she met my dad at uni in Edinburgh when he was studying abroad."

"Where's he from?"

"America, kind of all over the country. His family moved a lot, but when he fell in love with my mum, he decided he wanted to try the whole small village life, put down roots, work a steady job, and spend Saturdays with the in-laws at the seashore."

"The American dream, but in England," Pip summarized.

"Exactly." Claire sipped from her glass of water. She hadn't wanted to risk alcohol consumption for fear of lowering her inhibitions around someone who was already too disarming for her tastes. "Only, jobs were hard to come by in North East England in those days . . . and, honestly, most days still are. They had me here, and my brother Matt two years later, and then apparently that was two mouths too many to feed in the local economy."

Pip nodded as if she understood such things when, really, how could she possibly? "So they moved away?"

"Yes. They were still pretty young and idealistic. I think they got it in their heads that if they wanted that American dream, they'd have to make a stab at the real American life. We moved to the States when I was three and I spent the rest of my childhood and youth there."

"Were you, like, so cool?" Pip asked in a passable version of a Valley Girl California accent. "Did you, like, go to the mall with your friends and surf big waves and eat apple pies at the baseball games?"

She tried not to laugh, and mostly she succeeded. "Yes to the mall, no to the surfing, yes to apple pie and baseball, though never together. You eat hot dogs at baseball games."

"I learned something new today," Pip said brightly. "You always hear about the two mentioned together. I assumed they happened simultaneously. Like you swung the bat and then you ran to the pie."

"Look," Claire said with mock seriousness, "I think what you just said is both blasphemy and a genius idea that someone should actually market."

"Brilliant, now who do you know in marketing back in America?"

"That's a big old nobody," Claire said quickly. "I've been in the UK for ten years now, but I don't know anyone good in marketing here either."

"Ten years? Why would you want to leave all the malls and the apple pies behind?"

"I hate to burst your bubble, but malls are terrible now."

Pip made a clutching motion at her chest. "Oh no, what about the pie?"

"You're safe there. Americans are really good at sweet pies, but the Brits win in the savoury department, so the pies are a wash. The rest of America is kind of a wash, too." Claire slipped deeper into the comfort of this topic. "There are things I miss pretty badly, but there are things I don't. As a teen, though, I wanted something different, something more worldly and cosmopolitan. My parents were living outside Atlanta, Georgia at the time, and to an eighteen-year-old girl in a suburban high school Europe felt like a fantastical dream."

"Europe, yes." Pip nodded. "Paris, Rome, Barcelona, Prague maybe, but Amberwick, England?"

"I didn't start out here. I went to London first," Claire

44

clarified. "I already had a British passport and citizenship, and I was accepted to the Royal College of Art in London."

Pip's eyebrows shot up, and she tipped her pint glass with an impressed nod, which was exactly the right response, and Claire warmed at the acknowledgement of her accomplishment even if it did feel like eons ago.

"So I went to school in the city and then stayed."

"Stayed and did what?"

"That's an even longer, more convoluted story," she said quickly.

"I like long, convoluted stories. They're kind of my thing."

"Kind of your thing?"

"I have a lot of things, mind you, but one of them is complex narratives."

Claire eyed her more closely, not just her relaxed posture, but her bright, engaging eyes, the open collar of her shirt, the way she sat forward in anticipation of her answer. "Why do I get the feeling you've spun quite a few of them for yourself?"

Pip smiled slowly. "For myself and for quite a few others, but that doesn't make me any less interested in hearing yours."

The easy admittance should have frightened her, and on some level it did. Pip wasn't even trying to hide the fact that she led a complicated life and she complicated the lives of others around her. How much more of a warning sign did Claire need?

She shouldn't sit here sharing her life story with this person. And what's more, it shouldn't be so easy for her to do so. She thought she'd learned this lesson already. She promised herself she'd be polite, keep a respectful distance, share a great meal, have surface-level conversations, and get out before either of them had a chance to go any deeper. She wanted that. She honestly did.

Mostly.

But she also sort of wanted to know more about the walking contradiction in front of her. She wanted to know how someone could be so haughty one minute and down to earth the next. How someone with a formal title could prefer being known simply as "Pip." How someone with the world at her fingers could sit in a rural pub as though there was no place she'd rather be. Perhaps more than anything, though, she wanted to know how someone could be so sure of themselves and yet seem totally interested in her.

Her curiosity got the better of her, and despite her intention to stay aloof she blurted out, "What are you doing here?"

Pip's electric blue eyes widened at the bluntness of the question, but so did her smile. "I'm having a stellar meal and an engaging conversation. I'm enjoying myself immensely. I'm getting to know you. And, if we're honest, I'm also hoping for dessert, both because I'm quite fond of banoffee pie, and because I'd like to extend my time with a woman who's proven herself rather adept at keeping me on my toes."

Claire sat back. All her defences crumbled around her on the floor, sinking into the puddle Pip's wit and sharp tongue melted her into. Somewhere amid all the rubble she must've found her wherewithal and the ability to process thoughts into meaningful sentences because she finally managed to say, "I like banoffee pie, too."

CHAPTER SIX

The waiter, who also appeared to be the bartender, and perhaps also the cook, set two slices of pie in front of them, and Pip did her best to remember her manners. She'd had them drilled into her for so many years they should've been second nature, but everything else about this evening had been so delightfully surprising she could hardly wait to see what else was in store for her.

Still, she did restrain herself enough to pick up a fork and nod to Claire. "Should I let the American render a verdict on the sweet pie, or should my less accustomed palate go first?"

"I'm happy to eat my pie while you watch, but I have to burst your bubble first."

"Again?" Pip gasped playfully. "Wasn't it enough to ruin malls for me?"

Claire smiled, and Pip got the sense she hadn't wanted to, but couldn't help herself.

"I'm ruthless about shattering illusions, so you might want to hold onto your hat here, because banoffee pie is not American."

"What?"

"It's not. Totally invented here. In Sussex to be exact."

"Shut up," Pip said in her co-opted American accent. "This

47

dish is not what anyone expects from the British palate."

"The toffee is a bit British."

"It's not a proper toffee, but like a caramel or dulce de leche. And bananas and whipped cream? It's artery-clogging gluttony."

"Which is why people associate it with American food," Claire agreed as she tossed a strand of hair over her shoulder. "But in this case at least, it's a stereotype. Most Americans don't even know what banoffee is, and never in fifteen years there did I see it on a stateside menu."

"You lied to me about Americans winning sweet pies." Pip shook her head in mock disappointment, greatly enjoying this glimpse of Claire's sense of humour.

"I wouldn't go that far. American pies are a masterpiece." Claire took a bite of her dessert, then closed her eyes and moaned. "Sweet mother of all things holy, that's divinely decadent. Okay, fine, I lied to you about Americans owning the sweet pie category."

"Triumph." Pip tapped the table with the butt of her fork. "England wins again."

"No," Claire said quickly, then shovelled another bite into her mouth before going on. "I'm just saying it's worth noting that Americans don't have absolute dominance. Banoffee pie should be in the conversation depending on the season."

"Banoffee knows no season," Pip prodded, finally digging into her own slice with a little groan of pleasure. "What can America possibly have to compete with this?"

"Cherry pie, apple pie, pumpkin pie, sweet potato pie, key lime pie, lemon meringue pie, Boston cream pie, pecan pie, and black bottom peanut butter pie." Claire flew through the options without so much as a breath. "All-American, all amazing, and all sweet enough to give you a toothache. Need I continue?"

Pip's jaw dropped, and she shook her head.

Claire's cheeks flushed a delightful shade of pink as she took another bite of her pie. "Sorry, I've got a bit of a competitive streak and a real affinity for pies. Also, some people might call me, I don't know, assertive?"

"I don't think anyone should apologize for any of those things, nor should you apologize for speaking your mind in my presence," Pip said, then after another mouthful of banoffee added more cautiously, "That's actually what I liked about you at our first meeting. You spoke your mind instead of falling back on insipid niceties."

"I guess you probably don't get that much."

Pip tilted her head to the side. "I wouldn't go that far. Members of my family make their opinions of me quite known, and occasionally the press weighs in on that count as well, but outside of those areas, no, most people don't often argue with me about things like the superiority of American sweet pies."

Claire's reluctant grin returned. "I guess I'm not like most people."

"But see, at the time we met, you didn't know who I was. You treated me like any other scruffy, suspicious character who literally rolled in off the street."

"Which you liked?"

"I did, but I wondered if once you learned my full name—"

"—and title . . ."

"—and title," she agreed. "I had my suspicions as to whether or not you'd still relate to me with the same sharp sense of humour you levelled at the scruffy, reckless intruder."

Claire polished off her pie and eyed her deliberately. "You're a lot less scruffy tonight."

A little spark ignited in the parts of Pip that had mostly been occupied by amusement as Claire's gaze lingered on her lips.

"But," Claire continued, "if you were worried I'd swoon and fall into your arms when I heard your title, then you had nothing to fear but fear itself."

"Good," Pip said resolutely, then backtracked. "Which isn't to say I'd mind if you fell into my arms."

"Yes, I sort of got that sense with all your needy hand-holding attempts."

Pip scoffed. "Oh, here we go again. God forbid I offer a bit of chivalry."

49

Claire rolled her eyes. "Chivalry, or socially acceptable ways to cop a feel?"

"On my honour, my intentions are pure." Pip started to cross her heart with her index finger, then laughed. "Okay, that was too much to say with a straight face, even for me."

"Care to try again?"

Pip shook her head and felt another strand of hair fall across her forehead as she watched Claire's eyes trace its trajectory. "Maybe I can't quite pull off the whole pure intentions bits. I get the sense you know full well where I hope these interactions lead, but if either of us do fall into any more illicit positions, I can honestly say I want it to be for the right reasons."

Claire smirked. "It's not something either of us has to worry about in the immediate future, and seeing how you don't seem like the type to stick around for any sort of distant future, it's likely a moot point. But to satisfy my curiosity, what, in your mind, would be the right reasons?"

Pip leaned forward, warming to the mirth in those green eyes. "What about the fact that I'm devilishly good-looking and an exceptional conversationalist? I'm in excellent shape. Ridiculously charming. Suave to a fault. An above average dancer with excellent taste in fashion, food, and wine. Oh, I've also got a zest for life with a hint of danger and an overabundance of passion paired with impeccable manners."

"Don't forget your humble and unpretentious nature."

Pip batted her eyelashes coyly. "I didn't want to sound braggadocious. I like to let people find these things out on their own, but you clearly already know about my looks and charm."

"Clearly."

"And yet I still sense hesitancy in you."

"And be honest, that drives you a bit nuts," Claire pushed.

"I would've gone with 'I find you intriguing,' but your Americanisms also amuse me. Please don't hold back. What other insights would you like to share?"

"I think you're someone who's used to getting what they want."

Pip clenched her teeth to keep from arguing.

"But the little twitch in your jaw right there makes me wonder what's behind your cool exterior, which I'm fully aware is likely a dangerous impulse given your, how did you phrase it? Absurd good looks and stupid level of suave?"

"I'm not sure that's exactly what I said, but again I like the way you twisted it, and the whole evening really."

"I twisted the evening? You said you wanted to thank me for busting your chops after a motorcycle wreck, and then you pry my life story out of me and respond by talking about all the reasons I should fall into bed with you."

Pip smiled at the blunt summary, and the hint of colour rising in Claire's cheeks once more. "And? Is it working for you?"

Claire stared at her, a little shocked, a little exasperated, and with more than a little delight dancing behind her eyes. She shook her head slowly, pursing her lips in a way that made Pip suspect she was working quite hard not to smile.

The subtle tension between restraint and indulgence wasn't much to hang her hopes on, but for tonight it was enough.

⚜ ⚜ ⚜

"Do you mind if we walk past the beach before we retire for the evening?" Pip asked as they left the Raven. "I quite like the sea."

"Who doesn't?" Claire turned toward the water without the smallest urge to argue. "This road loops down to the estuary, along the shore, and back up to town."

"Lovely," Pip said. Claire felt her eyes on her as they strolled, and she tried not to be warmed by the gaze.

"This is quite a picturesque village." Pip slowed at a spot where well-kept row houses bent away like the river below. Reeds and tall grass cascaded down over dunes that levelled into a wide stretch of beach before blending into the azure sea.

"When I was smaller and we'd visit my grandparents, I thought all of England must look like this."

Pip made a little sound in her throat, maybe agreement or

amusement, and Claire finally turned to look at her, backlit in the golden hue of fading light. The breeze stirred a few strands of her hair, and the sea shone in her blue eyes.

She could have been a movie star or some fantasy heroine in this moment, and the only thing that kept Claire from buckling was the suspicion that Pip understood exactly how much she wanted to. Well, perhaps that and the knowledge that as soon as she bent to Pip's will, the illusion would shatter.

"My home has a view of the sea, as least from its upper reaches," Pip said without meeting her eyes. "As a child I knew England was an island, so I believed if I could only get high enough, I might be able to see the water on all sides."

A piece of Claire's resolve faltered.

"And then when I got old enough to understand my . . ." Her voice trailed off.

"Your what?"

"Nothing." Pip sighed and scanned the beach as if looking for something else to grab hold of until her eyes settled on a group of locals busting about down the shoreline. "What are they doing?"

"I don't know."

They started in that direction, and Claire tried not to wonder at what Pip had kept from saying, or the hint of wistfulness she'd heard behind the unspoken.

As they veered onto a narrow dirt path at the top of a dune, it became clear the people below were measuring something at an angle parallel to the surf. They had a long length of rope and appeared to be staking circles a few feet wide and an equal distance apart. Claire recognized several of the town's middle-aged men in the group, and just past the breaking waves one of the smaller lifeboats floated lazily.

"Oh, volcanoes."

Pip gave her a quizzical look.

"I'm not sure about all the details, but I think they're measuring for Volcano Night."

"I must admit geology was never my strong suit, but I didn't know the northeast coast of England had significant seismic activity, much less volcanic threats."

Claire laughed lightly. "Volcano Night is a fundraiser for the local lifeboats. I've never been here for it, but the town seems to go all out for the competition. Teams have a set amount of time to build volcanos out of sand, then stack them with wood and leaves and whatnot. Then they light it on fire as the tide comes in, and the last one burning wins."

Pip's eyebrows rose in a mix of confusion and disbelief. "Did you just make that up?"

"Trust me, my imagination isn't good enough to conjure something like that. In my parents' retelling, it always sounded almost fantastical, the shore lined with little fires fighting against the onslaught of waves and crumbling earth, while people cheer their victories and mourn their collapses collectively. I'm dying to watch it all unfold this year."

"Watch it? Why not join in?"

She shrugged, trying not to belie how much she wished she could. "Maybe next year. I've only been in town about six months, and I'm still getting my sense of the place."

"How so?"

"The only people I know are my grandparents' friends, and they're a little too old to be excited about playing in the sand or with fire."

"I wouldn't think anyone would be too old for such things."

Claire cast her a sideways glance. "I suspect you might not ever outgrow them."

"Thank you," Pip said sincerely, as if she'd been paid a great compliment, and maybe she had.

"But that only leaves my friend Emma. I'm sure she'd make a go of it with me, and maybe wrangle Brogan, whom you met at the pub, into it too, but three people hardly make a strong team."

"I don't pretend to know what constitutes a strong volcano-building contingent, but I'd be happy to offer my services."

Claire laughed outright this time.

"What's funny?"

"The idea of you doing manual labour, digging in the sand, getting dirty and wet and smoky."

Pip's grin turned a little crooked. "I could."

"I'd like to see you try," Claire admitted, then with a hint of sadness added, "but I'm not sure four is enough either. In the pictures I've seen most of the teams have, like, seven to ten people, though I think I read children count as half of an adult human."

"Rude. I generally find children more fully human than most adults."

"Fair, but their digging capacity might be compromised, though come to think of it kids probably have a lot more recent experience in that department than adults. Do you happen to have an army of children at your disposal?"

Pip shook her head as if she actually found this idea a bit disappointing. "Unfortunately, the children I know aren't encouraged to dig or play with fire, or play with me for that matter."

Claire shrugged again. The thought had been nice while it lasted. She turned from the beach and started up the hill back toward her little gallery and loft.

Pip followed quietly with one more glance back to the beach. "Are you walking back to work or home?"

"Both," Claire said. "I run the gallery and sleep in a loft space over the storerooms."

"Convenient."

"Undoubtedly. What it lacks in glamour, it makes up for with the short commute. I roll out of bed and climb down a ladder, and I'm ready for the workday."

"Barefoot?"

Claire arched an eyebrow.

"You were barefoot when I met you," Pip clarified.

"You noticed that?"

"I think I noticed everything I could about you in one flashing moment when I turned toward the sound of your laughter."

The comment caused a catch in her chest.

"When I saw your bare toes in the grass, I wondered if you'd recently awakened or if you worked that way."

"Both, actually. I'd only been awake a few minutes, but I'd come outside hoping to paint, which I often do barefoot, at least in the summer."

"Does it help you connect to the landscape?"

There was no mocking in the question, and Claire warmed to the insight. "It does."

Pip nodded, accepting the reply easily.

They crossed the little roundabout and skirted the Land Rover to arrive on the doorstep of the gallery.

"Maybe someday I'll see some of your paintings," Pip said with a hint of hope that made Claire nervous once more. She wasn't ready to invite her in, not to her home, not to her creative space, and not any deeper into her personal space than she'd already come.

"Business hours are from 9 to 6 Tuesday through Saturday, and Sunday twelve to four."

Pip smiled. "I'm glad to know I don't need a reservation to stop and see you again."

"That wasn't what I meant."

"I know." Pip leaned a little closer, dark eyelashes sweeping low as her gaze dropped to Claire's lips. "But I very much enjoy your company."

"And I—" she rolled her head to the side, a knot of tension tightening at her shoulders as she warred between what she should say and the truth. "I had a better time tonight than I wanted to."

Pip laughed, a quick throaty rumble that pulled at Claire's core. "Such a ringing endorsement. Has anyone ever told you that you have a real poetic grasp on the English language?"

She shook her head, but as Pip stepped forward, she didn't pull back.

"You do," Pip said softly, leaning closer still, warm breath fluttering against Claire's cheek.

The body before her overwhelmed her senses with its proximity, all heat and solidity and the scent of toffee. She didn't want to want any of it, and she closed her eyes against the onslaught of emotions their presence conjured.

"You intrigue me more than anyone I've met in a long time." Pip ran her palm along Claire's cheek, tenderly tilting her chin upward before skimming her thumb lightly over her lips.

Claire's jaw twitched at the touch, and she opened her eyes to meet the blue ones she'd worried about getting this close to. It turned out her fear had been more than warranted as she froze. It had been so long since anyone had looked at her with the singular focus Pip lavished on her now. Too long since she'd been touched with such exquisite tenderness. Too long since she'd let herself make a mistake of this magnitude, and she hated how much she longed to melt into everything Pip offered.

But before she had the chance to surrender to the gloriousness of her weakest impulse, Pip stepped back, breaking the contact between them and biting her own lip as if the move required a great deal of restraint.

Then, with a slow breath, Pip visibly gathered herself, straightening to her full height and curling the corners of her mouth into a more polite smile. "I had a lovely time with you this evening, and I'd like more time with you in the near future."

Claire blinked dumbly as she struggled to process the withdrawal.

"I'd also very much like to kiss you," Pip said, only a slightly breathy undercurrent belying the restraint behind the comment. "But I get the sense you don't trust me yet, so I won't push."

A voice in Claire's head screamed, suggesting a large part of her wanted Pip to push, but she took a step back once more.

"As much as I hate to wait for something I suspect we'd both enjoy immensely," Pip continued, "I'm willing to do so until you want to kiss me as much as I want to kiss you."

"What makes you think I'll ever want to kiss you as much as you want to kiss me?"

Pip's smile grew in size and certainty. "I'm not sure at all, which makes this gamble all the more enthralling, but despite my predilection for risk-taking, I'm also an optimist, and you're exactly the type of woman I want to have kiss me."

Claire's breath caught, and she parted her lips to try to pull in more air.

"So," Pip said with more resolve, "I'm willing to put in the time and the energy to do this like a gentleman. Which is why I feel certain we'll see each other again soon. What happens then will be entirely up to you."

And with that, she turned, climbed into the Rover, and drove away without a backward glance.

For the first time Claire envied her. Not for her money or title or charm, or even her confidence, though she would've gladly welcomed some of the latter for herself. No, what she coveted most about the person who'd just left her standing in a puddle of her own desire and indecision was her fortitude and her ability to channel it into restraint.

Both of those were things Claire felt lacking in this moment, and in every moment she spent in Pip's presence.

CHAPTER SEVEN

Pip lay back on a settee and stared up at the gilded crown moulding around her guest suite in Penchant castle.

She'd spent much of the day busying her mind on mechanics while doing a full inventory of the damage to the Triumph, both from the wreck and the underlying issues that had caused it. She'd taken apart several key components and cleaned others to discern which needed to be replaced and which could be salvaged. Tomorrow she'd connect with Vic's valet to begin tracking down some harder to find parts. With any luck they could source everything by the end of this week and spend the next doing repairs. Best case scenario, she could ride out under her own power without having to pull in any professional labour. Still, antique motorcycles rarely conformed to the best case scenario.

The wait hadn't seemed daunting last night. Nothing seemed too daunting in Claire's company, not even the woman herself. Pip smiled thinking about how Claire would hate to know she saw through her thin walls and weak defences. If Pip had been willing to take what she desired, Claire wouldn't have mustered any resistance, but the fact that she'd wanted to bothered Pip, who generally had to put women off rather than the other way around.

She furrowed her brow as she remembered Claire's dark lips soft against her thumb, contrasting with the tightness of her jaw. The woman was a swarm of conflict and complexities, and Pip wanted to sort them out, or at least stand in the middle of the chaos, relishing the rush of it all. However, she knew how it felt to not be welcomed in a space, and she never wanted to experience that feeling when pressed against a woman's body.

Especially not Claire's body, all strong and soft. She wanted to bend around those curves the way her bike leaned into a hairpin turn. Pip closed her eyes and imagined herself shifting her weight, into Claire, onto her, against her, the swell of her breasts, the indent of her waist, the press of her mouth, the length of those legs.

She groaned and gritted her teeth as her lower body coiled.

Pushing quickly up off the settee, she paced the room. She wasn't some sex-starved teenager. She was a confident, charismatic adult who never had trouble finding someone to satisfy her urges, but she didn't *need* anything in the moment other than a distraction. She was merely bored and unaccustomed to spending much time in her own head.

Without overthinking, she walked through her suite of rooms and down the hall. The castle was relatively quiet in the evenings, and the residence all but deserted this time of year. Still, no estate this large ever lay dormant. Perhaps she could cajole the security staff into a poker game or flirt with a housemaid simply to prove she could, but as she passed the family library, a better option presented itself in the form of Victoria and Sophia.

They'd both changed out of their business attire, but Sophia had done a better job of dressing down in yoga pants and hooded sweatshirt, while Vic managed only jeans and a loose, cream-coloured blouse. Still, she sat with her legs kicked out across the sofa and resting in her wife's lap, looking rather cosy as they both read in companionable silence. Pip's chest tightened for some reason she definitely didn't want to examine, and she cleared her throat, causing them to both look up.

"Good evening, Pippa," Vic said kindly. "What trouble are

you up to?"

"None." She flopped into an armchair.

"Not for lack of trying, surely." Vic shuffled some of the papers.

"It's too quiet for trouble tonight. I'm not sure how either of you stand the silence."

"These days we relish it."

Pip shook her head and turned to Sophia. "Are you to blame for domesticating my cousin?"

Sophia feigned offence as she tossed her copy of a Talia Stamos novel onto the coffee table in front of them. "Hey now, what a terrible thing to say to a fellow rabble-rouser. I'm the bad influence in this relationship, thank you."

"Oh yeah, you two certainly have a wild look about you. I can tell you're bracing for something epic any moment now."

Vic snorted. "What makes you think we haven't already done something epic and you've merely walked in on the aftermath?"

"I hope you're talking about something naughty and not your big premiere bash, which was days ago."

"It was also the culmination of months' worth of international press junkets and a UK tour, combined promotion- and foundation-building for future projects, location, filming variances—"

Pip yawned loudly. "Sorry, what? I dosed off listening to your buttoned-up to do list."

"Oh, sod off," Vic grumbled. "We can't all live up to your busy schedule of wrecking motorcycles and bedding actresses."

Sophia snickered. "You managed to live up to one of those items, darling."

Vic's cheeks coloured, causing Pip and Sophia to laugh.

"Forgive my wife," Sophia continued. "She's not boring. She's exhausted, and this is a rare opportunity for some non-chaperoned downtime. Do you have any idea what it's like to share your home, even a large one, with your entire family?"

"Actually I do," Pip shot back.

"Of course you do." Sophia rolled her eyes. "Then I can only hope that someday you get to experience it with your in-laws."

Pip shivered at the thought of living with Sophia's in-laws, but she kept herself from saying she'd have picked better in-laws because clearly Vic was worth all the baggage her family brought to the relationship. Still, as she bit her tongue, she wondered how many people could possibly live in Claire's little schoolhouse-turned-gallery apartment.

Then she blanched. She wasn't looking to have any in-laws with anyone, not in general and certainly not with a specific woman she'd only known a few days, but she did find the idea amusing if only for the fact that Claire would find it laughable. About as laughable as the idea of her doing Volcano Night.

"What are you grinning about?" Sophia leaned forward conspiratorially.

"Because she's up to something." Victoria set her papers aside. "She's always up to something."

"I'm not up to anything."

"She is," Vic said firmly. "She's been up to something since she was old enough to walk. She's mischievous, always has been."

Sophia smiled at her wife and then turned, allowing the expression to include Pip. "I kind of miss mischievous."

"I'm not being mischievous." She didn't sound convincing, even to herself.

"If you're sitting here with us on a warm summer evening and still grinning, you're plotting," Vic said pointedly as she sat up, and then angling closer to Sophia added, "and you'll only encourage her."

"I would encourage you," Sophia confirmed with a wink to Pip and a quick twirl of her wife's hair. "Come on, let me in on the good stuff."

"I swear, I'm not up to anything, good, bad, or otherwise. I merely smiled because I remembered a conversation I had last night."

"With whom?" Vic asked at the same time Sophia said, "About what?"

"With the woman whose field I wrecked in, and about some

local tradition called 'Volcano Night.'"

"What's Volcano Night?" Sophia asked.

"It's a fundraiser for the lifeboats, a bit of a contest of sorts," Vic explained. "Though I can't see what about the event would catch Pippa's fickle attention."

"What do you mean? You get to play in the sand and light things on fire. What about that doesn't strike you as appealing for me?"

The corner of Vic's mouth curled up. "You do like to play with fire, but Volcano Night is wholesome family fun, respectable community entertainment, and a charitable endeavour."

"So right up your alley then, no?" Pip asked as an idea began to form.

Vic's eyes narrowed. "What are you getting at?"

"Nothing." She shrugged. "I simply hadn't thought of it as an intersection of our interests until this moment."

"And now that you have?" Sophia asked.

"I think you've sold me."

"I wasn't selling anything," Vic grumbled.

"No, it's fine. You're right. We're talking about a fundraiser for one of your favourite charities, a chance to get out among your people, which I've heard is important to your style of leadership, and I suppose I could offer a hand with the actual competition, given my skill set."

"Your skill set?" Sophia laughed. "Is this a competition to see who can sneak out of castles without waking the woman in the bed?"

Pip tried not to laugh. "No, there'd be no real challenge there. On Volcano Night, each team has to build something and then set it on fire to see how long it can burn."

Sophia's eyes widened. "Do careers count? What about reputations? If so, I might be good at this game."

Vic groaned. "I told you she'd encourage you."

"We'd make a good team," Pip pushed, "and I know some locals, one called Claire, and she said a friend of yours might join in, the Volant woman."

"Emma wants to play?" Vic's voice softened.

"Yes, and possibly her partner, who appears to possess the build of a minor god."

Sophia snorted. "Brogan, yes. Please tell her that so we can watch her face turn as red as her hair."

"So, you're in?" Her excitement grew.

"I don't know," Vic hemmed. "It would be a fun night with friends, and also a good chance to be seen among our people, but I've never taken part in something like this from a competitive standpoint. I'm not sure it would be a good idea if we can't make a good showing."

"No worries." Pip stood resolutely. "Leave the details with me. I have plenty of experience burning things down."

Sophia gave a giddy little squeak. "I still don't even understand the rules, but when you put it that way, the poor locals don't stand a chance against this lot."

⚘ ⚘ ⚘

Claire glanced at the clock for the third time in ten minutes, then returned her bored stare to the front door of the shop. No one had come through all day. Wednesdays were terrible lately, as most of the long-term holiday travellers trickled off, their family beach vacations hampered by their children's impending returns to school, and their wallets drained by fees and new uniforms in the coming weeks. At least this weekend should be busier than normal with all the excitement around Volcano Night.

She glanced at a flyer for the festivities on her front window and tried not to feel left out. She'd have fun watching alone or with her grandparents, and by this time next year maybe she'd have more friends in the area.

Then again that's what she'd told herself for months, but aside from Emma and Brogan, she couldn't think of anyone else even remotely close to friend territory. If she'd stayed in the city, she'd have plenty of people she could have called on, but then again if she lived in the city, there wouldn't be a Volcano Night to take part in. Even if there were, she probably would have been scheduled to work at one of the many jobs she had needed to sustain a life in London. The same catch-22 had brought her here in the first place.

And she didn't regret her decision, not really. At least she had time to paint. Which she should have been doing right now. She'd set up her canvas and even chosen several shades of blue, hoping to paint a turbulent seascape, but every time she dipped her brush she came up with the brightest hue, the electric one that reminded her of Pip's eyes.

She blew out a frustrated breath as emotions swirled through her chest.

"I like Pip," she said aloud. "There. Fine. I admit it."

She wasn't sure who she'd confessed to, as no one else could hear her, but saying the words into the void at least released them from her core. "I like Pip because of course I do." She shook her head. "Who wouldn't like Pip?"

Pip held all the qualities the whole world was drawn to. She oozed wit and charm. She was attentive, easygoing, and so fecking good-looking she appeared almost unreal at times, and none of those things even factored in her wealth and privilege. No one with a pulse could resist that combo, which was the point. Pip could have anyone who amused her, and Claire knew better than to think she'd amuse her for long.

The little chime atop the front door jingled, and she whirled, both surprised by and desperate for the distraction. She didn't care if it was a customer, a bill collector, or even a religious zealot come to ask her where she planned to spend eternity. Instead, her eyes fell on Reg.

The teenager closed the door before turning to face Claire with an expression serious beyond her youth. "Good afternoon, Ms. Bailey."

"Good afternoon, Ms. McKay." Claire matched her formal tone.

"My last name's Yates, like my dad."

She grimaced. "Sorry, I see the red hair and think of your relations."

The girl shrugged. "I get that a lot around here, but you can just call me Reg."

"Only if you call me Claire."

"My teacher said we're supposed to address prospective employers with their title and their surname to show professionalism." Reg straightened her shoulders and looked Claire right in the eye. Had she been that tall a few months ago?

"Prospective employers?"

"Yes. I'm sixteen now," she said with great gravity. "I'm starting my A-levels."

Claire cocked her head to the side. "I'm sorry, I went to American school. I'm still a little fuzzy on the British system. 'A-levels' means you're getting ready for university, right?"

"I'm not even sure I want to go to uni. I don't know what I want to do at all, but my parents want me to keep my options open."

"Smart," Claire agreed. "Don't lock yourself in. Life has a way of rearranging our plans."

Reg wrinkled her freckled nose. "I'm sort of seeing that, 'cause for part of our classes this year we're supposed to try different jobs, but we aren't supposed to work for our family members, which, well, is complicated here."

Claire laughed as she realized what she meant. "You're related to more than half the town, and they're all small-business owners. You can't work for the post office, or the pub, or the boats, or the taxi. Here I was thinking I hardly know anybody, and you're related to everybody."

Reg's green eyes met hers more directly. "I'm not related to you, and you do know me. Maybe we could be a good pair."

Claire registered the hope in the comment, but also something deeper. She eyed Reg more closely, from her hair, cut close on the side and curly on the top, to her square jaw and broad shoulders as they swept down into limbs still a little too long for her frame, as if she'd recently gone through a growth spurt.

Reg squirmed a little under her appraisal. "I don't have a lot of experience with art, mind you, but I can work a register, and I can kind of do inventory, and with a family as busy as mine you better believe I know how to clean. Plus, I ran errands and such when the movie crew came to town. I can follow directions and order things and fetch things if you need."

"I don't doubt it," Claire said quickly. "You'd make the perfect assistant for me or for any new business owner. I imagine you're clever and hardworking, and I know you're well liked in town."

The kid blushed, but she seemed pleased with the compliment, and the way she worried her lip to keep from smiling pinged Claire's gaydar.

"If I had a job open, I'd absolutely hire you. Heck, I'd beg you to come work for me, but I don't even make enough money to pay myself these days, much less someone else."

Reg's expression faltered. "Are you trying to let me down easy?"

"No. I'm serious. You're welcome to look in my cupboards, and you'll find an inordinate amount of ramen noodles because I'm living on those and the seventy-nine pence frozen hand pies from Aldi."

Reg's eyes went wide. "Are you honestly?"

"I swear." Claire had never felt so glad to be truthfully lacking in genuine food. "Trust me, I'd love nothing more than to have your help and company, but you deserve better than I can pay because what I can pay is nothing."

Reg thought for a moment, her lips pressed in a thin, earnest line. "Maybe I could help you."

"I just told you, I'd love—"

"No, I meant maybe I could help you make some money. For you, not for me. I don't need to get paid."

"Don't sell yourself short."

"I won't. I need experience more than anything, and then maybe I could get my credit for my school projects, and if I did a good job, you could write a reference for me. Then I could have a real resume instead of a list of jobs I've done for my family."

Claire stayed quiet while the girl found her voice and began to pace with purpose. "I could come in after school or on Saturday and learn the business or maybe use some of what I'm learning in my studies to help you grow."

Claire smiled at her enthusiasm and her eagerness to help. Most teenagers would've heard they weren't getting paid and bolted, but Reg saw a problem and jumped in to help fix it. Claire suspected someday soon more than a few young women would swoon as those qualities grew into a butch sense of honour, but for now Reg managed to be quite endearing in that blend of awkward stages between tomboy and what might come next.

The thought made her think of Pip for some reason. Had she ever been this rough around the edges? Had she chafed under the societal expectations of her station and her budding awareness of who she wanted to be? Had anyone thrown her a line and offered to help pull her more into herself, or had she been forced to muddle through on her own? It was hard to picture Pip muddling at anything, but even the idea of it softened the last of her resolve.

"Okay. I still feel guilty about not being able to pay you, but if you want to try for a couple of months, I'd appreciate your help and your insights. If nothing else, there's always dusting to be done in a gallery."

Reg's smile finally broke through, brilliant and youthful in its exuberance. "Thank you. I won't let you down."

"I know, I'm more likely to do the letting down around here. I hardly know anyone, and I—" Her phone rang cutting off her self-deprecation. She held up a finger to Reg and answered. "Hello?"

"Hiya, Claire." Pip's smooth voice registered with more familiarity than ever, and Claire closed her eyes against her pleasure at the easy greeting. "It's Pip, remember, the one you enjoy roasting every chance you get?"

"What makes you think I'm not like that with everyone?"

"Ah, and here I thought I was special. I suppose I'll have to distinguish myself in some other way."

"What did you have in mind?" Claire heard the flirtatious drop in her voice and suspected Pip did as well, but she hoped Reg wasn't aware enough to pick up on the shift yet.

"I've a great many ideas, but how about Saturday night, a seashore, a picnic basket, a bottle of wine, a few shovels, and a box of matches?"

"Wow, that turned dark quickly. Should I bring my own zip ties and a body bag?"

Pip laughed, deeply, genuinely. "See, this is what I'm talking about. You have an uncanny way of meeting my challenge and then raising the stakes. However, rather than edge our relationship into anything illicit too quickly, why don't we take our time, enjoy the foreplay, and let me provide you with a jump on your Volcano Night team?"

"What?" Claire felt both relieved and disappointed at the unexpected turn onto safer topics.

"I didn't want to be presumptuous."

"Yes, you did."

"Okay, fine, I did. So I spoke to my cousin and her wife about Volcano Night."

"By your cousin and her wife, you mean Lady Penchant and the movie star-turned-director?"

"You're making it hard for me to sound down-to-earth here."

"Sorry," she said without sounding like she meant it, which she didn't. "Continue. What did you speak to them about?"

"About Volcano Night and how it sounded like a great deal of fun, mixed with a chance to show some community spirit and interact with the locals, including one local in particular I'm angling to spend some more time with."

"Who's that?"

"Emma Volant," Pip deadpanned, "so be sure to invite her and her partner, and whoever else you'd like to add to our team of six."

Something in Claire bucked up against the idea of someone else making plans for her, but that part was dwarfed by her excitement. Pip gave her something to be a part of, something to look forward to, and a chance to do something she'd wanted to do since childhood. While Claire wasn't naive enough to mistake the woman's motives as altruistic, she was quickly approaching the point where she no longer cared, and for the first time in a long time she let herself revel in that feeling. "Thank you."

"You're most welcome, and I look forward to seeing you on the shore soon."

They disconnected. Claire covered her face with her hands and tried not to scream into her palms.

"Are you okay?" Reg asked, causing Claire to jump.

She'd forgotten the teenager was still there and scrambled to pull herself back together. "Yes. Yes. Sorry, just shifting plans."

"Is there anything I can do to help?" Reg asked, her seriousness returning in force.

"No." Claire started, eager to reassert herself as the adult in the room, then caught herself. "Actually, now that you mention it . . . how good are you at digging?"

Chapter Eight

"Brogan!" Vic shouted in greeting as she led Pip onto Amberwick's beautiful beach. As they stepped between two dunes and onto the softer sand, Pip wasn't sure she'd ever seen a more picturesque seashore in all of England, with the wide, sandy slope, the gentle tide, the rugged dunes rolling up to the river's mouth, and the stone houses of the village nestled neatly amid it all. She didn't find it odd that this spot had been claimed by a novelist, a film director, and a painter alike. She did, however, find it odd to be included in their ranks this evening. She had no talent of her own to speak of, but as she followed Vic and Sophia into the crowd, she thrilled at the radiant warmth of their welcome.

"I've already signed us in. Here's our plot." Brogan gestured to a circle drawn in the sand, about a meter in diameter.

Vic put her hands on her hips and surveyed the circle, then squinted at the sea. "Seems as good a place as any to stake our claim."

"As if you would know." Sophia elbowed her in the ribs and reached around her wife to hug Brogan in greeting.

"Hey now, I used to work in land acquisitions."

"You specialized in contracts."

"Contracts for land."

"How many volcanos did you purchase?" a fair-haired woman asked as she joined them with a gangly teenager in tow. The kid seemed out of place next to the woman who had to be Emma Volant as she spoke softly and exuded the kind of quiet grace that appeared inborn rather than taught the way Vic and Pip had their decorum drilled into them.

"No fair ganging up on me." Vic laughed, and more hugs were exchanged.

"Hello, your Ladyship," an older man said as he walked by, his arms piled high with scrap wood.

"Hi, Tom," Vic called back, even as she glanced up to watch a drone waft overhead.

"Wave to Ollie," Sophia said, saluting the camera in the practiced way only someone of her film background could.

The drone dipped low on her, and she laughed before saying, "He better come find me later so I can make notes on the footage."

"No working tonight." Emma nudged her. "I need all the gossip from after we left the party."

Sophia looped an arm through hers. "Girl, I have tales to tell."

"While they devolve into sharing my relations' dirty laundry," Vic said to Brogan, "tell me more about our strategy."

"I have a plan." The teenager hopped up to them enthusiastically, and Pip suffered a wave of envy at the way Vic and Sophia eased right into this cadre of locals.

They were obviously not just admired, but adored on a personal level. They knew these people and allowed themselves to be known in return. There was a bravery there most of the family would find distasteful at best and reckless at worst, but standing on the outside of the circle watching easy affection and genuine interactions, she understood that Vic and Sophia were forging something deeper and more powerful than any form of nobility Pip had seen modelled. They wore their status well— elegant, efficient, and aspirational, while still maintaining truly authentic relationships with the people they strove to serve. Pip had always been taught she had to choose between the two, and had never managed to do either gracefully.

"You're Lady Mulgrave, yes?" Emma finally noticed her standing off to the side.

She clenched her teeth and nodded before extending her hand. "Please, call me anything else."

"*Anything* else?" The teenager asked. "Like Johnny Bobby, or Shoehorn, or Bacon Butty or —"

Brogan caught the kid by the arm and pulled her up short. "I'm sorry, your Ladyship. This is our niece, Reggie, and she doesn't realize who she's speaking to. I'm Brogan McKay."

She shook Brogan's hand. "I remember you from the pub. Excellent meal, by the way, and my estimation of you has only grown since then, as I've heard many good things from my cousin here. Though I have to admit, Reggie and I are likely to become the fastest of friends because I swear on my honour I'd rather be addressed as Bacon Butty than 'your Ladyship.'"

Reggie grinned and rocked forward on her toes triumphantly.

Brogan sighed. "Why does everyone around here encourage her?"

Vic gestured to Pip. "Same with this one. Always getting away with everything because they're so naturally endearing. And we all call her Pip, so I suppose you should, too."

"I don't know," Sophia stood back. "Bacon Butty could grow on me."

Emma smiled, and Vic rolled her eyes. "I'm not sure I can survive them as chums."

"I can." Emma threw her arm around Reg's shoulder and extended her other hand to Pip. "I like Pip better, and I'm glad you're here."

She warmed at both the statement and the woman's welcoming appraisal. "Thank you."

"Is this your first Volcano Night?" Emma asked.

"Indeed."

"Mine, too," Sophia said.

"And mine," Vic added. "Well, my first time competing anyway. I've watched before."

"Same," Emma said. "It looks like we've given poor Brogan and Reg here a team full of rookies. What possessed us all to jump off this cliff together?"

Vic and Sophia turned to Pip, but as they did, something up the beach caught her attention, and the justification she'd barely started to form withered away at the sight of Claire.

She wore jeans and a lightweight sweater, the collar of which scooped low enough to show the hint of her shoulders. The cream colour amplified her smooth skin, and the subtle hint of honey curls stirred on the breeze, giving her an almost ethereal aura as her eyes shone on Pip with the kind of focus she'd only moments ago ached for. Her loneliness evaporated, along with any other longings, all of them replaced by a fullness that came from being seen by this woman.

She had no idea how long she stood transfixed by the sight of her, but when they finally drew close enough for the electricity to arc between them, Claire said, "You came."

In the statement Pip heard a hint of doubt she'd hoped to have dispelled, but also a smidge of wonder that stirred hope.

Then Claire turned to include the others in her greeting. "And you brought reinforcements."

"You invited me," Reg cut in and moved to stand next to Claire.

"Yes," Pip sighed heavily. "You brought the useful members. I only rounded up the useless posh lot over here, but we did nick a load of shovels and some dried shrubbery clippings from the castle landscaping department."

Reg glanced at the pile they'd dropped near Brogan and beamed, then clapped Pip on the shoulder. "Well done, Bacon Butty. You have, like, a small tree there. I'm going to work it into my plans."

"Bacon Butty?" Claire asked.

Pip shook her head but couldn't hold in her smile. "Just go with it."

"Yeah, we don't have time, and seeing as how you're all new, I think I should give everyone their assignments because we're about to start." Reg scanned her team, seemingly pleased to find no objections to her self-appointed authority. "In the first stage we should build as big a mound of sand as possible and pack it down. We need a wide base with all our fortifications pointed toward the sea."

Pip glanced at Claire, amusement welling at the enthusiasm of their young general. "Who is this kid?"

Claire's mouth quirked up. "You can't have her. I just hired her for myself."

"Good on you."

"Brogan, Lady Victoria, Sophia, Bacon, and I should all shovel, but since Emma and Claire are more artistic, they should work on sculpting the volcano. Make sure you leave a good tabletop for us to build the fire on, and pack it down sturdy."

"I love how I got relegated to manual labour while you get artistic license." Pip grinned.

Claire gave a one-shoulder shrug. "It's not my fault you royal types don't have any useful skills."

Pip snorted but didn't disagree.

"Places, everyone," an official-looking gentleman with a clipboard and stopwatch called. "Ready, steady."

Pip picked up a shovel and shot one last glance at Claire, who eyed her with a hint of challenge.

Then an air horn sounded, and everyone jumped into action.

They dug frantically, piling sand rapidly as Reg shouted instructions to pat it down or add more to various sections. Everywhere around them voices rose in excitement as people called out and children ran down the shore comparing the entries.

It didn't take long for Pip to break a sweat, but she didn't dare slow. She didn't even want to. The strain of her muscles felt meaningful and productive. She relished the burn of activity and the thrill of pulling together with others in a task that yielded such quick and visible results.

Claire worked alongside her, patting down each surge of sand. Nimble and quick. She darted under Pip's shovel and brushed up against her a time or two, but Pip's intention never wavered from the work. Slowly their mountain rose, its growth proof of their effectiveness as a team, and it took shape, smoothed with hands Pip couldn't help but find a little distracting even amid the barely controlled chaos.

The air horn sounded again.

"Drop the shovels," Reggie shouted. "No more sand. Build the fire."

No one dared contradict her, and Pip had to grin at the kid's ability to successfully boss around a team of people who were much more used to giving direction than taking it.

"Bacon, get your tree in the middle."

She grabbed what was really the top half of a decorative hedge some gardener had lopped off and left to dry until its branches and sparse remaining leaves grew brittle. She planted the trunk in the tabletop of their sand hill, and immediately Claire pressed beside her, working to form a sturdy base of packed earth as the subtle smell of her citrus shampoo mingled with the scent of the sea.

The others worked around them, shoring up the tree with bits of scrap wood to box it all in. Somewhere in the recesses of her brain she registered that Brogan, Reggie, and Vic had begun kindling a fire, but she didn't want to step away yet. She needed to make sure what they'd built in those frantic moments would stand.

Pip stayed, chest pressed to the sand, arms clutching tightly to the trunk until smoke filled her eyes and flames licked up into the lowest branches. Even then she stepped back only reluctantly, and held her breath to see if their creation could withstand the heat.

The fire caught hold and climbed, spreading and consuming until it roared atop their volcano. A cheer went up from the people gathered around, and for the first time she noticed they'd drawn a crowd. She scanned the smiling faces of both her teammates and their admirers, but none of them made much impact until she settled on the person closest to her in more ways than one. Claire's shoulders nearly brushed her own as they rose and fell on heavy breaths, her cheeks flushed either from the exertion or the excitement. The reflection of the blaze before them shone in her eyes and held Pip mesmerized.

She remained transfixed as the tide rolled in. The waves echoed elements far from her control as they rushed toward them, and she wasn't naive enough to believe what they'd built wouldn't crumble eventually, but a part of her dared to hope that even the forces of nature couldn't extinguish the fire they'd stoked until it consumed everything it touched.

Claire reached out, closing the inches between them enough to brush their hands together, and this time she didn't pull quickly away. Instead, she hooked her index finger around Pip's. Only the barest of links, but she gave a little squeeze and somehow managed to convey more meaning than any touch Pip had felt in a long time.

ʕʘʕ ʕʘʕ ʕʘʕ

"Third place out of forty teams is quite good, Reg." Claire clasped her newest and only employee on the shoulder. "And you led us there."

"I thought we had a chance to win it all."

"We were close," Emma said.

"And we have your leadership to thank for our success," Lady Victoria Penchant added kindly. "You took a ragtag team of inexperienced enthusiasts into the top tier."

"If they gave awards for the most valuable manager, you'd have taken home the trophy for sure," Sophia agreed amiably, and Claire marvelled that the daughter of a duke and a movie star were genuinely helping to pep up her young friend.

Reg squared her shoulders. "You think so?"

"Indeed," Pip piled on. "You not only succeeded with a green crew, as Claire pointed out, but also at least three of us have no propensity for manual labour. You probably could have done more with people who actually work for a living."

Sophia gave her a little shove. "Don't throw me in with your kind. I grew up poorer than anyone here. I've always worked for a living, unlike you two."

Victoria shook her head. "Come on, I work for a living now."

Pip laughed. "I don't, Reg, and I never have, but I hope I didn't drag down your average too much."

Reggie shook her head. "You did good, Bacon Butty. The tree planting was brilliant."

Pip lifted her chin, seeming legitimately pleased with the compliment, and another little piece of Claire's resistance crumbled. Sort of like their trip to the pub, she kept waiting for Pip to do or say something that showed how utterly out of place she was in the life Claire had dedicated herself to building here. Instead, the longer she stayed, the harder it was to remember why she had to go. Which, of course, was the danger in women like Pip.

"And it's all for a good cause," Reg said with the seriousness that so often undercut her youth. Then she looked to Brogan for confirmation. Claire saw clearly who she held up as a role model, and things made a little more sense.

"Right," Brogan confirmed. "On that note, let's go see how much money we raised for the lifeboats."

"I'll accompany you," Vic said. "It'll be nice to check in with the organizers and offer my formal thanks, as I am the patron of this lifeboat station."

"Ugh, do I have to go, too?" Sophia grimaced. "I don't know a thing about boats."

"We could work on that," Brogan offered. "You're welcome to sail with my family any time. But for today, Vic, Reg, and I can handle the formalities."

"I'll round out the contingent if you need another noble to glad-hand," Pip said. "I wanted to make a donation anyway."

Vic arched an eyebrow, making Claire suspect she found the offer unusual, but said, "It would be an honour to have a Mulgrave beside me in my patronage."

Pip nodded, chin all the way to her chest as the flash of something more practiced came over her. "Would you care to accompany us, Claire?"

She would have gone. The realization surprised her a little. She would've taken her arm this time and accompanied Pip to do whatever thing ultrarich and powerful people did in these situations. Thankfully, Emma saved her from herself by catching her arm and pulling her toward a blanket she'd spread out on the beach.

"No. She's going to stay here with me and Sophia, and we're going to gossip about you while you're gone."

Vic and Brogan both frowned, but Pip flashed them a winning smile. "In that case, we'll be sure to provide you with ample time."

Then, before walking away, she winked at Claire.

Honest to God winked at her.

Claire stared at her retreating form in a mix of disbelief, petty annoyance, and a disconcerting amount of attraction. Who winked at women? And even worse, what kind of person actually pulled it off?

"Oh girl." Emma gave her hand another tug as she curled up on the blanket. "What is happening right now?"

She groaned and sank down beside her. "I don't know."

"Okay, but something's happening, right?"

"I didn't encourage it, or at least I didn't mean to. She wrecked her motorcycle in front of me last weekend in one of those little twists of fate, but come on, people like her don't stick around with women they meet on the roadside." She turned to Sophia, who lounged with her long legs in front of her and her hands in the sand. "Do they?"

"Believe it or not, I don't actually have a lot of experience with women who stick around. I'm still sort of new to the whole concept."

"Some women do," Claire said. "You only have to look at Brogan, and you know she's a good one who won't let anyone down."

Emma glanced in the direction her wife had walked and smiled sheepishly. "Sorry, yeah. I can't argue there."

"And you shouldn't. You found a keeper, and I don't really know you, Sophia, but I get the very limited impression Lady Victoria is the rare breed who actually takes all her ancient responsibilities seriously?"

Sophia sighed. "Serious as a heart attack."

Claire rolled her eyes heavenward. "Good for both of you. You did things the way you're supposed to. You found these model women and fell in love, and everything you read about in books and watch in movies teaches us you're destined to live happily ever after, but Pip is not Brogan McKay, and she's not Lady Victoria. She's the player, she's the charmer, she's the one who teaches women hard lessons about why they should learn to be attracted to someone steadier and more stable. Honest to God, I can't even believe she's still here."

"Still here as in 'here in the village' or still here as in 'still chasing you even though you didn't immediately swoon for her'?" Emma asked.

"Either. Both?" Claire fell back and stared up at the light as it faded from golden to orange around them. "She apparently lives in a castle somewhere. I didn't ask for the details because I don't want to know, but clearly she has options. She doesn't have to stay here because she broke her motorbike, right?"

Sophia snorted. "No. Vic offered to lend her any number of vehicles so we could finally have some privacy."

Her chest tightened at the confirmation. "I promise I haven't encouraged her to hang around. Hell, I've been downright rude a time or two. I laughed at her when she wrecked. That was our first interaction. She could have broken her neck, and I mocked her."

Emma and Sophia shared a conspiratorial grin.

"What?" She sat back up.

Emma giggled. "It's just so classic."

"What's classic?"

"She's a glutton for punishment." Sophia shook her head.

"I mean, I knew it ran in the family, but I always got the sense Pip wasn't much like the rest of the family. Then again, maybe it runs on the queer side, because Vic and I almost got into a sword fight when we first met."

"No! You two are like model citizens."

Sophia gasped. "Shut your mouth. I nearly destroyed the whole family line. I can't believe some ne'er-do-well cousin is going to come along and upset my reputation, but you're not wrong to be bemused. Pippa's not known for sticking around. I'm not sure I've spent more than a few hours in the same room with her in the last two years."

"So why now?" Claire asked.

"Women like Pip like a challenge," Emma said matter-of-factly, "and you've been challenging. You've told her no and tried to maintain some boundaries, which I think she probably doesn't run into often."

"If she's not used to being told no, shouldn't that make her dislike me?"

"Quite the opposite," Emma explained. "It's similar to the laws of physics. She likes you because you're not like all the other girls. The question is, what do you like?"

Claire rolled her eyes again. "If my dating history is any indication, I only like people who are horrible for me. And also, yeah, since you brought it up, I do have a type, one with a very specific profile."

Emma tilted her head to the side. "Care to share the profile?"

She gestured off down the beach in the general direction Pip had gone. "Her. She's the profile. If I could've drawn an over-the-top caricature of the type of person who consistently breaks my heart and then turned the cartoon into a person, the person would be Pip."

"Wow."

"Right? It's stupid how much she should come with a warning sticker plastered on her perfectly smooth forehead that reads 'Claire Bailey, do not do this again.'"

"Again?" Sophia asked.

"So much again. I have a ten-year track record of falling for people just like her. She's charming and privileged and reckless and self-absorbed, and the thing is I can't even blame her. How could she not be with that jaw and her androgynous frame and those eyes?"

"The eyes run in the family," Sophia admitted. "Vic and her sister both have them, but I'll admit, with Pip's dark hair, the colour seems more vibrant. Not prettier, but somehow, more . . . I don't know, just more."

"Yes," Claire exclaimed. "More . . . too much really."

"Too much to handle or too much to resist?" Emma asked.

"Both! With Pip it always seems to be both. I thought if I did my best to fend her off, she'd lose interest because I'm not at all interesting, and it's been my experience that once people like Pip figure that out, they bolt."

Her mind wandered back to a long train of people bolting in myriad ways; then she pulled herself back to the present. "Which is why with all the others I worked so hard to be more engaging and more exciting and more interesting, but this time I thought if I were simply my surly, average, and contrary self straight away, we could skip to the point where I get left holding the bill or the guilt or my heart in my hands."

Emma squeezed her fingers sympathetically, but Sophia took the more sardonic approach. "How's that working out for you?"

She shook her head until she focused on Pip as she strode back toward them, eyes bright, smile knowing, and a swagger in her step. "Good."

"Good?" Emma's voice took on a new lilt of amusement.

"I mean, not good," she corrected, blinking and forcing her eyes off Pip before confessing, "bad, actually, but I think we've reached the point where the going bad has started to feel good."

CHAPTER NINE

Pip smiled at the three women on the oversized beach blanket and held up a bottle of champagne.

"Where did you steal the bubbly from?" Sophia asked, a mix of pleasure and disbelief in her voice.

"I don't have to steal to get what I want." She handed the bottle to Claire and added, "People always give me what I want eventually."

"Seriously?" Emma asked with a hint of awe. "You went for a walk on the beach and someone gifted you a bottle of champagne?"

"There was a little more to it than that." Vic grinned. "But not much actually. We stopped in at the organizers' table. I said a few words, Brogan showed off the plans for a new lift addition to the docks, Pip flirted with everyone, and Ester practically begged her to take the bubbly back to our team."

Pip shrugged. "I also made a donation to put them over the edge for their fundraising goal, but I'm not going to lie, I do hope I won the bubbly with my charm rather than my bank account."

"Knowing Ester, I wouldn't doubt it," Emma said. "The older women in this town are shameless flirts."

"Something you have in common," Claire quipped, looking up at Pip with a hint of mischief in her eyes.

"I brought some Victoria sponge to share with everyone." Emma gestured to a picnic basket behind them. "But I wasn't planning on champagne, so I didn't pack any glasses."

"I can run up to our house and get some," Reg offered quickly. "Mum's got posh ones for parties."

"I'm closer," Claire said, and stood. "I can get up to my place faster, and I've got plenty of cups left over from the gallery's former life as a tearoom. That'll save time and save Reg's hide from getting tanned when her mom finds out she brought her good stemware to Volcano Night."

Reg grinned sheepishly. "Probably a good call."

"I'll walk with you," Pip said. "They who bring the bubbly must carry the cup, right?"

Claire rolled her eyes. "No one says that."

Pip shrugged. "I made it up. I'm kind of wise."

Claire gave a little snort and turned away to head up toward the dune, but Pip chose to think the move covered up a smile, and followed along.

She caught up as they stepped from the soft sand onto a hard-packed path. "So, was this your clever plan to get me alone?"

Claire shot her some side-eye.

"What?"

"I was wondering the same thing about you."

"I'm not that clever, but I'm glad you are. I'm also glad you have such an entertaining and friendly village."

Claire's expression softened. "I do. Sometimes I forget, what with the lack of business and entertainment, but I shouldn't complain. I have a place to live, a space to indulge my artistic impulses, nice neighbours, and good scenery."

Pip glanced over her shoulder and corrected her. "Stellar scenery."

Claire sighed. "Truly."

"And good friends."

"That's new," Claire admitted as they crested the hill

approaching the roundabout between town and the gallery. "Tonight's the first real event we planned together."

"Really? You seemed awful chummy on the blanket. Would you say that's due to the strength of the friendship or the salaciousness of the conversation?"

"Wouldn't you like to know?" Claire bumped Pip's shoulder with her own and then crossed the street.

Pip followed, amused both by the casual touch and the realization she honestly did want to know. She was more than used to being talked about, in both good and bad ways, and while she tried to convince herself there was no such thing as bad publicity, she hoped the conversation between the three women worked in her favour. But Claire kept her cards so close she couldn't tell.

Claire opened the door to the converted schoolhouse and let them in. The front room was a smaller sort of foyer without much distinction except for a rack of postcards and brochures for local attractions. A large window overlooked the village with glimpses of the sea, and along the back wall a counter housed a tablet and credit card reader. Claire walked around it and through a doorway, but Pip's attention wandered to a much larger space off to the left. As she stepped into the wide-open doorway, she got her first peek at the gallery space. It was clear to see where Claire had invested her time and resources, from the high vaulted ceilings to the natural light to the array of art on the walls and pedestals throughout the room, creating flow rather than clutter.

However, before she had a chance to examine any one piece in detail, Claire called, "I found the cups. Come make yourself useful."

Reluctantly Pip obeyed, disappointed to be pulled away from something that felt important, but the sight of Claire standing atop an industrial worktop inspired only pleasure. "What do you think goes better with champagne? Granny-style flowery tea mugs, or plastic children's cups with lids?"

Claire held up one option in each hand for Pip to inspect.

"Don't get me wrong. Those flowery mugs are something to behold, but I'm regularly told I'm childish, so I'd appreciate the lid."

"Fair." Claire hopped down. "You don't seem like the kind to be trusted with breakable things."

"I didn't know this was a loaded question steeped in metaphor."

Claire raised an eyebrow and studied her for a second. "Maybe that's my own prejudices coming out, but I do think plastic would be easier to care for and clean at the seashore. Do you need me to find anything to help you open the champagne?"

"No. Believe it or not, popping corks is one of the few life skills I actually possess."

Claire laughed, and the bubbly sort of unguarded effervescence went right to Pip's head in a way the champagne had little hope of doing. She liked that sound. She liked this woman. She'd actually liked everything about this evening. Pip took a few seconds to let those thoughts sink in. She wasn't usually the type to seek out small-town fun, or to work hard to win a woman's attention. She rarely worked at anything at all, but then again tonight hadn't been work. Easy and uncomplicated enjoyment were two things she didn't usually encounter. For the first time in ages she didn't feel like she was floundering in one way or another. She wasn't parsing herself or trying to walk any tightropes, which in turn meant she wasn't looking to the horizon, counting down to anything, or subconsciously plotting her escape.

"Claire," Pip said. They turned back down the hill toward the beach.

"Yes?"

"Thank you."

"For getting the cups?"

"No. Well, yes, that too, but also thank you for this whole evening, and for including me in it."

Claire looked over her shoulder with a brilliant smile and a teasing raise of her eyebrow. "You have things backward. You're the one who included me in your master plan."

"But I would've never even known about Volcano Night if not for you."

Claire shrugged as she kept walking. "I wouldn't have thought to even tell someone like you about Volcano Night if we hadn't stumbled across the preparations on Monday, but I'm glad you had fun slumming it for a night."

The comment hit Pip like a dart to the chest. Claire had fired several similar barbs, but for some reason this one stung more than any of the others. Maybe it was just a step too far on the self-deprecation front, or maybe it encompassed too much to be deflected, or perhaps her own affinity for this woman had grown too strong to be mocked.

Acting on pure, rash instinct she grasped Claire's shoulder, halting her forward motion and pulling her around so they faced each other.

Claire's lips parted on a gasp of surprise as she eyed Pip from under thick lashes, testing every ounce of fortitude Pip possessed.

She slid her free hand down Claire's arm and along her side until it settled on the sumptuous curve of her waist.

Claire closed her eyes and lifted her chin, once again giving every sign of someone willing to let herself be kissed, and Pip fought the urge to take her right there in the street. They could melt into each other so easily, and the surrender would feel equally sweet from both sides of the equation. She might not have been strong enough to resist were it not for the echo of that last comment still rumbling through her brain.

Taking a deep breath, she leaned as close as she dared and said, "I don't think of tonight as slumming it."

Claire's eyes blinked open, full of confusion.

"You don't trust me, and I understand why you won't let yourself, but even if you can't believe me when I say tonight was the most fun I've had in ages, you should at least see the value you brought to the experience."

Claire tried to take a step back, but Pip applied only the

slightest pressure to her side, and she stayed.

"I relished the opportunity to be a part of something meaningful, something that wasn't chosen for me by someone else, but most of all it felt good to be accepted into such wonderful company as myself rather than what other people expected me to be. I don't get to experience that often in my circles, and so I'm all the more appreciative you allowed me to be included in yours."

The rigid set of Claire's body softened. "I'm sorry."

Pip finally took a step back, breaking the contact between them, and trying to hide how much the loss of connection grieved her. "I don't need apologies. I merely ached to make myself understood. I didn't mean to come on too strong, though."

"You didn't," Claire said quickly. "I was being unfair, but it's not you. It's me. I mean it's also you, but it's not your fault you stumbled into some well-conditioned protective mechanisms I know are my own baggage to carry. I shouldn't take it out on you, but I'm so freaking conflicted I don't know how else to process the questions and warning bells racking my brain right now."

"Maybe if you ask some of those questions in your out-loud voice, I could try to answer a few of them."

Claire rolled her eyes and started walking again, but more slowly.

"Why is that such a terrible idea? I seem to be part of this conflict. Why couldn't I be part of the solution?"

Claire bit her lower lip, and Pip had the overwhelming urge to do that job for her.

"Come on. Ask me the biggest, most pressing question."

Claire lifted her hands, still holding a couple of children's cups aloft for a few seconds before finally blurting out, "If I give you what you're after, will you go away?"

All the air left Pip's lungs in a rush as if she'd been kicked. All she could manage was a totally inarticulate, "What?"

"I mean, I know you'll go. This isn't my first time playing with fire. I know I'm going to get burned, but I don't know your timeline. Do you leave when I kiss you? When I sleep with you?

When I fall for you?"

Pip had never, in a life full of surreal interactions, had someone ask such a question so bluntly. All her social graces faltered as she stuttered, "Who says I'm going to leave?"

"Don't bullshit me." Claire kept walking, leaving Pip struggling to keep up both physically and emotionally. "We both know you're going to leave, and I'm not asking you to stay. There's no legitimate scenario where this leads to happily ever after."

Claire was right of course. Pip wasn't the happily ever after type, and for more reasons than the woman could possibly fathom. A million images flashed through her mind, from members of her family to ancient contracts to the spires of her home, golden in the setting sun, to empty beds all accompanied by the echo of words she dreaded to hear spoken, and the deafening silences of the ones that never could be.

Claire finally turned to look at her full on. "Are you okay?"

She nodded.

"You've gone all pale. Are you going to faint because I asked about your estimated departure time?"

"No," Pip croaked. "I've just never been asked the question outright before. I had some of my own baggage to work through quickly there, but none of it's relevant. You asked for honesty, and I want to give you that."

"I didn't mean to pain you. I thought you probably had more experience, and I wanted to set realistic expectations. Are we talking a night? A week? A month? A season?" She shook her head quickly as if she realized she had crossed a line and needed to back up. "No more than a season because I'm not taking you to holiday parties or introducing you to my family."

"Wow," Pip marvelled at her once more.

"If we're going to play this game, I don't want to drag a bunch of other people into it."

"What game?"

"The one that you've been trying to play all along and, honestly, that I suspect you're very good at."

88

"I'm starting to suspect I'm not, because I'm not sure I even know what game you're referencing."

"The one where you seduce me."

"Oh." Pip helplessly wondered if she'd ever be able to speak, or even breathe effortlessly again. "I know I'm not very good at that one."

Claire laughed, and shocked her even further by looping an arm loosely through her own as they reached the beach once more. "Now who's selling themselves short?"

"I'm not even sure who's selling what right now."

"I'm not selling so much as surrendering to the setup where you do whatever it is you do to sweep me off my feet and then get your fill of me, however long that takes, and then move on with your life while I pick up the pieces of mine."

"Why would either one of us sign up for a game with those goals?" Pip asked earnestly, for the first time actually examining a familiar pattern in the bright light of day.

Claire smiled at her in a new way, one that suggested she knew things Pip didn't, and found the prospect utterly empowering.

In that instant the tables turned. Pip was the one to lean closer. Pip was the one to wonder at her own resolve. Pip was the one left suspended, full of questions and a dark undercurrent of desire as Claire shrugged and offered the kind of answer Pip could only hope to summon in her most suave moments.

"Because we'll probably both have an exceedingly good time while it lasts."

CHAPTER TEN

Claire set up an easel on the threshold of the sliding glass doors between the main gallery and her back patio, so she faced outward while the artwork faced in. The arrangement had the effect of making her feel both sheltered and expansive at the same time. She needed the former, but still craved the latter, which might also be why she'd begun painting a sea scene even while looking out across the gently rolling pasture.

Behind her she heard the faint shuffle of Reggie's feet as she moved around the large open room with her dust rag. Today was the teenager's first official day on the job, and Claire had almost called her off, once again conflicted about how little work she could offer. However, Reg hadn't seemed at all bothered by the prospect of spending her day wiping down sculptures and picture frames. She'd gotten right to work with quiet focus, and what's more she went about her task with almost a reverence for Claire's artistic process. She moved through the gallery lightly and quietly, as if afraid to disturb the sanctity of a sacred space, and even though they weren't speaking, Claire found herself grateful for the presence of another person in the usually empty room.

She hadn't talked to Pip in two days, which shouldn't bother

her, but the fact that she'd thought of little else since then suggested it did. She tried not to care, but she'd felt as though they'd been close to something powerful as they'd returned to the beach arm in arm as if ready to face a kind of adventure together. But as they rejoined their friends and the champagne flowed, Pip had retreated behind her polished shell once more.

She hadn't withdrawn socially. On the contrary, she'd remained as engaging as ever, still jumping into the conversation with frequent ease. She'd laughed at everyone's jokes and often added her own witty retorts to the constant flow of banter, but she seemed more a part of the group than singularly focused on Claire the way she'd been earlier.

At one point Claire'd caught Pip studying her, gaze intense and curious, but before they'd had time to trade little more than a raised eyebrow, their friends had begun to pack up for the evening. Pip had left with Vic and Sophia while Claire walked back to the village with Emma, Brogan, and Reggie.

Any other night she would've relished the sense of camaraderie that came from time spent with people she'd started to genuinely think of as friends, but after a few stolen moments of something honest and anticipatory with Pip, she somehow found less comfort in being comfortable compared to the thrill that coursed through her while dancing near a flame.

Only now, after days of silence, she'd begun to fear that maybe she'd let the fire run a little too hot. Maybe she had scared Pip off with her boldness or perhaps by making her acknowledge what they were risking in allowing the heat between them to go unchecked. She tried to tell herself that might be the best possible outcome, and the one she'd initially wanted, but she'd be lying if she tried to pretend she didn't feel a prick of disappointment at the prospect of Pip shrinking from a challenge.

She blinked away the memory of Pip staring down at her with heavy lids over those electric eyes and forced herself to refocus on the paint she had been mindlessly daubing on her canvas. With more than a smidge of surprise, she noticed that the scene had turned dark and cloudy. The sea pitched in tumult with deep blue waves, capped in swirls of turbulent white and violet. The image spoke to power and chaos, with a kind of magnetic undercurrent. Technically, the work had more than a few compelling aspects, or at least that's what she told herself to balance the knowledge that no tourist would ever buy it.

A door opened behind her, and she suspected Reg had simply gone to shake out her dust rag, but as footsteps fell more firmly across the room, there was no mistaking the presence of a woman she feared she might have summoned with her own mood.

"What's got you all stirred up?" a rich, smooth voice intoned close to her ear.

The hair on the back of her neck stood on end the way it might while a rollercoaster car paused atop the big drop. "Who knows what drives an artistic impulse? Could be anything."

"Far be it from me to armchair analyse anything the artist herself doesn't ascribe to the work," Pip said, the scent of worn leather and salt air mingling around them. "But in case there were any connection between your stormy sea and, say, loose ends or unanswered questions, would a cup of tea and a few millionaire's shortbreads do anything to calm the surf?"

She lifted one shoulder. "There's one way to find out."

"Then by all means, let's."

She finally turned to look at the woman wreaking havoc on her senses. Pip wore camel-coloured chinos and a grey Henley with a pair of boat shoes, and a set of sunglasses atop her perfectly blown-back hair. The look was effortlessly stylish, and yet did nothing to lessen the air of practiced casualness or easy elegance about her as she held out a travel cup and a white paper bag.

Claire grabbed the pastry sack first as she did, in fact, want the shortbreads, but the jury was still out on the rest of Pip's agenda. "What are you doing here?"

"I thought I was supposed to be sweeping you off your feet?"

"Oh, are we doing that?" Claire hoped the slight rise in

her voice didn't convey the way her pulse accelerated at the prospect. "I wasn't sure, what with the total lack of response to the proposition on your end."

Pip rocked forward from heel to toe and grinned. "Honestly, I wasn't sure either. You caught me off guard, which I think you both knew and enjoyed."

Claire didn't deny either charge.

"No one's ever made me a proposition quite like yours before, and that's saying something because I actually get propositioned a lot."

Claire finally cracked a smile. "I bet you do."

"I needed time to process everything you said, but I haven't been able to think about much else since I last saw you, which is new for me. In fact, everything about you is out of the ordinary for me."

"And?"

"And I like that immensely, but it also makes me nervous."

"You?" Claire laughed. "*I* make *you* nervous?"

"You do, nervous and excited and intrigued and amused and confused. And maybe I'm a little mental for wanting more, but I've decided I do."

"How magnanimous of you to take two whole days to decide I'm worth such a bold statement."

Pip rolled her eyes. "I wasn't finished."

"By all means, don't let me stop you."

"I decided immediately I wanted to take you up on your, erm . . . ," she glanced over her shoulder to where Reg stood with her back to them, but not quite out of earshot, ". . . your offer of more time together, but I wanted to do it right."

"What does that mean for you?"

"That's what it took two days to start sorting out. I'm not used to acknowledging some of what you spoke bluntly about on Saturday, which made me examine things I've always taken for granted. I don't want to take anything for granted with you."

Claire sighed as she softened for this woman once more.

"I want to throw out whatever unwritten playbooks either

of us has stored in our head or heart from whatever games we've won or lost in the past, but no matter how I try to write up new plans on my own, I can't. I need you and your wildly unsettling ways of looking at these things. Which is why I'm here today."

"You want to lay down ground rules?"

"Something like that. At the very least, I hope we might continue, as openly and honestly as possible, the conversation you sprung on me Saturday night."

"I suppose we could sit on the patio, sip some tea, and lay out some general guidelines for seduction if you need me to hold your hand through that process," Claire said with a hint of teasing before adding, "but I must admit I'm surprised you're such a rule follower."

Pip shook her head as she ambled past her out the door. "Wanting clarity on the rules and following them are two different impulses."

❧ ❧ ❧

Pip stood at the edge of Claire's back garden, staring out over the hedgerow boundary toward the spot where she'd crash-landed a mere ten days earlier. Then she shook her head. Merely? Why did ten days feel like such a rush around this woman, when ten hours with the others had often seemed eternal? At various times over the past week and a half she'd tried to tell herself she needed only one more part for the motorcycle to arrive and she'd be gone, but even with all the practice she had lying to herself, she couldn't believe that one. She had made more impressive getaways with much less time or effort. If she wanted to run, she could have done so by now.

No, there was no need to lie, not to herself, and apparently not to Claire, who called out a quick word to Reg, then closed the French doors behind them.

Pip didn't turn right away, but she felt Claire's eyes on her back, and the act of being seen warmed her more than the September sun.

"I'm going to need some of this chocolate, caramel, and shortbread in my system before we have this conversation." Claire finally broke the ice. "You want some?"

"Please." Pip joined her at the table, easing into the wooden chair and crossing one ankle atop her knee, hoping to seem more relaxed than she felt.

Claire slid one of the rectangles of gooey-topped goodness across the table and then shoved half of one into her mouth and chewed for a few seconds. "Okay, that's delicious, and also maybe a good starting point because it illustrates that I'm not some dainty supermodel or high-end etiquette girl. I like food. I like to laugh. I swear. I like dresses, but only in moderation. I often have paint on my clothes, on my hands, even in my hair, and while you might get me to spruce up for a night out, you won't change me."

"Nor do I want to," Pip said sincerely. "I just finished telling you how much I enjoy the fact that you're unlike the women I'm accustomed to sharing my time with. What other concerns do you have?"

"I don't want to meet your family."

"Pardon?"

"Other than Vic and Sophia, whom I actually had a great time with, I don't want to meet anyone else."

"That's no hardship for me, but may I inquire why?"

"Because it would feel too real. I'd have to confront things I don't want to think about. Besides, if I met them, I'd disappoint them, and I'd feel judged or self-conscious, which isn't fun for me."

Pip wanted to argue. Her family wasn't as bad as many people might imagine. Still, while most families would love for their child to bring home a woman like Claire—smart, funny, self-sufficient, and talented—she knew better than to believe those attributes could outweigh the expectations that came with either a title or a rather large estate. She did have some bit of loyalty stamped on her DNA, though, so she managed to mumble a weak, "Some of them would like you."

"I'm sure they're lovely for the landed gentry and all, but I'm still mostly American. I don't even know how to curtsy."

"You'd only have to curtsy to my grandmother."

"Then I definitely don't want to meet her or go to any fancy balls or eat at any other places where they use more than two forks."

Pip's grin spread to the point where it hurt her cheeks.

"What, are those things a problem for you?" Claire asked.

"Not at all, I'm merely noting a few more ways in which you're very different from most of the women I've dated."

Claire drew her knees to her chest, bare feet curled over the edge of her chair, as she took more time to nibble on her shortbread. "You're very much like most of the people I've dated."

"See? That's what I'm talking about. Women don't say those things to me, even though it's probably true for a lot of them." She stopped to think about that for the first time only after saying it aloud. "Once women know who I am, or at least who I'm related to, because few of them ever take the time to learn who I am, they immediately want to meet my family. Most of them devise grand plans to work their way in, then start conniving ways to work toward some extravagant fairy-tale wedding."

"No worries there," Claire said. "No part of me wants to marry you. You'd be a disaster as a spouse."

"Hey now—" her natural defences rose again "—I wouldn't go that far."

"Really? What do you tell these poor women who do want to marry you?"

"I usually tell them I'd be a disaster as a spouse."

Claire threw back her head and laughed, such a lovely, easy sound that Pip couldn't help but join in even at her own expense.

"Okay," she finally said. "Back on track here. You've told me a lot about what you don't want, but what about what you do?"

Claire popped the last of the shortbread into her mouth and savoured, which gave her time to think and Pip time to hold her breath uncomfortably. She wasn't even sure what she hoped the answer would be, but she wanted, almost painfully so, to know.

To know her, to know what they might become.

"What it comes down to for me is honesty and fun."

"Seriously? All this and you could've boiled everything down to honesty and fun?"

"I'm not complicated. I cannot let us become complicated," Claire emphasized. "This whole thing is predicated on us setting realistic expectations, so honesty is key. You want something, you say it. I don't want something, I say that. We get to be completely ourselves, and no one pushes the other for anything more."

Pip breathed a heavy sigh of relief. No one had ever started any interaction with her with such openness. Not ever. "I'm on board, probably more than you can imagine. However, I'd like to hear more about this fun you speak of."

Claire's smile turned coy, almost conspiratorial, as she leaned forward. "Good, because while I can't speak for you, I'm bored out of my skull. I know I'm supposed to want something stable and dependable, and I do. God help me, I do, but I also want some pleasure, some romance, and to be swept off my feet."

"Don't we all?"

"Do you?"

Pip nodded, a little tingle running up her spine at the flash of genuine interest in Claire's expression. "Don't act surprised. I may chase those urges in different ways than you do, but who doesn't want to lose themselves, to get carried away, to make rash decisions based on desire, consequences be damned?"

"Yes," Claire called enthusiastically. "Damn them all, at least for now. So what if I've made this mistake before? I know what I'm getting into this time. We're both adults. If this ends up being a terrible decision, at least I made it with my eyes wide open, and I'll remember that when it ends. Hell, I may even revel in it then."

"Wait." Pip held up her hand as her head spun again. "I was with you until the last part. You're eager for us to end?"

Claire tilted her head to the side. "Not before we get our fill, but once the flame burns itself out, it will still have served a long-term purpose for me."

"How so?"

"It'll be like a virus that's run its course, one I've already had and know how to handle so it won't be as painful as last time, but enough to serve as a sort of inoculation against future cases."

Pip sat back, not sure exactly how to take the unflattering comparison to a mild case of measles. "Has anyone ever told you that you have a real way with words? It's as if you know exactly what someone needs to hear to feel special."

Claire laughed again. "Don't worry. I think we're basically on the same page, so we can finally get to the good stuff, and I suspect once we do we'll both find some ways to make each other feel pretty special."

"Not so fast." Pip shook her head as she processed the last comment and some of the blood left her brain on a southward path. "I mean, yes to feeling special, because, please. But also my rules, as in, what about them?"

Claire laughed. "I love it when you lose access to your impressive vocabulary, but I didn't know you had any rules."

"I didn't either until I heard yours, but if I'm to play within the parameters you've set, then I want them to go both ways."

Claire nodded. "Seems fair."

"I get to be myself, too, not some lofty image you have of modern nobility. I can dress up or dress down as I please. I can go sailing or horseback riding or to a pub if it amuses me, so long as I don't take you anywhere with more than two forks. I can lie around all day doing nothing, or I can make a dramatic entrance to a lavish party."

"Okay, so far you've described exactly the lofty image I hold of modern nobility, but all of those things sound fun to me. Anything else?"

"You never tell anyone my title. It's mine to disclose or withhold."

Claire narrowed her eyes. "Agreed. No aristocratic outing allowed. What else?"

"You ride the motorcycle with me when it's fixed."

"Hard no," Claire said. "Those things are death traps, and

you're bad at driving."

"They aren't, and I'm not. Besides, if I'm going to whisk you away, you deserve to feel the wind on your skin as we make our great escape."

"Ugh." Claire threw back her head. "I don't like it when you go all poetic about dangerous things. You make me nervous."

Pip leaned forward, enjoying the flush in Claire's complexion as she wrestled against her more reasonable nature. "Nervous or excited?"

"I don't see why we have to draw that as a binary. Can't we think of all things related to *us* as a continuum?"

Pip's heart gave a little lurch. "I'd appreciate that very much."

Claire reached across the table, laying her hand palm up, the interest in her eyes expanding to include a hint of concern. "I know I've been standoffish with you up until this point, but it's only because I felt genuinely drawn to you. *You* the person, not you the title or the money or the privilege. If there's something you want me to know or see or understand, I promise I'll give you back as much as you're willing to put in."

A small bubble of emotion rose through Pip's chest and lodged in her throat, temporarily affecting her ability to speak, but she accepted Claire's offered hand and the comfort it provided.

"And—" Claire gave a little squeeze "—I'm willing to at least consider the motorcycle at some point if you promise me one more thing I didn't have the nerve to ask for earlier."

"Anything," Pip said rashly, but she meant it. In this moment, in the warmth of Claire's eyes and the security of her soft skin, she wouldn't deny Claire any request within her power to grant.

"No sneaking out."

Pip arched an eyebrow.

"When this ends, I'll understand. But, in that moment, I need you to look me in the eye and promise you'll always remember me before you say good-bye."

Pip's chest constricted, both at the challenge and at the insecurity behind it. She had never made any such promise to any woman in her life, not even close to it, but then again, it had already become abundantly clear she'd never met a woman like Claire Bailey before. So, holding her gaze steady and clasping tightly the hand beneath her own, Pip vowed, "On my honour, you have my word."

CHAPTER ELEVEN

Ready to be whisked away?

Pip's text message pinged Claire out of her inventory of the kitchen supplies, and she eagerly accepted the distraction. She'd lived here for more than six months without going through all the boxes tucked away on upper shelves in the pantry. One more day wouldn't hurt.

She carried her phone outside and sat in the same chair she'd used during their conversation earlier in the week before typing back, *I thought you'd never ask.*

She sat with her face turned toward the midday sun, soaking up the relatively warm weather while she could. Winters were dreary and damp in this region, and she intended to make the most of every golden ray she had left. She smiled as another message came in, reminding her she'd set a similar intention with Pip.

Eight o'clock tonight. Meet me at the entrance to the castle gardens.

She'd barely read the text when another one popped up to forestall arguments she hadn't even formed.

I know how you feel about castles, and I promise we won't set foot inside, gardens only, and the event is open to the public.

They're letting the riffraff in?

Indeed, which is why none of my family will be there. Not even Vic and Sophia, who are in London for the weekend.

She waited, not because she harboured concerns, but because she didn't want Pip to think her a foregone conclusion, even if she was. Drawing things out was part of the fun.

Also, no forks.

No forks? she shot back.

None, Pip confirmed quickly, then in another text added, *Hors d'oeuvres only.*

I guess I better pre-eat.

Pre-eat?

You know, when you're going someplace posh or experimental and suspect there won't be enough food or what's served won't be anything you actually want to eat? You have a meal before you go so the second meal is less disappointing.

Has anyone ever told you you're a bloody genius?

She laughed loudly enough to startle a few nearby sheep. *Maybe a time or two.*

Sad. I'd hoped to be the first.

You're not my first anything, she typed, *except my first castle garden party. What's the attire for this shindig?*

Anything you like, but cocktail attire is the usual.

Got it, she wrote, though she wasn't at all sure she did. She'd figure it out.

Figuring it out took much of the rest of the day. She'd located a little black dress easily enough, as she had several from her days working as a gallery attendant, but she had to dig through a few more unopened boxes to find anything resembling appropriate footwear and still came up with only some black suede ballet flats.

As she walked up the path to the castle gardens, she felt a prick of relief she hadn't located any heels, both because of the uneven stone walkway and the way her knees wobbled at the sight of Pip, dressed to the nines, waiting for her.

Claire took the chance to luxuriate in the view of her long

form stretched out leisurely as she leaned her shoulder against a wrought-iron gate. Pip wore a crisp white shirt tucked into slim-fitting black pants and a sleek suit coat that had clearly been custom made as it curved in perfectly at the waist to give a hint of feminine figure amid drool-worthy androgynous style.

Then Pip turned toward her, their eyes met, and the temperature of the evening air shot up at least ten degrees due to the electricity sparking between them.

"Good evening, Ms Bailey."

"Good evening yourself. Do you always travel with suits, or did you have it commissioned for the occasion?"

"Sadly, I don't have a tailor on retainer." Pip's tone suggested that fact might actually pain her. "I had this one with me for the movie premiere, which brought me to the area in the first place."

"You're wearing the outfit to two events in the same season? How gauche."

Pip nodded solemnly. "A grave embarrassment to say the least, but the nobility isn't what it used to be."

Claire glanced over her shoulder at the entrance to the lavish gardens as the soft strains of a violin wafted out amid the sounds of murmured excitement. "However will you survive your meagre circumstances?"

"I suppose we'll have to keep calm and carry on, stiff upper lip and all." Pip finally grinned.

"That's the spirit." Claire laughed lightly. She couldn't remember the last time she'd let herself slip from the burdens of her business, her future, her uncertainty so easily as she did with this beautiful human leading her under a high archway in the towering hedgerow. The scene before them danced with magic. Fairy lights flickered as the sun dipped toward the horizon. Off to every side, paths spiralled under trellises or around topiaries. Tangled vines undercut the orderly layout, carving natural pavilions and secluded side shoots all meandering their way back to a mammoth, cascading water feature reminiscent of a grand stairway with each terraced pool spilling into the one below. The entire scene shimmered as it beckoned her forward, its fragrance of hydrangea and fine wine soaking through her senses.

"It's breathtaking."

Pip's lips curled up as if she took the compliment personally. "My aunt's doing. She and I don't see eye to eye on most things, but she's got a taste for beauty and an ability to suss out what people are drawn to."

"Show it off to me," Claire requested. "I want to see it all."

Pip nodded, and they veered to the right, down a path strewn with bamboo and the last of the year's most stubborn rosebuds. They passed a waiter in a white jacket, and Pip snagged two small servings of *brie en croute* with apricot jam for them as they ambled.

"That's divine," Claire said.

"Indeed. Next time he comes by, let's trip him and take the entire tray."

"I like the way you think."

They ambled around a lazy bend in the path, which led them back toward the centre of the garden, and Claire's eyes fell on a large stone and steel feature overflowing with water running in rivulets to a horseshoe-shaped pool below.

"So soothing." Claire closed her eyes to focus on the sounds. "I'm fascinated with the ways in which elemental forces can be harnessed to create moods, like the combination of water and stone and the scent of herbs or flowers. Rain and roses do different things for the brain and body than, say, waves and citrus."

Pip nodded slowly. "I'd never given any thought to those combinations before, but of course you're correct."

"Of course." Claire gave her arm a little squeeze. "I'd like to do more with my outdoors at the gallery."

"How so?"

"Expand it for one. Open up the hedgerows to feel more expansive, but also spruce it up. Maybe a trellis with some vines, but not enough to dim the light. I'd love for it to become an extension of the gallery, a transition from inside to out."

"What would you do with it?" Pip asked as they strolled into a more open area where they could hear the opening strains of a string quartet taking up their bows.

"I'd paint out there, but more importantly I'd love to hold events like this, though maybe not quite as posh. I'd want a place where people felt comfortable staying for a bit, to connect, to ponder, to unwind. Sort of nicer than a beer garden, but not refined enough to make anyone put on airs."

Pip glanced pointedly at their attire. "No, we wouldn't want them to do that."

She laughed. "They could get dressed up if they wanted. I'd like a space where people felt like they belonged, however they see themselves at their best. I'm a big believer in place."

"Tell me what place means to you," Pip encouraged, eyes so intent Claire didn't have any choice but to trust in the genuineness of her interest.

"Places have personalities and moods like people, and they can rub off on us the same way people do. When I lived in London, I became a part of the city, and it became a part of me. I immersed myself and let its essence into my pores until it seeped into my bloodstream."

"And now that you've moved?"

She frowned slightly. "I feel close sometimes—the sea, the dunes, the river; it's all there with no lack of character—but I'm not part of it all yet, and what's more I haven't been able to foster the connection for other people, which is something I'd planned on doing at the gallery when I took over from my grandparents."

Pip flagged down another roving waiter and accepted a bit of fig wrapped in prosciutto.

Claire popped the entire thing in her mouth and tried not to make yummy noises as the sweet and salty both hit her at once. She barely finished chewing before saying, "Now that's a combination, but I want to find the kinds of connections unique to here, and not just in food."

"What else?" Pip prodded gently.

"Local everything. Obviously, I've started with local painters and sculptors, but I want to surround myself with indigenous plants and serve local gin at my openings, and hire local musicians to play under starlit skies. I want every taste and touch and smell, and to immerse my patrons in a sensory sort of recognition of both uniqueness and—" she suddenly became aware that not only was she rambling, but she'd begun to gesture as her voice verged on the line between excited and manic, "I'm sorry."

Pip stopped strolling. "Whatever for?"

"Blathering on about all my half-formed, esoteric ideas."

"Don't apologize for having dreams. I'm interested in what you think of things."

"Thank you for saying so, but I don't want to monopolize the conversation."

"Please do," Pip said with an earnestness that felt out of place on her. "Trust me, your ideas are more engaging than anything I've busied my mind with today."

"No." Claire wouldn't let her deflect, or maybe she would have before, but she'd seen too many glimpses under Pip's polished exterior to fall for the easy redirects anymore. "I've been thinking a lot about what you said the other day about wanting this thing we're doing to go both ways, and I'll admit I hadn't given it any thought until then."

"You believed you were looking for romance, and I merely wanted a quick shag?"

She shrugged. "It's happened to me enough times to expect that trade-off, but if not merely to score, I thought you probably got some sort of thrill from being fawned over."

"Who doesn't?" Pip asked airily.

Claire caught her hand and pulled her up short. "But the more I get to know you, the more I realize maybe you do enjoy being fawned over, *and* also something more. Which means if I merely trade my genuine emotions for your charm and your amusement and your body, I may end up being little more for you than I initially worried you'd be for me."

"I appreciate that, but I also hope at some point you do use me for my body."

Claire laughed and gave her a light shove. "God, you're maddening. And I don't even know you enough to be sure if that's a deflection or a confirmation."

"We're working on a very queer continuum here. Can't I confirm and deflect all at once?"

"I suppose, but if you're going to do so, I should get to ask questions of you, too. I want to know more about your continuums, all of them."

A rush of emotions played across Pip's smooth face. The quick twitch of lips, the subtle expansion of pupils, a flex of wrinkles across her pristine brow—they all fluttered away before Claire could even register, much less read them, and Pip smiled politely. "Would you like a drink?"

Claire blinked, uncertain she'd really seen what she had, and searched for more signs, but Pip retreated behind the beautiful mask once more.

Pip pointed to a porch-style swing hung in an alcove surrounded on three sides by arborvitae. "Why don't you wait right there, and I'll return momentarily."

Claire glanced at the swing and then back to Pip, her mouth open to object, but before she could, Pip nodded and jogged off so quickly the back of her coat billowed a bit on her retreat.

Claire watched her go, confused at the abrupt change and feeling Pip's absence more than she should have.

∽ ∽ ∽

Pip reached the centre of the garden out of breath from more than the easy jog.

She didn't know what had come over her. Perhaps it was the contrast of Claire's dreams butting up against her own lack of direction, or maybe the way the woman seemed to see into her. Most people wanted only the illusion and didn't look any deeper for fear if they did it would shatter. Now Pip felt the same fear pulsing at her core as she approached the bar.

"Good evening, Lady Mulgrave," the young bartender said immediately.

Pip's mouth twisted at the title, but the normal admonition didn't rise to her lips. The "lady" part still irked, but the assertion of who she was, or at least who she was expected to be, soothed in ways Pip both craved and hated. There were expectations of the title that didn't involve queerness or continuums. Hell, it didn't even allow for them. Her chest constricted in a new way, and she glanced up to see the bartender staring expectantly.

"Two champagne flutes and one bottle, please."

"As you wish." The man turned toward his ample supply, and she fished a sizeable tip from her wallet, glad to have at least the trappings of a life she felt at ease in.

Then she pursed her lips. Was this comfort or merely familiarity?

Pip slipped the glasses into her inside jacket pockets, accepted the bottle, and strode back through the garden. For better or for worse she felt comfortable in the role she'd played for so long. She knew how to inhabit pretty places filled with pretty people, and the setting tonight certainly qualified. Darkness had fallen, and the fairy lights flickered like fireflies, lighting her path and leading her back to one of the most genuinely beautiful people she'd ever spent time with. As the string quartet took up a sweet, romantic refrain, she couldn't deny that Claire's beauty went deeper than her own.

She enjoyed listening to Claire talk about art and purpose and all the dreams she had for her own little corner of the world. She strongly suspected Claire would find her role, her people, her sense of belonging. She might stumble or lose her path a time or two along the way, but even the stumbling seemed a luxury Pip couldn't afford. Her place had been set before her birth, and she'd never fully fit into it.

She couldn't fit into Claire's place either, no matter how much she might long to, and therein lay the danger of this game they'd decided to play.

"There you are," Claire said as Pip rounded the corner to see her sitting with one leg crossed over the other and the hem of her dress riding up enough to make Pip's mouth go dry.

Still too parched to speak, she held up the bottle of champagne as a sort of offering to the celestial being before her, and was thrilled that the move was met with a sardonic smile.

"Do you have bottles of bubbly thrown at you wherever you go?"

Pip paused to ponder the question. "Now that you mention it . . ."

Claire laughed. "You live a charmed life. Show me your one useful skill and pop the cork."

Pip obliged, and since they were outside, she allowed for a little flourish to let the cork fly unrestrained, then held everything at arm's length to avoid the impressive arc of ichor.

"Not a drop on your perfect shoes." Claire rewarded her with a golf clap. "Do I need to go rummage through some cupboards and find us glasses again, or shall we drink straight from the bottle?"

"Actually," Pip said, still holding the fizzing bottle by the neck, "reach into my pocket."

"Pervy."

Pip rolled her eyes. "My jacket pocket, not my trousers."

"Less fun, but more appropriate for the setting," Claire teased as she fished both glass flutes from the coat and held them up for Pip to fill, but when Pip moved to sit beside her on the swing, Claire set her glass down and said, "Not so fast. You have to earn this seat."

"Bringing the champagne isn't enough to pay the toll?"

"Not hardly. You all but admitted people throw the stuff at you. I can't be one of many when you've clearly demonstrated how much you like a challenge."

Pip breathed deeply in through her nose and straightened her shoulders. "Fair enough. How about I make a toast in your honour?"

"Not sure that'll be enough, but I'll allow you to try."

Her doubt only made Pip want to raise her game. Lifting

her glass, she met the woman's eyes and held them. "Here's to honesty, to fun, to dreams and days in the sun, evenings dancing under starlight, and making memories that inspire art even in the darkest nights."

Claire's chest rose and fell more dramatically than before, drawing Pip's eyes to the hint of cleavage at the low scoop neck of her little black dress before Pip pulled her gaze back up to the quirk of a smile on the lips she ached to tease with her tongue.

Claire seemed aware she was being ogled, and didn't appear bothered by the prospect as she took her time sipping her champagne. She closed her eyes as she tipped her head back and exposed the curve of her neck for Pip to admire, then meeting her gaze again shrugged lightly. "Not bad, but not nearly as revealing as my rambling endlessly about my half-baked ideas. A little tit for tat is only fair."

Pip's eyes flicked over Claire's chest once more, and this time she didn't try to hide her grin.

"God, one minute you're like some royal Adonis, and the next you're a teenage boy."

"And do you find the combination irresistible?" Pip asked with an exaggerated sort of smoothness, eager to get them back on more comfortable footing.

Claire rolled her eyes playfully. "I think I've already proved I do, but if you want to snuggle a little closer, you'll have to offer me something more. I told you some of the ideas I'm trying to wrap my future around. The least you can do is give me the same in return."

Pip sighed, the sound more wistful than she wanted. "If I had such a thing to give, I wouldn't withhold it from you, but I fear you'll find I lack even your freedom to grapple with those concepts."

Claire merely slid over and patted the seat next to her, which Pip accepted with gratitude before continuing. "When you spoke about the things you wanted to figure out, I suffered a prick of envy, because when it comes to a sense of place and parameters around purpose, all these things were settled before

I was born."

"You have no choice at all?"

"I wouldn't go that far," Pip admitted. "It's no longer as if my father could trade me in marriage by providing the right dowry, or force me into a life of servitude, no matter how much it may feel that way when I have to sit through endless formal events. But the freedom that social progress and feminism brought to my station traded golden shackles for, well, fences perhaps."

"And let me guess, you're the sort who doesn't take to being penned in?"

"No, and I get that I'm incredibly privileged. I'm not comparing my life to people who live in poverty or under the threat of violence, but for someone with my connections, the choices I'm often given feel rather, well, rubbish."

"Like what?"

"Like when I went to university, I was initially told I could study finance, law, or politics."

"I don't see you in any of those."

"Right?" Pip said excitedly, then remembered to lower her voice. "I've a sister who's an architect, but I wasn't good enough at maths. And my other sister chose finance like a good daughter. My brother studied law."

"What did you want to do?"

She shrugged. "I never got to entertain those questions, not seriously. After I dropped out of Oxford, I—"

Claire put a hand on her arm. "You did what?"

"Long story. I'll tell you sometime when I've had more to drink."

"I'm going to hold you to that, but go on."

"Anyway, I thought I might fancy a go in the theatre, but it turns out I was terrible."

"That's surprising."

"Yes, to me as well." Pip laughed to cover the ache in her chest. "So, I tried to sit down and come up with some sort of counteroffer for my parents, some way I could do something I cared about at all, and I tried to make a list of things I'm good at, and it turned out to be a very short list."

"What was on it?"

"Sailing landed at the top, fencing, reading, and I quite liked art and music, though I don't have much aptitude for either."

"And what conclusion did you reach?"

"None, that's the whole point. I couldn't come up with a single thing my family would've allowed me to squander my name on, and as much as I admire the bohemian lifestyle, my tastes mean I'm simply not cut out for austerity."

Claire laughed, and rolled her head onto Pip's shoulder. "That's the funniest way I've heard anyone convey that idea, but yes, you're too pretty to live in a hovel eating beans on toast."

Pip didn't know whether to accept the backhanded compliment, or pout about Claire's easy agreement. "If I'd been born a thousand years ago, I could've been a pirate."

"Why a pirate?"

"It actually used to be a rather logical choice for the fourth child of the aristocracy," Pip explained. "The firstborn always inherited everything: land, title, money. The second one went to the military, and the third to the priesthood, which left the fourth to make their own way with the list of skills I shared, and a great many chose to regain the trappings of their upbringing through piracy. I suspect the lifestyle would've suited me."

"It would indeed." Claire smiled sweetly as she pulled a lock of hair from the place where Pip had combed it earlier and swept it across her forehead, as if picturing her as a little more rakish. "But you said you had two sisters, so one would've been sold off to a rich merchant and the other to a nunnery, which would leave you to the military."

She grimaced, then grinned, grateful Claire hadn't lumped her into the femininely acceptable career paths along with her sisters. "I would look rather dashing in a royal uniform."

"Obviously."

"But rules and ranks and discipline aren't my cup of tea."

"Maybe they would have drilled some respectability into you." Claire's voice took on a lightness to suggest she found the idea entertaining.

"I doubt it, but even if they had, where would that leave me? Not on a motorcycle to wreck at your doorstep, and not sipping champagne under the stars at your side."

Claire leaned close enough to brush her lips against Pip's ear as she whispered, "Then I'm glad you're a pirate."

CHAPTER TWELVE

"Did you ever think Pip looks a bit like a young Jack Kennedy?" Emma asked as she and Claire sat next to each other on a low bench seat that curved along the side of Brogan's family sailboat.

"I hadn't until you mentioned it." Claire inspected Pip, who worked fluidly alongside Brogan to hoist the sails. Today she wore her hair feathered more to the side than swept to the back, and every time a little breeze stirred, the layers fell effortlessly back into place. She wore a cream-coloured sweater, and camel-coloured pants hugged her perfect backside when she bent over to secure ropes from the rigging. Claire didn't know a damn thing about the ins and outs of sailing, but from where she sat, Pip seemed good at it.

"So how many dates have you been on?"

"If you count today, then two."

"Why wouldn't you count today?"

"I don't know. I guess you would, but I wasn't emotionally prepared. Last time I had plenty of warning to obsess about what we were doing, but today she showed up looking like someone who ambled her way down from 1960s Cape Cod and carrying a picnic basket. When did she rope you into her little plans?"

"I think Brogan got a call first thing Saturday morning."

"So less than twelve hours after our first date ended."

"Wow." Emma bumped her shoulder. "Must've been a good date."

She didn't argue. Their evening in the garden had been so much more than she could have imagined. Of course, Pip had been swoon-worthy, but swooning didn't surprise her from a woman with a body like a demigod and the skin of a supermodel, especially when they had a castle and its entire grounds at their disposal. But in those quiet moments hidden away in a world all their own, Pip had also revealed a hint of depth she hadn't counted on.

"You got awfully quiet, awfully fast. Is that a dreamy silence or a darker sort of pensive?"

"Maybe a little bit of both, but yes, a very good date from my end. I just wasn't sure if Pip felt the same way, given how we left things."

"Cryptic."

"We had a lovely time. She was everything you'd imagine and then some, but when she walked me to the car, I didn't kiss her."

"Oh."

"Yeah," Claire agreed with all the unspoken. She'd been kicking herself ever since, but was also a bit afraid of how much regret she carried over one missed kiss. That wasn't normal. It wasn't reasonable. It wasn't safe, but in those moments when Pip had talked about the options off-limits to her, the wistfulness she'd tried to cover with talk of pirates, the softness to her features as she'd avoided the topic of dropping out of school, none of it felt like a game.

"So you're taking things slow?"

"We weren't supposed to. That wasn't part of the deal we made."

"Deal?" Emma's voice rose slightly more than a mundane question might warrant.

"Long story short, we both know what we're getting into, but falling feels like flying right up until the moment of impact, and we want to enjoy the ride for a while."

Emma looked a trifle queasy even though the North Sea barely even rippled before them, so Claire quickly changed the subject. "She does seem to know her way around a boat."

"Better than I do," Emma admitted. "When Brogan and I come out on our own, I'm barely allowed to steady the till, even after years together. Pip acts like she was born on deck."

"Maybe she wasn't far off base when she said she missed her calling among the pirates."

"Pirates?" Emma asked.

"What about them?" Brogan asked, putting her back into tying off another rope. "None on the horizon I hope."

"No, but there's one on your bow." Claire's eyes raked over Pip's lean form once more. "Show us your best pirate captain impression, Pip."

Without so much as a questioning glance, Pip did exactly as she was told, as if she'd been waiting for her cue. She kicked one foot up on the rail and planted a fist on her hip, then with a subtle squaring of the shoulders, a defiant lift of the chin completed the picture. Not even the preppiest attire could negate the glint in those electric eyes as they put the azure ocean to shame. Pip could've sailed any sea, struck fear into her enemies, and made every damsel swoon if only the fates had afforded her half the chance.

Emma applauded beside Claire, a rude reminder that Pip couldn't simply drag her below decks and provide her the ravishing that last little bit of fantasy had been heading toward.

"Well done. I actually wrote a book about a pirate woman once. If I'd known you then, I might've used you as a cover model."

Pip's grin oozed a natural sort of confidence. "There's always time for a sequel."

"Maybe Sophia will cast you in the movie," Brogan suggested, sitting next to her wife and taking the tiller as she steered them toward a small island in the distance. "She's hinted about wanting the rights to that one, too."

Pip's smile twisted so quickly most people would've missed it. Even Claire might've missed it if she weren't still studying her against the image of her ideal pirate. "Sadly, I'd never inflict my meagre thespian abilities on such a worthy project. Not even my brilliant cousin-in-law could direct me into something passable."

"Maybe it's for the best. My friend Talia is working on a book of her own at the moment, so she's not free to take on the screenplay yet," Emma explained, "and I'm in no hurry to do anything but see the puffins today."

Claire groaned. "Not you, too. This whole town is puffin obsessed."

"They're so cute!" Emma exclaimed.

"And they're good for business," Brogan added.

"You don't like the puffins?" Pip asked, sitting next to her as their course arced farther to the south but still away from shore.

"It's nothing personal," she defended. "I find them as darling as the next animal, but it's all people bang on about when they come into the gallery. Puffin pictures, puffin postcards, puffin paintings."

"Lean into it," Brogan advised. "In about a month the little buggers will fly away, and soon after the skies will turn grey. By the end of Bonfire Night there won't be any more people asking for much of anything until spring rolls around again."

"Not if Claire has her way." Pip stretched out her arm along the back of the bench seat, not exactly around Claire's shoulder, but close enough for her to feel the warmth through her own thin sweater, and she leaned toward that heat.

"You have big plans?" Brogan asked casually, as if she didn't find it odd at all to see her snuggled next to this dreamy, pretty pirate who set her brain to boil.

"She's going to make this village about much more than puffins," Pip boasted. "She's developing a sense of place filled with art and music and food that tastes like the uniqueness of the region."

Slowly the realization slipped through her hazy brain that Pip was talking about her dreams as if they were some cemented certainty.

"Oh and gin," Pip continued. "She's going to do events at her new outdoor area in the gallery and feature local gins."

"Brilliant," Brogan said enthusiastically. "Have you considered tasting nights for local artisan ales? We're always getting drop-ins from local brewers at the pub, but we can't possibly accommodate all of them."

"I haven't given much thought to them . . . or anything really." She flushed. "It's more of a wild dream at the moment."

"You should think about it more," Emma encouraged. "Some of the ladies in town have been on me forever about starting a literary arts salon, but I don't have the time or space, and we tried the pub, which was too loud and doesn't lend itself to deep discussion. Your gallery would be perfect."

"I haven't done much with it yet." She began scuttling backward, at least mentally, and perhaps she might've backed up physically too, if doing so wouldn't have put her in the sea.

"It's got to be a step up from the pub," Emma said. "I've been meaning to stop in anyway. Maybe I could come by next week?"

"And what's this about a new outdoor space?" Brogan asked.

"Nothing more than a dream at the moment."

"She's going to expand the back garden."

"You should talk to Reg," Emma offered. "She planned my entire garden when she was a tiny kid. What are you hoping to do?"

"String it with lights and have a space for local musicians, and use it like an extension of the gallery space." Excitement bloomed as Pip answered for her once more. "Sort of nicer than a beer garden, but comfortable enough for people to enjoy art openings or tastings, or—"

"Pip," Claire finally grumbled in a mix of embarrassment and annoyance, "it's a silly idea. I have no actual tenable plans, much less funds."

Pip frowned as if the thought hadn't occurred to her, probably because someone with her means and connections generally had her wishes and wants fulfilled.

"Well," Emma cut back in kindly, "I for one think it's a

wonderful idea, and if it's funds you need, then we'll have to make sure we drum up some business for you."

Claire smiled weakly. She appreciated the sentiment, but she hadn't sold a single painting all week, and Brogan's earlier comments about the impending end of the tourist season weighed heavily on her, which was the exact opposite of what she wanted during a beautiful day on the water with people she was coming to care for a great deal. Of course, now she could think of little else.

"I've got a few puffin cruises scheduled this week, and a full slate next weekend. I'll put in a good word with the birdwatchers," Brogan said, and then with a cheeky grin added, "but they'll definitely want puffin pictures after I get done with them."

Claire managed a small laugh. "Then I guess I better get a closer look at the little bastards."

She rose and walked to the front of the bow. Holding onto one of the ropes, she scanned the island as they approached. Little round heads popped up from between the rocks, orange beaks and bright feet standing out against the craggy, grey shore. She sighed as a couple of them took flight, their white bellies all but skimming the water as they glided low over the gentle surf. They were compelling creatures, as much as she hated to admit it.

"I suspect I owe you an apology," Pip said softly.

Claire startled, surprised she hadn't noticed her approach, especially since she felt her closeness acutely now, though she wasn't sure if she wanted to cling to her or push her overboard.

"I didn't know your plans were a secret."

She shrugged. "They aren't secrets so much as pipe dreams. I don't want to have visions of grandeur just to end up disappointing everyone."

"Everyone including you?" Pip asked.

"Probably."

"I suspect my opinion on such matters doesn't carry much weight at the moment, but for what it's worth, I don't think you will. You spoke with such joy and passion a few nights ago.

That sort of thing is contagious, and I'm proof. You called me a virus once, yes?"

Claire smiled slightly in spite of her lingering concerns. "I may have made a comparison."

"The same goes for you. I got some of your excitement, and some of your vision infected my brain too, and I hate to break it to you, but I fear we've exposed Brogan and Emma to the contagion as well."

She rolled her eyes.

"Scoff if you want," Pip said lightly, "but you're compelling, Claire, and so are your dreams. You can do with that whatever you will."

She didn't argue, not because she didn't think she could, but because she didn't want to.

∾ ∾ ∾

Pip helped Brogan lower both the sails and the anchor about thirty yards offshore a little island inhabited only by a small lighthouse and a couple hundred puffins. She'd never seen so many of them, and now that she did, she also saw the appeal. In their land-based state they looked more like stuffed animals than actual birds, and when they took flight, their grace seemed discordant with their squat forms and perfectly rounded heads.

"Okay, fine." Claire threw up her hands. "I see the attraction, I really do. Doesn't mean I want to paint puffins and only puffins all day, but from this distance, it's hard not to be a little enthralled by them."

"This is as close as you get, though. We can't go ashore," Brogan explained. "It's designated as a bird sanctuary."

"But we can spread out a blanket above deck," Emma offered, "because I've been wondering what's in the picnic basket ever since you came on board."

"I assumed it's holding a bottle of champagne," Claire teased. "Pip travels with them most days."

"Must be nice," Brogan said.

Pip laughed, wanting to deny the charge, but she had in fact packed a bottle of champagne. She'd come to think of it as their thing, and since it amused Claire, she'd continued to do so. Pip loved to see that sardonic grin seemingly reserved only for her. "I also brought cheeses and biscuits and chutney."

"And I brought some scones Brogan's mother dropped by this morning," Emma added.

"A veritable feast," Pip declared as they set to work laying everything out and settling down on some cushions from the cabin below.

"Lord, this is good." Claire took a rather large bite of cracker she'd slathered with Camembert and topped with chutney. "I've eaten noodles out of little microwaveable cups for two nights in a row."

The others all grimaced.

"Don't pretend you haven't done it," she said, then turned to Pip and said, "Okay maybe you haven't."

"No, I have," Pip said sadly. "I gave the bohemian life a go, got a little fifth-story walk-up in Edinburgh one summer, much to my parents' horror. They refused to pay a penny, and I spent several weeks starving. No one would hire me, as I couldn't provide a single reference that didn't give away who I was, and if I'd provided them from people who did know me, they would have promptly told any prospective employers I was unfit for anything other than being sent straight home."

"How long did you last?" Claire asked.

"About a month, and the first two weeks were the best of my life. I slept all day and roamed haunted streets at night. I listened to original music, saw an all-transgender version of Macbeth performed in an old dungeon, and woke up atop Arthur's Seat one morning."

"Then what happened?" Emma asked.

"I ran out of money, and none of my new friends found me quite as amusing when I needed to sleep on their couches, so I limped back to Cambridge when the new term started."

"Cambridge?" Claire arched an eyebrow. "I thought you

dropped out of Oxford."

"I did, again long story. When I finally got back to my studies and regained access to my trust fund, I squandered ridiculous amounts of money on motorcycles and caviar and custom tuxedos."

"Good lord," Brogan sounded properly horrified, but Emma laughed.

"I bet you look smashing in a tux."

"I like to think so, and my grandmother hates me in them, which was the original point."

"Does she expect you to wear dresses?"

She shrugged and popped a bit of ham into her mouth. "Occasionally."

"For what it's worth, I think you'd look smashing in a dress as well," Emma said.

Pip grinned. "You aren't alone in that opinion either."

"Does it bother you?" Brogan asked.

"Wearing dresses?" She shook her head even as she clenched her teeth. "It's part of the job, though heels irk me, especially around a castle with all the uneven surfaces. Trousers are more comfortable, physically and emotionally."

"No kidding," Brogan agreed, "but I meant other people telling you what to wear."

"Oh yes, that does in fact drive me mad." A hint of fire crept into her voice. "People telling me how to live in any way always chafes, but attire is one of the few ways I have to truly express myself, to play, to explore, and to have that infringed upon always rankles."

"What about gender-wise?" Claire asked.

"I suppose it's all performative." Pip hoped the comment sounded more casual than she felt. "I don't have the luxury of becoming attached to any of my whims, so I've learned to treat gender as a sort of plaything."

Claire's eyes narrowed as if she were squinting into the sun, or attempting to see deeper into her. "Why do I get the feeling you've learned to treat the whole world as your plaything when you need to?"

Pip managed a smile despite the truth of the statement and the sting of having her favourite coping method so summarily stated by someone who'd known her such a short time. Unable to make sense of the twist, much less respond to it, she stared out across the water shimmering in the sun as the waves rolled steadily toward the shore.

"If there's one thing Emma and I have learned, it's that we have to find our own ways to make it through," Brogan said kindly.

"And those paths rarely lead where we expect them to," Emma added, passing her a scone. "A few years ago, I'd planned to live out the rest of my life as a hermit spinster. That's how I ended up in Amberwick broken, frail, and a total mess."

"You?" Pip asked, genuinely surprised. "You're a famous, vibrant author. I assumed you two had been together for all eternity."

Emma's eyes danced with amusement. "The first time I met Brogan, I had to present her with my divorce papers to prove my identity, and I ended up practically sobbing in front of her."

"And don't forget the screaming," Brogan added. "She scared me half to death."

"I've never heard this story," Claire said.

"That's basically it, but suffice it to say, we all have traumas to carry or let go of in our own time. Money, fame, or success don't negate our humanity."

"No," Pip agreed, "and I'm grateful I landed in Amberwick, if only because of a motorcycle crash. From the sound of your story, I got off relatively easily."

"How's the bike?" Brogan asked. "I know Charlie's loved helping you track down parts."

"He's a good sort," Pip said, eager to move the subject onto lighter topics. "I also met your older brother, Archie. Are you constantly surrounded by good people?"

"Yes, but don't tell Archie I said so. Or Charlie either, for that matter."

"How many siblings do you have?"

"How much time do you have?"

And just like that, the conversation took off once more as they floated easily atop deep water in the fading warmth of a summer sun sinking slowly toward autumn.

❧ ❧ ❧

Claire watched Pip. She watched her shoulder muscles work as she hoisted the sails. She watched the wind blow through her hair without mussing it up. She watched the reflection of the waves in her eyes as she studied the shore. She watched the corners of her lips twitch up or down and wondered what lay beneath the cool surface of her polished exterior. Mostly, though, she watched for any crack in the shell, like the ones she'd sensed when Pip opened up for those few seconds as she talked about not making her own decisions or becoming too attached to her whims. The topic had come up twice now, and both times Claire had sensed a tremble in that usually smooth voice.

A part of her didn't want to know because she wanted this thing between them to be easy, simple, and fun. She'd heard the pride and the excitement in Pip's voice as she'd recounted Claire's dreams. Those were genuine emotions, and she'd be damned if she didn't want to return them, to offer something real and honest back to Pip. So, as they said good-bye to Emma and Brogan after docking the boat, she took Pip's hand and tugged her away from the road and down toward the beach.

"Thank you for a perfect day."

Pip smiled. "Thank you for accompanying me, and for sharing your friends."

"The thing is, until you burst into my life, they were little more than polite acquaintances. We'd wave when we passed around town or chat at the pub if we happened to be there at the same time, but we'd never done things together, and now we've had two outings in two weeks. We're sharing gossip and telling our stories."

"I suspect you would have gotten there on your own eventually. I merely helped speed up the inevitable."

Claire turned to study her as they walked along the sand. "You disagree?"

"No, and I guess that's what I find surprising. You seem to have an air of inevitability about you; it feels as if everything you do in my life is almost preordained."

"No pressure, though, right?"

Claire snorted. "None at all."

They walked a little farther down the shore. Up ahead a woman threw a stick into the water for a border terrier to chase, and two children hunted for sea creatures amid the rocks left exposed by the receding tide.

Without speaking, Claire steered them from the beach and onto a sandy dune path before saying, "Tell me the long story about dropping out of Oxford."

Pip's hand tightened reflexively around her own, but her voice stayed light. "You don't want to hear that one."

"I do."

"You just said today was perfect. Why shatter the illusion by letting you see behind the curtain?"

"Because we promised honesty, and without it that's all you and I will ever be. An illusion."

Pip worried her lower lip as if trying to decide if that were a trade worth making, the truth for a beautiful mirage. Claire held her breath as they started up an incline in the path.

"There'd never been any real doubt I'd go to Oxford. Both my parents had, and all three of my older siblings had. Margaret was still there at Blackfriars, and I'd always gotten good marks at school."

"Really?"

She grinned. "Don't sound so surprised. I like to read, I write well, and I'm charming. Even my instructors found my antics entertaining from time to time."

"I wouldn't have thought that quite enough to get into Oxford."

125

"You aren't alone in that assessment. When I made my application, my father apparently decided to shore up my borderline case by inviting a few trustees and administrators to Mulgrave for a weekend."

"Oh."

"I'm sure he used a great bit of tact. He wouldn't be so coarse as to bribe anyone. He couched the visit as his way of saying thank you for everything the university has provided for many generations of Mulgraves and reminded them how strong those bonds have been. My older siblings were paraded out as proof, my brother Henry having recently stepped into his title as Viscount Whitby and the undisputed heir to the earldom."

"Wow."

"Yes, he's rather impressive. Handsome, smart, the picture of modern nobility, and a scratch golfer. By the time I was introduced, everyone was so busy salivating over his patronage they hardly noticed."

"Do you think that's what did it for you?"

Pip's breath hitched, either from the topic or from the steady upward climb. "That question haunted me for eighteen months in the city of dreaming spires. Every time I donned the robes I wondered if I'd earned the right to do so. And the thing is, I might have. My test scores were good. My marks were better. I spoke well in my interviews, but the not knowing drove me a bit mad."

"How so?"

"I became erratic as a student, swinging wildly between working incessantly to prove I belonged and blowing off classes and assignments because what did it matter anyway? Even if I had gotten in on my own, no one would believe it or even care."

"But obviously *you* cared."

"Not that it made any difference. No one worries about Lady Mulgrave's sense of self, and honestly, who can blame them?"

"Having a title doesn't preclude you from having feelings or insecurities or dreams," Claire pushed, eager to pull Pip back from the emotional withdrawal as her tone shifted from intensely introspective back to a sardonic sense of humour. "It speaks to your character that you wanted to see what you were made of. Many people wouldn't even have wondered. I bet there are hundreds, if not thousands, of people in this country riding the coattails of their lineage without a lick of self-awareness, and drowning in entitlement without a passing thought to their own deserving."

Pip laughed. "I'm related to a great many of them."

"And yet you welcomed being tested."

"Something like that. The idea wasn't fully formed, though. I simply withdrew one day in June without taking my exams, packed up everything I could fit into my rucksack, told no one, and fled to Scotland."

"I bet that went over well."

"You can only imagine my parents' vast embarrassment when they heard, weeks after the fact."

Claire grimaced. She had no frame of reference for Pip's family, but she knew how her own parents would have taken the news, and it wouldn't have been pretty. They reached the top of a high, grassy rise, and stood, mildly winded but still holding tightly to one another as they looked over the village and beach and the wide expanse of endless sea below.

"My naïveté knew no end back then," Pip continued after a moment. "I applied to attend Cambridge the next year and made some of the same mistakes again, along with a few painfully new ones, but that's a story for another day. I've done enough to ruin the mood of an otherwise lovely outing."

"You didn't." Claire turned to face her, the world in her eyes even more alluring than the view they'd climbed so high to enjoy. "You didn't ruin anything."

Pip rolled her eyes playfully, but Claire caught hold of her cheek and held her gently.

"You didn't, and I need you to understand me when I say the sailing, the picnic, and even those blasted puffins were all magical."

"But?"

"Perhaps a bit too magical, because it hadn't quite felt real until I got to see your face filled with authentic emotion and hear your voice tell me part of your story. I didn't want to fall for an illusion, and I had no interest in kissing a mirage."

Pip's eyebrows arched in a hopeful sort of question.

Claire smiled. "You heard me, but I want to make it abundantly clear what I'm about to do isn't in spite of those confessions, but because of them. Got it?"

Pip nodded.

Then Claire guided them toward each other until their lips met, and the rest of the world faded away.

Pip's mouth was soft and tender, keeping her promise to let Claire make this move in her own time, but she was there now, all the way, and if she'd only known sooner how her knees would buckle at the first press of their bodies, she might not have had the fortitude to wait this long.

Sensing Claire's increased confidence, or perhaps surging back into her own, Pip wrapped one arm around her waist and snugged them closer together, the fit of their planes and curves too much to deny.

Opening up her heart, her mind, her mouth, Claire welcomed more, and Pip stepped into the invitation. Deepening the kiss, Claire soaked up the scent of salt and the taste of champagne, aching to imprint every sensory detail into some part of herself she could summon at will. Pip's other arm worked around her shoulders, clutching her and enveloping her in both strength and tenderness, compelling her to dream of things she hadn't let herself dare.

CHAPTER THIRTEEN

Two days of kissing Claire hadn't been enough. The thought should have troubled Pip, and maybe if she'd let herself stop to think long enough it may have, but she'd become a pro at holding serious questions at bay, which was why she'd returned to Amberwick every day since their sailing trip. First, she used the excuse of needing to retrieve the picnic basket she'd left in Brogan's care. Then she needed to test her newly repaired motorcycle. Today, with the weather too rainy to ride, she decided the time was ripe to test-drive some of Claire's dreams she found so inspiring.

Only Claire wasn't cooperating.

"I can't go to the pub in the middle of a workday."

"But testing local ales is your work," she argued. "Ales and autumn would go together. You could get a big fire pit and do something for Bonfire Night with local brews. Both would help people stay warm."

"I don't have the time or the money."

"Two months is plenty of room to plan. And all you have to do is pick the ales and sell enough paintings for a fire pit. Or maybe I could buy—"

"No!" Claire said firmly. "It's bad enough you come in here

129

making me want to kiss you all day, every day."

"I'm sorry."

"You're not. And I'm not either, but the point is, you're starting to leave your mark on me, and as much as I'm having fun with your sweet side and your romantic nature and your amazing mouth, I also know we're barrelling toward some undisclosed expiration date."

Pip didn't disagree, but for the first time a hint of resistance bubbled up—only she didn't have time to examine the new impulse before Claire ploughed forward.

"You can't lend any sort of permanence to this thing we're doing. You can't plant seeds you aren't going to water, and I can't let my business depend on your funds or connections."

"What about—"

"No." Claire cut her off. "New rule: no buying me things."

"Not even a drink?"

"Okay, maybe like normal date things, but not rich people date things. No jewellery or meals that cost more than, I don't know, fish and chips."

"The cheese I brought on the boat cost more than fish and chips," Pip defended, more out of self-respect than any desire to eat at five-star restaurants. "Can't the under-three-fork rule still stand for meals?"

"Fair, but, like, no renting cruise ships or private jets to go get sandwiches in Paris like some *Pretty Woman* bullshit."

Pip burst out laughing. "Have I mentioned lately how unlike any other woman I've ever met you are?"

"Not in the last week."

"Then enter it into the record again, because virtually every other business owner in this village would eagerly accept my funds or my connections, even the ones who aren't eager to kiss me."

Claire snorted. "I think there might be a great many who'd be eager to kiss you if they were honest with themselves, and that drives me a little mad, too."

"Other women wanting to kiss me?"

"Yes, or men for that matter. You have other options, and one of them will catch your eyes soon enough. We've never shied away from the facts of our limited amount of time together, and I don't want to let you work your way into my dreams. This was supposed to be the fun of a moment."

"Well," Pip drew out the word, creating time to parse out the many things in that statement. "I thought having ales in the middle of the workday would be rather fun, but I also enjoy when you talk about your sense of place and your sense of purpose. Both of those concepts are rather scattered in my own life."

"They're pretty scattered in mine, too."

"Yes, but you have a vision, one that resonates with me in ways few things have for a long time." Pip hadn't given much thought to the statement until it came out of her mouth, and once it did she paused to let the impact slide back over her.

"Are you okay?" Claire asked softly.

She shook her head.

"No?"

"I mean, yes, I'm fine. You just make me think about things I'd never let myself ponder before."

"Sounds serious."

"Perhaps." Pip began to share some of Claire's concern. "I didn't mean to leave my mark on your dreams. I didn't formulate any plans at all beyond today, and I did make those plans with fun in mind."

"But?"

Was there a *but*? Again, she hadn't thought so until Claire turned toward her, expression expectant. "Maybe I subconsciously wanted to coopt your sense of purpose for a bit, perhaps see how it felt to have choices to make and a future worth working toward."

Claire stared at her for a heavy second, then blew a strand of hair out of her eyes, only to have it fall right back.

Pip tucked it behind Claire's ear, then let her hand trail down her cheek until she brushed her thumb against those full lips. Claire closed her eyes and leaned into the touch. The sight of her, serene and slipping into surrender, caused Pip's heart to do a disconcerting stutter step against her ribs. "I'm sorry if I overstepped."

Instead of answering, Claire pressed a quick kiss to her thumb—then, taking Pip's hand in her own, kissed her palm and her wrist, before emitting a low growl in her throat. "Okay. Fine."

Pip blinked her surprise and squeaked out a little, "Hmm?"

"We can go test the ales."

Despite such a blunt statement, Pip still needed a few seconds to process that she'd been granted her original request, because in the time since she'd made it, she'd also started to want several other things. Most of them couldn't be granted in the time they had together or maybe ever, but at least one of them could.

She leaned in and kissed Claire soundly.

                           ❧ ❧ ❧

"Good afternoon, you two," Brogan greeted as Claire and Pip entered the Raven, dripping the rain they'd done a poor job of dodging on their way down the block.

Claire hoped they could slide in quietly without arousing too much notice from the locals as she didn't want to get a reputation for day drinking.

Pip, on the other hand, had no such qualms, and greeted their new friend enthusiastically as she shook a few lingering drops from her wet and yet still-perfect hair. "Good lord, I know it's a small village, but how do you manage to be multiple places at once?"

Brogan laughed. "I've merely swapped shifts with one of our other bartenders so I could have my first Friday off in months."

"Good trade." Pip slapped a hand on the bar. "Claire and I wanted to get the inside scoop on those local ales you don't have room on the menu for."

Brogan brightened. "You want to give the craft brew scene

a good look, er, taste?"

Claire sighed. "Small tastes."

"I could do some flights like posh places do with wine."

"Perfect," Pip cut back in. "Put it on my tab."

Claire shot Pip a look, but before they could get back into their previous discussion, Brogan forestalled her by saying, "No worries. I've got several sample packs. I don't think anyone would have a problem with me sharing them in this case since we all want the same thing."

Did they? Claire wouldn't have thought herself on a dovetailing business path with a bartender or a brewer, and she still couldn't figure out what path Pip was on, which of course was why she'd caved in the first place. She simply didn't know how to resist those hints of humanity under the gorgeous façade. The idea of Pip being lost or helpless or living vicariously through her didn't mesh with any of her past experience, or with any of the others who had taught her to be wary in the first place.

Claire wasn't Pip's keeper, she wasn't even her girlfriend, and she certainly wasn't a bartender. She was a gallery owner, and, honestly, she only did that so she could be a painter. That's what she'd moved here for, and yet she hadn't set up her own easel in days. Still when Brogan told them to take a seat in the corner booth, she didn't argue.

She did, however, tense as soon as the door opened and Ester bustled in, followed on her heel by one of the people she loved most, and the last one she wanted to bump into right now.

"Shite," she muttered.

Pip turned to her, then followed her line of sight to the door.

"It's my gran and her best friend."

"Lovely," Pip said. Then reading her expression more closely, she frowned. "Or not. Are they wicked?"

Claire laughed a little. "No, they're adorable and generally entertaining, but also nosy, and sort of like those dogs whose jaws lock when they get their teeth around something."

"How troublingly descriptive. Are you worried they'll get a piece of you?"

"No. You."

As if on cue, both women spotted them in the corner, and their eyes lit up in unison.

"Hello, love." Gran beamed at her. "Fancy meeting you here, with a friend."

"And a friend I recognize," Ester piled on with a less than fluid curtsy. "Lady Mulgrave, how nice to see you again."

Pip rose swiftly and held up a hand. "No need for formality here."

"And you don't curtsy to her or her parents." Claire recounted their earlier conversation. "Only her grandparents."

"Whom Claire's sworn never to meet, but seeing as how I made no such vows, it's a pleasure to make your acquaintance, Claire's gran, and to see you again Ms. . . . Ester, yes?" Pip finished with a little flourish of a bow.

The women about swooned and practically hopped into the booth.

Claire rolled her eyes as Pip eased back in beside her, looking rather amused and more than a little content to be fawned over.

"I didn't know you had plans to stay in town after Volcano Night," Ester said.

"I'm not much for making plans, but when I saw your adorable village with all its charms—" she shot a pointed glance at Claire, "—I decided to stick around and explore a bit."

"She wrecked her motorcycle in my back field and got stuck here," Claire deadpanned.

"And after seeing Claire's beautiful gallery along with all its potential for expansion," Pip continued undeterred, "I've urged her to sample some local craft ales in hopes of sussing out some potential event partners."

As if on cue, Brogan came around the bar carrying a wooden cutting board loaded with two lines of five-ounce tasting glasses.

"Fancy that." Ester marvelled at the presentation. "I didn't even know our little pub did tastings."

"We don't," Brogan said flatly, "and don't go getting any ideas. The last thing I need is one more job. Between Emma's travel schedule, the puffin cruises, and the bump in tourist traffic now the movie's been released, I haven't slept in months."

"Which is why you're plying us with free ale and begging me to offer a competing event space," Claire surmised.

Brogan laughed. "I guess I'm not one for subterfuge, but yes, for the love of all things holy, give this town somewhere else to spend a bloody evening every now and again."

They all laughed, and Pip held up one of the glasses. "It sounds like drinking these right now is simply the neighbourly thing to do."

"Yes, I've got two sets here." Brogan eyed Ester and Claire's gran, Diane. "I suppose it's enough to share."

"Can we really?" Ester asked excitedly.

"The more the merrier," Pip answered before Claire could even consider the full implications of the four of them drinking together.

At least splitting the alcohol would mitigate the risk of getting tipsy.

"We can share this lot." Pip slid the board a little closer, then indicated the women across from them should take the other row.

"They're produced in Northland or Newcastle, and arranged lightest to darkest," Brogan explained. "I'm not going to tell you any more than that. You taste them, let me know which you like best, and then I'll write up a list for you."

"You're a good sort, Brogan," Pip said with a genuineness that warmed Claire's heart, and her smile must've given her away, because when she turned back toward their group, her gran gave her a questioning look only a grandmother could.

She quickly distracted herself by taking a sip of the first drink. It was light and refreshing and crisp. While served at the same temperature as everything else she'd ever had to drink in this pub, it somehow felt cooler. "I wish I'd known about this one all summer."

"Right?" Pip asked. "It's got the weight of an ale but the ease of a cider."

"I could drink this," Gran said, "and you know I'm not a fan of ales."

"I'm a fan of everything." Ester took the glass from her friend and sipped before adding, "including this."

Claire reached for the next glass, both encouraged and eager to get on with the process before any of them got too comfortable, but Gran reached out a gentle hand. "You have to let it settle on your palette first, and then you need to sip some water to clear it off before going on to the next one."

She snorted softly. "When did you become an ale tasting expert?"

"Don't sass me. We've been drinking in this pub since your mother was merely an idea."

"That's right," Ester echoed. "We used to sneak into the beer garden after our parents had gone home and make eyes at the sailors and railroad workers who came in after the families cleared out. You can't rush these things. Draw them out to get your kicks."

Pip laughed. "I like your Gran and her friends."

"You seem like the type who knows how to find some fun," Gran said pointedly. "How does that sit with your family?"

"About as well as you might imagine."

"But you get on with Vic and Sophia?"

"Yes. Vic was like a third sister to me while growing up. She's the same age as my brother, and her younger sister overlapped with me at Cheltenham, so she always checked in on us."

"And your brother is?" Diane prodded.

"The Viscount Whitby."

The older two women froze, and Claire's stomach tightened at the sense they'd stumbled into something she didn't want to know.

Pip shifted in her seat, but forced a placating smile. "If you need help filling in the family tree from there, let me know."

"I don't think there's any need," Claire said quickly.

"Your father is Earl Mulgrave, and your mother is . . ."

"Countess Mulgrave, and also sister to Victoria's mother,

Lady Penchant the elder, though I wouldn't suggest calling her that, or calling her anything, as I don't recommend ever meeting her."

Ester tutted. "We know Victoria enough to know that, love. Is your mother more mellow?"

"Generally," Pip said, "or perhaps my station as a fourth child afforded me a certain freedom, though my older sister would tell you my parents were merely too old and exhausted to parent properly by the time I came along."

"How about the next ale?" Claire suggested, grateful for Pip's easy openness and her ability to use self-deprecating humour to deflect the larger questions hovering about this topic.

Sadly, her grandmother wasn't easily redirected. "Your father's not also a prince, is he?"

"Why, Gran," Claire said as Pip stiffened slightly on the seat of the booth, although her smile never faltered. "You're not a royal watcher, are you?"

"Not hardly. I'm merely old enough to remember a bit of the history we had to learn in school. Though I'm not sure I know all the rules anymore."

"I think you do," Pip said. "All males descended directly from the sovereign are princes, which means my father and, incidentally, my brother meet the qualifications, though neither of them is styled as such."

"What does that mean?" Ester asked, leaning forward with interest. "Are you related to Princess Sasha?"

"She's my first cousin once removed," Pip said easily. "She's closer in age to my eldest sister. They went to school together."

"Can't we go back to the bit about titles verses styles?" Gran prodded.

"We didn't come here to grill Pip on her heritage," Claire cut back in.

"No, it's quite all right," Pip said with her usual amiability.

Only Claire didn't agree. She didn't think it was all right. She didn't want to know any of this. She didn't want anyone else in her small circle to know it either. She'd worked hard not to think about anything outside the little cocoon they were still trying to spin around themselves. She didn't want to think about anyone but them, and especially not princes and sovereigns and all the horrible realizations that came with their level of duty or public scrutiny. She didn't want Pip to belong to anyone but her.

"Most nobility are entitled, quite literally, to a great many different labels. Princes are often earls or dukes, or both," Pip explained with the rote delivery of someone who'd done this before. "Most people can't keep it all sorted, and it's rather unwieldy to use in addressing us, so while all the titles remain in effect, we get something called a styling or a short address based on the title we're most strongly tied to."

"And your father is Lord Mulgrave."

"Yes. As he was the third son of a prince and by the time of his wedding well out of the realm of immediate succession, the family chose to style him as an earl rather than a prince, and he took on one of his father's subsidiary peerages."

Claire didn't understand half of those words, and in that moment suffered a wash of utter gratitude for her American schooling, which allowed her plausible deniability, but Gran's pensive expression and narrowed eyes made it look as though she were pondering a math problem she totally expected to find the answer to. For the first time Claire longed to kick her own grandmother squarely in the shin or dive across the table and smother whatever conclusion she'd come to. Better yet, she wanted to run back to the gallery, dragging Pip behind her and right into her bed before anyone could shatter the illusions they hadn't even had the chance to fully form, much less enjoy.

Instead, she sat in quiet horror as her grandmother blurted out, "Your great-grandfather was the king of England."

Pip's complexion paled lightly as she turned to Claire. "I feel as though I might need to apologize for that?"

Claire shook her head even as her vision swam.

"You still don't have to curtsy to anyone."

Claire nodded numbly.

"Or even meet them."

She nodded again.

Pip picked up the next ale in their row and took a healthy swig before passing it to Claire. She accepted it, relishing the cool glass against her warm skin, then pressed it to her forehead for a second before downing the remainder of its contents.

"It's fine," she finally said. "This one's fine. I'm sure they're all fine. Everything's fine."

She definitely wasn't in over her head at all.

CHAPTER FOURTEEN

"I'm sorry," Pip said as they walked back to the gallery.

"No, I'm sorry." Claire didn't look at her. She'd barely looked at her for the last hour and a half.

"I shouldn't have pushed you to go drinking or invited your gran to join us. You tried to warn me."

"I did," Claire admitted, "but I get it. They look like a pair of adorable old ladies. No one expects the Spanish inquisition . . . oh God, can I even say that? You aren't related to Isabella and Ferdinand, are you?"

Pip burst out laughing. "Probably, but you have to know, I care even less for them than I do most of my extended family, which is a low bar to set. Do you need me to renounce the whole lot of them?"

Claire shook her head.

"I will. Fuck the whole lot of them," Pip swore, desperate to see this woman smile at her again. "My title isn't the kind you can abdicate. I mean, if you want to be honest, I don't even really have a title. I was born with a vagina."

Claire's eyes went wide.

"Okay, not the best statement I've ever made."

"It's a pretty decent statement," Claire said. "There's a lot to unpack there."

Pip sagged. "You have no idea."

Claire stepped closer and finally met her gaze. "I didn't want to have any idea. I wanted us to be easy and fun. I didn't want to know anything complicated."

"I know."

"But I also want us to be open and honest, so maybe I need to know. If not about your family, at least about you."

"It's all intertwined."

"Okay." Claire pulled open the door and held it for her. "Help me untangle it."

"I'm not sure how."

"I don't give a fig about castles or money or stylings, but I do care about the little things I see in you when the topic comes up. You wince like someone jabbed you with a needle when anyone calls you 'Lady Mulgrave.' At first I thought you wanted to keep your profile low, or maybe you wanted to play pauper for kicks, but now I think it has something to do with having a vagina, which is super confusing to me."

Pip's chest constricted. "Super confusing is as good an explanation as any."

"Then let's start with confusion." Claire led her to the kitchen. "And also tea. You're apparently ridiculously English, so I feel obligated to put on a kettle."

She chuckled in spite of the ale and bile churning in her stomach.

"I don't have a fancy tea set, mind you."

"No worries." Then using the overture to springboard into the deep end, Pip added, "I won't deny I have champagne tastes, but even those were handed down to me without awareness. Everything about me was handed down without any ownership at all."

"How so?"

"The house, or rather castle, I grew up in belonged to my father as it belonged to his father and someday will belong to my brother. I certainly benefitted tremendously from all those

141

connections, but none of it's mine, not the house, not the legacy, and certainly not my title."

"I don't get that." Claire carried two cups and the kettle to a small table near the front window. "I mean, I understand your brother will get the big house and your dad's title, but you're still you, right?"

Pip's face grew warm at how close the question came to hitting her heart. She steadied herself against the table while taking the seat opposite Claire, who filled both their mugs.

"No matter how long I live in this country, I still feel like a little girl playing tea party every time I pour tea for another human," Claire said, "and now we're going to talk about nobility and stuff. I worry maybe I should put on a fancy hat and gloves."

Pip smiled genuinely at Claire's ability to somehow both convey the seriousness of the situation and mock her simultaneously. "I fear it won't be the kind of conversation most little girls dream of at their childhood tea parties."

"Good. I was never like most little girls. Give me the dirt, because I'm getting the sense there's a lot of sexist bullshit, what with the mention of vaginas and inheritance."

Pip actually laughed. "Maybe that'll be the title of my autobiography someday: *Vaginas and Inheritance*."

"Catchy. Can I get an advance copy?"

"The short story is women can't inherit titles. They can't even hold most of them. There's different rules for the sovereign, but for the rest of us, we're only as honourable as the man we're most closely related to."

"Lovely. Can I get a for instance?"

"For instance, my eldest sister, who's one of the few family members I actually adore, used to also be styled as Lady Mulgrave because she's the daughter of Lord Mulgrave, but she married the son of a duke, so now she's Lady Halston. She'll never be a duchess in her own right, but she'll have the title because she married well."

"Lucky her, but correct me if I'm way off base here. You don't plan to marry a man."

142

"You catch on quickly."

"What if you married a woman? Would she get your title?"

"I don't have a title to give. I'm merely styled as a lady as a reflection of my father's title, a title he can only give to my brother at the moment."

"At the moment?"

"Incidentally, you've already met the person most likely to challenge the sexism there."

"Vic?"

She nodded. "My favourite cousin may fight to inherit her father's title, but she could only do so because my uncle has no male heir. I have a brother. I have no claim to any title in my own right, and I have no plans to marry a man who will lend me his."

"So, if you marry a commoner, you can't give her your title, and if you marry an aristocratic woman, she can't give you hers either, but will you lose your title?"

"Again, it's not my title to lose. I'm always the progeny of an earl, and without another man in the picture, I could be Lady Mulgrave for the rest of my life." Pip didn't quite manage to keep the steel edge from her voice, and she sipped her still too hot tea to banish the taste of metal from her mouth.

"What about the styling business you mentioned back at the pub? It sounds like people choose all sorts of different things from princes to dukes."

"Traditionally, children are styled by their parents at birth, and then come into their adult title on the occasion of their marriage, male or female."

"Holy shit, back to the marrying thing. There's a lot of assumptions there."

"So many." Pip fought the urge to fold in on herself. Only her relief that Claire seemed to understand those assumptions and the pressure they produced kept her skin from crawling the way it normally did in these conversations.

"And because the title isn't yours to give, it's also not yours to throw away?"

"That's complicated."

"More complicated than what we've already covered?"

Pip bit her lip. "Yes."

"Because?" Claire pushed gently.

"Because." Pip started then stopped, unsure how to proceed. Normally she abandoned this line of conversation long before she allowed it to creep so close. Most people wanted only the rote explanation. A few wanted larger conversations about sexism or classism. Everyone focused on the system in some way or another, but as Claire waited patiently, her eyes kind and concerned, Pip suspected she wanted something more personal, and for the first time a part of her wanted to offer that. "The whole subject is both personal and also predicated on so many troubling things: class, bloodline, birth order, marital status, and gender. A person has to make peace with every piece in order to function with any semblance of sanity, or risk losing them all."

Claire's eye filled with understanding. "And you have one you can't reconcile."

Pip worried her bottom lip with her teeth. They were close now, and this woman saw her too clearly. Even if Pip didn't say the words, Claire would know. And if Pip ran now, Claire would also see her cowardice. For the first time that fear outweighed the others. "Maybe a better person would wrestle with the class or birth order or the bloodline. There are plenty of legitimate bones to pick in those areas."

"*Lady* Mulgave," Claire said, only she didn't direct the title at her like an address so much as a thing one might lift up to the light as if trying to see through a cloudy glass. "The title is given only by a man, and only to a woman. It's not just sexist. It's restrictive in its femininity."

Pip's heart pulsed in her throat as she willed Claire to take the next step, the one she'd never dared take on her own for fear of falling off the edge of a cliff she'd clung to her whole life.

"And you're . . . not."

"Well, I am, but—"

"You don't want to be," Claire said quickly.

"It's not that simple."

"Why not?"

"Because I don't know what I want." The words rushed out like a tidal wave. "And I've never had the chance to figure it out. I don't have the freedom of exploration or expression needed to play around with thousands of years of history. I don't get to deconstruct one piece of who I am without risking all of the others."

Claire's smile spread as she stared at her. "You do now."

Pip's heart leapt, painfully pressing against her ribs.

"I don't care about the rest of it." Claire pressed on. "I only care about us. This is our game. It's our experiment, our escape. If we're in for a penny, let's go in for a pound."

"I don't even know what that would look like."

"Me either." Claire laughed. "That's what makes this so exciting."

"Exciting or nauseating?"

"Both. That's your answer, right?" Claire pushed her fingers through her hair roughly. "This is so much bigger than I realized. When we were laying out the ground rules, I didn't understand what you meant about this thing between us going both ways. I was so wrapped up in my fear of how you might hurt me I didn't hear your own need and nuance."

"I didn't want you to."

"I suspect you did, somewhere deep down. I stereotyped you as a rich kid out for kicks, and I was willing to go along with you, but this is much more interesting."

"Interesting like a science experiment?"

"Interesting like a whole human being." Claire caught her hand and squeezed tightly. "You are a whole person, Pip. I worry you haven't let yourself acknowledge that, and I'm sorry I haven't either. I should've put things together sooner. The way you chafe under the title, your talk of continuums, and—oh God, you told me to call you Flip."

"No," she said. "I don't need you to call me Flip. I don't even know why it came out of my mouth."

"Because something's pushing up from your core, and no

145

matter how much you try to push it down with champagne and motorcycles and one-night stands, it's still going to be there. Let's take that part of you and invite it to join us for tea or a walk on the beach."

Pip's chest ached, and sweat pricked a thousand pores. The idea was so terrible and exhilarating her vision went white around the edges.

"I'm an artist." A hint of calm returned to Claire's voice. "It's my job to see reality and project it back to people in ways that convey truth they couldn't see on their own. Let's do that for each other."

"It's not what you signed up for." Pip squeaked out the last emergency exit, the last chance for them both to hop off this ride before either of them lost their lunch, or something far worse. "You wanted fun."

"This will be fun, but also so much more."

"You wanted easy, you wanted simple, you wanted to be swept off your feet by someone who knows what they're doing."

"I wanted to be swept off my feet by you."

"I don't know who I am without the confines of my title, and while a part of me relishes the chance to find out, another part of me fears there's nothing left down that road but disappointment."

"But you said yourself you don't know for sure. What if there's something wonderful and freeing and real?"

"It's a big risk. And that's not what you initially asked for."

"No, it's not." Claire lifted Pip's hand to her lips and kissed the palm. "It's something better."

CHAPTER FIFTEEN

Claire lifted her head at a low rumble in the distance and tuned her ear, trying to discern the whine of a particular engine. She didn't want to be the kind of person who sat listening for the hoof beats of a white knight coming to whisk her away, but her body still hummed with the electricity of last night's conversation. It felt as though lightning had split the clouds over them, and in a single, blinding flash she'd finally seen the person who'd stood in front of her for weeks.

It wasn't her place to push someone else into their own identity, and the trepidation in those electric blue eyes served as a warning to tread carefully. Nothing they were doing together seemed like a game anymore, and that awareness only made Pip more alluring. This force of nature who'd grown used to doing everything fast needed her to go slow.

She found the prospect both alluring and endearing, and while she had many questions, she'd settled for kissing Pip soulfully and had staved off the urge to ask her to stay the night.

It had been the right call, but as a little blue Fiat came around the bend toward town, she sank deeper into her disappointment. She tried to distract herself by flipping through an art supply catalogue, occasionally marking the place of something she couldn't afford to buy. Mostly, though, she stared out the open sliding glass door to ponder the grazing sheep or smile at the serious crease in her young assistant's forehead.

Claire had accepted Emma's advice and asked Reggie to work up several different designs for an expanded outdoor space, and the teen took to the task with all the earnest solemnity one might expect. Reg sat on the ground with one pencil pressed to a sketch pad and another tucked behind her ear along with a little red curl. She adjusted her tape measure, muttered something under her breath, and then erased the line she'd drawn before glancing up to see Claire staring.

A pink flush spread under a sprinkling of freckles. "Was I talking to myself?"

"Most artists do."

"I'm not an artist."

"Of course you are. You're making something out of nothing." Claire held out her hand. "Let me see what you've got."

Reg stood and brushed off the back of her jeans before stepping inside to hand over the pad. "I've actually got three different plans, or at least two and a half."

Claire's eyes wandered over the pages, taking in the details. The diagrams offered a study in discipline, with clean lines and neatly transcribed dimensions, but they also held hints of true beauty: a flourish to denote light, a spiral design in the stones, a wispy drawing of a water feature.

"Reg." She didn't even know what else to say.

The kid shifted from one foot to the other. "The last one needs more work."

"Even *Hamlet* could've used another draft."

"What does that mean?"

Claire tousled her hair. "It means every artist sees room for improvement, but this is very *very* good. I'm impressed, and the last one is my favourite. I love the way you've drawn the vines around the trellis, as well as the lights, and all the potted ficuses give me options to move them, sort of like natural barriers to shape according to what we need."

"You could remove them completely when you need open space, or use them to funnel people in a specific direction if you wanted."

"That's brill." She was already picturing different setups when another low mechanical whine caught her ear. She squinted into the sun as it sank low over the hills until a ray of light reflected off the gleaming metal frame of a motorcycle.

Her ribs tightened around her heart and lungs, making it hard to breathe, much less finish her previous thought as Pip leaned into a turn and arced toward the village. Claire's mouth went dry at the way her body moulded to the bike as if she weren't steering, so much as gliding.

"Is Bacon Butty your girlfriend?" Reg asked in a low, quiet voice.

She blinked, tearing herself way from Pip and the yearning her approach sparked. Focusing on the girl beside her, she let the question soak through her haze before rebelling at the idea. "No. She's . . . hmm, Pip is not a girlfriend."

The term didn't fit on so many levels that she didn't have to examine any of them too closely.

"But you like her?"

She nodded, finding the second query easier to answer than the first. "I do. I consider Pip a friend definitely, but I guess a special kind of one."

Reg rolled her eyes. "I'm not a baby. I know what 'special friend' means, and I kind of thought that might be what you two are, but I didn't know what to call it."

"I know what you mean," she said as the sound of the engine cut off nearby. People like Pip might simply defy definition. "I don't have the right word either."

"The right word for what?" Pip asked, appearing around the corner of the gallery and ambling into the garden.

Claire let her eyes rake over her, unabashed in her appraisal of the tight-fitting black pants and the bright blue canvas jacket that managed to almost match those alluring eyes. As usual, Pip's hair fell like a wave of dominos tipped over in perfectly cascading layers. "The right word to describe what you are to me."

"Hmm." Pip gave a low little hum. "I think the word you're looking for might be irresistible."

Claire snorted softly. "I'm not sure that's it."

"Let me know when you think of it." Pip swung open the gate, and without the barrier between them, Claire could no longer control herself. Grabbing hold of Pip's jacket, she gave a little tug, and they collided, mouth first.

The feel of those lips on hers, soft and skilled, made every joint in her body a little weaker, and if not for the sound of Reg clearing her throat, she might've clung to Pip all evening, but she managed to assert a modicum of decorum, and stepped back.

"Hiya, Reg," Pip managed, sounding only a little breathy. "What are you up to today?"

"I was working on some drawings of the garden, but I think I better go."

"Not on my account, I hope."

"No, it's almost teatime. I promised my mum I'd be home to help." She said the words evenly enough but glanced away, making Claire wonder if they were totally true.

"You're a good sort, too, Reg." Pip nudged her. "Tell me, does it run in your family?"

The kid gave a weak smile. "Probably."

"Along with your shy grin and the red top." Pip gave a low whistle. "You must drive the ladies wild."

Claire's breath caught, and Reg's eyes went wide. Was this the first time anyone had given voice to the assumption so many must have made? They stood suspended for too long to be comfortable, and almost long enough for Claire to step in, but before she thought of a graceful way to do so, Reg squeaked out, "Not really."

"Are you sure?" Pip asked with a conspiratorial smile.

The flush returned under her freckles. "None of the girls at my school even know I'm alive."

"I remember those days," Pip said.

"Me too," Claire added.

Reg looked from one of them to the other. "Both of you?"

They laughed.

"I think it's universal," Pip said. "The waiting and wondering, worrying you might be the only one, but you're not, and you're sitting right on the cusp. My guess is it'll happen any time now if you keep being you."

"Being me isn't exciting."

Claire laughed. "I still feel the same way most days. But you're wrong, and so am I."

"She's right on both counts," Pip confirmed. "You're both perfect."

"She is," Reg blurted, then grimaced.

"And you are, too," Claire shot back. "You're ahead of the curve. You have to give the girls a chance to catch up. You're good-looking and kind and smart and steady. Plus, these drawings—how many people know you can do this?"

"Do what?" Pip leaned over Claire's shoulder to see the sketch pad.

"The specs for possible garden remodels."

"Blimey, Reg." Pip snatched up the drawing and oriented it to where they stood. "You've been holding out on us. You didn't introduce yourself as a landscape artist."

"I'm not."

"I think you are." Pip tapped a couple of boxes off the edge of the trellis. "Tell me about these."

"Those are sort of like flower boxes, but instead of being built on the frame, or up from the ground, I could anchor them with the sturdy hooks. That way they give the vines a higher starting point in the spring so they don't have as far to travel before the summer sun takes hold. Then in the winter you can prune them back and bring the boxes inside to keep them from freezing."

"Wow," Claire said. "I've never heard of such a thing."

"Me either," Reg admitted, "but I could build them to hook onto the inside of your windows in the winter and still fit the

151

trellis in warm weather."

Claire's mind whirred with all the possibilities. "I set out to expand my gallery space into nature, but you went a step further and brought the nature in for me during those long grey days when I can't paint outside. You managed to make both spaces more fluid and functional at once."

Pip clasped Reg on the shoulder. "It's truly a work of genius, friend, and what's more, I think you helped Claire find the words she was looking for earlier."

Reg squinted up at them. "I did?"

"Yes. She and I are striving for fluid and functional."

Claire laughed, glad to see Pip's humour hadn't fled in the wake of big revelations. "There you have it. You've solved all my problems today, so while I'll let you get back to your mother, tell her I insist you return tomorrow and put the finishing touches on this drawing."

Reg appeared to be trying to contain a much larger smile as she collected her things. "I'll be back after school for sure."

They watched her go until she disappeared between a row of village houses, then turned to each other almost tentatively.

"You did a good thing there," Claire finally said.

"I sort of worried I'd outed her for a few horrible seconds."

"Oh no, I think you totally did, but you handled it well, and what would you have given to have had a coming out with two people who immediately told you women were mere months from swooning over you?"

Pip rubbed the back of her own neck. "Honestly, I can't even imagine."

"Me either."

Pip shifted from one foot to the other, much the way Reg had earlier, only on her the shyness seemed much more foreign. Did all the talk of coming out make her feel as raw and vulnerable as Reg had in that moment?

Claire couldn't bear the thought of Pip waiting, wondering, worrying. It simply didn't suit someone of her skill and beauty to be so unsure, and Claire ached to inject the same assuredness

Pip had given Reg. Only with Pip, she suspected the task would be less innocent and a lot more enjoyable.

Clasping Pip by the lapels of her jacket once more, she pulled them together, and this time, decorum be damned, she didn't stop at one kiss. Parting her lips, she deepened the connection, then swept her tongue along Pip's as an invitation. She wanted to draw the sexy force of nature back to the surface, to hear the blood rush in her ears, and to feel stolen breath brush against her skin. She worked her hands up to clutch Pip's smooth face, then continued until the tips of her fingers sank into silky strands of hair. Giving a little tug, she thrilled at the way Pip's hips pushed into her, and she ground forward to meet the pressure.

The jolt of baser instinct grabbed hold of something deep inside her and spread, consuming like hunger and tasting like honey. She wanted more. She wanted Pip raw and wild. She wanted something reckless. She wanted parts of this person no one else had ever known. Most of all, she wanted something real, even if only to be remembered.

Pulling back, she panted, her hands still in Pip's hair. "Let's go for a ride on your bike."

❧ ❧ ❧

Pip settled trembling hands onto Claire's hips and soaked up her steady power. If she'd only known what she was getting into with the woman, would she have taken the deal? She wasn't sure she wanted to know. They were here now, and that's what mattered. The fact that Claire continued to be here, revelation after revelation, may have mattered more than anything ever had, but she didn't let her mind wander down that path. Instead, she focused on the matters of the moment. Even with all the apprehension she'd expressed early on and everything she'd learned since then, Claire had asked to ride with her.

Pip nuzzled her neck and kissed the pulse point there before whispering, "I promise I don't take risks on this bike, despite what you may have seen in other areas of my life."

153

Claire met her eyes. "I trust you."

Lord, this woman moved through her in all sorts of wonderful ways, but now she had to ask something slightly different of her. "Move with me."

"What?"

She took her spare helmet off the back of the Triumph and set it gently atop Claire's head. "When we ride, you can put your hands anywhere you want."

"Anywhere?"

"Yes, but when I lean, you lean, and when I ease up, you do too."

"What if I don't want to ease up?"

Pip smiled and threw one leg over the bike. "Then we'll find somewhere to pull over. Remember, I may be driving, but you can always tell me when to throw on the brakes."

Claire kissed her so soundly their helmets knocked together, before climbing on behind her. "I appreciate that to no end, but this moment I don't even want to slow down."

That was all Pip needed. Easing open the throttle and lifting her foot, they rolled forward. Within seconds they picked up speed and headed downhill toward the coast. Claire wrapped her arms around Pip's waist, clasping her hands across her stomach.

Shifting steadily with her foot, Pip barely felt the cool breeze on her face with the warmth of Claire's body enveloping her. As they approached a sweeping turn, she leaned to the left, and Claire went with her. They shifted their weight back in unison as Claire tightened her legs against Pip's thighs. To their right, the sea shimmered azure and white as the wind skittered in ripples toward the shore.

Pip often felt like she was flying when she rode up the coast, but with Claire wrapped around her, even flight seemed too constricting a metaphor. Together they glided, they soared, they skimmed above the surface racing by below.

"I didn't expect it to be soothing," Claire called over the wind, the rumble of her voice reverberating along Pip's spine.

"It's not always."

"Why today?"

"Because you're wrapped around me."

Claire responded by leaning her cheek against Pip's shoulder blade, with her face to the water, and Pip wondered idly if she'd provided Claire with even a hint of the peace she'd offered by simply seeing her and not turning away.

They rode for miles up the coast until she recognised the square castle keep towering over the dunes in the distance. She pointed it out to Claire. "Bamburgh Castle."

"Does yours look like that?"

Pip arched an eyebrow though Claire couldn't see the expression. It was the first unprovoked question about the life she lived outside of this dream state they shared. Instead of answering, she chose to downshift and veer into a wide lay-by between two stretches of dunes.

"Why did we stop?" Claire sat back, but didn't move her hands from their snug spot across Pip's abdomen.

"Because you're the first person I've ever wanted to carry on a conversation with while riding."

Pip felt Claire's intake of breath more than heard it.

"And," she continued before she lost her nerve, "because you displayed a great deal of reckless bravery this evening, I wanted to return your show of faith before darkness fell."

Claire glanced at the sun sinking low over the rolling hills, then back to Pip. "What did you have in mind?"

They dismounted the bike but kept their helmets with them as Pip took Claire's hand and led her down a sandy path. They stopped before reaching the beach and tucked themselves into a small hollow surrounded by reedy grass, which offered a swaying sort of shelter from the wind.

Pip sat in the sand and pulled Claire into the crook of her arm before pointing up to the distant castle keep, only its top ramparts visible between the dunes. A green and yellow standard flew stiff and steady in the breeze. "My home doesn't look much like the castle up ahead, except from this vantage."

"The ridges at the top?"

155

Pip nodded. "And the flag, though ours is charcoal grey with red and gold accents. Our castle is more grey than brown, too, but we have a tall, square keep at one end, and at the other a tower to face the sea. Between those two features, it looks like a much more modern estate house, but if you lie on your back in the dunes and stare up, you don't see anything but the ancient aspects."

"Is that how you prefer to view it?"

Pip gave a little hum of pleasure and pulled Claire down until they reclined against the dune side by side. "I spent hours like this as a kid, and honestly even right up until I neared Reggie's age."

"What changed then?"

"I'm not sure. Less time at home, less time to spare, less freedom to scramble down the rocks to the shore," Pip answered, then thought some more before adding the rest of the truth. "Also, Henry got engaged."

"Your brother?"

"Yes."

"And the marrying age is also the title-styling age." Claire filled in the blanks flawlessly.

"You're a quick study for an American."

"Half American, and the things I found boring in history books seem much more interesting when I see them written across your face."

Pip turned to face her, back to the castle now. "We'd always just felt like siblings living under our father's roof, all of us related to Henry and to each other until then. With the estate firmly secured into Henry's line, it became less like my home and more like his."

Claire nodded.

"Mind you, he's never once rubbed that in, at least not as an adult. When he was a teen, he used to threaten to have me thrown out on a regular basis. As viscount, he's all but assured me I'll always have a place under his roof, but it will be his roof someday. It'll never be mine. I can transition from black sheep sister to spinster aunt to his kids."

Claire popped onto her elbow. "What are your pronouns?"

Pip blanched at the quick subject change. "Pardon?"

"You keep referring to yourself as sister and aunt, so I assumed 'she' and 'her,' but then I remembered our conversation last night and the damage assumptions can do. I want to stop the cycle and actually ask which pronouns you prefer."

"I don't know." Pip tried not to sound panicked by the emotion the question sparked. "No one's ever asked me before."

"Well, if 'she' and 'her' feel good, there's no need to change, but you can if you want."

"What if they feel okay only because they're what I'm used to?"

"Then you can get used to something that feels better. Or you can try different ones on until you know which fits best in which moments."

"I don't think I'm a 'he,'" Pip said, though the thought hadn't been clear until the words were spoken.

"Okay."

"But I don't know. What if I'm not a 'he' because it's too big a jump? What if it's a bunch of little jumps?"

Claire smiled. "I love the image of you hopping from rock to rock until you get where you want to be."

"Won't it be unsettling to you if the target keeps moving?"

"Not at all. No matter what someone calls you, I like *you*, Pip. Finding better ways to convey who you are doesn't change who you are. You're not moving the target. You're bringing it into better focus."

"Why are you so good at this?"

"Because I'm trying to get you into bed."

"Wait." Pip laughed. "I thought I was trying to get *you* into bed."

"You were at first, but we keep swapping roles, and now I've come to think that's part of the fun. We're both people being people together."

The idea, or maybe the affection with which Claire conveyed

it, soothed frayed nerves enough to return to the earlier question. "What are the right pronouns for people being people together?"

Claire grinned. "I don't know. Let's try them out."

Pip blew out a heavy breath as if bracing for something solemn. "Okay."

"This is Pip. She's my person today," Claire tried.

"Not bad. It's what I expect."

"This is Pip. He is my person today."

Pip's eyebrow twitched, but what did that even mean?

"This is Pip. They are my person today."

This time the twitch came around the lips and pulled up instead of down. "That one doesn't come with any expectations, does it?"

Claire shook her head.

"You don't know if they wear a skirt or trousers, if they're a lady or a lord, and it doesn't have to be either."

"Could be both, could be neither."

"I could be anything."

Claire's eyes sparkled, and in them Pip saw a new reflection. "You want to take 'they' for a test drive?"

She nodded. No, *they* nodded. "Only if you want to ride with me."

Claire leaned forward and kissed their lips lightly. "When you move, I move."

CHAPTER SIXTEEN

Claire stared at Reggie's finished drawing of her back garden blueprints. She'd thrown it into a frame and hung it on the wall next to her retail counter. The move seemed to both please and embarrass Reg, who still maintained she wasn't an artist and her sketch didn't belong on a wall, especially a wall near so many other amazing paintings. Claire disagreed on all counts. The drawing was beautiful and inspiring, and she wanted to keep it in her line of sight, even when it hurt to think about how long it might be before she had the funds to start the project.

Especially then.

She'd sold some puffin postcards this morning, but for a Saturday the gallery had been impossibly quiet, even though the village was still in shoulder season with the lonely winter months off in the dreaded distance. She didn't have to pay rent, as her grandparents had all but given her the gallery space when they retired, but she had plenty of utility bills and a regular need to eat. She needed some new canvases if she wanted to keep painting, but in order to afford them she needed to sell some of the ones she'd already finished. Would there ever come a time when she wasn't merely scraping by?

The low rumble of a motorcycle alerted her to Pip's

impending arrival, and she practically vaulted over the counter to get to them. She had enough wherewithal to realize that seeing Pip as the only bright spot in her life set a dangerous precedent, but she didn't have the strength to resist the surge of excitement coursing through her at the sight of them, standing all windblown and glorious.

"Good afternoon, gorgeous." Pip removed their helmet and shook out perfectly feathered hair.

"Do you do that to drive me wild?"

Pip paused. "Do what?"

"Take off your helmet like you're in a movie, and the camera's going to zoom in on the heartthrob with their perfect hair and perfect chin and ridiculous eyes."

Pip's grin spread to something that could only be described as cocky. "I've never given a second thought to how I take off my helmet, but I can assure you, from here on out I will because this is basically the best greeting I've ever received."

"Ugh." Claire sagged onto a strong shoulder. "Who are you turning me into?"

"I'm just making you a person who's really into another person."

"I don't feel like a person today. I feel like a ball of anxiety and lust. I want you to put me on the back of the bike and drive us into oblivion, and that's not who I am."

"But maybe it's who you want to be." Pip caught hold of her chin and kissed her.

The press of those confident lips slowed some of the whirring in her brain, or perhaps that was a function of all the blood flowing southward. She hated herself for pulling away and for not immediately hopping onto the back of the motorcycle.

"Wanting and needing are two very different things. I may *want* to run away like a wild woman, but I *need* to sell some paintings, which means the gallery needs to be open today."

"And I want to be as good and supportive of you as you've been of me," Pip said sincerely. "I don't want my issues to divert from sweeping you off your feet, and magic and romance and fun."

"You could never divert from those things. You ooze them, but, alas, I genuinely have to work today."

"Alas." Pip grinned. "Believe it or not, I do understand obligations. What's more, I saw Brogan loading a boat full of tourists in the estuary, so maybe she'll direct the puffin crowd up here when they disembark after their sail 'round the sanctuary."

Claire rolled her eyes. "Great, I can sell another three quid worth of puffin postcards."

"Aww, are you still hating on those adorable little birds?"

"No, I get the appeal."

"But you haven't painted them any proper portraits yet."

"If I wanted to paint cheap, quick kitsch, I would've stayed in London." She sighed. "I thought if I moved somewhere more affordable, I'd have more time, more freedom, more . . . food that doesn't come shrink-wrapped."

Pip pulled her into a hug. "Sometimes we have to do the things we need to do in order to be able to do the things we love to do."

She tilted her chin up to regard Pip more seriously. "Rather profound for someone so pretty."

They laughed. "I've had some practice with both duty and brooding. It's a balancing act. How about we knock out a couple of puffin paintings to give the people what *they* want this afternoon, and then this evening we can do whatever *we* want."

"You say 'we' like you're going to share the labour."

"Why not? It's not as though puffins are hard to paint."

"Easy for you to say. I'm the one doing the painting, unless of course you intend to tag-team these portraits?"

"I wouldn't dare suggest I have anything to offer on work of your quality, but how about we each paint one of our own?"

The idea of the two of them painting side by side charmed Claire greatly, causing a little spark of something warm and sweet to flicker inside her core.

"If that's not too presumptuous," Pip added, a hint of a grimace starting.

"No," Claire said quickly. "I love the idea."

Within a few minutes she'd set up two canvases and given them each a full palette of oil paints. Pip insisted on arranging the easels back to back so they couldn't see the other's artwork unfolding.

"I don't want to have performance anxiety," they said.

"I wouldn't think that's something you'd have to worry about . . . or admit to."

"It doesn't extend to any other areas of my life," Pip clarified, "only art."

"Whatever you have to tell yourself."

"Can't we change the subject please?" Pip picked up a brush. "You're not helping my inferiority complex about having to paint in the presence of true talent."

"Okay, fair enough. I promise I won't judge you. Art is expressive. You do your thing and I'll do mine."

"Perfect." Pip began to paint, and Claire did her best not to sneak a peek even though her curiosity niggled at her. She wouldn't be surprised by anything the person across from her did at this point. Stick figure puffins, dogs playing poker, a modern Mona Lisa. With Pip anything seemed possible.

"Tell me more about moving up from London," Pip asked only a minute into their work time.

"I basically told you all there is to know. I lived there for ten years and made enough to survive, but never enough to thrive. I always worked at least two jobs to keep my chin above water."

"What type of jobs?"

"I tried to stay as close to the art world as possible. I mostly worked in galleries and a few different museums. I was probably best off working as a personal assistant to an art dealer, at least financially anyway, and it kept me in the art scene." She sighed and tried to keep painting. "I loved the energy of the city, the bright lights, the pretty people, and the conversations constantly flowing about form and technique and inspiration, but I never had time to focus on my own work."

Pip nodded but didn't interrupt, and Claire's mind wandered backward down old, divergent paths. "My own artistic impulses were always a bit too traditional for the avant-garde, but never quite classical enough to get noticed by traditionalists. I ended up settling for things I could paint and sell quickly, but I never grew. In ten years, I never went under, but I never managed to match my vision with my reality either."

The muscles in her arm began to twitch. She took a step away from the canvas and rolled her head to release the tension in her shoulders. "I was run down by living constantly betwixt and between, you know?"

Pip's lips pressed into a tight line, and Claire suspected she had her answer. She would never have thought it possible a few weeks ago, but now she wondered if the two of them weren't fighting similar struggles in wildly different arenas.

"What finally made the decision for you?"

"I'd been going back and forth for about a year, not about moving up here, but about moving back to America. My parents still live near Atlanta, and I have plenty of friends all along the East Coast. It seemed the logical choice, but I hated admitting defeat. In one of my bouts of self-pity, I let Gran and Granddad buy me a train ticket up to visit them, worried it might be my last chance for a while."

She stared at her painting for a bit, surprised to see it coming together despite the way her mind drifted. Perhaps Pip had been right about the ease of painting puffins.

"So, when you came up here, you weren't intending to take over the gallery?"

"There wasn't any gallery to take over," Claire said, getting back to work. "At the time the building was a tourist shop. This main space housed all sorts of knickknacks and a vast array of tea towels."

"What are tea towels?"

"You know, the thin towels people hang in their kitchens."

Pip cocked their head to the side and frowned as if unable to pull up an image.

"They're good for drying dishes, but people also use them decoratively," Claire tried. "You've probably seen them hanging off your nan's cupboards or on the front of her oven."

"My grandmama is Her Royal Highness, Princess Alice, and the Dowager Countess Mulgrave. I've never seen her in a kitchen."

Claire stared for a few moments, waiting for Pip to realize how absurd the statement came across, but when they simply kept painting, she grudgingly moved on. "Okay, maybe not *your* nan's kitchen, but normal people give them as housewarming gifts or commemorative mementos. It's beside the point. This place was a quaint tourist trap with a little tearoom up by the entryway, and my gran ran it most of her life, but she wanted to retire."

Claire smiled at the memory of Gran moaning about how she always hoped one of her daughters would take it over, and her vast disappointment at having raised a bunch of city dwellers, all gallivanting off to London or Leeds or, worst of all, Atlanta. "After days of her going on about her lost legacy, I asked if I took it over, would I have to keep it the same, or could I make it my own."

Pip paused and arched an eyebrow.

"She kissed my cheek and told me every generation has to make their own way."

Pip's arms fell, dropping a line of paint along their trousers and nearly knocking their palette to the floor before straightening quickly once more.

"Are you okay?"

They nodded.

Claire stepped closer. "Sure?"

"Yes, perhaps a bit surprised, or envious."

"Envious?"

"To have someone in your life who would not only hand you their legacy, but trust you to change it, shape it, make something new." Pip bit their bottom lip, then shrugged. "Thank you for telling me that story."

"I hope it's merely the start of a story," Claire said softly, not quite sure what to make of Pip's reaction, or her own, at this point. She'd always seen her move north as sort of a failure. Even when she began to feel at home or built the beginnings of big ideas, they were always tempered with the fear they weren't that big after all, and maybe she'd settled for something small compared to the life she'd wanted.

"It will be if we sell these paintings today, and now that I have a better understanding of what's at stake, I'm honour-bound to help." Pip punctuated the statement with one last dab of their brush before stepping back with a dramatic bow. "And I'm finished with mine."

"What? Already?"

"I did less talking and more painting."

"You asked me questions. I had to answer." Claire started to peek around, but Pip held up a hand.

"Finish yours before you look at mine. I don't want you to copy."

"It's not like school. I can't check my test answers against yours." She pouted playfully but did as instructed. She'd chosen a simple enough design. A single large puffin, its round head turned in profile to inspect its squat shadow across the stark, white canvas. She had put most of her work into the bright details of its beak and feet, creating a lifelike feathering around its single visible eye, and giving the little fellow an almost introspective gaze. The subject was hardly complex, but as she dabbed a bit of texture to the webbed feet, she didn't hate the outcome.

"Wow," Pip said, close enough for their warm breath to flutter across her neck.

"Hey now, we weren't supposed to look yet."

"I'm allowed to see yours, just not the other way around."

"How do you figure?"

"First of all, I already finished mine. Second, the rules governing commoners don't generally apply to me."

Claire snorted softly at the blunt truth, spoken so matter-of-factly. "Fine, but I do need a break to let mine dry before I add a few finishing details. The design is set, though. I'm free to see yours without fear of compromising my artistic integrity."

"But after seeing yours, I don't want you to see mine." Pip caught her around the waist. "You did, like, an actual puffin. I feel as though I need to stand back, as he might hop off the canvas and onto the floor. There's no such concern with mine."

"I already told you, I don't judge art. I mean I do when I have to make a decision on whether or not to show it in the gallery, but never anything done for fun, and painting beside you was the most fun I've had at work since . . . I can't even remember when. Plus, you got me to paint a puffin. That's a big deal no matter what style you choose for yours."

"I chose the only style my abilities allowed," Pip said, but they still loosened their grip on Claire's waist, letting her step over to the other easel.

As she peeked around the painting, a smile exploded from her chest to her lips.

Pip had painted a full scene of grey rocks tumbling toward blue water, and dotted them with several small shapes in black and white with tiny yellow beaks and feet. There was no doubt the creatures were puffins, but not puffins in the dynamically expressive sense so much as puffins whittled down to their most endearing essence, as one might draw them in the illustration of a children's book.

"It's adorable."

"It's not very realistic."

"Not conventionally, but you captured the cuteness people are drawn to. It's evocative in its lighthearted simplicity."

"Ah, when you put it that way . . ." Pip grinned. "Who am I to argue with an expert?"

"I'm only an expert in what I like. I have no idea what the puffin crowd wants in a painting." She gestured around to art along the walls. "Obviously, I'm still trying to gauge the local market."

"The market isn't something you gauge. It's something you shape."

"Is it now? Care to shape it for me along with your mini-masterpiece there?"

"I could. If you want, I'll sell it straight away."

"I don't know what's bigger, your ego or your bravado."

Pip shrugged. "Have I ever failed to live up to either of them when it matters to you?"

Claire thought back through their early encounters and failed to produce a memory that left her cold. "Not yet."

Pip rocked forward on their toes, tongue in cheek. "And you haven't even seen my best work yet."

"Is that a reference to your painting or to a tawdrier innuendo?"

"Why not keep up our trend and call it both?"

"Ah yes, both. When will I learn?"

Pip pulled her close once more and kissed her soundly before leaning back only far enough to say, "I like the way you see me."

Claire pressed her forehead to theirs and, staring into those eyes, whispered, "I like what I see *in* you."

❧ ❧ ❧

Pip sat atop the counter dividing the kitchen from the rest of the space and watched Claire rummage through the lower bins of the refrigerator.

"We've got a couple frozen pies," Claire called. "Do people of your stature eat such things?"

Pip traced a visual line up Claire's thighs over the curve of her backside, and ached to trace the path with their hands, and then maybe their mouth.

"Hello." Claire glanced up and must've quickly read Pip's expression because her cheeks flushed and her pupils expanded. "Do you want the pies, or should I bend over again and look for something else so you can enjoy the view a little longer?"

Pip grinned, not at all chagrined at having been caught. Women like Claire deserved to be looked at. "Pies are fine, but so are you."

"Too smooth." Claire chuckled a bit as she grabbed a small

sheet pan off the hob, then held up two items in thin plastic sleeves. "Do you want the bacon-mushroom pie, or the chicken curry?"

"I don't have a preference."

"Because you've never tried these?"

"Correct."

"Then let's go halfsies."

"Halfsies?"

"We each get half."

"Like a miniature pie flight." Pip nodded. "Brilliant."

"Yes, I'm quite the culinary genius." Claire dumped the little frozen food bricks onto the pan. "I can teach you the joys of cheap frozen food to repay you for teaching me about how titles work."

"I'm not sure that's a fair trade, as yours is a useful skill and mine is steeped in ancient absurdities, but I'll take what I can get."

Claire waggled her eyebrows. "If you play your cards right, you might be able to get quite a lot tonight."

Now it was Pip's turn to feel flush. It didn't matter what they did. They'd rarely had anyone in their life who could hold pace with their cheekiest impulses, much less raise the bar. To find that quality in someone with beautiful eyes, kissable lips, and dangerous curves almost made Pip wonder if they had actually suffered a head injury during the motorcycle crash. Perhaps the last few weeks had merely been a fever dream, only they'd never even dared to dream of the welcome, the acceptance, and the challenge a woman like Claire offered.

A lump of emotion rose against the dryness of Pip's throat, and they struggled to force it down. Those sorts of thoughts and feelings had never been part of the deal. Fingers twitched against the urge to reach for something steady—only if they allowed that, they'd undoubtedly reach for Claire.

Pip hopped off the counter, and Claire looked up questioningly.

"Little cramp," they lied. "I need to walk around a bit."

Pip strolled back into the gallery under the guise of stretching when what they needed was distance. They moved along the wall, studying various paintings in turn. Some were on consignment from other artists whose names Pip didn't recognize, but about half of the art bore Claire's mark in the corner. Pip felt drawn to those the same way they felt drawn to the artist herself, in that the work both excited and soothed. This whole place seemed alive with those senses, and more like home than anywhere else, including their actual home.

The sound of a bell signalled the arrival of someone else, and Pip turned to see an older woman bustle through the door. She wore a green fleece a bit too heavy for the weather, along with thick boots and glasses.

"Hullo," she greeted Pip warmly and tried fruitlessly to pat down slightly damp curls.

"Good afternoon."

"I've just come off the puffin cruise down at the estuary, and the strapping young woman on the boat said you might have some art to help me commemorate the most wonderful voyage."

"Of course." Pip made a wide, sweeping gesture toward the gallery. "We've got several beautiful seashore scenes to offer."

The woman entered the main gallery and inspected several pieces on the wall without much reaction. She paused for a few seconds in front of a stormy seascape, her eyes hovering over the turbulent waves for a moment before turning back. "I do like this one quite a bit, but I was sort of hoping for something brighter or more, I don't know, happy."

Pip nodded seriously. "I can certainly understand that after a day in such a quaint village."

The woman brightened. "It is quite picturesque. I honestly had no idea. I've lived in Yorkshire all my life and never ventured this far up the coast."

"You've been missing out." Pip gave the woman a warm smile. "How long will you be in town?"

"I'm only here for the day, though I wish I could stay longer."

"Then I see why you'd want to take a piece of this place home

169

with you. Every time you look at it you'll feel just as you have during your visit. And any art that captures a happy memory is a good investment from both a collection standpoint and an emotional one."

The woman gave a happy little chuckle as she kept walking along the row of paintings. "My thoughts exactly."

Pip glanced up to see Claire watching from the doorway, eyes sparkling with amusement. She made a little rolling motion with her hand as if she wanted them to keep going.

As the woman reached the easels, Pip poured on a little extra charm and slid up beside her. "This piece here hasn't been hung yet because the paint hasn't even completely dried. The artist was here this morning."

The woman turned to study Pip's painting, and the corners of her mouth curled. "Who's the artist? Someone local?"

"Very much so, and also rather mysterious. They're a close friend of the gallery owner who wants to support her, which is why they dropped by to paint with her, even though they've never done a public showing in the past."

"Never?"

Pip shook their head with mock seriousness. "Only privately commissioned work up until this point."

"Sounds rather exclusive."

"Very." Pip affected their most aristocratic accent. "The artist merely said they believe in the mission of this new venture to showcase Northlandian talent, and desperately want to be a part of conveying the rich uniqueness of the region."

The woman wrung her hands. "We were just talking about that richness, were we not?"

"Indeed."

"How much is it?"

Pip grimaced. "We haven't even discussed it yet. We'd planned to frame it and have it hung in a place of honour to increase traffic to the gallery. Perhaps even have some prints made from the original."

"Prints of the original?" The woman bounced a bit at the

prospect. "What if I made an offer on the original first?"

"I'd have to talk it over with the owner, but I'm not sure she'd want to let this one go so quickly. Would you consider leaving it here for a few more weeks as a show of support for the business? We'd put a sticker on the frame, of course, to mark it as sold, and you could certainly tell your friends it's on its way to your collection."

"Wouldn't that be exciting?"

"And it would give you an excuse to return in a few weeks to collect it, or we could see to its proper shipping."

"Oh no." The woman shook her head. "I'd collect it personally. Perhaps even make a weekend out of the trip. I'm sure a few of my girlfriends would tag along."

"What a splendid idea." Pip put on the same tone they used when speaking to the acquaintances of their parents they'd been ordered to keep happy at official functions. "I like the way you think. You get an original piece of art and a holiday simultaneously."

The woman straightened her shoulders, appearing rather chuffed. "May I speak with the proprietor?"

"Of course. Here she is now." Pip gave Claire a cheeky grin behind the woman's back before introducing them. "Ms. Bailey, this lovely lady is interested in the work from P.A. Farnes, and she's willing to leave it on display for a while. I know we hadn't planned to sell it so quickly, but I've got a good feeling about her. I think she's made a genuine connection to the piece."

Claire nodded seriously. "Connection is always the goal of good art. If my salesperson here speaks on your behalf, I'd be happy to entertain an offer."

From there Claire took over, playing her part beautifully, not quite bad cop to Pip's good cop, but certainly stepping more into the role of businesswoman, and by the time the woman bustled happily out the door, Claire had a sizeable wad of cash in her hand and a credit card number on file to process the rest upon pickup.

They both waited in quiet stillness until the door closed

firmly and their customer fully crossed the roundabout before dissolving into giddy squeals of near manic laughter.

They clutched each other and kissed fervently before breaking apart to dance a little more.

"You crazy bastard." Claire finally broke away and punched Pip in the arm.

"Is that a compliment in America?"

"Yes. Well, sometimes. But, in this case, yes. You sold your painting for a ridiculous amount of money with your 'never shown publicly before' and 'only takes private commissions' bit."

"It's the truth. Once my governess's boyfriend paid me twenty squid to go paint a portrait of our dogs in the garden. I was ten, and I suspect they used the quiet time to have a quickie in the tool shed, but it doesn't change the facts. I have only ever been paid for my art by private clients. I told no lies."

Claire nearly doubled over laughing for a full minute before standing up and handing over the stack of money. "Okay then, P.A. Farnes, it's all yours."

"Not at all." Pip refused. "I believe the artist and the gallery share the profits."

"I won't argue." Claire split the bills and handed Pip half before pocketing the rest.

Pip took it, then handed half of it back. "I also owe you for the paint and the canvas and rental on the art space. Also the pies."

Claire took all but one bill. "The pies are on me to celebrate the momentous occasion of your first sale, both as an artist and as an art dealer."

"Art dealer." Pip's heart gave a happy little tap on their ribs. "I like the sound of that. Pretentious enough to suit my rank, plus I can make all kinds of quips about having a refined eye and a taste for beauty."

Claire scoffed. "I think you've already made those claims, but come on. I'll let you tell me tales of your glory while we eat lunch."

Pip followed her to the kitchen and beamed proudly at the

money still in their hands while Claire pulled the pan out of the oven and plated two small, rectangular pastries before dividing them so they each had half. Then Pip followed her back to the small table near the entry.

They barely wanted to set down their commission long enough to pick up a fork, but the pies did smell surprisingly good for something out of a plastic sleeve.

"This is not bad at all," Pip said after a tentative first bite. "The way you talked about it I feared for my taste buds, but it mostly tastes like chicken curry in a pie."

"Such descriptive language skills you have there."

"I used all my flowery vocabulary for the day on my massive first commission. You have to admit, I was thoroughly impressive with my skills of persuasion."

Claire glanced at the bills sitting on the table and nodded grudgingly. "Actually, I found the salesmanship more impressive than the art itself, which is saying a lot because I did find the painting utterly charming. You were the total package today."

Pip sat a little straighter, stomach tightening with a surge of pride.

"I wish I had something nicer to offer you in way of celebration, but I'm fresh out of champagne. Maybe we should go to town and buy a bottle with your fat stack of cash."

"You're thinking too small."

Claire frowned. "Force of habit. What did you have in mind?"

Pip sat forward, a grin spreading almost conspiratorially. "There's a local artist I've got a thing for, but she doesn't like me spending my inheritance on anything too frivolous for her. So, seeing as how I earned this money the old-fashioned way and she sort of owes me now, I thought she might let me finally take her someplace posh for dinner tonight."

Claire pursed her pretty lips together. "How posh are you thinking?"

"Two forks maximum, I promise, and no private jets or yachts to get there."

"What about public jets or yachts?"

Pip laughed. "Totally normal means of transportation, no castles, no funny business, and also no food out of plastic wrap. Simply a nice, normal, and only slightly upscale celebration of the first money I've ever made entirely on my own."

Claire finally smiled. "When you put it that way, how could a girl refuse?"

CHAPTER SEVENTEEN

Pip was perfect in so many ways Claire admired. Looks, obviously, were the first thing to come to mind, and she'd let her mind linger there on many occasions, but the more time they spent together, the more Claire fixated on other things as well. The delicious blend of confidence and self-deprecation. Their flawless way with words mixed with a willingness to admit what they didn't know. The impeccable social graces tinged with an emerging vulnerability. The respect Pip showed for her dreams, her talent, her fears, combined with an almost compulsive desire to test those boundaries right up to the limit before easing back with a smile and a sure hand.

All those contradictions swirled around her as they strolled arm and arm through the oldest parts of Edinburgh. The fading light cast long shadows that covered even the widest streets in this area of the city, and Claire clung to Pip's strong arm for fear of stumbling over the uneven cobblestone crosswalks.

"If I'd known where you were taking me, I would have worn lower heels."

"And what a shame that would've been," Pip said breezily. "Also, you might not have boarded the train."

"First class was a bit much for a forty-five-minute ride."

Pip grinned as they had while they'd led Claire down the narrow aisle of the train into the lush seats where they were served drinks before they'd even fully picked up speed. "And yet I saw no other nobility in our vicinity, just normal businesspeople making a late return from the city, proving there was nothing aristocratic about our mode of travel."

"How can you be sure? Do you know every aristocrat in the country?"

Pip laughed. "I almost certainly do, and what with all the inbreeding, I'm related to most of them. Why do you think my sister's off in Italy to find a husband? She's hoping to diversify the gene pool."

Claire laughed.

"You think I'm joking? I've got six toes on one foot."

Claire's feet faltered. "Do you really?"

Pip paused long enough to concern her before grinning again. "No, but you wouldn't have been shocked, would you?"

"I'm not sure anything about you could shock me at this point."

"That sounds like the most wonderful challenge."

"I don't think you need to put any effort into the chase. You manage to do fine while being yourself."

Pip snugged her arm closer, pulling Claire flush against their side. "And yet you're still here."

"Yes." Claire regarded them more closely, the proud chin, the slant of their nose, the glint in those eyes, and her body reacted the way it always did as a steady dose of arousal dripped into her veins. "I suppose this virus hasn't run its course yet because I still feel a little feverish when I get too close to you."

"Now that you mention it, I felt a little woozy earlier when you kissed me."

"Then you're still symptomatic. My legs grew a little weak when you walked in wearing that ... that ... perfection." The last word came out more like a growl as she raked her eyes over Pip's slim-cut black slacks and cream-coloured suitcoat with black trim. Her gaze followed the subtle indent of a well-tailored waist and back up the length of a black tie. The ensemble would've been a bit too high-fashion on most of the world's population, but on Pip it merely looked amazing without being over the top.

"Me? I almost couldn't keep my eyes on the road during the short drive to the railway station. I know you thought the train a bit much, but I'd not have survived a coastal drive with your thighs peeking out from the hem of your dress."

Claire flushed and would have gladly written off the compliment as flattering hyperbole had she not felt the warmth of Pip's gaze on her legs every time she crossed them during the ride up. A hunger pulsed at her core in a way they couldn't satisfy in any restaurant.

She'd seriously begun to consider ducking into one of the many narrow alleyways they'd passed and ravishing—

"Here we are." Pip pointed to a blue door in an old stone building, jolting Claire out of her dark fantasies. Inside, warm golden light shone softly on white tablecloths while waiters in formalwear weaved among the diners, carrying large trays piled high with culinary masterpieces.

"Are you sure this place only has two forks?"

"Positive," Pip said. "It's one of my favourite places in the city, and I can't wait to share it with you."

Her heart kicked up another tick at the sincerity of the comment and the sparkle in those blue eyes. "Then, by all means, lead the way."

Before they even reached the hostess stand, a maître d' stepped forward. "Welcome, Ms. Bailey, Lady Mulgrave. Allow me to show you to your table for the evening."

Claire arched an eyebrow at Pip, who frowned slightly. "They know me here. There's no way to make a reservation without revealing myself."

Claire pondered that fact and the phrasing as they worked their way through the restaurant to a secluded table in the back corner. As an artist she understood the act of revealing oneself to the world in all sorts of vulnerable ways. She hung her heart on the gallery walls daily, offering it up for inspection and even critique. She depended on emotional openness for her entire livelihood. She would have thought she had a better handle than most on what it meant to put herself out there for the world to see, but every time she chose to do so, it was exactly that, her choice.

She might not control who saw her work, but she controlled when, where, and how. She also had the choice to hold certain parts of herself back or bring others to the forefront. Pip didn't. By merely existing in public, they revealed the parts of their life most defined by other people and the one they held the least control over.

The thought lingered as they each ordered a glass of wine and perused the menu, which Claire found to be a mouth-watering combination of seafood and modern Italian. She could hardly imagine how she'd narrow down her choices when Pip brightened across the table from her. "Halfsies!"

"What?"

"I can't decide what I want, but then I remembered lunch, and couldn't recall what you'd dubbed the serving style."

"I'm not sure halfsies counts as a formal serving style, but I like the way you think."

Pip's smile softened around the edges. "A fact which continually surprises me even as I keep waiting for the other shoe to drop."

"Your shoe or my shoe?"

"Either, I suppose. Since candour has served us well so far, I won't lie about my track record with long relationships."

"Is there a record of such things? I suspected those were mere myths."

"Touché, and to answer your question, not recently," Pip admitted without a hint of chagrin. "I wouldn't say there's been much over the forty-eight-hour mark since my time at Cambridge, but be honest. You've considered pulling the plug here too, right?"

Claire sipped her chardonnay and regarded Pip over the rim of her glass, heart beating faster this time for reasons outside her arousal. "Maybe a time or two at the beginning, but not recently, which now that you mention it worries me."

"It should," Pip shot back quickly. "I've told entirely too many truths for you to want to stick around. Even the most dedicated gold-diggers I've ever known have seen the folly of trying to traipse down that road with the likes of me much faster than you have, which makes me wonder, what kind of masochist underpinnings are holding you here?"

Claire took a second to give the question its due. If someone had asked her three weeks ago how long they might last, she certainly wouldn't have bet on this long. What's more, she'd stopped holding her breath waiting to find out if each kiss were the last. Still, she hadn't wanted any of them to be the end yet. She couldn't speak for why Pip hadn't taken off, but for her plenty of reasons came to mind.

"You still entertain me, you're a good kisser, you intrigue me, you make me think about things I took for granted, and you're apparently quite good at selling puffin paintings." Claire lifted her glass. "Shall I go on?"

"You've already given a more comprehensive list than anyone I've ever known."

"Then maybe you're spending time with the wrong kind of people."

"I don't doubt it, but then again, perhaps I'm also the wrong kind of people."

"For some, maybe." Claire didn't see any need to deny what Pip already knew. "But you've said yourself, I'm not like the people you usually run around with, so if you're waiting for me to get scared off by the person underneath the façade, you're going to have to work harder at being less interesting."

❧ ❧ ❧

"To puffins." Pip raised their second glass of wine over their meals.

"To the salesperson who marketed them beautifully." Claire

clinked her glass against Pip's, and they each sipped.

"The selling wasn't nearly as hard as the painting." Pip twisted a strand of linguini on their fork, then stabbed a scallop before taking a bite.

Claire eyed them with a hint of suspicion. "Are you joking?"

They shook their head, not wanting to talk with their mouth full, but also not wanting to rush the meal.

"Look, I don't want to detract from the painting. You created something genuinely appealing and relatable, and you captured something true without leaning on realism."

Pip finally swallowed. "You don't need to pile on the praise. I liked my painting, but I've studied enough art to know the difference between my doodles and what you do."

"Good," Claire said resolutely, "because what you painted was cute, and there's clearly a market for that, but there's also a million other people who could replicate your style and flood the same market without much trouble."

Pip nodded and shovelled a bit more food in without tasting it this time. They didn't need to argue with Claire's assessment. They'd known for some time they had no special talents to speak of.

"But," Claire continued quickly, "there aren't a million people who could have sold your painting for a stupid amount of money. In fact, I've worked in some of the top galleries alongside high-end art dealers who couldn't have done what you did today."

"I'm sure you could've—"

"No." Claire cut them off quickly. "I can't. Not with all my degrees, not with ten years of experience in the field, not with my highly trained eye or all of my artistic talent."

Pip's heartbeat provided a bass thump to the passion rising in Claire's voice.

"In more than six months of working and marketing and relationship building, I've never sold a painting for that much in this region. I wasn't even sure it was possible. The art—"

"It's not about the art," Pip jumped in, their own certainty inspired by Claire's. "I didn't sell a painting to a region or a market. I connected a piece of art to a person."

"And that—" Claire stabbed her lobster-filled ravioli emphatically, "—is an art form in itself."

Pip started to wave her off, but Claire didn't stop.

"You're good at reading people. You're charming and funny and quick-witted. You think on your feet and draw connections I would've missed."

"I'm glad to see my finishing school wasn't completely lost on me."

"Don't get me wrong, those sorts of things can probably be practiced and refined, but they can't be taught, not fully. You were born with those talents as much as I was born to paint or sculpt. Of course, we both studied and learned and were shaped by our experiences, but you've honed genuine talents as much as any artist I know."

Pip struggled not to let the compliment get under their skin, but they couldn't deny that the warmth spreading through their core had little to do with the wine.

"Hell, you're not only as talented as I am, you're talented in the way I fall short. You're talented in the one area I hate about my job. You're talented in the area I worry will lead to my ultimate failure in the one dream I have left."

Pip set down the fork and reached across the table to take Claire's hand. "You're not going to fail."

"I may, unless I learn to do what you did today."

"I merely did what I've been brought up to do. When you're raised with my title, you learn to lean on the tools at your disposal."

"Only you didn't lean on the title today." Claire lifted Pip's hand to kiss the tips of their fingers lightly. "You could have told the woman who you were, or you could have told her the painting came from the house of Mulgrave, or even some generic nobility. You could have labelled it with all the haughty intrigue of the aristocracy, and yet you played the part of the lowly commissioned gallery worker promoting a local artist."

A new sensation seeped into the tight ball of resistance at

Pip's core. They'd been aware of not wanting to use the title, but the choice had stemmed more from a desire to maintain the bubble Claire had built around them. But in refusing to drop the title on some unsuspecting art buyer, they'd also made a shift in how they let someone else view them and, most importantly, the exchange hadn't been a disaster. If Claire were to be believed, they'd actually done something quite, well . . . entirely on their own.

"Hey," Claire whispered, "you still with me?"

"Very much so. Maybe more than I've ever been before. Thank you for helping me see things differently. You're right. I didn't use my title today. I sold the painting completely on my own, though I did perhaps embellish the story a bit for dramatic effect."

"Li'l bit," Claire agreed, "but you didn't lie."

"No, I didn't tell her I'd done the painting, but I also didn't tell her any of the things about myself I have no control over."

"Is that a hard line to walk?"

Pip snorted and took another swig of wine, hoping to cover the bitterness coating their tongue. "My entire life is a tightrope walk. I want to be who I'm expected to be, but I also want to be myself, and in all fullness I'm not sure I even truly know who either of those people are. Lady Mulgrave will always hinder Pip, and Pip will always undercut Lady Mulgrave."

"I'm not sure that has to be true forever simply because it has been in the past. You've taken some huge steps lately."

"I've tried taking them before. I failed, spectacularly. I don't want to go back to those moments. As much as I hate how much the title defines me, I hate even more knowing that without it I'm nothing."

Claire gasped softly. "How can you even say such a thing, much less believe it?"

"Because I lived it," Pip shot back so forcefully several people at nearby tables turned to stare at them, but Claire didn't flinch.

"Okay." She nodded. "This is important to you. I want to understand. I want to know all of it, not just the pretty parts or the smooth parts or the proper parts. However, first, I want you to take a deep breath."

They obeyed.

"Then I want you to take another sip of wine."

Pip did as instructed, going through the motions even though they didn't taste anything this time.

"Then I want you to pass your plate over and trade it for mine, because I was promised halfsies."

Pip laughed. "Seriously? You're over there thinking about my linguine?"

"Why does it sound dirty when you say it that way?" Claire snickered. "But yes, because whatever you're about to tell me seems like it'll be hard, and we may need to fortify ourselves with carbs and wine, but I also know we'll take it in stride because that's what we do for each other, right?"

Pip didn't answer, at least not verbally, what with the emotion so thick in the air and in their throat. Instead, they swapped plates with Claire. Then, clinging to the idea of a defence system built on carbohydrates, they took some delicious bites to soothe a few frayed nerves.

"Now," Claire finally said, "let's rip off the Band-Aid. Does this have something to do with a relationship lasting more than forty-eight hours?"

"How'd you know?"

"Because you're a terrible poker player, and you told me once your time at Cambridge was another long story."

Pip swirled some wine in their glass, then set it down without sipping. "I told you I went there after things fell apart at Oxford, and then I fell apart on my own."

Claire nodded.

"For a brief moment I had the dim idea that I'd apply to another school without telling my parents, so they couldn't possibly intercede."

"And then you'd know the accomplishment was yours alone."

"Right. A lovely idea in theory, and yet utterly imbecilic in practice. When I rolled up on my motorcycle with nothing but a small rucksack, a valet met me at the door to my new accommodations. It took all of fifteen minutes to realize everyone living in my immediate vicinity possessed a similar title."

Claire groaned in sympathy.

"Only a nineteen-year-old would think one of the world's most prestigious universities wouldn't research their students' parents and net worth."

"What did you do?"

"In the depth of my idiocy, or perhaps my desperation, I found an advert for some theatre students who needed a flatmate, and I moved in with them."

"Another crack at the bohemian lifestyle?"

"Yes, though this time with the safety net of my trust fund intact."

"How'd that go?"

"Blissfully for about a year. I made friends on my own for the first time in my life. We had parties, we travelled together, we spent days lying about discussing art and books and music. Before long they convinced me to audition for plays with them, and I always got parts."

"Really?"

"It surprised me. I had no real training, not like the rest of them, but I always found my way into their productions. Small parts, but people took notice, first the directors, then the actresses."

"Which doesn't surprise me a bit," Claire said with a wry grin, "and then came the audience adoration?"

They frowned. "No, which should've been my first clue, followed by the fact that the parts never changed much, but I didn't notice, as I soon suffered from a rather rabid case of puppy love."

"Ah, your longer-than-forty-eight-hours relationship."

"Nella," Pip corrected, trying not to let the ache in their chest take hold after all this time. "She had genuine talent, big dreams, and eyes for me. I'd finally found my niche. New friends, new hobby, a new love all of my own making. My first

184

year radiated golden magic, right up until the moment it didn't."

Claire offered a weak smile as she gave Pip more time and space than they wanted to relive the horrible night when the last of the illusions shattered.

"I hosted a cast party after a show closed. Nella had been drinking, and the more she drank, the louder she got. She always had to be the centre of attention, and she generally deserved to be, but she'd received some bad reviews for this particular play, so she was down and a bit defensive, and . . ." They sighed. "I don't know why I'm defending her. She'd gone full-on diva and grown jealous of the attention the other principal cast was getting, but instead of turning on them, she turned on me."

"You?"

"Apparently I was an easy target." Pip shrugged. "One of the new actresses introduced herself to me, and I just said my name was 'Pip,' but Nella told the girl I was Lady Phillipa Anne Marion Farne-Sacksley of Mulgrave."

Claire grimaced.

"The girl curtsied, and Nella cackled. Everyone turned to stare, and once she had their attention, she wouldn't lose it. I tried to laugh it off and say I was 'Pip' among friends, and we were all on equal footing here, but Nella disagreed."

"Why?"

"My question exactly, and Nella answered in full. She told me and the girl and everyone listening that while we all liked to think of the theatre as a meritocracy, someone had to pay the bills, so they were all planning for the future by keeping me around."

"What?"

"Apparently every young actor or actress dreams of dedicated patrons, and they were all setting the stage for me to play that part. Every role I'd been given had merely been an investment toward their financial goal."

"No."

"Yes." Pip laughed humourlessly. "Nella went through them one by one, telling me they'd sat around trying to find places in each ensemble where I could basically play parts resembling my real life: an heiress, the daughter of a duke, a spoiled socialite, an unruly castoff. I could affect all the trappings of wealth and status they struggled with because those things felt natural to me, not because I had any actual talent."

"She didn't actually say that?"

"She did, loudly and repeatedly, going into great detail about how I was always good in roles where I only had to stand there and look pretty, seeing as I'd had so much practice, but that was the extent of my range."

"What did you do?"

"I sort of smiled politely until I realized I was doing exactly what she accused me of, playing the good-natured host, plastering on a fake expression, standing stock still while the lead actress held her audience captive. Then I turned to my friends for help, but none of them would meet my eyes."

"Oh Pip."

"I silently pleaded for them to tell me there was more to our friendship than hopes of future patronage, but not one of them did. Not the people who'd worked beside me, not the people who'd cast me, not even my roommates. That's when I knew."

"Knew what?"

"There'd never be any accomplishment I could claim, and no friend I could trust to take me one hundred percent on my own. As long as I lived, I'd never be able to tell if I had any genuine merit or if people merely hoped to gain something by convincing me I did."

"That's not true."

"You weren't there," Pip scoffed. "A room full of actors, and not one of them could summon a convincing enough performance to combat a truth of that magnitude. I moved back into my original house the next day. I put my head down and did what I needed to get a degree in art history. Then I went home, secure in the knowledge that no matter how hard I worked, the title would always matter more, and I did my best to make peace with my reality."

"Why make peace with something that hurts you?"

"Because I finally understood the title was the only remarkable thing about me." Pip shook their head and picked up the wine glass once more to have something to do with their hands. "And without it, there'd be nothing to say about me at all."

"You're wrong," Claire said emphatically. "They were wrong about you."

Pip shrugged. "There's no need to argue now. It's all settled and past."

"Except it's not, because I'm here right now, and I've never lied to you. Honesty is what we do."

"Honesty and fun," Pip corrected, "though it seems we might be slipping on both counts at the moment."

"You might be, but I'm not. I hate your title," Claire said. "I hate how it makes me feel insecure. I hate how it creases your stunning features. I hate how it limits your expression. I hate how it makes people think they know you when they clearly don't even see you. I hate how it causes you to grimace and clam up, because that takes you away from me for even a second, and I want you with me ceaselessly."

Pip's breath caught in their chest and wouldn't allow any sound, much less coherent words, to pass.

"And if you don't believe me," Claire continued with a ferocity Pip had never heard before, "then believe in what happened today. You said yourself you sold your own work to a woman who had no idea about your title."

"It's just one exchange."

"The first of many if you want them. The first line of a new narrative to supersede the one you've let others tell you for entirely too long."

"I don't know."

"Good." Claire lifted her wine glass. "Here's to not knowing, because not knowing is better than knowing the wrong things."

Pip clinked Claire's glass with their own and sipped, the flavours once again returning along with creeping sensations they hadn't registered in a long time. Hope? Peace? Pride? It was too soon to tell whether any of them were real or whether they could last, but they did know one thing: those emotions hadn't been sparked by selling a painting. They were tied inextricably to the woman sitting across the table.

Chapter Eighteen

They finished dinner in a more subdued fashion, and sweetened the experience by also going halfsies on some crème brulee and tiramisu, but even after Pip did an admirable job of pulling the conversation back to happier topics, Claire's anger still simmered. Pip shouldn't have had to buck up or wrestle things back on track. Pip shouldn't have honed those skills over years of settling for a shell of who they could be.

Pip paid the waiter and rose from the table with a smile that seemed both genuine and tired, and Claire's internal compass warred between the urge to offer comfort and the desire to spark something more consuming.

"Shall we?" Pip extended their arm and she took it, unsure when that had shifted. Her willingness to be guided seemed like such a small swing compared to the others they'd experienced over the last few weeks, but she suspected it signified more than she had acknowledged. There'd been a time not long ago when she'd believed they could keep things light and simple.

She chuckled, and Pip cast her a sidelong glance in the yellow glow of a streetlight.

"Sorry, I just remembered how bad I am at keeping things casual."

Pip tensed. "I'm the one who's come up short there tonight."

"You didn't force anything on me. I kept pulling at the thread, and I worry I won't be able to stop until I have you fully unravelled."

"Maybe I need to be unravelled."

She tugged on Pip's arm until they faced each other. "Do you mean that?"

"I don't know. That's the point, Claire: I don't know what I mean, what I am, what I want in anything more than a moment. I've only let myself live in stolen seconds until you started asking your questions."

"There's nothing wrong with wanting something in a moment. What do you want right now?"

"You."

The single word reached into her chest and stole her breath away. She couldn't think. She couldn't speak. She couldn't even find it in herself to wish for anything other than this person up against her. Pulling Pip flush to her body, she crushed their mouths together.

Pip caught hold of her and clung tightly to her shoulder, to her waist. Then their hands were on her face and in her hair. They kissed as if the only air left in the world came from the other's lungs.

They weren't going to make it back to Amberwick, not without being cited for indecent exposure on the train. Claire understood this with a certainty that might've terrified her if it weren't also laced with lust. Cracking open her eyelids enough to glance around, she searched for an alley or even a deep doorway. This city with its dark, haunted nights was known for magic, and she needed some now.

Frantically half-searching while against Pip, she spied a narrow offshoot and backed toward it without breaking the kiss. Pip seemed too wrapped up in her body to notice they weren't stumbling aimlessly until Claire's back bumped against the stone building whose shadow she sought.

"Sorry," Pip mumbled between kisses.

"A few more steps," Claire muttered.

The comment took extra seconds to sink in before Pip glanced up. Then a slow smile spread across those tantalizing lips. "Why, Ms. Bailey, I never pegged you for the dark alley kind of woman."

"I never have been before," she admitted, still holding tight to them, "but I will not survive a train ride tonight."

"Good," Pip muttered, "but I know of another option, one with fewer rough edges."

Claire wasn't entirely sure she wanted to smooth all the roughness away, but the cold stone against her back suggested that a bit more comfort might be warranted.

"It's near the station," Pip explained even as they worked one thigh between Claire's leg. "We could spend the night and still catch the early train home in time to open the gallery as scheduled."

Her brain refused to compute words like *time, gallery,* and *schedule,* but the appeal of having Pip's body fully undressed against her own made her consider the offer. "Where?"

"Another block or so, but in the spirit of honesty, the money I have left from the sale of the painting likely won't cover the whole bill."

"Fine." Claire didn't care how they got to where they needed to at this point, as evidenced by her initial plan to ravish Pip in an alley. "Use your allowance or pocket money or whatever rich people call it if you wish."

Pip pulled back and met her eyes. "I do wish."

She fought down the urge to overthink. "Your title has exacted its pound of flesh often enough. It can damn well pay for a little healing, too."

Pip released a rush of warm breath into the cool night air, then grabbing Claire's hand, strode off with a purpose that left her head spinning.

Claire had barely shaken the haze of lust from the edges of her vision when Pip led her up the steps of the Scotsman hotel, but if the walk hadn't sobered her up, the ornate lobby would have. She had been inside posh buildings before, but the contrast between their luxurious surroundings and the alleyway she'd opted for left her suffering a bit of cognitive dissonance.

The brightness made her squint as her eyes adjusted from the street outside, the sense of dark magic driven away by the overwhelming assault of opulence. Marble walls and columns soared into vaulted ceilings dripping with massive chandeliers that threw light across the ornate balconies circling the second floor. She blinked several times before she could even process everything, then decided against inspecting any of the details for fear they might overtake her completely.

Pip cast her a glance filled with both hope and concern, then arched an eyebrow as if offering one more chance to draw her line in the sand.

Claire laughed nervously. "The alleyway would have worked for me. I don't need this in order to make me want you."

"That's why I want to give it to you."

She understood the impulse. She would have granted this image of perfection in human form anything she had the power to give.

"I told you I'd bend the rules eventually." Pip grinned, some of the cockiness coming back and making Claire swoon once more.

"You chose your moment well."

Pip kissed her hand before releasing it, and approached the reception desk alone, leaving Claire a bit exposed in the cavernous space. She tried to act natural, as though she did this sort of thing all the time. At least she was still dressed to the nines, so her attire didn't lend to her feeling out of place, but even in a black dress and heels, she didn't move with the confidence Pip had baked into their DNA. She eyed them as they chatted calmly with the desk staff and pulled out a credit card that undoubtedly carried a limit the likes of which Claire couldn't even fathom.

Still, as she worked to keep her focus on Pip and not on her surroundings, she found it easy to anchor herself to the confident set of their shoulders, the ease with which they handled the transaction, the way the low timbre of their voice vibrated across the marble even with words too quiet to distinguish.

How many times had Pip done this very thing with other women? She wasn't naive enough to think herself the first. Pip had known the way. They had come into the space as though they owned it and had spoken to the clerk with a familiarity that couldn't be completely conflated with class. They carried an air of practice about them, and that understanding didn't bother Claire, nor did she entertain ideas about being the last woman to wait patiently for Pip to make arrangements of this nature. Still, as she raked her eyes over their stellar form, lean and at ease, clad in clothes styled specifically to showcase flawlessness and surrounded by a luxury suited to their grace, Claire did harbour a fantasy that she might be the only one to know them beyond the image they projected to the world.

She wanted to be the one who saw them, unfiltered in their fullness, to strip away the layers of presentation and the protection of prestige to make them feel her undiluted desire.

As Pip returned and led them up a grand staircase to their room, she needed to make her point before losing control. She wanted to be different than the others, and she needed almost desperately for Pip to understand why they were here.

Closing the door behind them, she caught hold of Pip and tugged them close, refusing to let either of them look around. "Eyes on me."

Pip complied without question, and everything around them faded as she anchored herself to the sea of electric blue.

"I need you to know I'm not here for any of this." She gestured around the room she had yet to even see, then brought her hand to Pip's chest before adding, "I'm here for all of this."

Pip kissed her, but she leaned back.

"I need you to acknowledge that before we go any further."

They nodded.

"I need more. I need to know you know it. I love that you found us a place to be safe and warm and open and together, but that place could've been anywhere as long as you're in it. I didn't ask for any of these trimmings any more than I care for your title. I don't want them between us tonight."

Pip smiled with a new hint of sweetness. "I understand. I'm not quite sure what to do with that understanding, though. My wealth and privilege have never been a mood killer before. Most women find them my most appealing qualities."

"Most women are trying to marry into your family. I'm trying to sleep with *you*."

"Me." Pip laughed as if they found the idea absurd, but Claire refused to let them pull away physically or emotionally.

She grabbed them by the lapels and gave a little shake. "I mean it. Selling the painting isn't the only thing you've done without your title today. I'm not going to bed with Lady Mulgrave. I want to make love to Pip, who's an entity unto themselves, fully dynamic and whole, and criminally sexy."

"You'd be the first."

Claire's smile spread as she ran her hands inside the suitcoat she'd clutched, then slipped it from taut shoulders before shoving Pip backward several steps until they fell across a large, lush bed. "I promise I'll be gentle . . . the first time."

❧ ❧ ❧

Pip lay on their back and bit their lip as Claire undressed, slipping first from her shoes, then slowly pulling the black dress over her head. How surreal to see the article of clothing that had driven Pip mad all evening reduced to a rumpled castoff in the shadow of the woman who held every ounce of their attention. Claire's glory exceeded all expectation, from the curve of her hips to the swell of her breasts beneath black lace, the delicate line of her collarbone, and the slight tremble in her legs.

"You're stunning."

Claire reached behind her for the clasp on her bra, but Pip held out a hand.

"Please, let me."

She nodded and leaned down, allowing Pip to guide her to the bed, then kiss her deeply as their hands began to move over each other.

Pip ran their palms over newly exposed expanses of skin while Claire fingered the buttons on their dress shirt. They wanted to be flush against this woman with a ferocity that rumbled through their core and rattled their brain. Claire's body exuded softness Pip ached to sink into, but when they tried to roll her onto her back, she broke the kiss.

Pip stared up at her, heart beating rapidly, unable to think clearly.

"I want to see you," Claire whispered as she flicked the last button open and tugged the bottom of Pip's shirt from the waistband of their trousers, splaying it open to reveal their tight white compression binder. "All of you."

"You do." Pip's voice sounded low and raspy in the quiet room. "You can. Anything you want."

Claire straddled their legs and unclasped Pip's belt. "I want to know what you want."

"I'm good. It's fine." Pip's throat constricted at the newness of the statement and all the emotion behind it.

Claire shook her head. "You're so much more than good and fine. You're the sexiest person I've ever been on top of, and I hope before the night is over you're also the sexiest human I've ever been under. But I want to make you feel seen and desired while I do the things I've been dreaming about since the moment you popped up in my back field looking too delectable to be real."

Pip's chest swelled, straining against the binder as pride filled both their lungs and their mind, but this was new territory. People generally expected them to take the lead. Once again Claire had shattered all the expectations by carving out an entirely different path.

Pip pulled her back down, relishing the weight of Claire's body as it settled across their hips and chest. They kissed her neck and unclasped her bra, feeling the lace go slack between their bodies, but they didn't rush to rip it away. Claire moved against them, creating friction and kissing a wet line up their jaw.

"I get the feeling you're very good at this," Claire whispered against their ear, "and I plan to enjoy that immensely, but we're not taking turns here. You don't get to teach me about your both/and philosophy and then not bring it to bed with us."

Pip's breath caught as Claire worked her hand between them to unfasten the belt on their trousers. The little sliver of space offered the perfect angle for Pip to discard the bra between them and explore Claire's breasts in all their perfection. They brought both hands up to palm their fullness, and Claire groaned her assent. She dropped her forehead to Pip's as her fingers faltered on the zipper.

"God, your hands are so hot."

Pip responded by circling their thumb around one hard nipple. Claire arched her chest into the touch and swayed slightly before pulling back to sit upright astride Pip's body once more.

"Look, I promised to be gentle only the first time," Claire said with a little growl that made Pip's hips jerk off the bed of their own accord, "so it might be a good idea to tell me if anything's off limits before I lose what's left of my control."

Pip shook their head, unable to think of anything they would deny this woman as she sat tall and exposed above them, hips circling subtly, breasts heavy and firm. They moved to sit up, intending to capture one of the pink nipples between their lips or maybe their teeth, but Claire interrupted the impulse with a firm hand on their shoulder.

"Tell me," she panted, "tell me how you like to be turned on."

"You're doing it. Or rather, you've done it," Pip said through gritted teeth, but still Claire waited patiently, attentively, clearly searching for more than blanket consent given in a sheen of need.

In the space that opened before them Pip's cheeks warmed, and their breath burned in their chest, giving them time to register the subtle disquiet they'd always rushed to fill with speed and abandon. In the gap Claire created, Pip glanced down at their own body with new eyes. "I, erm, it's not anything serious . . ."

Claire massaged the muscles tightening beneath her fingers.

"It's just my . . ." The word caught in their throat as their eyes flicked down to their compression top once more.

What was happening? They'd never had any trouble labelling the female anatomy before. Then again, they usually used those terms to describe the bodies of women they slept with instead of dwelling on their own, the same way they jumped into Claire's dreams while refusing to think about their own future. The realization sent them spiralling, but before they could fall, Claire sank a hand into their hair and tugged their head back until Pip met her eyes.

She was so stunning, so steady, so sure, Pip had no choice but to return to the arousal connecting them like a cord.

Still holding fast to Pip's hair, Claire slid her other hand over the compression binder to the zipper down the front. "Can I take this off?"

It would've been easy to ignore the niggling tells of discontent in favour of the oblivion, but for the first time Pip didn't want to. Claire never shied away from reaching for something better, and that quality inspired courage. Sadly, it didn't inspire a better grasp on the English language. "You can undo the zipper, but it takes a while for my . . . um . . . shite."

Claire kissed them again, swallowing their frustration as she tugged the zipper all the way down in one swift motion, then, splaying the binder open, placed her palm flat across Pip's sternum. "Tell me more."

Pip glanced down once again, this time focusing not on their own anatomy but on the feel of Claire against it even as a comfortable word refused to come. "My . . . I like it when my . . ."

"Chest?" Claire offered, seeming to understand the conflict.

"Yes," Pip rasped as gratitude flooded into desire. "My chest gets really sensitive eventually, but not right away."

"Something to look forward to." Claire smiled. "I won't start there, but I'll be sure to circle back."

Pip groaned. "Please."

"God, that's a sexy word on your lips." Claire kissed them again, sweeping her tongue through Pip's mouth before pushing them onto the bed once more. She kissed her way down along their throat, dipping into the hollow at the base before drawing a wet, hot path in a straight line to their straining abs.

Pip watched her, transfixed, as she circled their navel before reaching up and raking her fingernails down the length of their sides and into the waistband of their slacks. She glanced up at Pip, pupils dark with desire and yet still conveying a question no one had ever stopped to ask.

"What else?"

This time the words came easier. "I'm already so hard."

"That's hot," Claire panted as she finished unfastening the trousers. Then, taking hold of both the waistband and the boxers below, she urged their hips up and freed them of the final barrier to Pip's body.

"Can I take you in my mouth?"

"Yes," Pip hissed through clenched teeth, then sucked the word right back into their lungs as Claire closed around their need. The tongue that had teased their lips over the last few weeks proved equally skilled as it swirled around the length of their sex, and Pip strained against the urge to simply surrender. It had been so long since anyone even offered them the option, but Claire wasn't asking for control or submission. She wasn't merely flipping a script. She was rewriting it, and Pip ached to be a part of the process at every level.

Struggling against the urge to sink first into the pillow and then into oblivion, Pip hauled the weight of their torso up onto their elbows, and lifted heavy lids to watch Claire work. Her head moved up and down with each stroke, and the eroticism of it all took hold of Pip's chest like a fist. They reached down to brush long strands of honey hair away from Claire's face, and ran a thumb along her open jaw.

Claire's eyes flicked up without slowing her mouth, and she

held Pip's gaze with an intimacy that shook through them. Pip trembled from their splayed thighs all the way to their scalp. They wanted this woman with a force that nearly cracked them open. They laced their fingers through Claire's hair, not to exert any pressure, but merely wanting to hold on as a sweet kind of tension coiled their muscles. They rocked in time to the rhythm of Claire's tongue until their roles reversed and Claire worked to keep up with the frantic pace of Pip's increased need.

Their head fell back, mouth open, white light tinging the edges of their eyelids, but in the final second Claire pulled back, causing Pip to jerk upright once more.

"Easy, champ," Claire cooed, her smile satisfied as her fingers took up the place her tongue had held. Then, crawling between Pip's legs, she urged them flat back onto the bed.

She kissed Pip's mouth quickly, lips slick with desire, before whispering, "I told you I'd be back up here when you were ready."

She used her sinfully skilled tongue to draw a circle around one of Pip's tight nipples while moving her fingers in a similar motion.

Pip groaned and reached for her, any part of her to crush against their own body. Breasts, hips, waist, they pawed their way toward purchase until finally brushing across the last remaining barrier between them. Claire's silky black underwear had grown slick with arousal, and Pip gave a fleeting thought to ripping them off, but even that would take longer than they could wait, so the next time Claire circled high, they merely slipped inside.

"Fuck," Claire stiffened, then groaned as Pip found her clit. "Yes."

They worked in unison, passion a mirror to pleasure as they rocked against each other, each one escalating in turn. Claire was so wet that Pip slipped lower unintentionally.

"Yes," Claire gasped, keeping them from reversing course.

"Yes?"

"Inside," Claire panted, "I want to feel you move inside me."

Pip's head grew light, then spun at the luxuriousness of Claire's body as they sank in fully with one push. Then without waiting they adjusted their hand and eased in another finger until tight muscles contracted around them.

Claire let out a grunt of satisfaction and pushed back against Pip's hand, then clamped her mouth around the nipple she'd been teasing.

Pip thrust up at the thrill shooting from one erogenous zone to the next, and in doing so curled their fingers deeper inside the woman, driving her mad with need.

"Claire," they gasped. "I'm not, oh hell, I'm close."

"You?" Claire laughed against their chest. "No one's touched me in six months."

Pip could hardly believe that, but even though they hadn't gone nearly as long between partners, none of the others had ever touched them like Claire.

"Come on," Claire urged, then flicked her tongue to Pip's other nipple. "Please stay with me now."

"Yes," Pip vowed without hesitation, "together."

They rocked, breath heavy, hearts racing, all hands and mouths and raw power.

"Yes." Claire tightened around Pip.

"Yes." They agreed as they lifted off the bed.

It was the only word either of them knew anymore, and the only one either of them wanted to hear. The chain reaction ricocheted through them both and reverberated through the room in hoarse cries and the clutch of fingernails and thighs and Claire's mouth hot over their heart.

Sweat prickled and turned cool while Pip waited for the urge to run, for the disconnect to crash through the clouds, for reality to rip through the fabric they'd tried to weave. They weren't naive enough to believe that the whispers filling their brain since the earliest age of awareness could be banished in a single evening, no matter how magical, but as they sank into the lush mattress with Claire still flush in the crook of their arm, the only sound Pip heard was the echo of their last words still ringing through the room.

Yes. Yes. Together.

CHAPTER NINETEEN

Claire awoke to a soft kiss on her temple and tried to snuggle a little closer to the body beside her. The crisp sheets rustled against her cheek, and she reached for the duvet to pull up over both of them.

"We're almost there," Pip whispered softly in her ear.

"I think we got there several times already."

Pip's low chuckle rumbled through her chest. "Undoubtedly, but in this case, I mean we're almost to our stop."

Claire didn't have the wherewithal to process the word 'stop' when she didn't even have the energy to start going in the first place. Her fingers kept searching for the duvet or even the sheet she seemed to be on top of instead of under, when her hand fell on something hard and cool to the touch. She wasn't amused with the mental work it would take to figure that out, and even less thrilled with the loud voice shouting in the distance.

"Five minutes to Amberwick. Next stop Amberwick."

She cracked open one eye enough to see her own hand wrapped around an armrest. Turning her head slightly her eyes drifted to the button of Pip's dress shirt below her nose. She groaned as her least favourite part of the last few hours came back to her.

They'd left the hotel in the dim light of morning wearing the same clothes they'd worn the night before and crossed the street into the train station. Thankfully, most of the staff and predawn commuters had been too busy with their own morning rush to pay much attention to two people stumbling aboard the train in evening wear, though the steward who'd offered them coffee did do a bit of a double take.

She hadn't managed to care in the moment as she curled into her plush first-class seat and promptly nodded off. Now with the sun rising, her own village coming into view, and nearly an hour's more sleep, she wondered why her embarrassment hadn't risen yet. She and Pip were clearly conveying all the outward signs of a walk of shame, or rather a train of shame, but she couldn't summon the corresponding emotions. She barely managed to feel chagrin as they stepped onto the platform filled with locals.

Pip took her hand, and they headed for Vic's Land Rover without a bag between them. The move soothed her in a way she couldn't have imagined even ten days ago. The easy, casual touch spoke to how much things had shifted between them, but she couldn't help wondering what other shifts might be in store. She hadn't even begun to process how the world had tilted on its axis over the last twelve hours. She simply didn't have the capacity yet. She would need large quantities of food and caffeine to even approximate a functioning status, followed by a long hot shower to ease the aches in the muscles they'd strained, and then maybe after a solid ten hours of uninterrupted sleep, she might be able to make sense of what she'd experienced in Pip's arms.

Pip turned out of the railway station car park and down toward the village. The sun had barely hoisted itself above the horizon and cast the usually blue sea in shimmering gold.

"I'm not usually up early enough to see the sun so low over the North Sea," Pip mused.

Claire yawned. "Are you a fan of the early morning light?"

Pip glanced away from the road long enough to meet Claire's eyes and flash one of those knowing smiles. "I am now."

"You're too smooth." Claire laughed.

"Has anyone ever told you, you have the best laugh in the whole world?"

"Maybe, but only when they were trying to get me into bed, not afterward. You really don't have to work so hard anymore."

"Complimenting you is never work."

Claire rolled her eyes, but as she turned to watch the estuary approach out the window, she fought a flutter in her stomach. How could the butterflies still take flight after everything they'd seen and done together?

A million memories played across her mind's eye, and she became absorbed in her own little world. She might have been content to move there permanently if not for the sight of two familiar figures waiting to cross the roundabout as Pip pulled up in front of the gallery.

She craned her neck in the hopes that her tired eyes were playing tricks on her, but her gran was most definitely walking toward them with Emma Volant in tow.

"Is it common for you to have company before you open to customers?" Pip asked.

"Not at all. It seems we've got impeccable timing."

"Should we get our stories straight?"

Claire snorted. "Can you sing? Maybe light a baton on fire? Because short of a truly spectacular show, there's no reasonable excuse for us to return home at this hour, dressed like this, which doesn't involve being out together all night."

"Is that terrible?"

"How much would you like to see your gran, the crown princess of whatever, when you rolled out of bed after a spontaneous night of seriously mind-blowing sex?"

Pip's grin spread in spite of the situation. "So you agree the sex was top tier?"

"I'm surprised someone of your calibre even has to ask."

Pip shrugged and looked as though they might say something more if not for a knock on the window of the Rover.

Claire shouted and jumped, though there was no reason to

be so startled by the arrival of two people they'd seen coming. She simply didn't seem to be high-functioning at the moment, and she had many factors she could blame, but chief among them was the fact that Pip had mentioned sex, which apparently had the power to short-circuit her brain entirely.

"Good morning," Pip called amiably as they exited the car. Maybe they weren't as frazzled, seeing as how they weren't facing their own grandmother, or perhaps they'd simply had more practice with these types of encounters. "To what do we owe the honour of such esteemed company at such an early hour?"

"I hardly sleep a wink anymore, so I baked some scones," Gran explained as Claire climbed out and managed to give Emma a conspiratorial grin.

"She brought them over to my house knowing I'm also an early riser, but I'd baked a batch myself," Emma added.

"And after a bit of a chat, we thought Claire might like a sweet treat to start her day." Gran moved her eyes pointedly over Pip's attire. "But I suspect she may have already had one."

Claire groaned. "Good morning to you, too, Gran."

"Hi, love." Gran kissed each of her cheeks, and the smell of fresh baked goods hit her senses, making her stomach growl loudly.

"Why don't you come in, and I'll put the kettle on."

"Are you sure?" Emma asked, her eyes flicking from Claire's dress to Pip.

"Of course," Pip answered for her. "Don't go on my account. I've actually got to be off."

"You do?" Claire asked, surprise and perhaps a hint of fear creeping in.

"As much as I hate to leave three beautiful women and a breakfast undoubtedly fit for a king, there's a mechanic coming to check the clutch on the motorbike this morning."

"A likely excuse," Claire grumbled, then under her breath added, "traitor."

"If I'd only known where the last twenty-four hours would take us, I assure you I'd have planned differently."

"Why don't we go on in and set the kettle for you," Emma offered, taking Gran by the arm. "It's always lovely to see you, Pip, no matter how briefly."

"Likewise."

"Perhaps next time you bring my granddaughter home shortly after dawn, you'll be able to stay a little longer."

"Gran," Claire snapped, but Pip only flashed their winning smile and gave her a little bow.

"It is my fervent hope I'm afforded the opportunity in the near future."

Gran shook her head as Emma gave her another little tug, but Claire thought she saw her smile as she unlocked the door to the shop.

"That could've gone worse," Pip said when they were finally out of earshot.

"Could it?" Claire's voice went up an octave. "Because as far as mornings-after go, having your grandmother basically accuse your lover of a booty call and then being left to face the charge alone doesn't rank high for me."

Pip smiled and pulled Claire close. "At least you'll get scones. I notice she didn't offer me one for the road."

"You don't deserve one until you prove you're not abandoning me for good."

Pip kissed her temple. "I'm sorry you even had to worry about such a thing."

"I didn't until it came out of my mouth," Claire admitted. "I thought we'd have more time, but you've slept with me, now things are awkward, and suddenly you're leaving. I wouldn't blame you if the whole mechanic bit turned out to be a rather convenient excuse to make your escape."

Pip nodded. "I wish I could find the charge unfounded, but it's not. In the past I would absolutely have done such a thing, but you're different, Claire, and I'm different around you."

She softened, and rested her forehead on Pip's shoulder. "I don't want to believe you. I never wanted that to be true."

"Then I suppose it would be a great disappointment to you

if I proved myself by returning this evening to try to make it up to you?"

Claire sighed. "I might not hate that."

"With such a ringing endorsement, how could I possibly resist?" Then before Claire could offer more in the way of comebacks, Pip caught hold of her chin and kissed her soundly on the mouth. Then they stepped back and glanced over their shoulder to where both Gran and Emma were clearly watching them. "Now go explain that to our audience."

"Ugh. Remember you promised me a real, honest good-bye."

"And you will get one, but not today, because I will see you tonight after you have cleared up all the questions waiting for you inside."

Claire shook her heard. "You are the worst."

Pip laughed as they got back in the Rover. "And you like that about me."

She didn't argue, and she didn't quite manage to hold in a small smile as she turned to face the music.

Emma and Gran both managed to look busy as she opened the door. The kettle gurgled in the kitchen while Emma set out the scones on the tiny table, along with some jam and clotted cream.

"I can't stay long, love," Gran said, bustling in with two teacups. "Your grandfather has a doctor's appointment up in Newpeth at nine. Spill the beans quickly."

"I'm not sure I have any beans to spill."

"Bollocks."

"Gran!"

"What? I might have been born in the dark, but it wasn't last night. You don't show up this early in an evening dress without having been out all night, and you don't stay out all night with someone like Lady Mulgrave unless you're up to no good."

Her face flamed, but before she could even consider a rebuttal, Gran continued.

"And don't get me wrong. I've no objections to a young woman having a bit of fun, and I never wanted you to be all on your own. I'm glad you've found someone your own age who's awfully easy on the eyes." Gran turned to Emma with an *am I right?* kind of expression.

Emma nodded in agreement. "Almost ridiculously pretty, or handsome maybe, but yes."

"Okay, what's the point, then? Pip and I went to dinner in Edinburgh and had such a good time we decided to spend the night. Doesn't that constitute a little fun?"

"The point is . . ." Her gran drew out an exasperated pause as only a grandmother could. "I want to make sure you understand that a little bit of fun is all it can ever be."

The words hit her square in the chest.

"You grew up in America. You don't understand how things work over here, but there's a way things are done, and someone with a title and castle, and a square jaw and dimpled chin, isn't going to stick around the likes of Amberwick indefinitely."

"I know."

"And the Mulgrave clan won't accept a poor artist into the upper echelons with anything other than animosity."

"I know," she said a little more forcefully.

"And it's all for the best anyway," Gran clucked. "Even if you did manage to win Pip over for long enough to make her forget the rules, you'd only end up with heartbreak on your hands."

"I won't," she said over the wild rush of her own pulse in her ears. "Pip and I are having a good time, but we're just having fun."

"Good." Gran patted her arm and kissed her cheek. "Because that girl is too good-looking to ever be faithful."

And then her lovely little old gran tottled out the door, leaving her big knife stuck right between Claire's ribs.

Emma must have seen it because she placed an arm around Claire's shoulders and eased her into the chair. "I'll get the tea."

She sat very still, trying to breathe evenly and not think at all as her friend bustled about, pouring tea and plating the scones. "Thanks."

Emma sat opposite her. "I'm happy to do it, and thrilled at

my timing. I suspect I picked exactly the right morning to pop in."

She smiled weakly.

"I'd been meaning to stop by all week, but if I'd showed up three days ago, I get the sense I wouldn't have had nearly as much gossip to catch up on."

"No, you definitely wouldn't," Claire admitted. "Despite what it may look like, Pip and I didn't just fall into bed."

"So last night . . .?"

"No, last night we totally fell into bed, but that was the first time."

"Oh wow. You didn't get much time to process before your grandmother jumped all over you."

Claire laughed, but the sound came across as more tired than humorous. "No, she's got a real knack for dropping truth bombs at the worst moments."

"Yes, I've met her. She's not one for beating around the bush, but I'm wondering after seeing you and Pip together on the boat and then this morning if Diane's little bomb was actually the truth."

"What do you mean?"

"I don't want to pry . . ." Emma paused to spread some cream on her scone. "And I know when you two met you intended to keep things casual. But, from where I'm sitting, it looks as though there might be more between you."

"Oh no." Claire quickly jammed a scone in her mouth before doctoring it.

"Okay," Emma said.

"I mean, I've been impressed with them in a few ways I didn't anticipate."

Emma nodded.

"They have more going on underneath those good looks, like there's a soft side there, and a lot more introspection than you'd expect for someone so steeped in privilege. And a self-deprecating sense of humour, like they get how good-looking they are and how suave they can be, but they also know when they are full of it, which is endearing."

Emma smiled. "Yes, sounds casual."

Claire groaned. "I might be in a little deeper than I initially wanted."

"Because of last night?"

"Last night didn't help. The sex was amazing, which I suppose shouldn't come as a shock since Pip has likely had more practice in that area than the average human."

"So, all the hype then?"

"Totally founded. They're passionate and skilled, and when they look at me with those eyes, it's something more." She didn't know how to explain without going into the vulnerability she'd seen in Pip last night, and she didn't want to break their trust or turn it into tawdry gossip, but she also didn't know how to process the emotions it sparked in her. Pip set the bar high and then hurdled it by staying so completely present even when Claire clearly deviated from the script. They brought all the sex appeal anyone could ever imagine to the experience, but they didn't stop there, and maybe if they had, Claire could've been more convincing in her continued assertion of their casualness, but certain parts of last night didn't feel casual.

She glanced up from stirring her tea to see Emma eyeing her intently. "I notice you're using they/them pronouns."

"Leave it to the writer." She shook her head. "I don't know what the final verdict will be. We're sort of trying it on."

"I like that," Emma said. "I actually like so many things about the two of you together."

"I do, too," Claire admitted. Then, with a tired sigh, she added, "but my Gran's not wrong. Pip and I come from completely different worlds."

"I don't disagree, and she's likely right about Pip's family, too. I've spent enough time around Vic and Sophia to know these nobility types are harder to break away from than the mafia."

Claire frowned.

"But I also know it can be done if it needs to be, if you're strong enough, and Pip is strong enough, and you both want it bad enough."

"Those are some pretty big ifs, don't you think?"

"Probably," Emma said sadly, "but I wouldn't rule it out because of that last thing your grandmother said. Pip's a person, and from what I've seen they are a lot more genuine and complex than anyone has ever given them credit for. Maybe if you're the first, you can spark some firsts for them, too. What have you got to lose?"

"Oh, nothing much," Claire scoffed. "Just my heart."

❧ ❧ ❧

Pip grabbed their rucksack and glanced around the bathroom for their toothbrush. Back home they left it out, but here the cleaning staff always put it away. The question was where?

They were still rummaging through drawers in the washstand when someone knocked on the door.

"Enter," Pip called.

Vic strode in and glanced at all the open drawers.

"I hope you lost something and you aren't merely trashing the place for sport."

"Your staff keeps taking my toothbrush."

Vic shook her head and pressed on a mirror that appeared flush with the wall, only to have it spring open and reveal a little cupboard. There on a shelf sat a pewter cup, and in it several of the toothbrushes she'd used over the last month.

"Are you serious? Secret cabinets? Like this place isn't big enough to get lost in already?"

"We like to keep our guests on their toes, which I suspect might run in the family, given how you're currently dodging phone calls from yours."

Pip's shoulders tightened. "I don't know what you mean."

"Is your phone dead, or have you found a way to program it so your mother and sisters go straight to voicemail? Because you seem to have no trouble getting messages from mechanics or Claire, and yet I've been fielding the calls you've avoided all day."

"I've been busy." Pip chose a toothbrush and closed the mirror.

"Uh-huh. As you so often are."

"It's not like that."

"Oh, so you're not sleeping with Claire?"

"Well . . ." Pip sighed. "I mean I am, but only recently."

"She made you wait. Good for her." Vic gave a little nod of respect. "But now that you've had your way, I assume you'll be moving along."

Both the charge and the flippancy with which it was delivered set Pip's teeth on edge, not because they were unfair, but because they weren't. Pip had no defence. They hadn't earned one, and quite frankly they hadn't ever wanted to. They'd built the patterns in their life because they worked.

"Hey," Vic whispered. "Are you okay?"

They shook their head.

"No?"

"Yeah. I mean no, I'm fine. I'm sorry you've been fielding calls for me all day. I didn't want to become an imposition."

Vic's expression softened. "You haven't. I've hardly seen you this whole time between my trips to London and your outings with Claire."

"I promised I wouldn't get in your way." Pip tried to scoot past her, but Vic caught them gently by the arm.

"I might have been a little brash when you asked to stay. I was tired, and I didn't know what you were up to."

"No worries. I'm generally up to something." Pip forced a grin. "Honestly, at the time I was up to something."

"And now?"

Pip bit their lip. They'd gotten much better about admitting what they didn't know, except they'd only done so with Claire. Vic was different. Vic was family. Family was complicated.

"You're worrying me. I don't think I've ever seen you search for an answer in your life."

"Maybe I've learned to give people the ones they want to hear."

Vic nodded. "Makes sense."

"Does it?"

"Maybe not to most people, but to me. Sometimes it's easier to meet expectations than to break them, but you can't go your whole life playing a role someone else cast you in."

"Can't I?" Pip shot back.

Vic laughed. "Calm down. I didn't say it as some sort of a challenge, and lord knows plenty of our people have done exactly that, but giving people what they want takes a toll. I understand that better than most."

"Yeah," Pip agreed. They'd been a teenager during Vic's divorce, but even at a young age they'd understood enough about the expectations of their lineage and how those expectations had taken someone as strong and honourable as Vic and brought her to her knees. They didn't want that, not for themselves, and not for anyone they cared about.

Even if they were one hundred percent certain of what they wanted and had the courage of their convictions, they didn't have Vic's grace or presence or pure heart for service. They'd never be a poster child or a role model or an ambassador for a greater cause. They had only questions and half-formed identities and an ache to be back in Claire's arms.

"You can talk to me," Vic offered.

"Claire gives me the freedom to explore who I might be without everything and everyone else screaming in my brain."

Vic's lips parted in surprise, and Pip tried to neither laugh nor cry at such a telling reaction. Vic clearly hadn't thought them capable of such reflection.

"I like who I am with her," Pip continued, "and I like the sense that I might yet become something more. She lets me grapple. She lets me play. She lets me enjoy the journey and never pressures me to know where we're going, or even to check some preset map."

Vic nodded. "And what are you learning along the way?"

"I'm not sure yet. Everything is still too fluid. I'm too fluid to pin down any answers, or maybe that's the answer. I am too fluid, period."

"I'll admit I don't have as good a grasp on fluid identities as I should. I spent so much time fighting for the right to cling to my very concrete one, but now that I have, I'd be honoured to learn more about yours."

Pip's emotions formed a knot in their throat, allowing only a strangled sound to emerge.

Vic smiled. "Phillipa of Mulgrave, speechless. Will wonders never cease?"

"Actually," Pip squeaked, then tried again. "Can we stick with Pip now, no title, no feminine names?"

"Of course. Pip has always suited you best of all," Vic agreed, "and I know a thing or two about wanting to chuck titles. Come on. Let's get some dinner, and we can trade horror stories."

"Thank you." Pip hoped the simple words conveyed their gratitude, even as they turned down the offer. "But I promised Claire I'd be back this evening. And I know someone of your honour wouldn't want me to break my word."

Vic's smile grew exponentially. "No, and for what it's worth, I'm glad you don't want to either."

Pip laughed. "Yeah, well, maybe I'm trying something new."

"Then you have my blessing, but can you do me one small favour before you do?"

"What's that?"

"Buck up and call your sister."

Their chest tightened. "Which one?"

Vic clasped them by the shoulder and gave an encouraging squeeze. "Margaret."

Then, like someone who'd dropped a lighted match near a vat of oil, her brave, bold, honour-bound cousin turned and practically ran from the room.

"Ugh." Pip shoved the toothbrush in their rucksack and fished out the phone. Turning it on for the first time in days, they noted several missed calls, not only from Margie, but also from Louisa, and even two from their mother. They hit the call-back button for Margie before they lost their nerve, but sent up a small prayer that maybe the younger of their two sisters wouldn't answer.

No luck. Margie picked up on the second ring and without so much as a "hello" squealed, "I'm engaged!"

"Wow."

"Right?" Margie laughed. "I'm going to be a countess someday! Marco finally popped the question. He had an orchestra, and of course he'd already asked for father's permission."

"Of course." Pip couldn't have withheld the eye roll even if Margie were right in front of them. Marco would ask their father for the right to transfer his daughter's title to his own. Lady Mulgrave would become Countess Riccini based on his claim to both her and the title inherent in his birth.

"And the ring. I have to send you a picture, but just you wait, Pippa."

They gritted their teeth against the name, and tried to focus on what Margie was saying about diamonds and sapphires and carats, but it all whirred into an unintelligible jumble. Margie was getting married, and while the marital status of their sister would have little effect on their life going forward, a wedding would derail months and months of freedom. A wedding, especially an international one between the children of two aristocratic families, would mean endless events and obligations and expectations. Travel, planning, attire, presentation, and so much prestige to uphold. There would be eyes everywhere and all the time, and none of that time would be scheduled to allow for exploration or escapes to Amberwick.

"So, you'll have to fly in no later than Friday, okay?"

The way Margie's voice rose in inflection alerted Pip to the fact that they'd been asked a question.

"Sorry. You cut out for a second there. What did you say at the end?"

"You'll have to fly in by midafternoon next Friday to make it for the engagement party."

"Next Friday?"

"October twelfth."

Pip sat on the edge of the bed. October twelfth. Was that the expiration date Claire had mentioned? The date when the real world would assert its dominion over them again? They whispered the words, trying them out the way one might practice a name they found hard to pronounce. "October twelfth."

"Don't pretend you need to check your schedule." Margie laughed. "I know you don't have anything more important to do."

Pip didn't argue. There wasn't any use trying to explain. No one in her family would find anything she did with Claire as important as keeping up appearances around such a momentous family event. Claire wasn't related to any Italian counts, and she didn't have money or a family name worth touting. How could Pip make them see how little those things mattered to them? Or maybe they did matter, because they made Pip like Claire even more, because it meant Claire had figured out her path entirely of her own accord. The fact that she'd struggled and kept searching made her all the more appealing, and the fact that Claire managed to be open, warm, understanding, and utterly enticing while still finding her own way gave her a quality Pip had never stayed around long enough to warm to in other women.

Then again, maybe the other women hadn't possessed those qualities, which was why Pip hadn't wanted to stick around . . . until now.

The realization hit Pip so hard their breath caught, and the sound must've been dramatic enough to cut through Margie's monologue about the engagement party because she stopped to say, "Everything okay there?"

"Yes. Sorry, dropped my, erm, toothbrush." The lie came out easier than admitting they'd seriously given thought to the desire to stick around, not for a night, not for a weekend, but indefinitely with a woman they were supposed to be having fun with. Sticking around wasn't an option either of them had ever allowed for.

"Ew," Margie said, "better trade it in for a new model."

Yes, that'd be her response. If something touched anything unpleasant, it must be discarded, and the thing was Pip couldn't even blame her, as they'd discarded much more over much less. The first time anything got awkward or boring, personal or challenging, or not challenging enough, they ran.

In keeping with that theme, they cleared their throat and said, "I'm happy for you, Margie. I can't wait to hug you in person, but I've actually got to get going."

"Oh, me too. Dinner with the future in-laws tonight." She gave another happy squeal, and Pip managed a weak smile. Margie might be a bit much for their tastes most days, but they didn't begrudge her any happiness.

"Love you, Pippa."

"Love you too, Madge."

They disconnected the phone and sighed. Why did everything have to be so complicated? They'd been having fun with Claire. Every minute with her had been engaging and brilliant, and all the challenges Pip had come to take for granted sparked to new life with her. The first date, the first kiss, the hunt for more, and the satisfaction of, well, reaching satisfaction—Claire had lived up to all her promises for honesty and fun along the way.

Only those bridges had been crossed now. Claire had hinted at it this morning, and Vic had said it outright. By every standard in Pip's playbook, the game should be over.

And yet, here they were, shoving a change of clothes, a toothbrush, and a few unmentionables into their trusty rucksack, every part of them itching to point their bike toward the coast, and more importantly toward Claire.

CHAPTER TWENTY

Claire tried not to notice the time or the gathering dusk outside. Pip had said "evening," and therefore they weren't late, perhaps later than Claire had expected, and definitely later than she'd hoped, but not actually late. And it wasn't as though she kept looking at the clock on her phone every three minutes. She couldn't help it if it just happened to be in her line of sight since she'd propped it up on her easel to display a photo of a puffin all in the name of professionalism. If she was going to start painting the little buggers, she might as well get the details down.

And judging by the fact that she was currently outlining her third puffin painting today, she intended to keep painting them. She tried to tell herself it made sense financially. If Pip could sell their simplistic design so quickly and for so much money, it couldn't hurt to have a few similar items in reserve. And she felt nearly certain her change of heart had nothing to do with her newfound affinity for the little birds who had helped spark some beautiful firsts with the person who always pushed her to think of things differently. At least that's what she kept telling herself, but even she had a hard time buying the purely business argument, and as soon as the sound of an approaching motorcycle broke the silence her best intentions faded with the last light of the day.

"You came back." The words left her mouth in a rush of relief before Pip even made it fully across the threshold.

Pip smiled in a way that didn't convey any confidence. "Did you think I wouldn't?"

"No. I mean, I thought you would, probably." Claire pulled them all the way into the gallery and flipped the lock on the door before kissing them quickly. "I was, like, eighty percent sure."

"Eighty percent is probably more faith than I've earned."

"No, you've more than kept up your end of the bargain. You've never lied to me. The other twenty percent comes from the part of me who's gotten a bit too used to being left. That part's a real pisser."

Pip encircled her waist loosely. "For what it's worth, I wanted to be back sooner. Or rather, I didn't want to go in the first place."

Claire rested her head on Pip's chest, breathing in the soothing scent of cologne and clean air. "You don't have to convince me."

"Nor am I trying to." Pip kissed the top of her hair. "I'm merely stating a fact you might not have been aware of, one that perhaps I wasn't even aware of until I'd already gone."

Claire glanced up to meet those blue eyes. "What? You mean in the moment you pulled up with me still in last night's clothes and saw my grandmother standing there you didn't immediately think, 'Yes, this is exactly how I wanted to spend my postcoital haze?'"

"Not exactly."

"Welcome to the club."

"Was it awful?"

Claire remembered her grandmother's comments about fun and faithfulness, but managed not to shudder. "It could have been worse. She didn't give me any morality lectures, and she didn't stay long."

"Good," Pip said, "but here's the real question: Did she leave any scones?"

Claire laughed. "Enough to eat on for days."

"God bless her."

Claire shook her head and stepped back. "Have you eaten anything yet?"

"Not since noon, and I'm famished in more ways than one."

"I can offer you tea and scones, or a couple of bananas brown enough to have turned into banana pâte."

"Decisions, decisions. I think I'll go with the tea and scones."

"How very civilized of you."

They set an easy rhythm of moving around each other in the kitchen. Pip gathered plates and cups without having to search for them while Claire warmed the scones and some hot water.

"You'll have sugar," Pip stated more than questioned.

"Yes, it's on the table from earlier, but you can grab the cream." When had they taken the time to learn how the other took their tea? She hadn't made a conscious effort to do so, though that could be said for so many things about Pip. She hadn't set out to get comfortable—quite the opposite. Still, when she glanced up to see Pip watching her, her heart gave an extra jump at the intensity of their gaze.

"What?"

"You're beautiful."

She shook her head. "You don't have to say that. I'm pretty much a sure thing for you right now. No need to keep working the flattery angle."

Pip didn't laugh. "I know, which is why you need to believe me. You're always stunning, but here, relaxed, at ease in your own skin, there's something special I've never seen in anyone else before."

"Perhaps that's because you never stick around to know the women you take to bed long enough for them to let down their guard."

Pip didn't back away from the charge. "The thought occurred to me, along with the possibility that most women never feel comfortable relaxing around me. They're trying to either impress me or get something from me."

"Which could be why you haven't made a habit of sticking

around."

Pip nodded slowly, the little muscles at the sides of their jaw twitching with a tension Claire wanted to soothe.

Instead, she set a plate of warm scones on the counter between them. "Time to carbo-load."

Pip's perfect lips quirked up. "Why ever do you think I'd need to fortify myself calorically?"

"If you can't figure that out on your own, maybe you've come to the wrong place."

Pip split a scone in half and slathered it in jam. "Maybe you'll help me figure it out."

"Helping you figure things out is kind of my thing."

Pip frowned again. "I hadn't thought of it that way."

"Hey," Claire said more seriously, "I'm just playing with you."

"But you're not mistaken." Pip chewed slowly as if buying time to process. "You have given me a great deal of space and support. You've given me more genuine encouragement than anyone I've ever known. You've pushed me to think about so many things differently, chief among them, how I think about myself."

This time Claire's heart didn't kick; it melted. She'd seen Pip's introspective side enough to know it existed, but she'd never had it pointed out to her quite so acutely. She didn't know what to say. Their usual quick quips didn't seem sufficient, nor did simply accepting credit for something as monumental as Pip's self-discovery. "You must have been ready to do that work. It's not the type of thing a person can do for you. Still, I'm glad I got to be the one to see it."

Pip finished their scone and began doctoring another before they finally looked up again. "It hasn't been a disappointment to you?"

"A disappointment?" Even repeating the phrase hurt a little bit. "Why would you think that?"

"I don't know. I . . . you signed up for something light and fun with the picture of class and frivolity, someone with slick moves and easy conversation and good hair. Then once we got going, I turned into someone who doesn't even know what to call themselves and who bangs on about having no real friends. I'm doing it even now. I'm killing the mood again."

Claire walked around the counter and took Pip's face in her hands. "Listen to me. You are all the things you advertised yourself as being. You've been so much fun, and in those suits you exude class for days. And, as far as conversations go, you've exceeded all expectations by being smart and funny, but also genuine and deep and thoughtful in ways no one with your head of hair should be able to be."

"People with good hair shouldn't be deep conversationalists?"

"Of course not. It's not fair for one person to have all the good attributes. There should be a more even distribution, but you got the goods in every department."

"But my body and my brain, they don't ... I can't always—" Pip sucked in a painful-sounding breath and released it in a jagged rush.

"Whoa," Claire whispered. "Your body and your brain are both perfect and complex, like the rest of you. You're strong and bold and brilliant and beautiful."

"But, no one else—"

"—matters." Claire finished the sentence in the only acceptable fashion. "You're the only one who inhabits your skin. You're entitled to complete ownership of your lived experience. No one else will ever know you the way *you* know you, and they don't get a say in how you wear your reality."

"Except they do."

"Not here. Not with me."

Pip rested their head on Claire's shoulder. "But what if I want you to have a say?"

"Then I'll say I think you're ridiculously sexy, mind and body. I want you so badly I can hardly breathe. Last night was the most completely satisfying sex I've ever had, and not in spite of the fact that you told me what you needed, but because of it."

Pip sighed, this time more softly.

"What's going on? Where did this come from?"

Pip shrugged. "Nowhere in particular."

The hair on the back of Claire's neck stood up. "Are you sure?"

Pip stood back a bit. "Yes, sorry if I gave you a bit of a fright there. The lack of sleep must be getting to me. As you may remember, someone kept me up all night."

Claire searched their eyes, then glanced back toward the scone. "I'm not sure I'm solely to blame."

"Hmm, seeing as how I'm an aristocrat and we're never held accountable for our actions, you'll have to take the fall anyway."

Claire laughed in spite of understanding that Pip had deliberately turned on their charm the way a normal person might flip on a light switch, but the faint chime of warning bells sounded so far off she didn't have a hard time ignoring them.

If something were wrong, she'd offered them the space to explore it. She didn't want to spend these moments steeped in worry or insecurity, so when Pip took her in their arms again, she didn't lean back.

Pip kissed her, slowly and sweetly at first, but it didn't take long for their tongue to press for more. She parted her lips, welcoming the intrusion and the rush of arousal it sent through her. She wanted to pull them in closer, deeper, more completely. Running her hands down Pip's back, she took a few seconds to cup the most deliciously curved ass before using both hands to crush their body against her own. She ground her hips against the increased pressure, but something new caught her attention.

Still kissing Pip, and grinding together, her mind struggled to process the length of something firm tucked along Pip's leg. She had the wherewithal to realize that definitely hadn't been there last night, and the clarity to make sense of the most likely possibility, but her curiosity still took hold. She worked her hand between them without breaking any more contact than the move absolutely required until her fingers traced the outline of a subtle bulge.

Her heart rate accelerated as a million nerve endings buzzed in anticipation, and she leaned back far enough to arch one eyebrow.

Pip's smile bordered on a playful kind of arrogance. "You said you wanted to be gentle only the first time."

Both the expression and the comment combined to send Claire's arousal levels into the stratosphere. This is the Pip she found almost maddeningly irresistible: playful, powerful, fully realized in all their complexities and confidence.

Claire ran her tongue along her suddenly dry lips as her fantasies took hold. "You better know how to use that thing properly because I really like kissing you while I come."

This time it was Pip's turn to growl. In an instant they had Claire in their arms, and in another they lifted her off the ground until her legs wrapped around their waist, seemingly of their own accord.

Pip kissed along her neck. "Where's the bedroom?"

"Remember the wooden ladder in the storeroom?"

"Are you fecking joking?"

"Come on." Claire slid down and, taking their hand, led them through the gallery and into the back room before stopping at the base of the ladder. She turned to them, intending to say something about the mess of the loft area, or maybe to apologize for the small space, but when her eyes met Pip's, the raw desire reflected in expanding pupils killed all coherent thought.

The short single-story ladder she climbed every day now seemed insurmountable under the weight of her need, and she caught hold of Pip by the base of the neck and yanked them forward once more.

Stumbling around in the delirium of the bruising kiss, she felt blindly for any surface to catch hold of until her fingers found the edge of a workbench. Leaning against it for balance, she took hold of Pip's waistband right at the fly. She flicked open the top button and tugged down the zipper, then slipped her hand inside.

Groaning into Pip's mouth as her palm slid down a smooth surface, she closed her fingers around the girth and pulled her new fixation free of its confines.

As much as she didn't want to break the kiss, she couldn't help sneaking a quick peek. There at the apex of Pip's thighs stood the most artistic strap-on she'd ever seen. A deep, royal purple, swirled with a thick splash of midnight blue, ran from a slightly flared tip all the way down to a gleaming silver ring set in a luscious leather harness.

She swayed at the sight of its perfection, though she shouldn't have been surprised. Pip had never been shy about their champagne tastes. She'd just never considered how those proclivities might work for her own pleasure in this particular fashion.

"Do you want this?"

"Yes." She managed as she started unfastening her own blue jeans.

"Ask for it."

She rolled her head from side to side as she struggled to find enough vocabulary to convey her needs through her lusty haze while also kicking off her shoes and pushing her jeans to the floor.

Thankfully, Pip understood where this was headed, and with one sweep of their arm brushed a myriad of art supplies off the counter and onto the floor.

Everything landed with a clatter that barely registered with her senses, and she shimmied out of her underwear before hopping onto the newly cleared space.

Pip stepped into the space between her splayed knees and eased forward until the strap-on hovered millimeters from her sex but went no further until Claire met their stare.

This time, she wasn't sure if the questions there stemmed from the need for consent or the need for control, but the impetus mattered little as both scenarios drove her right up to the edge of reason. Clutching the front of Pip's shirt, she managed only two words. "Fuck me."

Pip pushed forward slowly, the muscles in their shoulders and neck tensed with the strain of patience, and Claire gasped as the head slipped inside. She needed little time to adjust to the fullness before she pulled on Pip's body once more. "Come on, Pip. I'm so wet for you."

The comment must've been the last bit of direction they needed, or perhaps the need in Claire's low, raspy tone simply broke the last of their restraint, because they surged forward in one steady thrust.

Claire threw back her head as the pleasure flashed through her. "Yes."

Pip worked in and out, first in short strokes, then in longer ones that shook the counter until everything rattled around them. They established a rapid rhythm that caused Claire's body to tighten and the edges of her vision to tinge red, then drew back, and eased into a way of rocking along every ridge inside her. Claire wrapped one leg loosely around Pip's waist, trying to both hold them close and let them move at the same time. She wanted to surrender to whatever path they set, because no matter what choice they made, it always seemed to be the right one. Maybe that was simply part of being with Pip. In all their fluidity, there were no wrong answers.

The thought filled her mind as Pip pushed her body to its limits over and over again, and the combination ripped through her in the form of an orgasm she hadn't even realized she'd been so close to. The convulsions caught her off guard in both their suddenness and their strength. She cried out, completely unrestrained as Pip pushed into her and pinned her to the counter.

Finding her mouth, Pip kissed her deeply as Claire's muscles contracted, released, and contracted again. Pip's tongue swept between her lips, heat prickled every inch of her body, and she grew dizzy with the rush of her own release. Their hips ground together, flush now save for the harness as the subtle tremors of the movement radiating through her with the final waves of climax gave way to afterglow.

Pip didn't withdraw even as they pulled their lips from hers and trailed down along her neck and back up her jaw before biting her earlobe and whispering, "You're perfect."

She gave a low laugh and let her heavy head rest against Pip's cheek.

"What's funny?"

"I was thinking the same thing about you."

⸙ ⸙ ⸙

Pip didn't even remember falling into Claire's bed last night, which said a lot, seeing as how they'd had to climb a ladder to do so, but when they awoke it didn't feel strange to open their eyes to a slanted ceiling and exposed rafters. Pip lay on their back and stared up at dark wood beams for quite a while, wondering at the new sensation of being nestled in a strange bed with Claire curled around them and not needing to run. Their fingers didn't even twitch with the impulse to peel back the blanket. The first time they'd slept together, they'd had to jump out of bed and stagger toward the train so early that a part of Pip assumed the quick movement filled their need to get up and go. Of course, Claire had gone with them then, but there'd still been a flurry of activity to serve as a diversion. This morning offered no such excuse.

Hell, the fact that there had been a second morning may have been disconcerting enough in most cases, but added to the fact that even with ample time to panic, they simply didn't, made Pip a little, well . . . panicked.

They rolled their eyes. What kind of person panics because they aren't panicking?

Claire snuggled closer, her head easing onto Pip's shoulder, palm resting lightly at the centre of their chest, her breath soft and warm where it fluttered across their neck. Pip timed their own breaths to Claire's as peace overtook them once more. It was a nice feeling, they decided: strange, but good. Did other people feel this contented all the time?

They were still pondering the question when a sound caught their attention. They strained their ear to listen. A key in the

226

lock, the sweep of a door opening, the click of it closing again. Pip tensed, hoping someone had merely dropped something off, but as footsteps fell across the wooden floor, they gave Claire a little shake.

"Someone's here."

Claire whimpered.

"There's a person in the gallery," they whispered again.

Claire yawned. "It's Reg."

"Oh." Pip relaxed only slightly before tensing again.

"All your clothes are on the floor in the storeroom."

That got Claire's attention, and she cracked open her eyes a sliver. "Where are yours?"

"Erm, I think mostly up here, but I don't remember all the details. I know I kicked my shoes off downstairs, and you took off my overshirt—"

Claire put her hand over Pip's mouth to quiet the recall exercise. "Where's the strap-on?"

They both sprang out of the bed in an instant.

"Hey, Reg," Claire called down the ladder, "there's scones in the kitchen. Why don't you heat some up, and I'll be right down."

"Right," Reg called. "Shall I put the kettle on?"

"I'll be forever in your debt."

"On it," Reg called as her footsteps fell away.

Pip stood stock still until they heard the sounds of Reg moving around the kitchen, then released a large sigh of relief.

Claire met their eyes and smiled. "Too close."

"The kid's got to learn some time."

"I'm all for offering support to the queer youth, but her stumbling on your strap-on in my workroom is a bit much for my level of mentorship."

Pip grinned. "It's good to have boundaries."

"How would you know?"

"Other people have told me."

Claire shook her head. "Why do I find you irresistible?"

They shrugged. "Just lucky I suppose."

Claire grabbed a few articles of clothing from various spots around the small room and pulled them on. "I'll go down and toss your bag up, then chat with Reg, but don't hide up here all day or sneak out or anything."

"I wouldn't dream of it," Pip said, then as the words sank in, marvelled that using Reggie's arrival as an excuse to bolt hadn't even occurred to them.

It was hard not to read too much into the realization as they sat on the edge of the bed waiting for their rucksack to come up the ladder. Even when it did and they set about dressing, then brushing teeth and hair in the cramped loo off to one side of the loft, they couldn't stop trying to put a finger on what was different about this morning, this place, this situation that made staying seem like a valid option. Glancing around at the unremarkable space one more time before slipping down the ladder, they had to finally admit their reason for staying had nothing to do with the location or circumstance, and everything to do with the woman waiting for them down below.

The thought didn't frighten Pip. They couldn't summon much apprehension when thinking of Claire. Even being apart for a few minutes left them eager to get back to her. How had they become one of those people who missed someone who'd just left? And worse, would they be able to keep from saying so when they came around the corner?

Thankfully, the vibration of their phone saved them from such a sappy statement, pulling their attention away. Grateful for the distraction, they made the rare mistake of answering it before checking to see who was calling. "Hello."

"Darling." Their mother's voice came through loudly. "I've grown so accustomed to addressing your voicemail I don't even know what to say now that you've answered."

"I could hang up and not answer when you call back."

"Don't you dare."

Claire peeked her head around the corner, and Pip gave a grimace while pointing to the phone.

Claire nodded, but her brow furrowed.

"I'm calling about your sister's wedding."

"Of course." They hadn't meant the comment to sound as droll as it did, and tried again to inject a little enthusiasm into their voice. "It's very exciting."

"Indeed. Exciting and important, which I know goes without saying, but I must reiterate how much this event means to our whole family."

"Understood."

"It's not every day a family like ours merges with one like Marco's, and this is a *family* affair, Phillippa."

They cleared their throat, intending to say something this time. "Pippa" was bad enough, but the dysphoria of being called "Phillippa" felt like needles under their fingernails. Before they could find the words, however, their mother pushed on.

"Margaret mentioned you hadn't gotten back to her about your flight arrangements."

"I only found out last night."

Claire's eyebrows shot up, and Pip lowered their voice. "I've hardly had time."

"I can't imagine what you've done since then that mattered more than your sister's big news."

Pip bit their lip and met Claire's eyes, their chest tightening. Her mother couldn't possibly understand the things they'd done this morning, the peace they'd experienced, the realizations they'd been processing.

They turned away and walked across the gallery, then out the sliding glass doors onto the patio. The cold air sobered them. When had autumn arrived since only a few days ago it had seemed like an endless summer?

Mother droned on about the wedding as though it were a merger between two companies rather than two people. Pip barely made out any of the words, but they understood the main idea. The event, or rather series of events, would take precedence over anything happening in any of their lives for the foreseeable future.

"So, I'll make your flight arrangements and forward

them to you."

What she meant was her assistant would do so, but there wasn't any use arguing finer points.

"You'll also need to coordinate your attire properly."

That finally caught their attention. "I'm relatively certain I can dress myself."

"As am I," Mummy cut back in, "which is why I'm giving you some choice in the matter, but I hope you won't make me regret the decision by showing up in tails and a top hat. This engagement party is neither the time nor the place to make statements."

"I'm not making statements. I merely dress in ways most comfortable for me."

"And I support your right to do so on your own time, love. However, this is your sister's moment. She deserves to be the centre of attention. Your right to self-expression stops where it takes the focus away from her or raises concerns about the very traditional family she's marrying into. Do you understand me?"

"You want me to wear a dress?"

"I'm not an uncaring ogre or an idiot. I understand a dress may be a bridge too far, but you could at least wear a feminine suit, a nice pastel blouse, perhaps, and for the love of God, dress it up with some heels."

"Mother—"

"Don't 'mother' me, Phillipa. Work with me. It's the minimum responsibility you owe to the family that keeps you in the lifestyle to which you've grown accustomed. Show up and play your part. Be gracious and charming, and you'll show some of the decorum you always seem to muster every time you have to get out of trouble or secure funds from your father."

Pip's jaw tightened. They were being asked to play the same part in which they'd always been cast: the heiress, the socialite, the daughter of nobility, the sister of the bride. A bit player who blended into the cast and never stole a scene.

"Do I make myself clear?"

They ground their teeth as they stared out across the soggy

field still shrouded in the remainder of the morning fog, but they didn't feel the chill anymore as a familiar numbness set in. "Yes, ma'am."

"Good. Then I do look forward to seeing you a week from Friday."

"Yes, ma'am."

"Don't be glum. We've missed you, and you're not off to the gallows. It'll be a star-studded event with amazing wine, decadent food, and pretty people. All your favourite things. I can't imagine anything that you've found in Northland can compare with that."

Pip glanced back over their shoulder to see Claire watching her, eyes filled with concern and a slight quirk of encouragement on her lips.

Arguing would only prolong a conversation they didn't want to be in, but standing there in the warmth of Claire's caring, neither could they agree with the statement, not even to keep the peace. "Good-bye, Mother."

⚛ ⚛ ⚛

Claire fought the urge to get up from the table and walk away from Reggie's story of some school drama. She didn't mean to ignore the teenager, but she couldn't take her eyes off Pip, who'd clearly hung up the phone but didn't seem in any hurry to come inside. The set of their strong shoulders spoke of a tension that radiated through Claire's own tight jaw. Clearly the phone call hadn't been good news, and the longer Pip stayed partially shrouded in the lingering fog, the more a sense of foreboding crept inside.

Still, if this were the end, Claire wouldn't cling to them or beg or cry. She'd already had more time with Pip than expected, or at least that's what she told herself.

Finally, Pip turned and came back in, their shoulders still hunched as if bracing themselves against a stiff wind and wearing a smile that barely bent their cheeks. "Sorry."

"Everything okay?" Claire asked, her voice higher than usual.

"Yes. My mother had a few things to catch me up on," Pip said quickly, then turned to their newest arrival. "Good morning, Reg."

"Morning," Reg said more softly, then with a slow smile added, "Bacon Butty."

Pip's expression softened as they walked to the table. Picking up a cup of tea, they sipped then made a sour face. "Not one for working a kettle, Reg?"

"That one was already here when I came in." Reg's face flushed. "Something must have interrupted teatime last night."

"Ah." Pip smiled at the memory even as Claire's own cheeks warmed. "I suppose day-old tea never killed anyone."

"Ew." Claire grabbed the cup. "It's got milk in it. Sometimes I worry you're part feral."

"A valid concern."

She didn't like the sound of that, or the worn edge of resignation in Pip's voice. She worked to keep her hands steady as she poured a fresh cup of tea and motioned for Pip to take a seat. "Are you sure everything's all right?"

Pip nodded, appearing both slightly embarrassed and a bit sad. "Quite."

Claire didn't believe them. She didn't believe any smile that didn't reach those electric eyes, and she didn't believe a benign phone call would have strained such a smooth voice. She believed anything that couldn't be shaken off by Pip's devil-may-care attitude posed a threat.

"Come on," Pip said with forced cheer. "Don't hoard all the scones, and don't let a momentary interruption mar the start to a lovely day spent in the best of company. What do you plan to work on today, Reg?"

"I might do a bit of dusting until the sun burns through the haar, and then I'll trim the garden hedges."

"I appreciate your sense of industry. It's an attribute I've never possessed," Pip said, then turned to Claire, "and I presume you'll continue working on the masterpiece whose progress I interrupted last night."

Claire sighed, wishing they could talk for a bit, but understanding that whatever emotions Pip insisted on burying weren't best unearthed in front of Reg. "I suppose I'd better if any of us hope to keep the lights on in this place."

"Then I'll use my only valid skill and supply you both with hot tea and scones as you work. Alas, I left my livery at home, so you'll have to stand me dressed like a commoner while I serve you."

Reg gave a little giggle. "I could get used to that."

Pip tousled her red hair and looked to Claire as if asking permission to take up the charade instead of sadness. "And you?"

"You'll have to clear the table while you're at it. Do you know how to do such a thing?"

"I've never tried," Pip said solemnly, "but I've seen others perform the chore."

"If you get lost, you can ask me," Reg said. "I've got plenty of practice."

"Very kind of you, squire."

"Don't expect a similar offer from me." Claire affected a snooty air. "My work is much too important to be disturbed by such trivial matters."

Pip gave a curt chin to chest nod. "As you wish, madam."

Claire smiled and then realized she'd fallen prey to a redirect via Pip's charm and sense of humour, but by then they were already whisking plates away to the kitchen, and there was something appealing about having the nobility do one's dishes. Plus, Pip hadn't wanted to let whatever happened on the phone ruin the day, and Claire could at least agree with that sentiment.

She rose and wandered to her easel, surveying the half-finished puffin and trying to decide where to pick back up. She'd already done a brightly coloured backdrop, and another one on a sunny shore. Perhaps she could give this one a charcoal background like a formal portrait to make his white belly stand out along with his orange beak and feet.

She'd just lifted her brush to the grey patch of paint on her palette when the bell over the door chimed.

She and Reg both glanced up as a middle-aged woman bustled in with small drops of water clinging to her coat and auburn bob of hair.

"Good morning," the woman greeted them cheerfully, despite her soggy state.

Claire smiled, but Pip jumped in before she could speak.

"Good morning, indeed." They stepped forward with a little flourish. "Can I take your coat for you? Perhaps offer you a cup of tea to warm up?"

"Wow, you're a full-service gallery."

"Anything to welcome a new friend." Pip flashed the woman a smile so bright that Claire's appreciation bordered on envy.

"I can do without the tea, but if you've got a place to hang my jacket, that might be best. I don't want to track any water anywhere near your art."

"Allow me." Pip helped her slip from her coat, and Claire tried not to notice how easy they made the move seem. It didn't take a great deal of skill, but any level of undressing strangers would have made her a little nervous, while the person she'd woken up with appeared to have ample practice in that area.

She shook her head slightly and focused on her painting. She was being silly. Pip's people skills were an attribute, not a threat. She simply felt off-kilter because of the phone call and Pip's reluctance to talk about it. They'd always been so forthcoming with each other. Still, everyone had a right to privacy, especially around something as personal as family, and Pip's family seemed more fraught than most. Honesty and healthy boundaries could coexist.

"I wanted a puffin painting for my grandchild's nursery," the woman was saying as Pip walked with her around the gallery, chatting amiably. "It's my first grandchild—that is, not my first nursery. I've three children of my own."

"How exciting. Have you thought about what you want the baby to call you?"

Claire smiled as the woman ran through a long list of

possibilities with Pip, who managed to seriously and joyfully ponder the pros and cons of everything from "Granny" to "Grandmama" until they came to the painting Claire had finished the morning before.

"I love how cheerful this one is." Pip stopped in front of the canvas. "And I particularly like it for a nursery because it would grow with the baby."

The woman paused to examine the painting. "How do you mean?"

"At birth babies can mostly see only black and white, so the puffin will be visible to the new bundle of joy basically from the beginning, but this splash of red over here will come into focus a few months in, then the other colours later. The baby will have something new to look at each time they grow."

Claire caught a look from Reg, who cocked her head to the side as if pondering the concept, and she didn't blame her. In all her years of painting she'd never once given any thought to how human sight developed. What a strange thing for Pip to bring to the forefront. Strange and wonderful.

"I love that idea," the woman said, "and I do love the colours. It makes the puffin seem more whimsical, which might make it well suited to a toddler's room, too."

"Plus, with many colours represented, it'll go with any décor," Pip added. "I think you're circling around the right choice here."

"Yes, I'll take this one, but another one over here keeps catching my attention." She glanced to the other side of the room where a large wall held some of Claire's nature scenes.

Claire ducked back behind her easel as the two of them came closer. She didn't want to break the spell Pip held over the woman by letting her own nervous exuberance show.

"What can you tell me about this one?" The woman indicated the stormy seascape, and Pip nodded seriously.

"You've landed on one of my favourite pieces in the entire gallery. Whenever I'm in here alone, I find myself drawn to this painting."

Claire's face flushed as she realized Pip hadn't merely said so for the woman's benefit. Claire had seen them pause in that area several times, though she'd never wondered why.

"I like the drama of the piece, the way you can practically feel the wind pushing the waves, and the churning colours from green to blue to almost purple. They have a depth to them, but see this ray of light?"

The woman nodded, her eyes training on the shaft of gold flooding down from a break in the storm clouds.

"You get the sense this is as bad as it'll get. This big wave right here is roiling and crashing, but when the light hits its peak, it's reached a glittering pinnacle." Pip sighed slightly, then smiled. "It's always struck me as turbulent yet optimistic."

"Yes!" the woman said excitedly. "I felt it even from across the room. A sense of hope amid chaos."

Pip flashed one of those brilliantly beautiful smiles. "And who isn't drawn to hope amid chaos?"

That did it. The deal was sealed right there. Claire watched the woman melt, no doubt feeling seen and heard and validated all at once. She'd never seen anyone so happy to part with so much money, and she'd never sold two full-sized works of art in the same transaction before.

After the door closed behind a happy customer, she threw her arms around Pip and kissed them ten, fifteen, twenty times, on the lips, on the cheeks, on the forehead, the tip of the nose, the little cleft in their chin. "Thank you, thank you, thank you!"

Pip laughed. "No, thank *you*. I've never received my commissions in kisses, but I think I prefer it."

"Oh, you'll get your commission, but I'll have to go to the bank first. I'm not sure I have enough on hand to pay you for both paintings." She got a little dizzy. "Two commissions at once."

"On your paintings," Pip pointed out. "Both of them were your work."

She continued to grow lightheaded and leaned against Pip. They were right. They might not have sold this puffin for a stupid amount like they had the other, but when you put both sales together and calculated both the gallery cut and the artist cut . . . she tried to do the math with her head spinning. "My work is going to pay some bills. I'm going to make payments on the life I want by doing the work I love."

This time she kissed Pip on the mouth, hard and long and deep. "How did you get so good at selling paintings?"

"Your paintings practically sell themselves."

"Not in my experience." Claire punched them in the shoulder. "Turbulent but optimistic? Where did you even get that?"

"From the painting." Pip's brow furrowed. "I know I sort of backed into it, but I did graduate with a degree in art history, and I have ample experience examining beautiful things."

Claire wanted to roll her eyes at the last bit, but she was too happy to do anything but kiss Pip again. When she finally stepped back, tears shimmered in her eyes. "How can I thank you?"

"The kiss was a toe-curlingly good start." Pip grinned. "But I'd also be honoured if you'd let me use my commission to invest in the business."

"What?"

"I'm serious." Pip rocked forward onto their toes, and the words spilled out in a rush. "I like this place. I like who I am in it. I like being a part of something, and we both know I have plenty of money. What I don't have is a sense of belonging or fit. I want to be a part of building it, even if it's a small part."

Claire took their hand, understanding this was important if not fully understanding what they meant. "You're welcome here, always. You don't have to pay to stay."

"And I won't be able to stay, always," Pip said, a gravity sinking into their voice that hadn't been there before, "but if I could help create something good, something to give back . . . I don't know, maybe it's silly."

"No. Go on."

Pip tapped one finger on Reggie's drawing in its frame on the wall. "I want to be a part of this."

"I'm a long way from being able to—"

"I know," Pip said quickly, "but maybe you could put my commission in a fund or a savings account as a first step. Then someday you'll be sitting under a string of lights, listening to a local musician play, sipping a local ale, watching your friends dance on the patio or your neighbours stroll in and out of the gallery, and some small part of the happiness you feel in that moment will come from this moment."

"And from you," Claire finished, her heart full to the point of aching.

Pip nodded.

"Okay. We'll start the fund on one condition."

"What's that?"

"You have to start fleshing out your ideas, too, because they're good ones."

"They're based on yours."

"Maybe, but you're good at filling in details. You envision things beyond what I have, and you're figuring out ways to make them work. I would never have contacted Brogan about linking up with the puffin cruises or scheduling ale tastings."

Pip waved her off. "Those things aren't hard. They come naturally once you get rolling."

"Not for me," Claire said quickly. "The painting comes easy for me and the dreaming too, but only to a certain point. The people and the parties and the planning make my head hurt."

Pip's eyes danced, and their lips curled up as if they thought she might be joking.

"I'm serious. You have a gift. I know you don't need a job, but if you did, you could easily get one planning your own events. You don't need to piggyback on my ideas to find a good fit."

Pip's smile turned wistful. "I've never found my own ideas as engaging as the ones I've shared with you."

CHAPTER TWENTY-ONE

"Hi, Bacon Butty," Reg said as she barged through the door to the gallery a few days later.

They glanced up from their spot at the table near the entryway, having taken up the post as it gave them a good angle to watch for approaching customers, or grandparents, while still offering a nice line of sight to where Claire stood painting at the threshold to the garden. The weather had turned a little too cool to stay outside all day, but the afternoon sun still warmed the floor enough for her to stay barefoot indoors, and Pip enjoyed the intimacy of watching her work.

Reg flopped into the chair opposite them and eyed Pip seriously.

After a moment of sweating under the inspection, they cracked. "What can I do for you?"

"I've been thinking."

They closed the book they'd been reading. "Sounds ominous."

Reg didn't so much as crack a smile, suggesting she didn't disagree with the assessment. "I want you to teach me to do what you do."

"Pardon?"

"Teach me."

"Teach you what specifically?"

"All of it," Reg said gravely, then, glancing at Claire, dropped her voice almost to a whisper. "How to talk to women, how to change people's minds, how to make them like you and listen to you."

They fought the urge to laugh. It wasn't funny exactly since the subject clearly mattered quite a bit to their young friend, but she was misguided if she thought Pip to be role model material. "I won't withhold any knowledge I've accumulated, but I fear I'll only disappoint you, as you seem to have acquired an inflated sense of my actual skill set."

Reg stared, then blinked a few times before saying, "See, like that, what you just said, teach me."

"I merely told you I don't know how to do anything useful."

"But you said it in a way that made you sound wicked cool."

"Ah." Pip nodded. "The vocabulary comes with the aristocracy, but I suppose you could pick it up by reading certain books or essays or following certain programmes."

Reg pulled out her phone and began to tap the screen. "Which kinds of programmes?"

"I suppose political programmes, as a lot of parliamentarians use an educated vernacular. Also, educational programmes like nature documentaries and such."

"I do like David Attenborough."

"Who doesn't? The man's a national treasure."

"Okay, what about making people like you?"

Pip's chest constricted. "I think you've already mastered that one."

Reg shook her head. "I don't need you to baby me."

"I'm not." Pip reached across the table and clasped her shoulder, desperate to undercut the insecurity in her voice. They couldn't stand the idea of someone as good and thoughtful as Reg contorting themselves into someone else. "I like you, Reg."

"But girls don't even notice I'm alive."

"Yet," Pip corrected.

"But maybe if I were more like you, I could talk to them the way you talked to the woman the other day when you sold the painting. Teach me those tricks."

"There's no trick. I listened to what she asked for. I followed her lead, and I paid attention to what she said, both with her words and with her body language. I noticed where her eyes lingered, when she paused, the little things you already do."

"I don't, though, not really."

"Of course you do." Pip sat back. "Consider the drawing you made for Claire. You listened to what she wanted, you asked questions, you minded the details, and you spent your time and energy on the things important to her."

"But that's a garden."

"It's the same skill set though, whether you're in a garden or a gallery or a castle garret."

"Really?"

"I swear," Pip said. Though they'd never had to articulate these ideas before, their confidence in the concepts grew the more they spoke. "You need to have some confidence in who you are no matter where you go or who you're talking to. You can't change who you are based on who you're with."

"And then everyone will like me?"

Pip finally did laugh. "No. Some people won't ever like you, for any number of reasons that don't matter, and you have no control over them, but if *you* like you, the right people will too."

Reg looked sceptical.

"Is there a girl you like now?"

"I like a lot of girls."

Pip nodded approvingly. "Well done, but is there one who has your attention in this moment?"

Reg shook her head, but her cheeks turned almost as red as her hair as she looked everywhere but across the room.

"Ah." The kid liked Claire. Claire liked Pip. Reg thought if she were more like them, she might attract the attention of the type of woman who liked them. They didn't want to patronize the kid or embarrass her further, so they sidestepped. "What about in the past?"

"When I was really young, I had a crush on Emma. Then when Sophia was filming the movie here, I liked Cobie Galloway."

"You've got excellent taste, my friend."

"Excellent taste in what?" Claire joined them. "What's all the whispering about?"

"Women," Pip said quickly. "Reg was filling me in about her type."

"Oh, what's your type?"

Reg's expression conveyed pure mortification. "In the past I liked Emma and then Cobie Galloway."

"I see nothing to argue with there." Claire smiled at her, but Reg about sank through the slats in the chair.

"Yeah, but with women like that—"

"But nothing." Pip turned to Claire. "We were talking about how the vocabulary might shift based on the situation, but the skill set's the same whether you're talking to the girl next door or a movie star. Be you. Be genuine. And don't let anyone else's opinion of you shake your own."

Reg nodded with the eagerness of someone desperate for this conversation to end. "Thanks. I'm going to go outside and check on the grade of the pasture where we want to expand the patio."

"Sounds thrilling," Claire said.

"Drainage is important during rainy season." Reg hopped up. "It might take awhile."

"Knock yourself out." Claire watched her go, then turned to Pip. "Was it something I did?"

"No, you merely existed."

Claire arched an eyebrow, and Pip pulled her down onto their lap, wrapping both arms around her waist. "You can't help being irresistible."

"Are you talking about yourself in the third person again?"

"I've never referred to myself in the third person, and while I may be playing with pronouns, I didn't muck up yours. Reg has a crush on you."

"No."

"Yes. Emma Volant, Cobie Galloway, and you."

"She's lowered her standards quite a bit as of late."

"Don't." Pip ducked under Claire's arm so it ran along their shoulder, and they could see each other's faces. "You're amazing, Claire, and as bad as I feel about treading on the kid's fantasy here, I'm not ready to give you up yet."

The words seemed to catch them both by surprise because Pip came up short and, from the rise and fall of Claire's chest, so did her breath.

"Anyway," they continued after the awkward pause, "I tried to give her the old to-thine-own-self-be-true pep talk to point her in a more general direction instead of at you in particular."

Claire ran her fingers through Pip's hair. "Do you really believe that's all you're doing here?"

"I don't know," they admitted. "Sometimes I feel as though I'm more myself here than I've ever been anywhere else, and at other times I feel as though I'm hiding."

"Like when your mother calls?"

Pip tensed again as they had every time Claire broached the subject. They had been hiding, both from their family and from Claire. Like an ostrich burying its head in the sand, they'd steadfastly refused to acknowledge what they didn't want to admit. They'd have to leave soon, and once they did the spell would be broken.

They didn't trust the person they'd only started becoming to hold up to the expectations people had for them to be the person they always had been in the past. Without the safety and freedom they'd had in this place, they'd revert back to the persona they'd created to offer comfortable illusions. And worse, without the strength and support Claire offered, they wouldn't have the courage to carve a new path amid old patterns.

"Hey." Claire tightened her fingers in Pip's hair and tugged their head back.

Pip stared into her eyes, wishing they could see them always because then they might find the fortitude to be worthy of all

243

the admiration they saw there.

"I have to go to Italy." The words poured out ahead of the fear behind them.

"What?"

"Friday next, a week from tomorrow. My sister got engaged."

"To the son of the count?"

"You remembered."

"Of course." Claire kissed their forehead. "I always remember things that overwhelm me. Your family more than fits the bill."

Pip's heart dropped into their stomach, but they forged on anyway, the risk of saying something seemingly less than the risk of not. "Come with me."

"To Italy?"

"My family's getting together with the count and his family for an engagement thing."

"An engagement thing?" Claire repeated. "With the count? In Italy?"

"Yes."

Claire threw her head back and laughed. For the first time the sound turned Pip's core cold instead of warm.

"It's not a big deal."

"Not a big deal?" Claire hopped off their lap. "The fact that you just said that shows how completely you've lost your grip on reality. Or maybe you're grabbing hold of your reality after a little hiatus, but it's not one I share with you."

"It's my family. I have to go."

"Then go."

"I want you to go with me."

"Am I even invited?"

Pip bit their lip. They hadn't thought to ask. They'd never asked before because they'd never wanted to bring anyone before. Ever. All of the implications of that realization rendered them speechless, and Claire stepped into the void left by their silence.

"I'm not crashing your sister's engagement festivities. You promised you'd push my boundaries, and I've let you, but what you're talking about breaks them."

Pip had no comeback, but that didn't stop Claire from elaborating.

"You want to fly me to another country, two strikes. You want me to meet your family, and not at a quiet, informal get-together, but at the engagement party hosted by a count, two more strikes. And I'm going to go out on a limb here and say there's going to be a considerable number of forks at dinner."

Pip nodded. "All the forks."

"Strike five."

Pip sighed. "I know that strikes have something to do with baseball, but I don't know how many one is allowed."

"Three."

"Oh." Pip frowned. "So five is out of the question?"

"Absolutely." Claire folded her arms across her chest, then must have noticed the dejection Pip couldn't quite school out of their expression. "You know I adore you, right?"

They shrugged.

"You know I do, but this is the you I like. Here, relaxed, free, and close enough for me to get my hands on without having to worry about who I scandalize with my common vulgarity."

"You're not common."

"I am, and maybe a part of me is afraid that if you see me amid all those people in your luxurious setting, you'll realize I'm not as shiny as you think."

"I won't," Pip said quickly, then worried the opposite might be true. Perhaps if Claire saw them outside this setting, someplace they weren't free or relaxed or even fluid, she might not like them either.

"Why risk it?" Claire pleaded. "Let's stay safe and golden and together. Or if you must go, how long do you have to stay?"

"I don't know. My mother intimated it might be a rather long process to plan a wedding."

"You're not just going to the party then?"

They shook their head.

Claire lowered herself into the other chair, and the small table stretched like an unfathomable chasm between them. "A week from tomorrow."

"I don't have to go," Pip said quickly.

"Honestly?"

"Yes." The word rolled off their tongue, born of the fervent wish for it to be true.

"Your sister's engagement party seems like kind of a big deal."

"No. I mean it is to her, but not to me." Pip's voice grew stronger the deeper they dug. "I promise. She won't even notice I'm missing. She'll have too many other people to impress. She might not even want me there. I have a history of mucking up these sorts of things."

"Are you sure?"

Pip nodded. They were sure. Maybe not sure of everything, or even most things, but with Claire sitting so close and feeling so far away, they were certain about the only thing that mattered.

They weren't ready for this to end.

Chapter Twenty-Two

Claire eyed Pip's mobile phone as it rattled on the nightstand next to her. She didn't mean to look, but after a steady stream of vibrations for the last five minutes, it was pretty hard not to notice that someone named Louisa wanted to get hold of Pip pretty badly.

Claire entertained the idea of texting Louisa back and telling her Pip was taking one of their notoriously long showers, but that might give the impression they'd call her back when finished, and Claire suspected neither implication was accurate. Pip had clearly been ignoring phone calls for over a week now, and a part of her worried about the real world attempting to push in, but another part of her loved Pip's refusal to let it. That had to mean something, didn't it?

All the others had been so eager to go they'd walked out of her life without glancing over their shoulder. No matter how Claire loved them or clung to them or rearranged her world for them, they each jumped ship at the slightest opportunity to do so. She didn't pretend to know what had come calling for Pip, but she was certain of one thing: they hadn't answered, at least not yet. Part of her began to consider the possibility they might not answer. They might not go. They might not break her heart.

She shuddered and pulled the blankets a little tighter around her. Hope still felt foreign against her skin.

"Are you cold?" Pip asked, startling Claire, who hadn't even heard them return.

"No," she said. Pip stood at the end of the bed, wearing only a pair of black boxer shorts and a smile.

"Are you sure?" Pip's grin turned lusty. "Because if you were feeling a little chilled, I'd offer to keep you warm."

Claire stared at them a bit longer in all their bare-chested glory. The sight made her feel anything but chill. Still, she pulled back the covers and nodded for Pip to jump in.

They obliged in an instant and curled around her body, all lush and hot and soft.

"God help me, I could get used to this."

Pip kissed her shoulder. "I think I already have."

It wasn't the first slip, or even the second, and the fact that neither of them tensed this time suggested they no longer found the allusions to permanence awkward.

Six weeks. A voice in her head whispered they'd known each other for only six weeks.

"Are you falling back to sleep?" Pip asked softly.

"I really shouldn't," she said, both in answer to the question and to the bigger issues swirling through her mind.

"I know, but doesn't this feel good?"

She bit her lip, and she must've tensed, because Pip sat up enough to lean on one elbow and look down at her. "Am I distracting you from work?"

"No." She smiled. "Well, yes, but it's okay."

"Then what's on your mind?"

"You."

"Me?" Pip kissed the corner of her mouth. "I want to make you smile. I don't like the thought of making you frown."

She sighed. "Then perhaps I wasn't really thinking of you. I was thinking of someone else."

"I'm not sure thinking about someone else while in bed with me is much better."

"Okay, I'm thinking of multiple other people. Better?"

"I'm not sure it is unless you're drawing favourable comparisons between me and those masses of people who don't quite stack up."

"I wouldn't go that far."

Pip rolled Claire fully onto her back and threw a leg over both of hers. "How far would you go?"

The press of toned muscle across her bare skin made it hard to remember anything but the familiar ache at the apex of her thighs. "Further than I said I'd let myself go with you apparently."

Pip kissed her slowly. "Does it scare you?"

"Yes, but not as much as it should."

"Because of the others?"

"The fear comes from them. The hope comes from you."

Pip stared down at her, those eyes more intense than she'd ever seen them. "I don't want to be like them. I never want to hurt you."

She noted Pip hadn't sworn not to be like them or not to hurt her. They'd merely stated they didn't want to. She couldn't help but wonder whether the others hadn't wanted to either.

"Tell me," Pip whispered. "What did they do to make you afraid?"

"They left," she said bluntly, "and there's no cardinal sin in leaving a relationship that isn't working for you—only they were working for me, or at least I was trying to make them work. I suppose I tried too hard, which only amplified the hurt."

Pip nodded. "It's much harder to be rejected when you care so much."

"I think I learned that lesson too late. I cared too much, too many times. Perhaps that's why I had to keep repeating the mistakes until I had it pounded through my thick skull."

"It's human to rebel against things we don't want to know."

She let out a humourless laugh. "Then I'm great at being human because I spent my time in London falling head over heels in love with one charming woman after another, only to be shattered repeatedly."

"I'm sorry."

"It's not your fault. It's mine. I clung to them and compromised myself and my own needs for them. First there was Annie, who strung me along, saying she wanted an open relationship."

"Open relationships can work if they're equally committed and based in mutual—"

"No," Claire said. "*She* wanted an open relationship for *her*. She didn't want me to have one. She needed me to be the steady one, to be her rock and her safe place to land."

"And you agreed to that?"

"She said it with a great deal of charm and gravity. I liked the idea of being the one who provided her with the security she craved, but in the end she didn't crave it very often until one day she didn't crave me at all, only she didn't tell me. She just stopped. I found out months later that she'd married someone else while I'd been waiting for her to return."

"I don't even know what to say."

"You don't have to say anything."

"But that's horrible."

"It's one example of many."

"Surely they aren't all utterly heartbreaking."

"Zenia had always dreamed of hiking across Europe. We moved in together to save money and plan for an epic trip. We had a dream board and collected maps and plotted an itinerary while eating tinned beans and boxed pasta so we could put all our spare change into a jar, but when we got close, she told me she needed a solo hike."

"No."

"Yep." Claire tried to keep the bitterness out of her voice. "She said she needed time to find herself, and she'd come back a better partner. Instead, she took all the money and sent me only one postcard from France saying she'd met someone else, and they were headed to the Pyrenees together."

Pip sank back onto the bed beside her. "How many times did this sort of thing happen?"

"They weren't all quite so traumatic. Some of them took 'breaks' they didn't come back from. Some of them cleaned their things out of my apartment when I was at work. Some simply went out with me for months, and then without explanation they were going out with someone else. No matter what method they chose, they all had one thing in common: they made sure I was the last one to know we were over."

After a long silence she rolled onto her side to find Pip staring at the low ceiling, their bottom lip between their teeth and their brow furrowed.

"Have you started to wonder what I did to make all of those women run away without ever looking back?"

"What?" Pip blinked away the haze in their eyes. "No."

"Why not? I did. I spent years wondering and worrying I'd become oppressive or cloying or too challenging or not challenging enough."

"It wasn't you," Pip said quietly.

She laughed again.

"I mean it." Pip sat up again, and this time they pulled Claire up, too. "I hate to say this now because I know it will reflect poorly on me, but I've left a lot of women in my life."

Claire's heart kicked against her ribs so hard she winced.

"I'm not proud of that," Pip pushed on. "I've never been proud of it, and I'm only bringing it up now because I need you to know from the perspective of the person on the other side, it's never the fault of the one who gets left."

"Lots of people break up for lots of valid reasons."

"I'm not talking about breaking up or deciding to part ways or consciously severing ties. I'm talking about running away, leaving someone behind for no reason or with no explanation." Pip swallowed, the words seeming to stick in their throat for a moment. "The person leaving is almost always the reason. Trust me, if they could've blamed you, they would have. They ran because they were lacking, and they couldn't face that."

Claire cupped Pip's face in her hands. "Hey, it's okay."

"It's not," Pip said empathically, "and you have to stop

thinking it had anything to do with you. If someone has that in them, there's nothing you could have done to change it for them. Maybe no one can ever change it, but if they can, it's on them, not you. You deserved better."

"Okay."

"Okay?"

She nodded, surprised to find she really did feel okay. Better than okay. Something about Pip's vehemence or perhaps their uncomfortable authority on the subject lent credence to what others had tried to tell her. Then again, maybe she merely believed in Pip more than she'd ever believed in anyone else.

Chapter Twenty-Three

Pip awoke on Friday morning with a tightness in their chest, neck, and shoulders. Stretching up out of Claire's bed, they raised their hands above their head until their palms flattened against the low ceiling of the loft, then bent over to press them to the ground. Muscles, sore from another passionate night, strained and flexed, but the pressure at Pip's core only grew, and they didn't dare linger to think about why. Thankfully, as they climbed down the ladder to find Claire barefoot at her easel, they found a compelling distraction.

"Good morning, sleepyhead." Claire cast a radiant smile over her shoulder at them, and Pip's heart constricted. "The light was too good to ignore. You're on your own for breakfast."

Pip wrapped their arms around her waist and nuzzled into her neck, breathing the scent of shampoo, clean laundry, and something deeper, more uniquely Claire. The aroma seeped through some of the tension. Nipping at her earlobe they whispered, "Maybe I'll have to nibble on you to sustain me."

"You could do more than nibble if you play your cards right."

They tightened their grip on her for a second before biting a little harder at her shoulder. "You're a temptress, but I refuse to rip an artist from her work."

"In that case, why don't you make yourself useful and pop down to the post office to grab some bread or muffins, anything fresh for breakfast and lunch."

Pip kissed her once more. "Aye aye, captain. Seeing as how we've got money to burn now, maybe I'll even spring for some Nutella."

"Look at you living large," Claire laughed, "but don't wander off and come back with a bottle of bubbly before ten. The neighbours will talk."

Pip pulled on the shoes they'd kicked off before climbing the ladder last night, grateful for a chance to burn off the remainder of their nervous energy. "Aren't their tongues already wagging?"

"What? You mean because your motorcycle has been parked out front for two weeks solid? Or because we've been to the pub three of the last five nights? Or maybe because you snogged me on the beach last night?"

"I'm pretty sure you did the snogging."

Claire's smile turned rather smug. "Why yes, yes I did, but to your original point, I do think the entire village knows I'm practically holding you captive up here."

"A willing captive, perhaps," Pip said, "one who's happy to do your bidding and return in short order."

"Don't go lollygagging along the way."

"Why? Will you miss me?"

"Endlessly."

Pip smiled as they stepped into the cool morning. The sunlight had burned away much of the fog, but a mist still covered the street and dampened the sounds of the small village coming awake. Somewhere down on the beach the calls of a few seagulls broke the rhythm of the waves as they strolled the short block to the village post office and general store. Pushing open the door, they were greeted by a woman they'd never met, but who still managed to look rather familiar.

"Good morning," she said cheerily.

"And to you," Pip said as they spied fresh crumpets on a rack near the door, alongside a loaf of crusty bread. They moved them both to the small checkout counter before hunting another shelf until they came upon a jar of Nutella. Then they spotted a block of mature cheddar in a nearby freezer, and next to it a package of locally produced sausage flavoured with sage. They could hardly pass those up. If it was local and delicious, it belonged at the gallery.

Smiling, they turned back to the woman at the till. "I've gone a bit off list here."

"You won't regret those." The woman pointed to the sausages, but something in her voice caught Pip's ear, and they inspected her more closely, from her red hair and green eyes to the warmth she exuded.

"You wouldn't happen to be the matriarch of the McKay clan, would you?"

"Indeed." The woman's smile grew. "And you are Lady—"

"Pip." They extended their hand in greeting. "Just Pip."

"It's nice to make your acquaintance, Just Pip. You've made quite an impression on my granddaughter."

"Reg has made quite an impression on me as well, as has your daughter."

"Which one?"

"Brogan, though I do hope I meet the others at some point. Oh, and you'd be Charlie's mother's also, yes?"

"Aye."

"Then I'm in your debt for raising so many truly helpful humans." Pip gave a little bow, and Mrs. McKay blushed.

"I see why you've won over much of the village."

"Again, the feeling's mutual. I'm quite thoroughly charmed."

"With the village or our resident artist?"

Pip grinned as they fished some pounds from their pocket. "I'm learning more and more that 'both' is a valid answer."

She chuckled. "Well done."

"Thank you," Pip said, "and I hope our paths cross again soon."

"Likewise."

Pip stepped a little lighter on the way back toward Claire.

This village housed a sort of magic, and for the first time they felt a part of it. They knew people here, and they were starting to make connections between them. And yes, the title had been the first thing out of Mrs. McKay's mouth, but she'd accepted the correction jovially. She hadn't mentioned Pip's parents. On the contrary she'd connected them to Claire and Reggie and Brogan and Charlie, good people, friends, relationships Pip had fostered entirely on their own.

They crossed the roundabout with a little skip, still clutching their armful of treats proudly as they glanced up and noticed a town car in front of the gallery. Immediately the tension not only returned, but amplified.

Closing their eyes, they tried to take a deep, steadying breath, but it caught as they realized whoever'd driven the car was likely now inside with Claire.

Opening the door to the gallery, they paused only long enough to process what Claire was saying. "I don't even know who you are. How am I supposed to know who your sister is?"

"Phillipa."

"It's nice to meet you, Phillipa." Claire still sounded confused.

"No. My sister is Phillipa." The frustration in Louisa's voice set Pip's senses on high alert.

"Oh," Claire said. "I'm sorry. I'm not sure I know—"

"Me." Pip stepped out of the entry and into their line of sight. "She's here for me."

Claire smiled broadly at the sight of them before making sense of what they'd said. "You? You're the . . . sister?"

They sighed and turned the label around in a slightly more comfortable direction. "Louisa is my sister, the oldest one, and in this case she's standing in for my mother."

Apprehension replaced the amusement in Claire's eyes. "If I'd known we were meeting family members this morning, I would have put on something a little nicer."

"If I'd known you were meeting family members, I would have at least told you so," Pip said through clenched teeth, "along with a great many other things."

"You would've known," Louisa finally cut back in, her voice cool, "if you'd deigned to check your messages any time in the last two days."

Pip whirled on their sister. "Did it ever occur to you that I didn't respond to your messages because I'd already said all I had to say on the subject?"

"You don't get any say on someone else's engagement party," Louisa shot back, "and a text message to our mother merely telling her something's come up and you can't make the biggest event of the season without apology or explanation doesn't come anywhere close to saying what needed to be said to appease her."

"Maybe I'm not interested in appeasing her anymore."

"Then you should have had it out with her, because now it's my problem, and I'm sick of that, Phillipa. I'm sick of bailing you out." Louisa's voice rose steadily as her eyes bore into Pip with the sternness of someone who'd played surrogate parent too many times. "I'm sick of getting called to track you down. I'm sick of having to drive all over the bloody north of England to drag you back where you belong."

Pip laughed bitterly, fighting against the urge to apologize and surrender like they always had. "What makes you think you know where I belong?"

"Because I know how you get and how you always come around when push comes to shove. I've been there time and time again to pick up the pieces. I know it's not always easy for you, but I also know where you belong." Louisa shook her head sadly and glanced around the gallery. "And I know where you don't."

Pip felt Claire stiffen, and their chest tightened, but they couldn't take their eyes off Louisa—their protector, their ally— seething and pleading in this space that had seemed so safe moments ago. The disconnect threatened to crack something inside of Pip. It shouldn't feel this way. Louisa's eyes on them tapped into something deep and formative, something strong and solid, someone they'd always known how to be. Then again, Claire, this woman, this place, made them feel other things too, something shifting and uncertain and new, but also real.

They shouldn't have to choose between the person who had always loved them in spite of everything and the woman who was teaching them to be more than they'd believed possible.

"What's happening?" Claire finally asked.

"We're leaving," Louisa said. "We have a flight to catch out of Newcastle in less than three hours."

"A flight?" Claire asked.

"To Italy," Pip said without turning to face her.

"You said you weren't going to Italy."

"I didn't plan to."

Louisa rolled her eyes. "As if you plan anything. Why are you being such a petulant child about this?"

Claire caught Pip's arm, the touch pulling them back. "You said it wouldn't be a problem. You promised no one would care."

"Oh, Pippa, you didn't." Louisa pinched the bridge of her nose. "Were you planning to leave this one without saying good-bye as well?"

Claire gasped and stepped back.

"No." Pip finally turned to her. "Claire, I promise you I didn't know she was coming. I didn't check the messages because I told them I couldn't go."

"But you knew you didn't have a choice, didn't you?" Claire's voice sounded strained. "You lied to me about needing to go."

"I don't *need* to go."

"Are you kidding me right now?" Louisa cut back in. "Are you seriously going to lie to her while standing in front of me?"

"Louisa, stop!" Pip snapped.

"No, you stop," Louisa shouted. Perfect, calm, cool, Louisa actually yelled, and the shock caused Pip to freeze once more.

"Mother was right, and damnit, you know how much I hate to say that, but you're being selfish." Louisa continued with a force Pip had never heard out of her. "Margie is planning the wedding of her dreams. Can't you just for once not muck everything up by making it harder than it has to be? Stop dragging this out. Stop stringing this poor girl along."

"I'm not stringing her along."

"Then you're lying to yourself." Louisa caught them by the shoulders and shook. "You have no skills. You have no money of your own. You have no plan. You've never shown an ounce of fortitude or resourcefulness in your life. And I love you to death, but you're scaring me. You have to stop pretending like you have any other valid option."

Pip clenched their fists at Louisa's words, and the fierceness behind them opened up another crack in the new identity they'd been building. They tried to fight the rising tide of dread, but their defence sounded weak even before it left their lips. "I can do things I've never done before. I can be someone else."

"Yes, you can." Louisa still clutched them firmly. "You can grow up and step into the role you were born to. You can think of your family, who knows your antics and loves you anyway. You can stop playing games that hurt everyone you claim to care about, and fulfil your duty."

Pip finally looked to Claire. They didn't want to hurt her. They didn't want to leave, but they couldn't deny Louisa's charges. If they mucked up this event, their family would never forgive them, and then what? They'd live in a loft with Claire? The idea would've sounded like heaven if not for the truth of Louisa's other charges. They had no skills or money or plan. Claire would be left to care for them while they tried to figure everything out, and there were no guarantees they would. They'd tried before and failed. Would they end up disappointing her in the end as well? The pain in Claire's expression suggested they already had.

Breaking away from Louisa's hold, Pip turned to face Claire once more. The old panic crept back in as they searched her eyes for some of the strength and certainty they'd grown accustomed to pulling from her. Only this time they found none of it. Faith had been replaced by confusion and hurt. Claire didn't see them the way she had this morning. In this moment she saw only the ways they'd come up short.

The tears shining in those green eyes broke them open. This is why they never stayed. This is why they always ran. This was the moment they always wanted to avoid seeing, the moment someone realized Pip would never be the person they'd believed Pip to be.

"Claire." They whispered her name like a prayer, or at least some deep kind of pleading.

"You're leaving."

"No," they said, then looked back to Louisa standing with her arms folded across her chest, and faltered.

Claire shook her head. "You are. God, I can see it in your eyes. You're trying to figure out how to play both sides."

"I'm not playing sides." Their voice cracked. "I'm getting ripped in two. I asked you to come with me."

"And I was honest with you about how I felt," Claire said. "I was honest with you every step of the way, but you didn't offer me the same in return. You lied to me, Pip. You lied to me then, and you've been lying to me for weeks."

They hung their head. They could tell her they'd wanted their words to be the truth. They wanted to stay even now, but not like this, not in a way that let everyone down and screwed everything up. Not in a way that made Claire look at them with her eyes full of pain and betrayal. No, it hurt enough to have Louisa regard them as a disappointment, but for Claire to do the same was too much to bear.

The burden of her disappointment paired with the pressure from Louisa and everything she represented finally overwhelmed Pip to the point of surrender. "Fine. I guess you're both right. No matter what I do here, I've already let everyone down, so I'll go."

They stared at Claire, silently begging her to contradict that narrative, to open it up and provide another path the way she always had, but this time she kept her lips pressed tightly together until Louisa finally broke the stalemate.

"Go collect your things. We all know you won't be back."

❧ ❧ ❧

Claire felt Pip's acquiescence like a knife to her chest. The wave of pain and regret threatened to drag her under. Only the sheer magnitude of her anger kept her upright. She should've known. And the worst part was she *had* known. She'd seen this moment in her mind the first time she'd watched Pip shake out their perfect hair in the golden morning sun. She'd known right then and there she was destined for heartbreak, but knowing something didn't seem to do anything to lessen its impact when the moment finally arrived.

"What an idiot," she murmured as Pip turned and reached the storeroom door.

Pip paused, but their sister stepped between them.

"Wait, there's a garment bag on the counter." Louisa grabbed it quickly and held it up to Pip. "You won't have time to change once we land."

Pip accepted it without meeting anyone's eyes, then closed the storeroom door while Claire replayed the comment in her mind. *You won't have time to change once we land.* How much time did Pip need to change? Apparently six weeks wasn't long enough. Or had they even really wanted to?

She shook her head. She didn't need to guess at such things right now. She wanted to cling to her anger, and she had plenty of fuel to keep the fire burning. Pip had lied to her. Pip swore there was nothing to worry about. Pip promised not to go, and promised every day for weeks that nothing was wrong. Maybe for them there wasn't. Maybe they'd intended to blow off their family, but they sure as hell hadn't been up front about that, not with Claire, and not with their sister, who currently stood mere feet away, still seething.

Claire couldn't stop herself from glancing at the woman. She wore a cream-coloured dress with black piping around the collar and down the three-quarter-length sleeves. The skirt came below her knees, and her peep-toe heels managed to be chic without seeming over the top for ten o'clock in the morning. Her dark hair curled flawlessly across her shoulders, sparking the only resemblance to Pip Claire could discern.

Louisa finally turned from one of the paintings to catch her looking, her smile weak and weary. "Are you the artist?"

She nodded.

"You're rather good."

Claire laughed.

"I'm sorry," Louisa said. "You'd think after all these years I'd know better what to say in these situations, but I never do."

Claire could at least relate to that sentiment. "I thought I was used to it by now as well. Imagine my surprise to find out it still fucking hurts this bad even when you know better."

Louisa grimaced.

"Sorry, am I not supposed to say 'fuck' in front of nobility?" She shrugged. "You'll have to forgive me. Or not. You could not. I'm sure saying 'fuck' is the least of my faux pas. You can tell everyone at the party tonight all about it."

Louisa shook her head. "We'll never speak of this again."

"Right." Claire snorted. "Good policy. Maybe I'll give it a try."

"This will all be over soon," Louisa said, seemingly more to herself than to Claire.

"For you maybe." But this would not be over soon for her. She would have to deal with the emptiness. She would have to tell her friends what had happened. She would have to face the pitying looks around the village when word got out. She'd have to explain to Reg that she didn't even warrant a proper good-bye from Pip. None of them did. Not only had Pip lied, they were going to walk away with no warning, no time to process, no time to reflect, or even speak their peace without an audience. Her anger surged, swift and strong. She clenched her fists until her fingernails cut into her palms, until the storeroom door opened and Pip stepped out.

Only, the person who shuffled into the room wasn't the person she'd fallen for, the person she'd been drawn to, the person she'd kissed or held or made love to.

This person wore a deep purple pantsuit with a light lavender blouse and silver heels. Claire did a double take and fought off a wave of offence at the sight.

"What the hell is happening right now?" The words flew out

of her mouth before she could think them through.

Pip refused to meet her eyes.

"Hey," she whispered in spite of her anger, "are you really doing this?"

Pip shrugged.

"Seriously?" she asked with more force this time. "I know there's a lot about your life I cannot understand, but you're going to walk out right now with no explanation, no fight, no honest good-bye?"

"What could I possibly say to make this okay?" Pip shot back without any strength or conviction.

Claire shook her head slowly, trying to think of anything that might help, but not even in her wildest fantasies could she summon a valid explanation that didn't mark Pip as a coward or a liar, or just plain weak.

"I asked so little of you," she finally said. "I wanted honesty and a proper good-bye. You couldn't even respect me enough to give me that."

Pip finally met her eyes and revealed that all the electricity had gone out of theirs. "Remember what I told you a few mornings ago? The person leaving is always the reason. The lacking is in me, not in my respect for you."

Claire took a step back as the pain in those words only amplified her own. "Then we're both to blame."

"No, it's me," Pip said. "I'm the one who couldn't be what you trusted I could. All you ever did was believe I could be something better."

"Yeah," she said bitterly, "and that's the mistake I have to live with now."

"Claire."

"Good-bye, Pip."

CHAPTER TWENTY-FOUR

Pip sank into their first-class seat on the British Airways flight to Milan and fought the urge to roll into a ball. They gave only a fleeting thought to how the position would wrinkle their pantsuit before biting back a sob. They wanted to rip every shred of fabric from its seams, and yet what would be the use? The damage had already been done. They'd traded something true and good for a painful lie, but pulling out the stitches right now wouldn't put them back together with Claire. They'd made their choice, and now they needed to make the best of it, but the prospect of going forward made it hurt to breathe.

"Can I get you anything to drink?" the flight attendant asked.

"Gin and tonic," Louisa said.

"And you, Your Ladyship?"

Pip clenched their teeth and shook their head.

"You should have something to settle your nerves." It was the first thing Louisa said directly to them since they'd left Claire's. They'd ridden the entire hour to Newcastle in a stew of grief and anger, then gone through the motions of valet, security, and boarding in an icy sort of rote utility.

"I'm fine."

"You're clearly not," Louisa said sharply, "and believe it or not, I am sorry you're upset."

Pip turned to face the window.

"I didn't mean to embarrass you," Louisa said quietly, "and I didn't mean to hurt your feelings either. I was angry at having to track you down, again, and horrified to have to tell yet another one of your conquests you wouldn't be sticking around. Do you have any idea what that's like for an older sister to have to do that over and over?"

They shook their head. They'd only ever given any real thought to having to do it themselves. They'd never stopped to wonder what it might be like for Louisa.

"It's not nice, Pippa. What you do to these women isn't nice. It's humiliating for them, and it's humiliating for me to stand there and watch the aftermath all the while knowing you've moved on and might well be doing the same thing to someone else."

"I wasn't," they croaked.

"What?"

"I wasn't moving on to someone else."

"*Yet*," Louisa clarified, "but you always do. You've been sleeping your way through Northland for weeks."

This time Pip turned to face her.

"Come on. You've been there since August. I know what that means. A new county full of fresh meat."

Pip shook their head, trying to make sense of that accounting. Louisa didn't know they'd been with Claire the whole time. She assumed Claire had been one of many flings, and why wouldn't she? Pip hadn't ever done anything different, and they hadn't told her they were doing something different this time.

"What is it?"

They shook their head, uncertain what good could come of telling the truth now, but the memory of Claire shrinking back, tears in her eyes as she said, "you lied to me" haunted them enough to try. "There's only been Claire."

"Pardon?"

"For the last six weeks. There haven't been any others. I've been with Claire the whole time."

The flight attendant chose that moment to return with Louisa's drink. She thanked her calmly, then lifted the glass to her lips and downed nearly half of it before turning back to Pip. "I'm going to need you to say that again."

They sighed, not wanting to, and not loving the gravity of their sister's reaction. "I met Claire the day I wrecked my motorcycle. I courted her the way I usually do, and she put up a fight, which I'll admit is what piqued my interest, but over time I found much more than the initial challenge. She's smart, she's got this caustic sense of humour, and she thinks differently than anyone else I've ever met."

"Then what you did is even worse," Louisa snapped as the plane taxied down the runway. "I didn't like it a bit when I thought you were sleeping your way through these women as a form of entertainment, but at least you were honest in the past. Leading her on for weeks and not telling her—"

"I told her." Anguish cracked Pip's voice. "I told her everything. I told her things I've never told anyone. I told her about our family and the futility of finding myself. I told her about not feeling at home in my own house. I told her about Oxford and Cambridge and Edinburgh. I told her about the roles open to me and the ones that aren't. I told her my worthlessness at being anything other than a socialite and my shame about that. I told her about the title's emptiness and how heavy it rests on my shoulders, but how without it, there isn't a single remarkable thing about me. I told her—"

"Stop it," Louisa commanded as the front wheels of the plane lifted, forcing them both back. "Stop saying all these things. None of them are true."

"All of them are true," Pip shouted.

"You are not useless."

Remembering where they were, they lowered their voice below the decibel level of the engines behind them. "Yes, I am. At least in every way that ever mattered to anyone until she came along." They let their head fall back onto the plush leather seat. "She made me feel something else for the first time in ages."

"What?" Louisa sat forward into their line of sight as the airplane levelled out. "What did she make you feel?"

"Understood. She looked at the mess I've become and didn't recoil. She saw so many possibilities. She saw potential, and she wanted to realize all of it. She chucked the title right out of the window when I told her how much I hate it."

"You don't hate it."

"I do. I hate being a lady in every form of the word. I hate being called Phillipa. I hate not being able to try different pronouns to see which one fits. I hate not being able to explore different identities. Did you know I can paint puffins?"

Louisa blinked as if waiting for more, then shook her head.

"I didn't either, and I hate that. I hate not knowing what I want to do with my life, even while I know I don't want to do what I've been doing. I hate having to know the answers all the time, and I hate having to make them align with someone else's idea of who I should be. Most of all, I hate not having the space or support to figure these things out on my own." They sighed. "Claire gave me that. For the first time in my life, someone accepted me right now, right here, in the mess and the struggle and uncertainty."

Louisa slapped them across the arm, then the chest, then the head.

"Ouch, hey, what—"

"You bloody fuckwit." Someone behind them gasped, and Louisa reined in her tirade. "You walked out on her."

"You said I had to go. You said I was mucking everything up. You said I had no skills or plans."

"And you let me believe you were hiding behind another one-night stand." Louisa punched them again. "You coward. You could've stopped this at any point. You could've told me what you just said when we were standing back at the gallery. You could have told me years ago how you felt instead of letting me believe you to be happy and carefree. Or you could have at least answered your phone days ago and told me then, like an adult instead of a sulky teenager."

"What difference would it have made? I still would have had to go."

Louisa stared at them as if they were daft. "You could have brought her with you."

Pip sagged. "I asked her."

"When?"

"Weeks ago." They cringed at the memory. "As soon as I talked to mother, I tried to get serious with Claire. I asked her to come to the engagement party as my date, but she said it broke all the rules. It gave me five strikes."

"What does that even mean?"

"It's an American thing, but you only get three of them, and meeting my family and dressing up and flying places with more than a couple of forks, it's too many strikes."

"None of that makes any sense. What kind of woman doesn't want to be whisked away to a gathering of multinational nobility?"

Pip finally smiled, weakly, but their first smile in hours. "She's not like anyone else we know. She doesn't want the money or the trappings or the formality. She doesn't care about the title or the castle or parties or our family line. She doesn't want that part of me. She wants the real parts."

"But they're all real parts."

"No."

"Yes," Louisa said. "They are *all* real parts, and I love that she let you explore new things about yourself. I want to hear all about them, and I want to learn new pronouns and whatever else feels good to you, but not at the exclusion of everything else."

"There's nothing else."

"I am something else, Pip," Louisa said softly. "I may not understand all of these new things, but I've loved you since the day you were born. I've watched you grow into someone strong, creative, and different from the rest of the family. I've seen you learn to stand out in a crowd and turn heads. I watched you come out and win over every person who wanted to look down on you. I've seen you charm heads of state and hold your head high in rooms where most people would be struck dumb."

Pip's heart raced. They wanted to argue, but Louisa's assessment wasn't far from things Claire had said to them in the past—only Louisa saw the same things in different settings.

"Claire has accepted a part of you your family hasn't even been aware of yet, but we haven't had the chance. Can you say the same thing about Claire?"

"I don't know." Pip's chest ached.

"I'm glad she opened doors for you to explore, but you can't let her close the others on us. Your upbringing is part of you. Your family is part of you. Your line, your title, your duty, even your privilege, they're all parts of you. Whether you want them, or know how to wear them comfortably yet, you cannot completely divorce who you've been from who you're becoming."

Pip's breath caught as the answer came to them with the same clarity they'd had when coming to other conclusions of the same ilk over the last few weeks. All this time they'd struggled to choose between who they wanted to be and who they were expected to be when the reason they'd felt ripped apart was because they were meant to be both.

"What is it?" Louisa asked, taking their hand.

"I'm supposed to be both."

"Both what?"

"Both sides of me. Or at least the better parts of both sides. That's why I can't let go of the title completely, and it's why I couldn't bring myself to tell Claire I had to leave. Both of those answers denied half of who I am, and I can't go on with half a heart, or a brain, or a sense of self."

Louisa cupped their face in her hands and planted a kiss on Pip's forehead. "That sounds like a great start to something better."

Pip wanted to share her optimism, and they may have if not for the echo of Claire's voice. *I asked so little of you . . . and you didn't respect me enough to even give me that.*

The pain seeped into every part of them now, carried forward on the fear that they'd burned that bridge beyond repair.

"I'm sorry. I let my anger get the better of me this morning," Louisa said. "I was so frustrated with you, and I think when I saw the way you looked at her, I got scared."

"Scared?"

"Yes. Scared of what would happen if you didn't come with me. Scared of mother. Scared for you and your future. But also, scared for what my life would be like if I lost you to something I couldn't understand."

"You don't have to worry about that now."

"I hope not, but looking back at the moment you turned away from me and toward her, I think that's why I said the things I said about you not having skills or resources or being selfish, because none of it's true, Pippa. Sorry, I mean Pip."

They smiled again, this time more sad and tired. "You weren't completely wrong."

"I was. You have lots of skills and lots of options, and being scared or confused or struggling to find your way doesn't make you selfish."

"Maybe, but you were right about the one thing that really mattered."

"What?"

Pip hung their head. "I did manage to muck everything up."

❧ ❧ ❧

Claire glanced down at the smooth hardwood floors, surprised her anger hadn't burned hot enough to leave scorch marks. She wasn't sure exactly what time it was, but from the low angle of the autumn sun coming through the back windows, she suspected she'd seethed her way through much of the day as she'd paced in circles for hours. Which isn't to say she hadn't experienced her fair share of other emotions since Pip had walked out. There'd been sadness, and she'd shed a few hot tears that they hadn't so much as looked back at her as they went. She might even have been tempted to close up shop and use what was left of her strength to climb the ladder to her bed, intending to stay there for weeks. However, the ladder seemed higher than ever, and the bed still smelled like Pip, which served only to make her sadder, which in turn made her angry.

Of course, as hard as she tried to hold onto her rage, she couldn't always keep the emotional door closed to confusion. Why hadn't Pip told her their family wouldn't let up? Why hadn't they thought Claire at least worthy of the truth? And even if they hadn't felt they owed her anything, why hadn't Pip at least stood their ground for their own sake? There was no way they wanted to wear a purple pantsuit and heels, but they hadn't even flinched when told to do so.

The *whys* would kill her or at the very least drive her mad. Experience had taught her the answers would never come. Pip had taken that sort of certainty with them when they'd walked out without any explanation, which brought her emotions right back to livid.

And she had an entire smorgasbord of rage-inducing aspects to turn over endlessly in her mind. Pip had lied, Pip had robbed them of good-bye, Pip hadn't looked back, Pip hadn't offered any explanation. The list went on and on, but no matter how many times she worked her way down it, the items always shifted on one pressure point: Claire had let it happen.

She'd known things would end this way all along, which was why she'd tried to make the rules in the first place. She'd deliberately demanded honesty because she'd known people like Pip didn't give it on their own. And she'd pleaded for a real good-bye because deep down she didn't expect one. As much as she wanted to believe Pip's final comments about their own lacking, she couldn't help but credit her own weakness. She'd spent their early encounters fighting it, and then weeks bracing for it in all sorts of ways, only to lose her grip on herself and fall completely into Pip.

She shook her head, then for good measure spoke aloud, "No. Not completely."

She could still pull herself out of this nosedive. She had her gallery. She had her art. She had a village to call home. She had friends and neighbours. She had some money in her pocket.

A small voice whispered she had the money only because Pip sold the paintings, but they'd been her paintings to sell, and she had every right to spend her earnings however she wanted. And right now, she wanted to spend them getting a little drunk.

Once the thought formed, she didn't even stop to grab her jacket before storming out the door and toward the pub. The cool air hit her almost immediately, but she'd made it most of the way down the main street of town before it seeped through the heat of her anger, and once she poured alcohol onto the fire, she doubted she'd be able to feel cold for quite some time.

She turned into the alley alongside the Raven, and moving through the evening shadows she pushed open the door with more force than the task warranted. Wood hit stone with a loud thud, and even before her eyes fully adjusted to the dim light, she felt people staring. She didn't care. She took the three steps necessary to reach the polished bar, and before Brogan even turned around, she said, "I'll take a scotch."

Green eyes went wide at the sight of her, but ever the good bartender, Brogan didn't argue. "Would you like to choose the label, or shall I?"

"I trust you." Such a silly simple statement, but it reminded her of all the things she couldn't trust. Pip—obviously, her own judgment, her emotions, her heart for sure, perhaps her tenuous grip on sanity.

Her eyes burned as Brogan poured the amber liquid over ice she hadn't asked for, but she'd no sooner wrapped her fingers around the cool glass than she felt a hand on her arm.

She spun, almost frantically, both surprised and too ready for a fight, only to register the concern on Emma's face.

"Sorry," she mumbled. "You startled me."

"I see." Emma looked her up and down as if she actually saw a lot of things. "Come join us?"

"Us?" Claire glanced to the corner nook to see Vic and

Sophia watching her. "Bad idea."

"No." Emma wrapped an arm around her shoulder and guided her toward them. "We're all friends."

"Are we still?"

"Of course," Vic said with a bright smile. "Why wouldn't we be?"

"I just thought . . . you probably know . . . I mean I'm sure Pip . . ."

Sophia and Vic shared a confused glance before Vic asked, "Where is Pip?"

Claire laughed. "I guess you didn't get a proper good-bye either."

Vic's shoulders tensed. "She didn't."

"They did." Claire slid into the booth beside Emma. "They had a party to get to in Italy."

Vic nodded. "Margaret's engagement. We were invited but declined."

Claire's heart twisted. "I was told that wasn't an option. Not by Pip, mind you. Pip told me they declined as well, and with all the casualness you just indicated, for weeks. Only when their sister showed up this morning did I learn otherwise."

"Whose sister?"

"Pip's. The older one, not the one who's getting engaged."

Sophia blew out a low whistle. "They sent Louisa to come get her."

"And Pip went. Louisa gave them a dressing-down, and Pip hung their head and jumped right into their pretty purple pantsuit."

"Purple pantsuit?" Sophia asked, but Vic had clearly gotten stuck further back.

"You're using they/them pronouns." Her sharp eyes narrowed. "This is part of the fluidity Pip spoke of?"

"One more thing they didn't mention?" Claire took a swig of her scotch, enjoying both its burn and the realization she wasn't the only person Pip kept in the dark. "I guess all the acceptance and the freedom and the unwavering support they claimed to crave must not have mattered in the end. A few weeks of playing house, or slumming it, or whatever they were trying on for size doesn't amount to much when your family yanks on the purse strings."

Vic's cheeks flushed. "I certainly understand your anger. I'm not fond of being kept in the dark either."

"I thought they might've at least told you the truth, but then again, what's the truth? Clearly not what I thought."

"I wouldn't go that far," Vic said softly. "A lot of things can be true at once."

"Not these things. You can't be the person who rails about wanting more options, more fluidity, more freedom, then fall back into every aspect of Lady Mulgrave when your sister snaps her fingers." Claire clenched her jaw against the pain blurring her vision now. "Either Pip was lying to me this morning, or they lied to me all along."

"Louisa dressed Pip in women's clothes?" Sophia asked softly.

"Right down to the heels."

Vic's jaw twitched. "And she showed up at your gallery unannounced?"

"She apparently called several times, but Pip ignored her messages."

"Damnit, Pippa."

"They don't like to be called that," Claire said, with a hint of protective reflexes she hadn't worked out of her system yet. "But I guess they'll have to get used to it again, because I doubt anyone at the fancy party will see them as anything other than Lady Mulgrave."

Sophia sighed heavily. "You're right. This family doesn't have much practice offering grace when it comes to breaking the mould."

"Something we're striving to change." Vic rose and extended her hand to Sophia, who accepted it and scooted out of the booth behind her.

"Wait. What does that mean?" Claire looked to Emma's sad

expression and back to Vic again. "Where are you going?"

"Apparently to Italy."

"You already declined the invite. You broke the pattern Pip didn't have the courage to even fight against. Why go now?"

"For all the reasons you just gave." Vic squared her shoulders and added, "I understand your anger with Pip. Believe me, I've been there more than a few times, and I have no doubt she, or rather they, earned it several times over. However, I still love them, and no one, no matter what they've done, should have to face this family alone in the middle of an identity crisis."

Claire's heart kicked her ribs so hard it jarred every part of her body and brain. "Are they really awful people?"

"No. As individuals they can be rather good, but you have to understand they were never given any more freedom or practice thinking creatively than Pip. The expectations inherent in the lifestyle warp people's understanding of what's acceptable to ask."

"She's more forgiving than I am." Sophia's voice dripped with a disdain that made Claire shiver. "If they are trying to rein Pip in, the purple pantsuit and heels were likely only the opening salvo."

"You clearly deserve more explanation than you were given, and I might wring Pip's neck for that later," Vic continued resolutely, "but please know I wouldn't be on the next plane to Milan unless I anticipated the possibility of utter disaster."

"Will you be able to stop it?" Emma asked softly.

Vic shook her head. "I doubt it, but at least I'll be able to make sure Pip doesn't have to face anything alone."

And with that she turned and left, Sophia falling in beside her.

Claire watched them go, but even after the door closed she couldn't shake the image from her mind, or the unsettled feeling from her stomach. Silence stretched around her for what seemed like a hollow eternity before the voices began to echo. Vic's, Louisa's, her own, Pip's—the whispers of words with new meaning haunted her memory, and she gritted her teeth against the onslaught.

"Are you okay?" Emma laid a gentle hand over her own.

"I don't think so." She lifted the scotch to her lips and swallowed, her throat dry in spite of the cool liquid.

"You've faced a lot today. It's okay to have some lingering questions."

She scoffed. "Lingering questions might be the understatement of my lifetime, but that was the right answer, wasn't it?"

"What?"

"What Vic said." She rubbed her face as it all sank in, past the anger and the confusion and the pain she hadn't wanted to feel, right to the heart of the pain she hadn't let herself see in someone she cared about. "I can be absolutely livid at Pip and still not want to see them hurt."

"Ah." Emma smiled sympathetically. "Yes. I believe both impulses can exist simultaneously and often do."

"How did she get there so fast?" Claire's voice rose. "How did Vic, in a single moment, get to where I'd taken all day to get and still not processed?"

"You're not the first person to be taken aback by the magnitude of Vic's chivalry, but I also imagine it has something to do with the fact that Vic hasn't recently had her heart broken by the person she's run off to protect."

"Point granted." The edges of Claire's vision tinged red once more. "It still hurts that they didn't trust me enough to be honest sooner, but I didn't give them much of a chance this morning, and now I worry Pip's not the only one to blame for the awful good-bye."

"Only you can answer that one."

She groaned. "I always knew it would end. And even if Pip insisted on making the choices they made this morning, I wish we'd had the chance to part on better terms, ones I could at least put into enough perspective to live with, instead of all this doubt and regret."

"Would it have made a difference in the long run if you

could have done so?"

"I don't know." She set her glass back on the table with undue force. "And now I'll never know."

"I wouldn't go quite that far," Emma said. "You might not be able to change what Pip needs, or what they'll ultimately choose, but as a novelist, let me assure you it's rarely too late to rewrite an ending from your own point of view."

Claire's chest tightened, this time with something other than dread. "What do you mean?"

Emma's expression turned almost conspiratorial. "I happen to know two people on their way to Italy tonight and, as rich as Vic is, she doesn't have a private jet waiting at the castle. They'll have to make arrangements, and perhaps if we get hold of them now, they can make room for one more on their reservation, but you have to make the call."

Claire nodded, her whole body trembling with the realization of what that plan might entail, but she'd already had a small, bitter taste of what inaction would cost her, and she was no longer willing to pay the price. "You dial the number. I'll take it from there."

Chapter Twenty-Five

"Pippa, darling, you look spectacular."

Pip feigned a smile as their father greeted their arrival at the party with a kiss on each cheek, his whiskers scratching against raw nerves.

"You should wear purple more often. It's quite regal, and it softens those hard edges."

They nodded instead of saying that's exactly why they didn't want to wear purple. While they occasionally found reason to appear regal, they never, under any circumstances, wanted to appear soft in front of the people who would pin expectations to them.

"I hear you spent the latter half of the summer at Penchant castle," their father continued, oblivious to their discomfort. Pip couldn't blame him. He was happy, and happy people, especially the rich ones, had a well-practiced skill at avoiding other people's misery. And Pip had enough practice hiding their discontent that only those who looked closely would see through the sheen of polite numbness they'd learned to affect in situations and settings like the ballroom which whirred with music, people, food, and frivolity.

"Yes. Or rather, around the area anyway."

He ignored the opening for genuine conversation. "I hope Victoria and Sophia were adequate hosts."

"Very much so." Pip took a glass of wine from a passing waiter and sipped without tasting.

"I'm glad you're getting on with them. I can't say I've agreed with all of their pursuits, but I admire their sense of industry and the grace with which they present their endeavours to the public."

"Indeed." Pip said the most innocuous thing they could think of.

"Have you spoken to your sister's future in-laws yet?"

"When I arrived, yes." Marco and his parents had welcomed each member of the family in front of their lavish villa before handing them off to staff to get situated quickly. "I thanked them for their hospitality and told them how much I look forward to the union of our families."

He beamed. "Well done, love. And have you spoken to your mother?"

"She greeted me when I came downstairs, but she's been rather busy." Pip tried not to let their resentment show at the fact that their mother only seemed interested in inspecting their appearance as one might check the floral arrangements or taste one of the appetizers to ensure they were palatable for the partygoers.

"No one works a room better, and she's quite in her element tonight." He smiled genuinely at his wife and then turned to include Pip in the expression. "And you're much like her in your ability to win over even the most aloof of crowds, so don't let me monopolize your attention. Go work your magic on the new Italian wing of the family."

Then before Pip could formulate an adequate response to the absurdity of that statement, he strode off, drink in hand and head held high with the confidence of someone who'd never fallen short in the estimation of the people he cared most about.

Pip, on the other hand, sagged the moment he turned his back. Thankfully, Louisa stepped in, taking the wine glass before it slipped and wrapping an arm protectively around their waist.

"Easy there," she whispered. "Only four more hours and you're done."

"I'm already done."

"You're not. Father's right; you've got Mother's ability to work a room. It's inborn."

Pip scoffed.

"It's true." Louisa squeezed tighter. "From the moment you could talk, you were a golden child. It drove me mad the way you had everyone wrapped around your little finger, even me. The things you've gotten away with in your lifetime would have left any normal person completely outcast from this family, and yet you never failed to charm your way out of trouble."

"I think my streak ended this morning." Pip reached for the wine glass, but Louisa held it out of reach.

"You took a hit this morning. What you're facing now, for the first time in your life, are the consequences of your own actions."

"Thanks."

"What happened with Claire is something new. You're used to women giving you your way, and when she didn't, you fell back on playing the one role you knew you could."

Pip's heart constricted painfully at the blunt truth. When challenged, they'd done exactly what they'd always done: frozen, then run. And in that moment, all the progress they'd made, both with Claire and on their own sense of self, blew away on the breeze created by their hasty retreat.

"But it's not too late to try something new now," Louisa continued. "You can take some time instead of acting on rash impulse. Gather up all your wit and charm, and use it for good instead of self-preservation. Figure out what you want to do and who you want to be, and then go win her over once again."

They wanted to believe her with all the ferocity of a child who still looked up to their older, wiser, more put-together sister, but Pip wasn't a child anymore. They knew things Louisa didn't, and they'd seen the pain in Claire's eyes. They'd watched the betrayal land across her beautiful features and the resolve it sparked ricochet off the memory of other losses. Pip had been exactly who Claire feared they would become and had confirmed every worst instinct either of them carried.

"It is too late," they said with sad finality. "You don't know her like I do. Her strength, her fortitude, everything she's already overcome. She might have forgiven me a lot of things, but not what I did this morning, and I don't blame her."

"Everyone deserves a second chance."

"She gave me so many chances, and she asked so little in return. I was a coward. I tried to play both sides rather than deal honestly with anyone, but I don't even know who I am when I'm not playing the role I've always played. Maybe it's better if I stick to being an heiress for a while. At least then I'm the only person who suffers."

Louisa grimaced. "I don't think that's a valid option for you anymore."

"This morning you said it was my only option, and you were right. I don't even know who I am or who I want to be when she's not around."

"But do you like who you are when you're with her?"

Pip nodded, their throat too thick with emotion to say more.

"Then buck up because the game just changed." Louisa gestured to the entry of the ballroom, and Pip turned, following Louisa's gaze to where Sophia and Vic had stepped into view, accompanied by Claire.

Their heart short-circuited at the sight of her in a black dress so alluring it should have been illegal. She wore her hair swept up in a twist that showed off her elegant neck, a hint of collarbone, and simple diamond studs in her earlobes. Pip could barely draw a full breath even before their eyes locked, and a slow smile teased Claire's lips.

"You're turning as purple as your pantsuit," Louisa said. "Pull yourself together before I retract all my compliments about your charm."

They blinked a couple of times to make sure their grief

hadn't caused them to hallucinate, but no matter how many times they reopened their eyes, Claire stood on the opposite side of the room.

"Go to her." Louisa punctuated the command with a shove, and Pip wound through the crowd, dodging multiple servers and one or two high-ranking officials eager to introduce themselves to the last eligible daughter of an earl. All the while Pip kept their eyes locked on Claire's until they stood close enough to see their own reflection there.

They opened their mouth, desperate to explain things they themselves still struggled to understand, and aching to make an impassioned plea for another chance they hadn't earned. Instead, all they managed to squeak out was an utterly inadequate, "I'm sorry."

Claire nodded, her sad smile full of compassion. "I didn't come for apologies."

"Why did you come? I didn't do anything to deserve such a gesture."

"You most certainly did not," Claire agreed quickly, but without venom. "I didn't come because I'm happy with you. I made the trip because no matter how angry you make me I still care about you and don't want to see you hurt. Not by yourself or anyone else, and no matter how you left I deserve a better good-bye."

"You do," Pip said. "You deserve a better everything than either of us got this morning, and I bear sole responsibility."

Again, Claire didn't argue. "I also came because, no matter what we are to each other now, you deserve a chance to be yourself in whatever world you choose to inhabit. If you need some support in order to do that, I'm here to offer it."

"As am I." Vic stepped up to clasp Pip on the shoulder.

"Me too," Sophia said.

"And I," Louisa added from behind her.

Pip fought back a sob as they looked from one woman to the next, completely overwhelmed until their gaze landed on Claire once more. "I don't even know what to say."

"You don't have to say anything." Claire took their hand and interlocked Pip's fingers with her own. "And you don't have to change a thing about you, but if you'd like to change that outfit, we brought the suit you wore in Edinburgh. It's in your suite if you want to take a step toward yourself."

Pip laughed, on the verge of tears as they glanced down at the purple monstrosity. "It looks horrible, right?"

Claire shook her head. "Nothing could look bad on you, but yes, on its own, it's heinous."

"Promise you'll still be here when I get back?"

Claire nodded. "I promise I won't leave your side for the rest of the night."

Pip heard the caveat. This wasn't forever. It wasn't even a reconciliation so much as a reprieve, but Claire had come all this way to stand beside them, five strikes and all. While they weren't entirely sure what that meant in the long run, tonight it meant more than they could have dreamed of.

CHAPTER TWENTY-SIX

Claire watched Pip jog up a grand marble staircase, their feet falling so lightly even the silver heels couldn't slow them down. Her eyes followed them all the way along an elegant balcony before the reality of her surroundings set in and her shoulders tensed. She'd barged into an extravagant engagement party at the lavish home of an Italian count. Sure, she'd had Sophia and Vic escort her in, but until this moment her only thought had been of Pip. Images of them had filled her mind every moment since leaving the pub. Throughout the entire flight, while Vic reviewed contracts and Sophia read scripts, she'd stared out the window trying fruitlessly to imagine what it would be like to see Pip again so far from the place they'd felt safe.

Then when their eyes met, Pip's pain superseded her own, and for those small magical moments all the extraneous details fell away. The connection was still there, under layers of hurt and confusion, and perhaps it ran even deeper than she'd let herself fathom, but it was also more complicated than she'd ever acknowledged.

Someone close by cleared their throat pointedly, and she braced to have her presence questioned, but when she glanced over her shoulder, she registered the serious expression on

Louisa's face.

"Lou," Vic said in a warning tone.

Louisa held up a hand. "I don't need an intermediary."

"There's a lot you don't understand," Vic started only to be cut off again.

"I agree. There are a great many things I don't know, and even more I didn't know this morning." Louisa sighed, her eyes more weary than wary now. "My youngest sibling doesn't have the best track record with women, and I've had one too many awkward conversations on her, or rather their, behalf to be blamed for the assumptions I made, but there's no excuse for bad manners. I sincerely apologize."

"Oh." Claire hadn't expected an apology, and didn't quite know what to say. "Thank you, and, honestly, I suppose I can't blame you for making your assumptions when I made a few of my own."

Louisa nodded. "Very gracious of you. I wish I'd given you the chance to process things more fully this morning because it seems that when given the opportunity, you came to a much better conclusion than I."

"I don't know about that." Claire glanced around the room once more, from the waiters to the string quartet to the crowd of beautiful people spilling out onto an elegant terrace.

"I can tell you're out of your element." Louisa's voice was even and kind. "But you weren't this morning, not at first anyway, and when I saw the way Pip looked at you, I think deep down I understood that they weren't either."

"What do you mean?"

Louisa smiled wryly. "I'm used to commanding attention. I'm the oldest, I've always had a soft spot for Pip, and they've always carried a reverence for me, but today they turned to you. They sought cues from you. They would have chosen you if only you'd demanded it."

"I needed them to choose me on their own, not because I demanded it."

"But you could have, and that scared me. I'd never seen my

baby sibling look at anyone the way they looked at you, and while the words I spoke came out in anger, they were rooted in fear."

"Fear of what?"

"Of losing them." Louisa's voice cracked. "I know this life isn't easy for Pip, and I guess I should have done more, but I prayed they'd grow into the role and settle down and find peace. Then today, for the first time, I worried they might seek peace by leaving all this, all of us, behind. We aren't a perfect family, but we do love each other."

Claire nodded. She heard the change in Louisa's tone and saw the way Pip's devotion to her sister must be tearing them apart. Those bonds ran deeper than obligation, and she didn't want any part in severing them. "Thank you for telling me, but I have no intention of breaking up families. I care about Pip, perhaps more than I understood, but our relationship isn't serious."

Louisa's smile turned sad. "I hope that changes."

She shook her head. She couldn't indulge the thought, not now, not here. There were too many complications, and she couldn't untangle them while performing the part she'd come to play tonight.

As if on cue, Louisa turned, and Claire followed her gaze back to the staircase as Pip descended, looking heart-stoppingly stunning in the suit. They smiled more genuinely, but with a lingering hint of nerves, and Claire returned both the expression and the sentiment.

Pip reached out tentatively, and Claire accepted their hand, not wanting it to feel as natural as it did, but glad to offer some tangible show of support.

"Ah, Lady Phillipa," an older gentleman said before either of them could speak to each other. "I'd come up to offer my company and catch up on your recent escapades, but I see you have already found someone to keep you occupied this evening."

Pip's jaw twitched. "Lord Croyden, allow me to introduce Miss Claire Bailey of Amberwick, a friend dear enough to accompany me this evening."

He shook her hand rather than kissing it, thankfully. "A pleasure to make your acquaintance, Miss Bailey. How long have you known Lady Phillipa?"

Claire shrugged. "A while now. Pip wrecked their motorcycle in the back garden of my gallery. The experience left quite an impact."

He laughed louder than the joke warranted.

"What's this?" A beautiful woman with dark hair and pale skin stepped forward and placed her hand softly on Pip's shoulder so the rings on her fingers glittered in the light of the chandeliers as she leaned in to kiss Pip on the cheek. "Are you going to let your mother in on the joke?"

"Your Ladyship," Lord Croyden greeted. "Miss Bailey was telling us how she met . . . What did you call her? Pip?"

"Yes." Lady Mulgrave smiled, though her eyes didn't crinkle so much as narrow when they flashed over Claire. "Pip is a childhood nickname I thought we'd outgrown, but it's always carried great affection."

"Mother," Louisa said, her tone low enough to match the matriarch's. "It's a preferred name."

"Is it now?" She smiled back at Lord Croyden. "You know children these days. How's a mother to keep up with their whims, and this one's harder to keep up with than most."

She then turned back to Pip. "I knew you were gallivanting around the north as of late, but I hadn't heard you'd damaged that bike of yours."

"Yes," Pip said, "though after that I did considerably less gallivanting. I've spent most of my time of late between Penchant castle and the village of Amberwick."

Pip's mother arched an eyebrow at the news.

"I've never heard of Amberwick," Lord Croyden said, seemingly oblivious to the undercurrents of the conversation.

"It's one of the true gems in the crown of Northland." Vic strode forward as if she'd sensed trouble brewing.

"Ah." Lady Mulgrave looked up. "Vic, be a love and go find

my husband, will you? I'm not sure he's had a chance to speak with his youngest daughter yet."

Claire wondered if that were the aristocratic way of saying, *Wait until your father sees what you've done.*

"Actually," Pip said, not seeming bothered, "we did speak earlier, but I'd love to introduce him to Claire."

Vic nodded, then gave Claire a little wink of encouragement, which surprisingly did leave her bolstered despite her suspicion she had no real read on the dynamics playing out around her.

Lady Mulgrave and Lord Croyden turned to watch her go, then had their attention diverted by someone else who stopped to greet them.

"Thank you," Pip whispered.

"For what?"

"Not being someone else here, or treating me as if I am."

Claire's heart squeezed. "Did you really think I could possibly call you Lady Phillipa?"

"There's a lot of pressure to conform."

"I see," Claire admitted, "but I'm not here for anyone but you, so if the others want to write off my lapse of decorum as the vulgarity of a commoner, I don't mind."

Pip worried their bottom lip as they leaned closer, and for a second Claire thought they might be fighting the urge to kiss her. She understood both the impulse and the need to fight it. They weren't who they'd been this morning, and their relationship wasn't the same either, but a reckless part of her ached to feel Pip's mouth on her own.

"Miss Bailey," Lady Mulgrave cut back in sharply, "did I hear correctly that you work at a gallery?"

"I do," she said.

"She owns the gallery," Pip corrected, a hint of pride in their voice, "and she's also an accomplished artist."

"Production and proprietor," Lady Mulgrave mused. "Quite an accomplishment."

"I favour the artistic side more than the business end, which is why Pip's been an asset as of late."

"A business asset?" Lady Mulgrave chuckled lightly.

"Very much so." Claire held her ground. "They've brokered deals on multiple paintings and helped flesh out the details on several ideas for expansion."

Lady Mulgrave turned her attention more pointedly to Pip. "Art dealing?"

"And one of the paintings they sold earned them double commission as both dealer and artist."

This time Louisa laughed. "Pipper, you painted a picture that someone actually bought?"

Pip grinned and rocked forward on their toes. "I did. Nothing as impressive as Claire's work, but enough to catch someone's eye. Then I spun a bit of a web to ensnare a customer afterward."

Louisa laughed again, and this time Pip joined in. The sound thawed some of the nerves Lady Mulgrave had chilled with her icy demeanour.

"What's all the fun about?" A middle-aged man approached. He had Pip's nose, though his eyes weren't quite as blue.

"Father," Pip said, their voice sounding rather official, "allow me to present my friend, Miss Claire Bailey."

His eyes landed on her then down to their joined hands. "Miss Bailey. Such a pleasure to finally meet one of Pippa's friends formally."

"Lovely to meet you as well," Claire said, trying to keep up with the conversations dancing around them.

Then Pip's father frowned slightly at his daughter. "Did you change clothes?"

"The new suit fits them better in every way," Louisa jumped in. "And Claire was regaling us all with tales of Pip's new artistic endeavours."

"Oh, is that what amused everyone?" He smiled. "I could've told you those stories, seeing as how I financed the worthless art degree she supposedly earned at Cambridge."

Pip's grip on Claire's hand tightened, inspiring her to action. "Actually, Your Lordship, you may have seen a delay on your returns, but I was telling the others how Pip's art background has proven rather useful of late."

"Useful how?"

"They have a keen eye and a wonderful ability to connect with art buyers, which helped broker several sales out of my gallery in the last few weeks."

He turned to Pip. "This young woman got you to do something productive with your education?"

Pip grinned. "She inspired me to explore sides of myself I hadn't acknowledged before, and while it's still early, she might not be off base to think I have some talent for dealing art."

Lord Croyden leaned forward. "You wouldn't have your eye on any nautical scenes, would you? I've got a bit of a collection from my time in the Navy."

"I may indeed." Pip cast a sideways glance at Claire, then with a hint of mischief added, "How do you feel about puffins?"

"Puffins?" The man's brow furrowed. "I can't say I know anything about them."

Claire's heart swelled at both the inside joke and the way Pip's smile crinkled the corners of their eyes once more. "I believe Pip could put you in touch with some pieces."

"Yes," Pip said brightly. "Mother, Father, would you excuse us a moment while I speak with Lord Croyden about a few listings that might suit him?"

Her mother opened her mouth as if she might object, but her husband spoke first. "Absolutely, love. I'm thrilled to see my investment bear fruit. Take all the time you need. We have other guests to greet."

"Yes, Mother." Louisa looped one of her arms through Lady Mulgrave's. "I haven't met any of Marco's siblings yet. You must introduce me so we can start planning the wedding."

Pip mouthed a quiet, *thank you*, to Louisa, then holding tightly to Claire's hand met her eyes with a look of gratitude that conveyed more than the situation would allow them to speak aloud.

Claire breathed a sigh of relief as they turned to Lord

Croyden and stepped into more comfortable topics. She didn't pretend to understand everything that had passed between Pip and their family, but the easy set of their shoulders and the low charm ebbing back into their voice suggested that, at the very least, they'd run a bit of a gauntlet together and come out the other side relatively unscathed.

She didn't know what that meant in the grand scheme of things, but she warmed at the confirmation that she'd made the right choice in coming. She only hoped she had the fortitude to continue doing the right things, especially since the night's biggest challenge still lay ahead.

⤜⤛ ⤜⤛ ⤜⤛

Pip waved good-bye to several people who said goodnight in passing, but they couldn't actually manage to take their eyes off Claire long enough to process anything else fully.

She stood at the rail of the terrace, her face cast in the yellow light flooding out through the open doors of the ballroom and from the full moon overhead. The heels, the dress, the hair, the earrings, they all worked together to accentuate her beauty, but there was something deeper there too, something that couldn't be accessorized or dressed up. Claire exuded a strength that spilled out of her and right into Pip.

They'd worked the room hand in hand as Claire spoke in the same tone and with the same interest to the waiters as she did to lords and ladies, much to the chagrin of the latter. They sat next to each other during the formal dinner and champagne toast portion of the evening. Pip had never felt more at home at any major function they'd ever attended. Even the speeches that usually dragged on for an eternity sounded more genuine and heartfelt with Claire sitting close enough for their legs to brush under the table.

Everything about her had been perfect, even the things others would have considered mistakes. She used her forks out of order, and Pip followed her lead. She didn't ever pretend to be anyone she wasn't, and she never shied away from questions, but neither did she offer enough of herself to be tied in knots. She told stories of her own upbringing when asked and made comedic asides with Sophia over dessert. She teased Pip gently when they got too serious, even going so far as to ask Louisa if they'd always been insanely good-looking, earning a slew of stories about their childhood and teenage escapades. However, the moment any conversation started to make Pip uncomfortable, she had always been the first to point out their finer features in a way that left little room for disagreement.

By the end of the evening several guests had stopped by to introduce themselves to "the artist" and the "art dealer." Even their father had made a point of saying he hoped to see her again soon, before retiring for the evening. Pip couldn't begin to number how many formal events they'd attended in their life, or recollect the myriad of ways they'd found to fill all those hours, but no game, no conquests or pursuits ever carried the appeal of the woman who turned to look at them now.

"What are you thinking?" Claire asked when she caught them staring.

"About how much you impressed me tonight. You didn't have to come, and I know you didn't want to. Simply showing up exceeded all my expectations, but you went so far beyond that. You gave me strength and peace and genuine confidence instead of the put-on kind I'd learned to use as a shield."

Claire smiled sadly, but Pip stepped closer and took her hand. "And you did all of those things while bearing your own sadness."

"I came here to focus on you."

"And I appreciate that, but I see you holding back parts of yourself to do so." Pip leaned closer into Claire's personal space, but she didn't meet them halfway, which only confirmed what Pip suspected. It wasn't merely the setting or the crowd or the formality of the evening. The hesitancy in Claire's eyes, her voice, her body centred on Pip.

"I cannot tell you how much it meant to have you here even

though I did nothing to earn your loyalty, but I'd like to start showing my gratitude tonight." Pip wrapped an arm around Claire's waist. "Please, come back to my rooms where I can hold you properly."

Claire placed a hand flat against their chest and fingered the button on Pip's dress shirt as if wanting to open it. Instead, she sighed, then pushed back. "I have to go."

Pip shook their head. "You don't."

"It's after midnight."

"You're not Cinderella." Pip tried to laugh, but it sounded strained.

"I kind of am. I have to be back at the airport in Milan by 3:30 to make my 5:00 a.m. return flight to Newcastle."

"We'll make other arrangements," Pip said, though they suspected the airline schedule was the least of their worries.

"It's time for me to go."

"Then let me tell Louisa good-bye. She will cover for me."

"I know she would." Claire smiled. "But that's all the more reason for you to stay. You need to start covering for yourself, and I need to take care of me now."

"Why can't we take care of each other?" Pip's voice broke.

Claire reached up and ran her hands through their hair, letting it sift through her fingers. Then she stepped back completely. "Because when push came to shove, you ran, and even before that you lied to me. You gave me your word, and then you broke it. You broke all the rules, and even though I understand why now, it doesn't change the fact that you also broke my heart."

"I am so sorry."

"I believe you," Claire said, her voice full of sincerity, "but I don't trust you not to do it again. I don't think you know how not to yet."

"I can learn." Pip said the words before they'd thought them through, but they wanted them to be true. For the first time in ages, they wanted to take the risk of trying to break the patterns that had kept them safe for so long.

"I hope you do," Claire said, "but it's not going to be easy, and it's not going to be quick. You need to wrestle through some things and figure out who you want to be, independent of your family and the title and the escape I provided."

Pip's breath came in shallow gasps. They'd already lost her once. They wanted to fight for her this time, but Claire didn't do her part. She didn't yell or accuse or make demands. How could she remain calm and reasonable while ripping Pip's heart out? "If you didn't want to figure it out together, why did you come tonight?"

Claire shook her head. "We both deserved a better good-bye, one that shows how much we meant to each other, one to offer closure and some kind of peace."

"Forgive me. I don't feel very peaceful right now."

"Then you should find a way to make peace with yourself because you don't owe me anything else."

"What if I can't do it without you?"

"You can," Claire said softly, "and you don't have to do it all at once, but you have to choose which direction you want to head, not for me, not for the title, not to hold onto something you're afraid to lose. You have to charge toward something you want to become."

"I want to be who I am with you," Pip pleaded.

"Except for this morning when your sister showed up. I watched you be ripped in two. Your conflict was real and powerful." Claire's voice caught, but she forged on. "You told me I wasn't the reason you left, that the impulse to run came from something inside of you, and there wasn't anything I could do to change it. I need to believe that's true."

The pain in her voice served only to amplify Pip's own. "It's true. I swear it, but I can change."

"I believe you can, but not if you're hiding, not if you're running from something else. You have to do it for you, and as much as it hurts, I have to learn to let you."

"So, that's the end?" Pip sagged against the finality of Claire's words. "You go back to your world, and I have to stay in mine?

What's the point of it all then?"

"I'm going back to my world, and you have to figure out yours, but now we both get to do our soul-searching without guilt, regret, or remorse. We always knew we'd reach this point. We started with this day in mind, and we promised to part on equal terms, better and stronger for the experience." Claire closed the remaining distance between them to place a gentle kiss on Pip's mouth, leaving with it the imprint of her lips and the taste of her tears before pulling back for the last time and turning to go.

Pip's bones felt as though they'd turned to sand in her wake, and they clutched the balcony railing to remain upright as they watched her run down the stairs and climb into a waiting town car without leaving so much as a single slipper behind.

No, that wasn't true. She'd left a great many things behind. Her heart, for one; her words, her faith in them; and a challenge Pip didn't yet dare believe they could meet.

Chapter Twenty-Seven

Claire flipped the calendar from October to November and tried not to count the days since she'd last seen Pip, but she knew it had been the better part of a month. What she didn't know was how to stop counting her days as pre- and post-Pip. Every part of her mind and body felt the time and distance, and only sheer force of will kept her from spending most of her days in bed, though the fear of financial ruin and starvation played a role as well.

And then there was Reggie.

God bless that baby lesbian. She'd taken one look at Claire two days after her return from Italy, set her jaw, and gone to work, quietly and steadily taking over one job after another until she'd learned to do everything at the gallery, other than paint the paintings. What's more, she'd taken to bringing homemade treats a few times a week as if worried Claire wouldn't eat otherwise, and she may have been right under other circumstances, but with plates of scones or biscuits appearing every other day, Claire managed to consume enough carbs to keep upright, if not actually productive.

"I dusted all the frames and swept the floors," Reg said as she came around the corner to find Claire still sitting at the table staring out the window. "Would you like me to do anything in the kitchen?"

She shook her head. "No, that's not part of your job description. Besides, I haven't used the kitchen lately."

"I know," Reg said. "I thought you might like me to use it. Brogan taught me how to cook a few things."

"You're the best, but really, I'm okay."

Reg pursed her lips, and the longer Claire sat under the teenager's intense gaze, the more she felt like a fraud. She wasn't, though—she *was* okay. Not great, but in the past when things had fallen apart, she had, too. This time the sadness weighed heavily on her shoulders, and the loneliness clung to her senses, but she hadn't gone under yet, and that had to mean something. Or at least that's what she insisted to herself in the darkest moments.

"Do you want me to do some work in the garden?" Reggie asked, then with a more optimistic edge in her voice, added, "The garden might make you happier, right?"

"I don't know what to do in the garden this time of year."

Reg brightened. "I could show you. None of it will be much to look at yet, but we're still in the window for planting bulbs, or anything with a big root ball."

Claire shook her head. "I don't know what that means."

Reg pulled her framed drawing off the wall and pointed to the perimeter as she'd marked it. "If we pull out this hedgerow and move this one back, we could ring this outer edge in bulbs that flower at different times. We could start with tulips. They grow well here, and then daffodils, and then for summer gladioluses."

Claire smiled, filled with a gently warming kind of affection for a teenager who cared about the flowering seasons of perennials at an age when most of her peers were obsessed with makeup, movies, and each other. While she didn't know many of the youth in the village, she suspected Reg was the best of them, and she couldn't help but wonder how long it would take for Reg to realize the same.

The thought made her think of Pip and all the horrible messages they'd internalized about their own better impulses and sense of self over the years. How long might it take to undo all the damage, and did Pip have what they needed to do that work?

"Emma has some lavender that's gotten quite big. If we transplant now, it might work, and we could add some smaller shoots in the spring when we start the climbing boxes for the trellis."

Reggie's words pulled her back as the thought of spring rattled through her consciousness. "I'm sorry, Reg. I love this dreamscape, but I'm a long way from planning for the long haul. I don't even know where I'll be in the spring."

The kid's expression turned stricken. "What do you mean?"

"Tourist season is about over, and I can't imagine I'll sell many paintings over the winter. I also don't paint as much during the long grey months. The colour goes out along with the light."

"Then you need to paint now."

She smiled sadly. "It's not as if I haven't tried."

"You haven't." Reg's voice took on a hint of desperation. "You haven't been at the easel for days."

Her face flushed, and if the accusation had come from anyone but the kid, she might have lashed out, but she saw her own fear reflected in those intense eyes, and it sent pain skittering through her.

"I know something bad happened with Pip," Reg said more softly, "but you can't give up on spring just because winter is coming."

Claire stared at her, shocked and struck dumb by the profoundness of the blunt statement.

"I'm sorry," Reg mumbled. "I didn't mean to yell at you."

"I'm glad you did."

"I'm not supposed to yell at adults."

Claire snorted. "I haven't felt much like an adult lately. I've felt like a sack of mush and emotions and self-pity, and you shook me out of that a bit."

"Really?"

She shrugged. "At least you made me think about things differently for a minute, which helps. And you're right, I don't know what winter will bring, but there's always a spring to look forward to. Why don't we plant a few bulbs?"

Reg furrowed her eyebrows suspiciously. "You're not saying that to make me feel better?"

"Nope, I'm saying that to make *me* feel better. I don't know how long it'll be before I can move forward with the big plans. Maybe I won't ever be able to, but planting seeds feels like an act of hope, and I could use some hope right now."

Reggie grinned. "Okay. I know where I can get some bulbs for free. Ester dug up a bunch. I'll go get them sorted and come back tomorrow so we can plant them together?"

"Sure," Claire said, both exhausted and grateful to have a plan. "You'll have to teach me, though."

Reg's grin spread. "You'll learn fast. Gardening is all about growth."

Claire tousled her hair. "You're pretty wise. Now, go get my bulbs."

"What are you going to do?" Reg asked, then said, "You should paint."

She blew out a breath and glanced around until her eyes landed on a stack of canvases leaning against a wall in the back corner. "I could at least go through the pile of things I started and didn't finish. Maybe something will speak to me."

Reg nodded as if she found the plan satisfactory. "Then I'll see you tomorrow."

"I look forward to it," Claire said truthfully as the teenager left her alone in the quiet space once more. She didn't love the quiet. Quiet felt too close to lonely, and she didn't want to go backward, so she got up and made good on her promise to at least sort through the canvases.

Still, even the effort of bracing herself mentally for any sort of productivity pushed her sad psyche to its straining point.

She picked up a canvas and saw the sketch of a sunny beach

scene before immediately setting it aside. Today's low light wasn't right for that one. The next held a shimmering sea and the first strokes of a billowing sail. She set it down before she could remember the sailing trip that had inspired the image.

She flipped through several more in similarly quick succession, all of them too bright, too bold, too brilliant; in other words too much like the person who'd filled her world when she'd begun them. Without Pip there with her, the colours they brought to her life dimmed to various shades of grey. She hated letting her sense of light and colour and texture become tied to someone else, but even in her most self-deprecating moments, she couldn't summon regret. Perhaps that was the biggest change of all. Even knowing everything she did now, she wouldn't trade the memories they'd made for who she'd been before they met, and she wouldn't undercut the person she'd seen Pip becoming for anything.

Maybe that was her own area of growth. She'd fixated on how Pip had come into their own and the things they needed to do to move forward on their path, but until this moment she hadn't given any thought to how the experience had changed her. Maybe that's what she needed to do now. The same way Reg spoke of planting for spring, perhaps her time with Pip had planted a few seeds as well. She'd been too deep in the dirt to see the sunlight, but she'd been growing, too. With Pip she'd found a voice. She'd found a backbone. She'd stood up for what she deserved, and she'd done right by someone she loved.

She did love Pip. She knew that now. It was the only way she could have let them go. And she'd made her own choice this time. She hadn't been left. She'd broken the pattern. She wasn't the person she'd been when they'd met, and now she had a long winter of lying in wait to figure out who she might become.

She tried to find the thought empowering rather than isolating, but as she pulled the final canvas away from the wall and turned it around, her eyes filled with tears. She recognized it instantly. Even though there were only a few brushstrokes on the stark white slate, still it transported her back to the aftermath of a crash, the spinning wheels of a motorcycle, the first rich tones of a smooth voice, the shake of perfectly feathered hair. The painting held none of that though, merely the fringes of a mottled background and two unmistakably blue eyes.

She smiled in spite of the tears and lifted the canvas to her easel. She might not have the same light around her anymore, but some images were burned so deeply in her memory she could have summoned them completely in the dark, and this was one work of art she didn't want to leave unfinished any longer.

Chapter Twenty-Eight

Pip tried to stroll through the villa with their normal ease, or at least project something close as they nodded to various members of staff. They'd come to recognize several others related to their future brother-in-law, though they hadn't figured them all out, as their mind had been occupied with other things.

Pip wanted to be present for Margie, who, to her credit, hadn't turned into a total bridezilla yet but was clearly battling excitement, nerves, and a great many new responsibilities. At least Louisa took the brunt of the emotional and organizational work along with their mother, as they'd planned weddings before, but Pip honestly did want to be of some use, which was a new impulse.

Their time at the gallery with Claire had left them craving a sense of purpose. For too long, their days had been aimless. They wanted more meaning and a sense of direction, but for now they'd settle for surviving today's first fitting of their bridesmaid dress. The thought of stepping into one of the floor-length burgundy dresses with an ivory lace overlay that Louisa had tried on yesterday made their stomach clench. They didn't want to fall into old patterns of self-centeredness, but they also didn't want to surrender all the progress they'd made either, which created a rather large disconnect. Pip spent a great deal of energy struggling to walk a line between their desire to be good and the desperate need to also be authentic.

Still, they had to square their shoulders and tighten their jaw as they swung open the door to the cavernous space set up as wedding central. It looked more like a war room than a stateroom. Tables covered in seating charts, flower arrangements, sample centrepieces, and piles of tulle lined one whole wall, while the entire back corner had been cordoned off with curtains to create a discreet fitting area ringed with sewing machines and a massive trifold mirror. They shivered a little, as they'd been avoiding mirrors as of late, another totally new experience for someone who had always relied heavily on their looks.

"You made it." Louisa appeared at their arm and kissed their cheek.

"Did you worry I'd run away overnight?"

She laughed lightly. "I wouldn't have blamed you if you had run back to Northland two weeks ago."

"Everyone else would have."

Louisa frowned. "You have to give them a chance. They love you, but they don't know how to show it."

"It's not their fault," Pip admitted. "No one can be held accountable for not knowing the real me when I don't even fully understand myself."

Louisa eyed them seriously. "That's remarkably insightful, and mature too. You've changed, Pip, and I'm not the only one who's noticed."

Louisa tugged their arm as she pulled back the fitting-area curtain to reveal Margie and Vic waiting for her.

Pip laughed nervously. "Where's everyone else? Too afraid of what havoc I might wreak to come within a mile of me in a dress?"

"No," Margie said, sounding a little flip. "We didn't invite anyone else because no one else's opinion matters on this front. It's my wedding and your outfit. None of the others get a say, and I told them as much."

Pip's head swam, and their palms began to sweat at the thought of anyone saying such a thing to their mother, much less Margie having cause to. She and their mother had been in lockstep over every aspect of this entire spectacle. What had happened?

"Don't look so bleak," Margie said quickly. "I can't stand it. You're always the one who brings the sunshine."

"Is this because Claire came to the engagement party or because of my clothes? I promise I'll wear whatever you tell me to wear to the ceremony."

Margie grinned. "We were sort of working toward a big reveal, but since you brought it up, I think we should start with the outfit."

Louisa rolled her eyes. "That's not what we agreed to. Vic was supposed to start first."

Pip glanced from one sister to the other, trying to figure out what was happening. Clearly, they'd had some sort of plan that had already gone off the rails, but Margie seemed giddy, which felt inconsistent with Pip being in trouble.

"I'll get it," Louisa relented, giving Pip a reassuring pat on the shoulder as she went back out of the changing room. Vic offered a calm, easy smile, and their heart rate dropped a couple of ticks as they eased into the empty chair.

"Close your eyes," Margie said.

"It's not a surprise party," Vic said.

"Sorry," Margie grumbled. "I've been to infinitely more surprise parties than interventions. I don't know the etiquette."

"Here." Louisa returned, holding a clothing hanger draped with one of the most exquisite suits Pip had ever seen. A light, smooth grey with a burgundy pocket square, the jacket was tailored slightly at the waist to give it a subtle curve. Beneath it, a silken ivory vest overlaid a rich burgundy dress shirt with an ivory bowtie fastened at the collar.

The image sparked both envy and confusion. "Is that a groomsman's suit?"

"No, theirs are black. Yours is unique," Margie said.

"Mine?"

"We had it made just for you." She bounced excitedly. "Because you're one of a kind."

"But we stuck with the bridesmaid colours, because that's where you belong. With us," Louisa added. "You're part of this family, and we don't want to lose you."

"But we don't want to change you either," Vic jumped in.

Pip's throat closed, almost completely blocked by emotion.

"We haven't always been good about showing it," Louisa went on, "and we've rarely understood what to do with your wilder impulses. I suspect we tried to direct them in ways that made us feel safer or you more manageable. I realize now our methods were deeply flawed, but they were never born out of shame or malice."

"We simply wanted you to be safe and close and part of the things that mattered to the rest of us," Margie said with uncharacteristic seriousness. "We didn't want to leave you out, so we tried to wrestle you in, because quite frankly you're the most fun family member."

Pip snorted.

"It's true," Louisa agreed. "From the moment you were born, you brought light and colour and entertainment to every situation. I know I've joked that Mummy and Father stopped parenting by the time you came along, but not because you were bad, only because none of us wanted to rein you in."

"At least not until you got a motorcycle," Vic clarified, "and then you kept trying to run away. It frightened us all a great deal, Pip."

They hung their head, remembering every mess they'd left in their wake.

"I imagine your parents overreacted and swung too far in their attempts to pull you closer," Vic continued. "I see now how those restrictions hurt you, however unintentionally. We all want to do better."

"What about Mummy and Father?" Pip once again made note of who wasn't in the room. "Why aren't they part of this little intervention?"

"They're coming around more slowly, but they will get there."

"They don't have a choice," Margie said firmly. "Times are changing. The world is changing, and the aristocracy will have to change with it or get left behind."

"Hear, hear," Vic echoed. "No one else gets to live our lives for us, and we're here right now to show you we'll have your back going forward."

"We're sorry we didn't do this sooner." Louisa clasped a hand on their shoulder and squeezed. "Honestly, we didn't realize you were hiding your real self until we saw the stark contrast between who you were with us compared to who you were with Claire."

Pip almost doubled over from the pain of their chest cracking open. They didn't know how to make room for all the love filling their heart as it butted up against the vast pain of knowing they'd only reached this point because of Claire.

Claire hadn't merely shown Pip who they could be. In doing so, she'd shown their whole family a model of how to relate to them on a higher plane. They said the only words they could squeeze out of their full and broken heart. "Claire's gone."

"Is she, though?" Louisa asked. "Because from what you told me, she didn't leave you. She gave you space to work things out."

"And I've been trying." The anguish poured out. "I'm ripping myself to shreds trying to make peace between the parts of myself I don't want to let go of here with you and the parts of myself I learned to love with her, but no matter how I try, I can't imagine a life where I sacrifice one for the other."

"What if you didn't have to?" Vic asked.

Pip shook their head. "I've worried it all to death, but I can't be an aristocrat with champagne tastes without feeling like a fraud while living above a gallery in a seaside village. And likewise, I cannot explore and bend and play with my identity, and still be Lady Mulgrave. God, Vic, you understand the constraints of those choices better than anyone else on the planet."

"I do." Vic nodded. "But I've also learned it's our generation's responsibility to find new ways of working within the old framework and to shape our traditions in response to the ways they've shaped us, which is why I'm here to help with the discussion of your styling."

"My styling?" Pip shook their head as the conversation took another unexpected turn. "I'm not the one getting married here. Margie is."

"My styling is set." Margie beamed. "And I'm quite happy. But, with me out of the way, you're next in line, baby sister— erm—sibling."

Pip smiled at the slipup. Their family was trying, and honestly the practice meant more than perfection at this point. It meant Pip wasn't alone in the struggle to make sense of their place in the world.

"You don't have to get married to amend your styling." Vic spoke with the formality of someone who'd already checked several reference books on the subject. "I actually ran this past your brother, and the two of us came to the same conclusion. Styling at the age of marriage is a tradition, not a mandate. Others have updated their styling upon coming of age or completion of military service or the birth of a child. I don't see why coming out couldn't work."

Pip didn't argue with the root sentiment, as they did very much feel as though they'd reached a crossroads, but they still didn't see a valid path forward. "None of the titles available to me fit. I'm not a lady, I'm not a lord, and I'm not sure I'm ready to be nothing."

"You will never be nothing," Louisa said fiercely. "Even if you forgo a title altogether, you will still be our bright, bold, brash wonder, but Victoria has found a creative solution we think might suit you better."

All eyes turned to Vic, who assumed her most official posture and tone. "My vast research on titles produced a gender-neutral styling historically afforded to both sons and daughters of peers, and its rules for usage are actually about as fluid as you."

"Very few things are as fluid as I am." Pip smiled as their spirits started to lift. "Are you going to tell me what it is?"

"I did have a little speech prepared," Vic teased, "but since

Margie already revealed the suit, I'll jump to the good part as well. The styling to which you're both entitled and in my mind deserving of is The Honourable."

"The Honourable," Pip repeated, trying it on for size.

"The Honourable Pip Farne-Sacksley. Do you like it?"

They nodded slowly. "I like the sound of it, but I'm not sure I've earned it."

"It's available to any child of certain peerage, or it can be certified by license of the crown if you'd rather go that route," Vic offered.

Pip shook their head. "I meant I'm not sure I'd feel comfortable wearing it until I've actually been honourable, and I haven't yet."

The others shifted somewhat uncomfortably.

"I know what I've put you all through," Pip admitted. "I am truly sorry. I appreciate the support you are showing me now, and I wish I'd given you the chance sooner instead of running, hiding, and leaving you to clean up after my selfish, reckless mistakes. We all deserved better."

They took a deep, shuddering breath before pushing on. "You were right when you said Claire's influence offered a contrast to the existence I'd led before. She helped bring the real me to life, and the fact that we're having this conversation is proof that more is possible than I imagined. But I didn't meet her faith and the freedom she gave me with anything close to honour, and while she managed to forgive me, I don't think I could assume the title until I made myself worthy of it in her eyes."

The other three stared at them for a long time, probably shocked, maybe confused, undoubtedly wondering who they were and what they'd done with the devil-may-care version of Pip. Finally, Louisa stepped forward and cupped Pip's face in her hands. "I have never been prouder of you than I am right now."

"But I don't know what to do."

"You will," Margie said with a certainty they wished they could share. "You will figure this out, and you'll keep challenging us to do the same, but please, if you must go now, promise you will hurry back to us, both in time for the wedding and always."

Pip's throat tightened once more and their eyes filled with tears, but they nodded their agreement moments before being pulled into multiple hugs at once.

❧ ❧ ❧

"Pssst, Reg," Pip stage whispered.

The teenager turned to look over her shoulder but didn't see them hiding down the narrow alleyway. Pip understood that calling to teenage girls from dark alleyways was actually sort of creepy, but they were too close to the gallery to take the chance of stepping out fully onto the main street of Amberwick.

"Reg, it's Bacon Butty," they tried again.

Reggie's back and shoulders tensed, making Pip suspect the whole alley thing might be the least of their concerns.

"I need to talk to you," they said sincerely.

Reg finally turned toward them, jaw set and eyes burning with a pure and instantaneous anger only a teenager could fully convey.

"Hey." Pip put up their hands, with the sudden urge to apologize for every wrongdoing they'd ever committed.

Reggie's fist struck out so quickly, Pip barely had time to duck out of her reach, their head hitting the stone wall with enough force to rattle their teeth.

"Feck." They rubbed their scalp and pulled their fingers away to see a hint of blood.

Reggie's eyes widened in shock before narrowing again. "Serves you right."

"Fair enough. Are you done swinging?"

Reg took longer to ponder the question than Pip felt comfortable with. "I don't know."

"Seriously?"

"You hurt Claire," Reg shouted as if the idea hurt her. "You were supposed to be good. You were supposed to show me. You broke her heart, and you didn't even say good-bye."

Pip registered the way Reg conflated Claire's pain with her own, and their chest constricted again. "I'm so sorry."

"It's a bit late. You need to leave her alone. She's barely started eating again, and painting, and if you're here to hurt everyone—" her voice shook as she clenched her fist again, "—then I'll . . . I'll punch you if I have to."

"You don't want to punch anyone." Pip spoke softly. "You're better than that. You don't want to hurt anyone."

Reg's lip trembled. "No, but I won't let you hurt her either."

Pip nodded. "I respect the impulse, my friend, and I admire you for being willing to do something hard to protect someone you care about. You have more honour in your little finger than I've exhibited in my whole life."

Reggie didn't seem to know what to do with the statement, but her hands dropped to her sides, so Pip continued, "But Claire's strong and smart, and she doesn't need you to protect her or defend her honour."

"She doesn't need you either."

Pip nodded. "I know. I've always known from the moment I saw her, which is why I let her go. I let her walk away because I thought she deserved better, and she does, but she also deserves someone to be there for her. She deserves someone who believes in her and puts their full faith in her and her dreams and her desires."

"I believe in her dreams."

"That's why I came to you first. Once, you asked me to show you what I knew, but now I'm asking you to show me what you know."

Reg frowned. "I don't know anything. I've been trying to help her, but she's so sad. She's trying so hard to paint, to garden, to eat, but it's like everything steals her energy."

Pip ground their teeth at the thought of Claire slogging through the kind of emotional gauntlet Pip faced without her, but they couldn't let the fear and futility drag them back there. They were here to break patterns, and even though the urge to run from that kind of vulnerability still coursed through their veins, for the first time they wanted to prove they could withstand it.

"You can't fix it," Pip finally said. "You can't control a woman's emotions. You can't control women at all. I made some sizeable mistakes, but Claire also made her own decisions. She stood up for herself, which she has every right to do, even when it's hard on us to watch."

"So you're not here to get her back?"

They sighed. "I don't deserve to ask for that yet. She doesn't trust me."

"I don't blame her."

"I don't either, but I want to show her I still believe in her even if she doesn't believe in me. I want to see her dreams come true even if she doesn't want me to be part of them. I want to be the person she deserves even if what she deserves is better than me."

Reg seemed to think for a moment, and the pressure pushed in on Pip from all sides. They didn't know what they'd do if the kid said no, not just from a practical standpoint, but also from an emotional one. If good, kind, honourable Reg found them totally irredeemable, they weren't sure they could ever look themselves in the mirror again.

Mercifully, Reg jammed her hands in her pockets and said, "I have a few ideas."

Pip's relief exploded through a smile that stretched their whole face. "I thought you might, and I want to go big."

"It's the least you can do." Reg's grin spread grudgingly. "I think I might know some people who can help."

Chapter Twenty-Nine

"Emma, I'm not much of a cook." Claire sounded a little pathetic, but it was the truth.

"I know," Emma said kindly. "You and I don't have to do much. The ladies will take care of the work. You're here to keep me company."

"I'm not any better company than I am a cook, and even worse in most social situations."

"That's not what I heard. Vic said you did very well at the big fancy party and everyone was very impressed." Emma threw an arm around her shoulder. "And Bonfire Night isn't nearly as intimidating as all that. Besides, all the locals have to be part of the village celebration."

"I hate to sound like a broken record, but I'm also not really up for a celebration."

Emma's smile turned sympathetic. "I'd hoped for a different outcome. When you ran off after Pip, I thought maybe the two of you might find a way to blend your worlds. I suppose part of me still hopes that. In the meantime, you have a community around you, and you owe it to yourself to at least try to join in."

The weight of responsibility settled heavily on Claire's chest. Her friends had been amazing over the last few weeks. Emma and Brogan stopped by at least every other day. Neighbours found multiple excuses to drop off scones or shortbread. Her grandparents took her out to dinner. She'd also had a few customers stop in to buy postcards or prints, and she strongly suspected they weren't random tourists so much as friends and family of full-time village residents sent to bolster her spirits.

She smiled through the hint of embarrassment at the thought of so many people working to prop her up. While she wished she could have bounced back faster, it had been a long time since anyone had cared enough to want to help. Their support offered further evidence that she wasn't the same person she used to be. She hadn't stopped functioning. She hadn't stayed curled into a ball of grief and pain. She didn't see her life in the dire terms she traditionally used after a breakup. She understood now that there were a million shades of grey to her evolution, and the process of healing was as fluid as . . . well, Pip.

With a sigh she nodded resignedly. "Okay, I can do a full day of community spirit."

"Yes, you can."

She checked one more time. "Are you sure it needs to be a full-day thing?"

"All day long," Emma confirmed. "Bring what you need for the duration because we're both in this together up until the bonfire burns out."

"Right." She forced a smile. "I can do that."

And she did. For hours she and Emma baked, which is to say Emma baked with a veritable stream of other villagers dropping in and out with supplies from picnic blankets to platters of treats, and each one of them stayed to chat or share a cup of tea. An outside observer might have thought she'd been doing this her whole life, and even Claire had to remind herself Emma had lived in the village only a few years as the day turned to evening and more people gathered to help them carry things down to the beach. Even her own grandparents stopped by to stroll with them along the dune path as the sun dipped below the rolling hills.

Emma waved to a group of redheaded children as they merged onto a wide stretch of sand, and Claire wondered why Reg wasn't with them.

"I'm surprised more of the young ones didn't pop in today," she mused.

"The kids have already been running up and down the beach for hours," Emma explained. "They're probably hoping to nick a few fireworks from the community pile for their own use."

Claire smiled. "Surely not Reg."

Emma shook her head quickly. "No, Reg is likely with Brogan and Charlie."

"I've never seen you and Brogan apart for so many hours."

"She's in her element, I'm sure; always big jobs to do before the main event."

Claire arched an eyebrow at the vagueness of that description.

"I'm sure she'll find us once the bonfire is lit." Emma gestured ahead to a giant structure with a mass of people busying about like ants near a mound.

Claire wasn't immune to the sense of building excitement, but the distant sound of a motorcycle caught her ear. She strained to hear it coming close only to have it fade, or be drowned out by the voices of her neighbours rising as the first flames licked the darkening sky. She might have convinced herself it had been a trick of her wistful mind had Emma not glanced up the hill toward the village with a hint of concern in her eyes.

No, she was reading too much into things. She'd imagined Pip's return too many times already. Emma had probably only been scanning the crowd in search of her wife. Then again, maybe she carried her own hopes. She had said earlier a part of her still believed Claire and Pip could find a way to work outside the box.

Claire hadn't even let herself consider the possibility on a long-term scale, not when they were together, and certainly not after saying good-bye. Early on, she'd been so afraid of getting left, but after realizing Pip really was different, she hadn't let herself consider the ways her own worldview had limited them as well. Pip's ability to blend and bend what had always been into something bolder and brighter had helped turn her into the type of person who could at least consider the possibilities of something more. But without them beside her to exude their "both/and" mentality, she didn't know what a shared future could look like.

As if sensing the wave of sadness barrelling toward Claire, Emma looped an arm through hers. "Come on, let's get closer to the fire. It'll keep us warm."

The evening hours ran together in a rush, much the same way the rest of the day had, only this time instead of baking the treats, they ate them, sprawled on a picnic blanket, listening to the rolling waves, the crackling fire, and the laughter of children. Warmth, comfort food, company—the festivities provided so many things a person needed to heal, and yet a part of her couldn't help listening for the low whine of the motorcycle once more.

As the night wore on, the strain of waiting and wondering where Pip was began to supplant the charm of the event, even as fireworks burst above them. Thankfully, Brogan chose that moment to finally make her appearance.

"Did you save me any cake?" She flopped onto the blanket beside Emma and dropped a kiss atop her head.

"You made it." Emma's relief seemed disproportionate for surviving a small community celebration.

"Looks like we all did." Brogan echoed the sentiment as they exchanged conspiratorial grins before turning to include her. "Hiya, Claire. How did you like your first Bonfire Night?"

"It's been lovely," she said truthfully, "and also exhausting."

"I agree on both counts," Emma said, "but I'm glad you stuck with me today. I don't know what I would have done without you."

"You would've managed fine, but I appreciate being included. I had the best day I've had in weeks, and you wore me out so thoroughly, I might actually sleep tonight."

Emma and Brogan exchanged another one of their cryptic looks.

"What?"

"I think we're probably ready to crash, too," Emma said. "Maybe we could walk you home on our way?"

Claire shook her head. "Brogan only just got here. You don't have to leave because I'm tired."

"You're not the only introvert in the village, friend. I've eaten my cake, the pyrotechnics are finished, and my love has returned." Emma rose and smiled down at them. "As far as I'm concerned, another successful Bonfire Night will be in the books as soon as we see you home."

Claire glanced around to see some of her neighbours packing up. Apparently, her grandparents and their friends had already slipped out during the fireworks. She frowned a bit that they hadn't said good night, but their escape made her own a little quicker. "You don't have to walk me home."

Brogan laughed. "And you don't have to argue with us, American. It's Bonfire Night. There might be shady characters about."

"Okay." She shrugged as they started up the hill together. "But I'm only half American."

"I barely feel even half these days," Emma admitted.

"Two half Americans equal one whole though, right?" Brogan teased as they reached the edge of the village, but Claire didn't laugh, and not simply due to the corniness of the joke. As they crested the hill, she saw her entire gallery lit up with golden light, and not just coming out the windows, but also rising like a halo from behind.

"What the hell?" She turned to Brogan and Emma, who smiled sheepishly.

"What's happening?"

"Go see," Emma urged.

"See what? What did you do?"

"Not us," Brogan said, "or at least we weren't at the helm of this one. Go on. They're waiting for you."

No pronoun had ever made her heart flutter like that one. Of course, she still understood that "they" could be any group of people, but her heart held a certainty that the "they" Brogan referred to was actually a person too big to be contained in a singular form.

She took off, jogged across the roundabout, and threw open the front door. The smell of warm food hit her senses, accentuated by the sounds of soft music playing from the back patio. She followed it in an almost dreamlike state and threw open the sliding door, but when she stepped outside, she entered another world rather than her own garden.

Overhead a hundred fairy lights twinkled as they dangled from a freshly assembled trellis spanning the entire space. Gone were the confining hedgerows, replaced along one side by a long stone bar, and along the other with potted plants and raised flower boxes. Against the wall to the gallery a water feature cascaded into a small pool with a gurgling fountain that offered a serene undertone to the light orchestral music playing through small speakers discreetly placed under the eaves. And in the centre of it all sat a large iron fire pit, beautifully rendered in swirls and flames, surrounded by wood and stone stools.

The entire area seemed impossibly enchanted, but as the fire flickered into the night sky, she couldn't settle on any of the delightful details until she landed on electric blue eyes as they danced in the glow surrounding them.

"Pip." She whispered the word as a cross between a prayer and a cry.

They stepped forward tentatively, smile nervous, hands jammed in the pockets of their suit trousers. "Do you like it?"

"I . . . how did you—? I mean, it's amazing," she stammered. "How?"

"I had some help." Pip nodded to the gallery behind her, and she turned to see Reggie standing back with Emma, Brogan, Charlie, even her grandparents and Ester.

"You rallied the whole town for me?" Her head spun.

They nodded. "Everyone agreed you deserve this and much more. And you deserve better than I was able to give you in the moment you needed it most," they said solemnly. "I'm sorry it took me so long, and I understand if I'm too late, but none of this is contingent on how you feel about me. It is entirely to show how I feel about you."

Claire's breath caught in her chest. "How do you feel about me?"

Pip laughed and looked around at the space, the light, the fire—and Claire knew. She saw all the elements and the depth of emotion they conveyed, but she didn't interrupt when they began to speak.

"You're the most singularly amazing human I've ever met. You inspire me, you embolden me, you show me things about myself I never had the courage to seek, but even independent of me, you stand out, entirely enthralling. Your art, your passion, your strength, your creativity all combine to make you a force that I'm not sure you comprehend yourself."

Claire shook her head.

"I want you to know," Pip continued, their voice low and intimate, "how deeply I believe in you. I want to see your dreams come true even if you don't see me as part of them. I want you to always live secure in the knowledge that you deserve everything your heart desires, and you're completely capable of achieving anything you imagine."

"And what about you?"

"What about me?" Pip asked hesitantly.

"It seems you're also part of my wildest imaginings, and you brought this one to life for me."

"You asked me to have faith in my own ideas, but the best of them all centre on you. I know I still have a lot of learning and growing ahead of me, but this is the least I could do to show my thanks for starting me on my new path."

"The least?" Claire looked around as the sentiment and the setting fed new ideas and new dreams she'd held at bay for so long. "What's the most you can do?"

"Pardon?"

"You said this, all this—" she gestured around them, "—was the least you could do, but what if I want more than your least?

What if I want the whole continuum you showed me? What if I want all of you, the wild and the sincere, the rich and the unruly, everything that shaped you and everything you're still becoming? What if I want your best, too? Are you in a place to offer me that?"

"My best is still muddled and confused. My best is not perfect, but . . ." They released a shaky breath. "You told me I didn't have to know everything at once. I only needed to decide on a direction of my own choosing. I've already taken some steps I think you'd be proud of, and while I'm still a long way from having everything figured out, I used the time you gave me to at least figure out the most important thing I needed to learn."

"What's that?"

"No matter where I go or what I do from here, the best version of myself will always be the one with you beside me." Pip hung their head. "I don't know if that's enough, but—"

"It is," Claire said quickly. "No need to say 'but' because it's enough. You are enough."

"Really?"

She laughed and took their face in her hands. "You're so much more than enough."

"I don't have all the answers yet."

She kissed their forehead, then stared into their eyes. "All I ever needed was for you to make the choice to stay. I needed you to choose us of your own free will and not out of fear."

"I'm not afraid," Pip said with strength in their voice. "Not anymore, not with you. I've made my choice, and whatever else happens along the way, I'll keep choosing you for as long as you'll let me."

"You promise?"

Pip stared deeply into her eyes with a measure of confirmation that outstripped any words.

"On my honour."

EPILOGUE

"Thank you so much for coming," Claire said as she walked Mrs. McKay to the door.

"Oh, I would not have missed it for the world." She patted Claire on the back. "Can you believe this is my first art opening in my whole life? And to have both my own daughter and granddaughter featured in the paintings made the whole endeavour magical."

Claire grinned at the description she couldn't disagree with. Then again, everything in her life had felt tinged with magic for months since Pip had returned in a dreamscape of their own making. She turned back to view the gallery now, taking it all in with as much wonder as she had that first night back in November. The building itself hadn't changed, but nearly everything else felt different now, fuller, brighter, more colourful.

Every bit of useable space on the walls overflowed with art, most of it hers these days. They'd titled the show "Both/And," which fit on a myriad of levels. The pieces they'd chosen to display ran the gamut of influences from the life of the village to the relationships she'd built there. Puffins, sailboats, seascapes, landscapes, and even a few portraits, speaking to the many sources of joy and peace filling her life. The sheer number of sales Pip had facilitated over the course of the evening suggested she might have conveyed those emotions to her friends and neighbours as well.

The oil painting of Reg amid her garden was earmarked as a thank you gift, and several of the McKay women had already cried over it, much to the teenager's vast embarrassment. And Louisa had offered a king's ransom for the one of Pip she'd started after their first meeting, but Claire had decided to keep that one for herself. Louisa had then insisted on commissioning her to paint another of Pip wearing her suit from the wedding, with the intention of adding it to the formal portraits in the great hall of their family estate.

Beyond those notable exceptions, virtually everything else had sold thanks to Pip's charisma, eye for art, and the connections they'd made in the larger art community over the winter.

The Honourable Pip Mulgrave had become quite a force as they established themself as one of the area's preeminent art dealers, and while they wandered everywhere from Mulgrave to Edinburgh in pursuit of local talent, they based all their commissions on Claire's gallery, giving her ample time to focus on her own work, and making sure she never spent a night alone. Claire wasn't sure which aspect of their new life caused the most shock among Pip's former social circle, the monogamy or the work ethic, but she knew which one made her happiest.

"We are heading out, love," Gran said as she and Claire's granddad moved toward the door with Ester in tow. "You have exhausted us with all this excitement, but we are so proud of you."

She took one hand from each grandparent and squeezed. "I couldn't have done any of this without you."

He chuckled. "That's what I told everyone here tonight."

She laughed. "Good, we wouldn't want Pip to take too much of the credit for all of those sales."

Ester shook her head. "They haven't, not once tonight. How you wrapped that one so tightly around your little finger is a marvel."

"Come on now," Pip called from the open doorway to the garden. "I can hear you."

"And do you deny the charge, Your Honour?" Ester asked without skipping a beat.

"Not in the least." They flashed her their most winning smile. "She's more than earned my complete loyalty and utter infatuation in a host of ways."

"Damn right she has," Granddad huffed, but he didn't manage to hide the quirk of a smile as he added, "and you better not forget it."

"I don't intend to, surely, but if I ever suffer amnesia, I trust you'll remind me." Pip gave him a slight bow, and Gran nudged him toward the door, winking back at them.

Claire waved as they wandered off into the evening, then closed the door and flipped the lock. "We made it."

"Indeed, we did." Pip wrapped an arm around her waist and pulled her so close she practically slipped inside their suitcoat. "The inner circle is gathered 'round the fire waiting to toast your success, but I'm sure they wouldn't miss us if we slipped upstairs for a few minutes."

Claire leaned into them, nuzzling their neck and breathing in the scent of them before whispering, "If I got you anywhere near a bed, I would need more than a few minutes."

Without missing a beat Pip gently bit her earlobe. "How about the storeroom then?"

She gave them a light shove and shook her head. "You're not dressed for that."

"How do you know?"

Her heart tap-danced across the inside of her ribcage, but before she had a chance to figure out if she was being teased or not, Vic stuck her head through the door to the garden and said, "There you are. We were beginning to take bets as to whether or not you'd abandoned us for better company."

Pip's grimace quickly morphed into a grin. "Better company than my favourite cousin?"

"And cousin-in-law," Sophia called from just outside. "Come

on, Claire, I thought we were going to teach the Brits how to make s'mores."

She kissed Pip on the cheek. "Sorry, love, American dessert duty calls."

"Nice of you to join us," Brogan said from behind the bar. "Can I refresh your drink?"

"I don't even have a drink to refresh," Claire said. "I've been entirely too anxious to allow for alcohol all evening."

"Well, I think the need for nerves has passed." Brogan snapped the cap off a bottle of cider and slid it over to her.

"It never existed in the first place." Emma looped an arm through hers and pulled her toward the fire. "You were already the talk of the town long before the doors even opened tonight. I haven't seen the village so excited about any event since the movie premiere."

"Our little art show hardly ranks next to a star-studded gala."

"Darling," Pip sing-songed, "you must stop undercutting your work."

She shook her head and sat down on a bench next to Reg, who was currently tending a roaring fire, then patted the spot next to her for Pip. "You're biased because you love me."

"Well, I mean, I do love you, but more importantly I'm trying to sell your work, so I take personal offence to your devaluing my trade."

The others laughed as they all took their places around the ring of seats.

"I hate to admit it," Vic said snuggling a little closer to Sophia, "but you have a valid business point, Your Honour."

Pip grinned. "Did it hurt a little bit for you to admit that?"

"Maybe not hurt so much, but it certainly feels odd to think of you and valid business points in the same sentence."

"Not to mention the word 'honour,'" Pip added.

"No," Vic said quickly, "that one's come around much quicker than one might have expected. The tightrope the two of you walked at Margie's wedding was quite a scene to behold."

"Or Christmas Day dinner with your mother." Sophia lifted her glass. "Here's to me no longer being the thing that offends her most on special occasions."

The others all laughed, but their easy habit of joking about society weddings and events at castles still made her head spin a bit. Vic and Sophia had taken to building them up and repeatedly telling them their presence and poise under pressure made them a raging success with everyone who actually mattered in the family, but most of the time she simply settled for keeping her wits about her without the added pressure of trying to impress anyone.

"How do you do it, Claire?" Emma asked as she accepted a glass from Brogan and pulled her down beside her. "What's your trick to living with one foot in the aristocracy and one here in bohemia?"

She rested her head on the strong shoulder beside her. "I don't know that I manage to do any of it very well, but I have learned that any time I feel in over my head, I can manage to stay afloat by keeping my eyes on Pip."

"Awww," the others all said in unison.

She could have left it there, but the defiant streak in her couldn't help but add, "And I've learned to protect my sanity by always using whichever fork I damn well please."

"Claire for King," Sophia called. "This damn family and their blasted fourteen pieces of silverware. I have greatly enjoyed joining you in that little act of rebellion."

"Well, I for one would like to know what kind of silverware one uses to eat these s'mores you keep promising," Reg cut in as she sat back from the blaze.

"Sticks," Claire stated at the same time Emma said, "Your hands."

"God, you Americans really are a classless lot," Pip teased.

"I don't know," Brogan said. "I rarely side with the nobility in this crowd, but if I'm to believe this correctly, you cook marshmallows while they dangle from yard waste and then use your hands to apply the molten sugar to melting chocolate and biscuits. Seems a bit of a mess."

"There you have it," Pip said. "If Brogan can't do it, no one can, for she is the best of us all."

"Hear, hear," Claire called, and they all lifted their glasses to Brogan, who blushed so profusely it could be seen even in the flickering firelight.

Emma placed a hand on Brogan's thigh and saved her the way she always did. "I can't believe you all haven't eaten a million s'mores in your lifetime. But don't worry, we will show you how to right this terrible travesty."

They set to work, all of them moving around each other with a casual comfort. Jokes were made, help given, love shared in the form of sugar and chocolate until each of them sat snuggled with their better halves making yummy noises.

Reg managed to find her voice first. "Where have these things been all my life?"

They all laughed.

"What, you mean all seventeen years of it?" Brogan licked a strand of marshmallow from the side of her hand. "You still stand a chance of making up for lost time. How do you think the rest of us feel?"

"Probably gutted," Reg mumbled as she started to make herself another.

Claire glanced around the fire to see each person watching her with a great deal of affection. She really was the last unknown of the group as she made her way both awkwardly and enthusiastically into the wider world. Emma and Brogan had settled into a life almost too beautifully idyllic to be believed. Vic and Sophia were a raving success in every arena they entered, be it public or personal. She and Pip didn't belong fully in either world but were charting their own course, not always with a complete sense of direction, but clearly, purposefully, and most importantly, together. Just as with so many of their other identities, they'd chosen to figure out their future along the way, and they were content to enjoy the journey.

No—more than content. They were happy.

She turned to face the breathtaking human beside her. They were still every bit as bright and bold as they had been on that first morning, when she'd stood in this very spot, unable to process the proximity of something so perfect literally crashing into her life. In that moment, she couldn't have possibly predicted where their winding path would take them, and even with the gift of hindsight, she still had a hard time putting the twists and turns into any sort of perspective.

Pip noticed her gaze and turned to meet it, eyes dancing with the reflection of sparks from the fire. "What are you thinking?"

She shrugged. "Just how far we've come from those moments when I was so afraid you were destined to hurt me."

Pip frowned. "I never wanted to hurt you."

"But we didn't know any other way. By the time you arrived in my life, I thought I had to choose between staying safe and small or living fully with the certainty of pain. Then you showed up and refused both binaries. You simply refused to see me as plain or expendable."

Pip touched their forehead to hers. "You did the same for me, you know?"

"I hope so, but I'm not sure I could have without your influence. You showed me a way to see the world beyond black and white, or even varying shades of grey. Your very existence proved there are a thousand hues to happiness, and you made me want to skip along that entire continuum."

"I can't believe I had anything to teach an artist of your calibre about colour." Pip grinned. "And to think you once compared me to a virus."

Claire threw back her head and laughed, causing everyone else around the fire to turn and stare at them.

"Are you going to let us in on the joke?" Reg finally asked.

Pip threw an arm around Claire's shoulder and gave her a little squeeze. "Just reminding my love here about a time when she compared me to a viral infection of sorts."

Vic tipped her glass toward them. "Only the one time? Why amend your assessment now?"

"Because viruses run their course and leave your system. I think this one intends to stay in my blood forever." Claire turned to Pip, giving them a quick kiss before adding, "I'm left with no choice but to upgrade your status to that of a chronic condition."

Acknowledgments

First of all, let me start by thanking you, dear reader, for making it this far into this book. The fact that you did so tells me you are at least open-minded, if not outright supportive of seeing more fluidity within your queer love stories. I appreciate your willingness to come along as part of this journey with me and these characters I love deeply. I know many of us are still learning and growing, as is our larger community, and 1 for one believe we are better and stronger when the stories we tell reflect that evolution.

Our stories are central to who we are as a people, and to a larger moment. Who we leave in and who we leave out tells us (and the larger world) what we value, what we care about, and what we want to carry forward with us. In that sense, this book is a value statement for me, but as is always true, it is also a love story on multiple levels. It details the love between two beautiful, capable, and whole people. It is a story about how falling in love can transform a person. And it is also a story about how being seen and loved for who you are can transform the way someone is able to view themselves. As I go through these acknowledgments, I want to thank folks, not just for their help in the creation of this particular book, but also in the larger task of creating strong foundations and safe spaces for all of us to share love stories with expansive boldness.

To start, I must acknowledge that the Bywater Books team has had my back on this front since day one. Not only have they been wonderful about my own personal shifts, they have always encouraged me to write diverse characters that reflect my own areas of interest. As I finished my first draft of this book, I gave my publisher Salem West a heads-up that a main character would use they/them pronouns, and instead of backing away or even asking for final approval, she responded, "This is thrilling . . . and if anyone has a problem with it, they can go pound sand." That kind of support helps give authors the confidence needed to really tackle a subject in authentic ways without worrying about possible backlash. Ann McMan created a great cover before I even conceived of the book this time . . . yes, she really is that good! The rest of the team—Marianne, Radar, Nancy, and Toni—all worked diligently to get the book out in a timely fashion amid a world full of shortages, holiday breaks, and clogged shipping channels. None of you would be reading it right now without their commitment and diligence.

Lynda Sandoval served not only as story editor, but also as sounding board to make sure we got the details right without at any point letting the characters' individual journeys detract from the romantic arc. I basically dumped this one in her lap and shouted, "Fix it, fix it," and she stayed calm and supportive, and multiple times reassured me that these characters were strong enough and capable enough to bear the burdens I pinned on them in my most hopeful moments. Beta readers Barb and Toni helped me stay in the romance wheelhouse, while Karen served again as my point person on all things British. Finally my awesome proofers (Diane, Wynn, Jenn, Meg, and Ann) cleaned up all those pesky typos that tried to sneak through. I also want to thank Parker, Finn, and all the other gender-nonconforming/queer folks who have acted as sounding boards for a myriad of questions and experiences. And thanks to my therapist, Leah, who constantly reminds me I have ownership over my stories and my emotions even when they don't match up with what others expect of me.

Now please allow me to shift from the logistical side of production to the emotional one because this book put me through the wringer in all the best ways. While I've done plenty of internal grappling over the last few years, having to articulate those concepts and conversations within the context of full and unique characters encased in a romantic arc took a new kind of toll and a whole lot of tools I'd never used before. I spent months getting swept up and sometimes overwhelmed by how all-consuming this story became. I want to thank my family of choice who were so spectacular in offering support from all sides. Anna Burke was there and excited for this project from the very moment I conceived it in a chat session. She never failed to ask how Pip and Claire were doing, and it helped to have someone else see them as being as real and central to my life as I did. Thank you to Georgia, Nikki, and Mel, who always love me even when I don't know my own pronouns, much less anyone else's, and who are always up for practicing new things even if I tell them I might have to try something else next week. And thank you to Alex and Jess, whose comfort with their own fluidity makes mine feel like so much fun.

Most importantly, I want to thank my amazing family, who put up with all my moods and wild ideas and wandering conversations that turn into plot points that then must be written down *right now*. I know it's not always easy to live with a writer, especially when I'm working on a project that pushes every button, but you all love me unconditionally even when I am a whiny, insecure baby about it. Thank you to Will Banks, who has always been the best at showing me how queering the idea of family offers so much more room for love. To Jackson, you blow my mind with your easy acceptance of so many people and life experiences. Please never lose your expansive worldview. And to Susie, blerg, I wish I had the words to properly thank you for all the work and love and growth and progress you've seen me through over the last year. Thank you for providing me with the space and security to keep chasing my dreams no matter how they shift and change. I love you, come what may.

And finally, thank you to my loving creator, redeemer, and sanctifier, from whom all these and many more blessings flow. *Soli Deo Gloria.*

ABOUT THE AUTHOR

Rachel Spangler never set out to be a *New York Times*-reviewed author. They were just so poor during seven years of college that they had to come up with creative forms of cheap entertainment. Their debut novel, *Learning Curve*, was born out of one such attempt. Since writing is more fun than a real job and so much cheaper than therapy, they continued to type away, leading to the publication of *Trails Merge*, *The Long Way Home*, *LoveLife*, *Spanish Heart*, *Does She Love You*, *Timeless*, *Heart of the Game*, *Perfect Pairing*, *Close to Home*, *Edge of Glory*, *In Development*, *Love All*, *Full English*, *Spanish Surrender*, *Fire and Ice*, *Straight Up*, *Modern English*, *Thrust*, and *Plain English*. Now a four-time Lambda Literary Award finalist; an IPPY, Goldie, and Rainbow Award winner; and the 2018 Alice B. Reader recipient, Rachel plans to continue writing as long as anyone, anywhere, will keep reading.

In 2018 Spangler joined the ranks of the Bywater Books substantive editing team. They now hold the title of senior romance editor for the company and love having the opportunity to mentor young authors.

Rachel lives in Western New York with their wife, Susan, and son, Jackson. Their family spends the long winters curling and skiing. In the summer, they love to travel and watch their beloved St. Louis Cardinals. Regardless of the season, Rachel always makes time for a good romance, whether reading it, writing it, or living it.

For more information, visit Rachel online at:
www.rachelspangler.com
or on Instagram, Facebook, Twitter, or Patreon.

Bywater Books is committed to bringing the very best of contemporary literature to a growing community of diverse readers. For more information about Bywater Books, our authors, and our titles, please visit our website.

www.bywaterbooks.com

We are all stories.